LISA CASSIDY

HEARTFIRE

THE MAGE CHRONICLES - BOOK 4

Tate House

 A catalogue record for this book is available from the National Library of Australia

National Library of Australia Cataloguing-in-Publication entry

Creator: Cassidy, Lisa, 2018 - author.

Title: Heartfire

ISBN: 978-0-9953589-7-3

Subjects: Young Adult fantasy

Series: The Mage Chronicles

First published 2018 by Tate House

Cover artwork and design by Jeff Brown Graphics

Map artwork by Chaim Holtjer

This one is for Andreas

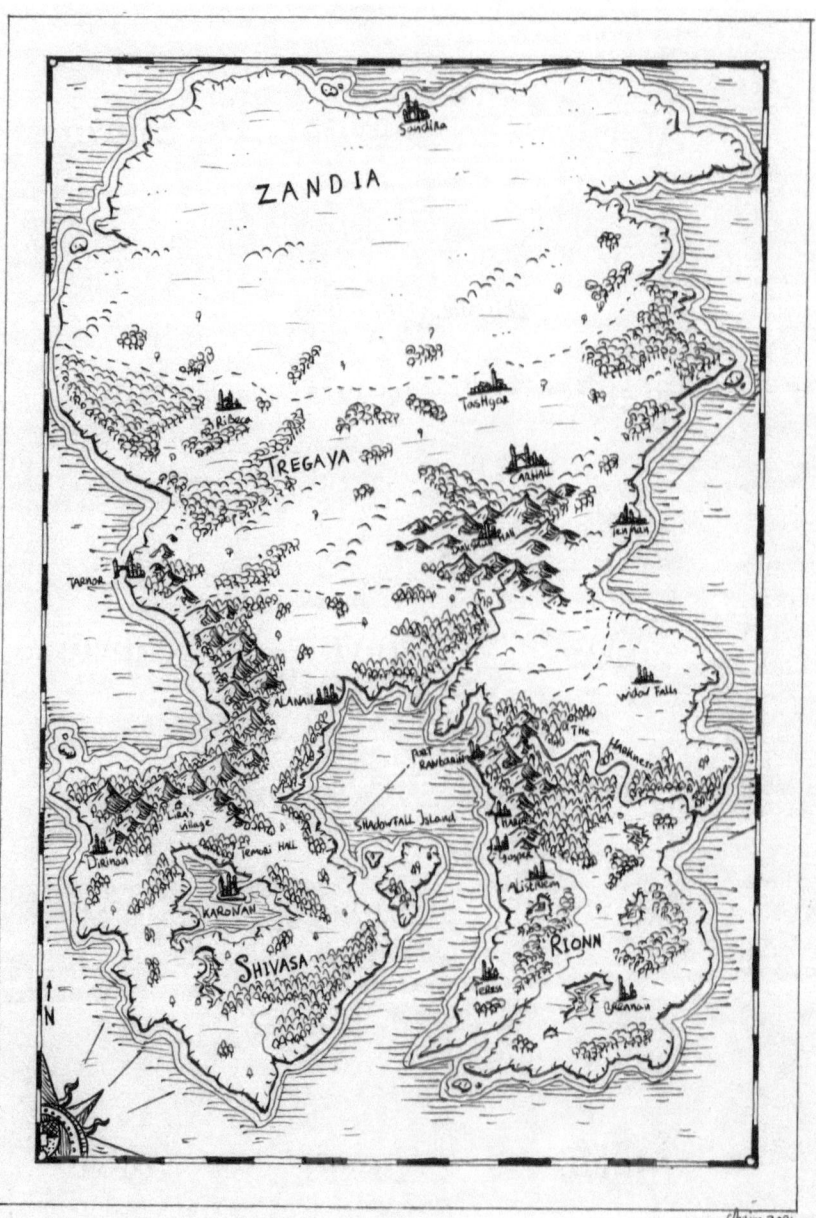

PART 1

CHAPTER 1

A distant thud permeated her dream. Then a second louder thud, followed by the sharp crack of splintering wood.

"Alyx, get up!"

Deeply asleep, she struggled to rise to consciousness. Someone grabbed her arm, shaking fiercely. Another voice cursed. Then came a series of shouts, followed by the distant ring of metal crashing on metal.

"Magor-lier!"

Rothai's cold voice in her ear finally broke the hold of sleep. Blinking, she shoved at the arm grabbing her—Tarrick—and scrambled to her feet. A thread of magic and her staff was flying to her hand, the touch of its smooth wood instantly reassuring. It took a moment to orient herself—she was in the guest wing of King Mastaran's palace just outside of Carhall.

"Hunters," Tarrick said tersely before she could ask.

"How close?" She struggled to gather her sleepy thoughts. Sleeping in a proper bed after months on the move had meant a deeper sleep than usual. Still, after being on the run for so long, she'd become well-practiced at moving quickly from sleep to battle readiness. Her magic sparked.

"Heading our way. Finn and Tari have gone to hold them off. We need to get you out via the escape route we practiced."

The distant crash of breaking glass emphasised his words. She moved to the door, readying her magic to fight, despite knowing Hunters would be impervious to it. "We have to make sure Cayr and his father are all right.

Mastaran too. It might not be me they're after this time—we only arrived yesterday."

The summit had been low key, discussions between the two kings on how to deal with the increasing Shiven incursions. Alyx and her mages had deliberately arrived late to reduce the risk of exactly this happening. And it had happened anyway. Frustration burned through her.

Tarrick took her arm again. "No. We need to get you out. I'll go first."

Frustration flared to anger. "I'm not—"

"Both kings' guards will be doing the same thing, Magor-lier," Rothai said before she could protest. "Trust them to do their jobs."

As soon as Tarrick cracked open the door, the sounds of fighting drifted in. A long corridor loomed to their left, the entrance to the guest wing only a few steps around the corner to the right. A scream of pain was so close it made her stomach twist. "How many are there? Surely I can help," she argued.

"Getting you out is the priority," Rothai snapped. "Quickly now!"

"Come on!" Tarrick urged, turning right into the corridor, away from the sound of fighting.

It was no use arguing with them. She'd tried it before, each time they'd been found by Shakar's Hunters and had to flee for their lives. They hadn't backed down before and they wouldn't now. The Magor-lier's life was the ultimate priority. And each time she had to abandon her comrades and run, it left more of a scar.

Her mind kept flashing to Cayr in the opposite wing of the palace, stomach churning with worry so potent her hands were trembling.

Neither man spoke as they shepherded her down a narrow servant staircase and into a tiny storage room at the back of the guest wing's kitchens. Rothai strode forward to shove several crates of potatoes aside, revealing a trapdoor in the floor.

Mastaran's personal militia guard had shown them this exit only the day before. Just like the palace in Alistriem, Mastaran's home was riddled with escape routes in the case of attack. Particularly necessary given his home sat outside the protective walls of Carhall City.

Tarrick urged her onto the ladder leading downwards after Rothai, then brought up the rear. Darkness closed around them when he shut the trapdoor, as heavy as her distress. It didn't take long before they reached the bottom. Flint scraped, and then there was a bright flicker as Rothai lit a small lamp.

"Quickly." Rothai's voice snapped out of the darkness.

She bit down on a sharp retort and pushed past him, determined to take the lead in *something*. Sometimes it felt as if the last year of her life had been nothing but listening to either Rothai or Tarrick telling her she needed to keep hiding, that she needed to learn more before she could face Shakar and destroy him.

And now they were running. Again.

The flicker of flamelight ahead had Rothai trying to push past her, but she thrust an arm out to stop him. Her pace quickened in relief as she recognised the cluster of figures in the tunnel. A matching expression crossed Cayr's face as he caught sight of her. He was surrounded by three Bluecoats.

"Your father?" she asked.

He gestured up to where an older man was climbing down a swaying rope ladder. Cayr's father. The king was pale, sweat beading his forehead despite the cool air of the tunnel. Above him, watching his king protectively, were two more Bluecoats—one of them Tijer's familiar face.

"Do you know what's happening?" Cayr asked Alyx.

"Hunters in the palace, that's all I know," she said. "They rushed me out before we could learn more. Did it seem like they were coming for you?"

"Unclear. Captain Tijer moved us out too quickly." Cayr looked grim but unafraid.

A flicker in Alyx's peripheral vision had her turning to see Jenna Aridlen, dressed in a beautiful gown, hovering just outside the light cast by the lantern one of the Bluecoats was holding. All three were casting her strange glances, as if wondering what she was doing with them.

"The rest of my father's attendants were staying in a different block of rooms," Cayr murmured, anticipating her question about Jenna. "They were taken out another way. Jenna insisted she come with us."

Bootsteps thudded as Cayr's father reached the ground, Tijer dropping lithely after him. The Bluecoat captain gave Alyx a nod of acknowledgement. "We should move. We can't be sure how long the rendezvous point will remain clear."

"I'll lead." Rothai pushed forward. "Tarrick, you bring up the rear."

"King Mastaran?" Alyx asked Tijer.

"Stayed in Carhall for the night, fortunately," he said, then rapped out a quick series of orders to the Bluecoats. They began moving along the tunnel. Alyx ran just behind Rothai with two Bluecoats close behind. Cayr, his father and Jenna followed, surrounded by Tijer and the remaining Bluecoats.

Her magic was still functioning which meant there weren't any Hunters close by. She wondered what their target had been, and hoped Finn and her other mage guards were okay. They knew where the rendezvous point was. At least Cayr and his father were out and safe. And Mastaran was still in Carhall... so either this was a poorly-planned attack, or the Hunters hadn't been after the Tregayan king.

Adrenalin thudded through her, making her heart race even though they were moving at a slow jog. The tunnel wasn't overly long—it would emerge into a thickly wooded area a good mile east of the palace. If Finn and her guard had fought clear, they would have gathered the horses and be waiting. King Darien's Bluecoats would be doing the same. If they hadn't... Alyx dismissed that thought. Fearing for her friends only skewed her focus. There was time for fear and worry once they were clear.

A shout from behind had them all stopping. Her heart thudded at the note of panic in Tijer's voice and she pushed through the two Bluecoats behind her to reach him. He had his arm around Cayr's father, who was staggering, head lolling back.

"What's wrong?" Cayr's voice was sharp with worry.

"I don't know." Tijer placed the king gently against the wall, and immediately he slumped to the ground. He was lathered in sweat, and he clutched at his chest, a rictus of pain etched into his features.

"Magor-lier, we should keep moving." Rothai's insistent voice sounded.

She ignored him, dropping to her knees beside the king. His breath was raspy, his skin turned the colour of milk. Short gasps escaped his mouth, which was moving, trying to form words but failing.

"It's his heart." Cayr stood over them, stricken. "He's been having problems. Ever since Casovar weakened him..."

"Lady Egalion, can you do anything?" Tijer looked as stricken as Cayr—she'd never, not once in her life, seen his serious face so scared.

She reached out, placed her palm on the king's clammy neck. His pulse jumped erratically, stopping and then starting. Her chest tightened in sympathy. "We need Finn. Dammit."

"Alyx, you can—"

"I haven't absorbed Finn's talent, Tarrick!" she almost shouted, utterly failing to rein in her mixed frustration and terror. "You know that healing ability is close to impossible to absorb."

She could give Darien strength, but that was the limit of her ability. It wasn't helping—that was obvious. No matter what she fed him with her magic, it made no difference to the struggling man. Pain rippled across his features, eyes rolling back in his head. He'd stopped trying to talk. She glanced up at Cayr. Tears made his blue eyes brighter than usual.

A shocked silence descended as realisation sunk in of what was happening. The king of Rionn was going to die here in this tunnel and Alyx couldn't do anything about it. Her best friend's father, and she was useless.

"Your Highness!" Tijer leaned over him, gripping his shoulders. "I'm going to carry you out of here. There's a mage healer, he'll be at the rendezvous point."

Darien shook his head. He wasn't going to make it that far. He managed to lift a shaking hand, covering Tijer's. His eyes flickered closed momentarily, as if he were summoning whatever strength he had left to speak. "My son...keep him safe."

"I will. I...dammit!" Tijer's voice mixed pain and helpless anger.

"Father!" Cayr was there then, pushing Alyx out of the way and pulling Darien into his arms. The king's eyes slid closed. When she touched his arm, his pulse had gone. Cayr's hand reached for hers, his eyes glassy. She squeezed back tightly.

"I'm so sorry," she whispered.

He swallowed, head bowed, muscles rigid. She didn't know what to do. What to say. It was all so unreal. So sudden. The king of Rionn had just died in a dark tunnel fleeing from a Hunter attack. Guilt sucked at her and her grip on Cayr's hand tightened.

For a long moment heavy silence filled the tunnel. Rothai and Tarrick hovered in the background. It was Tijer who spoke first, standing and stepping away from Darien Llancarvan's body.

"We must get the king to safety," he said.

As one, every glance shifted to Cayr, still kneeling over his father's body. Now the king of Rionn.

A rustling sound broke the silence. Alyx looked over to where Jenna was stripping off the skirts of her dress, revealing breeches underneath. Next went her bodice. Under that was a thin shirt. Alyx leapt to her feet, pushing Jenna back into the shadows before she could draw the sword she'd been concealing in a rolled-up cloak.

"What are you doing?" Alyx hissed. "If you reveal yourself as a Taliath—"

"My prince is now my king. His life is worth more than mine. It is my duty to keep him safe, and I cannot do that while pretending to be other than I am." Jenna gave Alyx a hard shove and walked back into the light, striding up to Tijer. "I will stay with the king and Lady Egalion. Your men will take point. We need to keep moving."

Cayr blinked, looking up helplessly at Alyx. Grief and guilt and regret all threatened to overwhelm her but she fought it back, managing to hold the emotions at bay long enough to reach out and rest her hand against his tear-streaked cheek. "You are king now, Cayr. I am so sorry, but we have to go." She fixed her gaze on his blue eyes. "You have to be strong. Mourning can come later."

He squeezed her hand again, so tightly it hurt, but then he gave her a nod. Her heart bled for her best friend, for the raw pain that spilled out of him, for the way he had to push his grief away and become a king.

It was a grim party that emerged into thick woods just after dawn. It had been raining, and water dripped from the leaves around them with a steady tapping sound. Hoofbeats thudded in the distance. Alyx threw out her telepathic magic.

"It's all right," she reported. "It's Finn, plus Tari and the rest of the Bluecoats."

Soon the clearing was a chaotic mess of milling horses and soldiers. Tijer shouted for some order. Finn and Tari came straight to Alyx, leading their horses. The sight of Finn made her heart twist in her chest. If only he'd been with them... if only he hadn't been off protecting *her,* Cayr's father might still be alive.

An odd silence fell over the clearing when the Bluecoats began to realise who Tijer was carrying in his arms. One by one they dismounted, taking their hats off and kneeling in the mud before Cayr.

The new king of Rionn sent a helpless glance Alyx's way, as if to ask what he was supposed to do now. She couldn't help him, not with this. Tarrick was already tugging at her arm, telling her they needed to move.

"Our priority is getting my father home to be buried," Cayr said eventually. There was a slight tremor to his voice, but she was proud of how straight he stood, how strong his words were. "There will be time for mourning then."

"Aye, Your Highness," Tijer spoke. At his words, the Bluecoats scrambled to their feet and returned to their horses. A disciplined, efficient unit, they were surrounding Cayr and ready to go in moments.

"Alyx, come on!" Tarrick urged. "We have to go."

Walking away from Cayr during what had to be the toughest moment of his life tore her apart. She met his gaze—he was mounted now with Tijer on one side and Jenna on the other—and tried to convey her regret and sorrow.

He bit his lip, looking lost and unsure. There was nothing more she wanted in that moment than to go to him.

"We have to go too, Lady Egalion." Tijer's voice was rough. "They could discover us at any moment."

She nodded, heart in her throat as she met Cayr's eyes. "Be safe."

He tried to smile for her but failed. "You too."

She couldn't even promise that she would see them again soon. Tears fought to fall and she ruthlessly held them back. "Goodbye, Cayr. I love you."

Once the Bluecoats were gone, they mounted in silence, Rothai leading the way, heading northeast at a fast gallop.

But no matter how far away they got, her thoughts lingered with Cayr. She was his best friend and he'd just lost his father. He was now king of Rionn. And she had to leave him.

She would never forgive herself for it.

CHAPTER 2

They hadn't entirely worked out how the Hunters kept finding them, no matter where they hid, but the general assumption was that Shakar was using his telepathic magic—or that of one of the mages that followed him—to track them. In their urgent departure from Carhall, nobody had time for thinking about it any further.

The plan had always been to remain in Carhall only a handful of days before travelling on to a safehouse in an abandoned underground copper mine in the isolated countryside of eastern Tregaya. And after ensuring they hadn't been followed, this was where Rothai led them.

It had been Finn who'd worked out that telepathic magic couldn't penetrate underground, and the mine had become a base of sorts for the ragged group of mages that had survived the attack on DarkSkull and chosen not to return to the Mage Council.

No mage who lacked a disciplined mental shield even knew about the place, let alone was ever brought there. Rothai kept Alyx's visits there short and infrequent. Still, it was the only central safe location they had.

They arrived just over a week after fleeing Carhall, weary to the bone. Rothai had pushed them hard and Alyx hadn't fought him on it. The exhaustion had helped keep her bitterness and grief at bay. As had her determination to do something, *anything* to make this better. The time in the saddle had allowed her to think, to come to a decision that at least would allay some of the terrible guilt she'd been feeling.

"I'm sorry about Cayr's father." Tarrick looked uncomfortable as they dismounted and saw to the horses.

"So am I," she said shortly. "I've been thinking about it ever since we left Carhall, and I want to talk about what happens next. I think we need to go to Sandira."

"Magor-lier, we talked about—"

"I know it's dangerous, and I know we just walked away from another Hunter attack, but the king of Rionn is dead!" Anger filled her voice. "What if Shakar sees that as a vulnerability and attacks? We need allies and we need Zandia's army."

"Cayr might be young, but he's not weak," Tarrick said.

"We know that, but Shakar doesn't. What is it you think comes next—more running from place to place? When does it stop? I need to *do* something."

"Tomorrow." Finn stepped between them, voice calm. "We're exhausted and upset. We can discuss this first thing tomorrow after rest."

She stared at him, chest heaving, wanting to keep shouting, wanting to force their agreement now. She wasn't sure she could sleep without feeling like she was doing something to help Cayr.

"Please, Alyx. None of us are thinking straight," Finn pleaded. "We'll talk tomorrow, I promise."

"Fine." She pushed past them both, stalking into the mine entrance without another word.

They occupied only a small section of the mine—the remainder of it too unstable after so long in disuse. Even so, Alyx managed to avoid running into any of the mages living there on her way to her private room, a tiny space carved into the rock which branched off a long, winding tunnel. Someone had left a fresh lamp burning, illuminating the narrow pallet and her few possessions scattered across the top of an old crate.

She pulled the curtain across the entrance and tugged her boots off before changing into an old, baggy sleeping shirt. Her stormy emotions were quickly fading in the face of physical exhaustion. Now all she felt was heartsick.

Once settled, she reached under her pillow and pulled out the small silver bracelet she kept hidden there. Tears welled in her eyes and she blew out the lamp before curling up on the pallet, hugging the blanket to her and finally allowing herself to think about Dashan.

Alyx hadn't seen him since that bright, sunny morning they'd said goodbye on the dock at Ester. His features had faded in her mind, but she still remembered those expressive dark Shiven eyes as if she'd seen them only yesterday. She'd never imagined they'd be apart so long; she missed him badly, and that feeling had only intensified in the time since she'd last seen him.

He'd only completed a half year of training on ShadowFall Island before her father had sent for him. Unrest in Shivasa had steadily worsened until much of the south of the country was in open revolt. With his Shiven blood and Taliath skill, Dashan was the perfect man to send into Shivasa to help the rebels in undermining the Shiven government. Her father had written to her about it, noting he hoped to cause enough problems in Shivasa that the military had to be diverted away from the Rionnan border to help quell the unrest.

Ladan too had left ShadowFall Island. He fought in the disputed area, helping to hold back the encroaching Shiven army, his life in danger every day. And when he wasn't there he was back at Widow Falls, helping to ensure the movement of supplies and weapons from Tregaya kept moving through safely.

Despite their best efforts, the Shiven gained inches more territory each month. Darien Llancarvan's death placed Rionn in a more precarious state than ever. The court had little choice but to accept such a young king, but Cayr might have to spend so much time and effort bringing them to his will that he had little left over for dealing with the Shiven pushing at their borders. And all amidst grieving his lost father.

She worried about all of them constantly. It wasn't only Dashan she ached at being apart from—those she loved most in the world were all fighting in one way or another. What if something happened to one of them and she wasn't there to help?

It would break her.

Unable to manage more than an hour or two of sleep, she was up early. A rusted iron ladder took her down to a large space they used to prepare food and drink. Over plain oats and hot tea she mused on what it was going to take to convince the others that a trip to Zandia was necessary.

The emperor commanded the most powerful armed forces on the continent aside from Shivasa, and his support would be crucial to any successful alliance. Alyx hoped that together they could first deal with the Shiven threat, which would then leave them free to focus all their resources on defeating Shakar. A much better strategy than relying on Alyx's magical abilities, no matter how strong they were.

When she'd first raised the idea a few months earlier, Rothai, Tarrick and Finn had all decided against it. A public trip would place Alyx in too much danger, they believed, leaving her vulnerable to a Hunter attack. But Darien's death had changed the balance. Rionn was in trouble, *Cayr* was in trouble, and she needed to do something to help.

"You mind some company?" Finn's head of messy curls appeared at the top of the ladder.

Alyx waved him in, her gaze searching him from head to toe for signs of injury. She'd been so upset in their escape from Carhall she hadn't properly checked if any of them were hurt. "You're okay?"

"Not a scratch," he assured her.

"This time," she muttered, anger surging despite her best efforts.

"Alyx, I know the king's death was upsetting, and that you wish you could be there for your friend." His understanding gaze met hers. "But at least, right now in this moment, we're safe. Appreciate that."

She scowled at him. "Not anymore, Finn. I can't *appreciate* being forcibly cooped up in here. Something has to change."

"We've talked about this." Finn's patience didn't help her irritation.

"Running away isn't going to help us defeat him. And now things are worse. You know as well as I do how vulnerable Rionn will be until Cayr can establish his rule."

"I get that, but it's also not going to do anybody any good if you get killed because you face Shakar when you aren't yet capable of defeating him," he pointed out. "Training and time will increase your chances of defeating Shakar."

Alyx shook her head. "Shakar is a mage of the higher order who has been alive far longer than I have. He has undoubtedly absorbed many more abilities and has had a lot of time to hone them. I can't ever catch up. And even if I could, he's invulnerable."

Silence filled the room, her words echoing around them with the inevitable ring of finality. It was the elephant in the room. The thing none of them had spoken aloud, but all knew in the backs of their minds. Mage of the higher order she might be. More powerful than any other mage, maybe. But Shakar was invulnerable to magic.

After a moment, Finn shook his head in obvious frustration. "It's not as simple as you keep making it sound. Yes, he's invulnerable, which means you can't touch him directly with your magic. It doesn't mean you couldn't use telekinetic power to pick up the chair you're sitting on and throw it at his head."

Around and around this argument always went. She bit down on her usual response: that invulnerable or not, Shakar was still stronger and more skilled, and forever would be. "I'm not talking about facing down Shakar tomorrow. I'm talking about travelling to Sandira to seek a military alliance with the emperor of Zandia. Cayr can't leave Alistriem now to do it, and I doubt Mastaran will be willing to venture outside the walls of Carhall anytime soon."

Finn sighed. "We just need to—"

"Magor-lier?"

Both turned to the narrow opening in the rocky wall opposite where they sat. The young warrior mage standing there lifted his eyebrows in surprise at the looks directed his way. Finn's patience with her had finally snapped, and irritation was written all over his face. Her disgruntlement came from a different source—she *detested* the title everyone insisted on giving her. Rothai had started it, but only because she was the strongest mage fighting against Shakar. She held no real power, evidenced by her confinement to whichever hiding place they'd found for the moment.

"What is it, Nordan?" Finn asked.

Tall and slim, the ice-mage's demeanour matched his mage ability perfectly. Slicked back dark hair framed a narrow, pale-skinned face and grey eyes. Beyond his faint indication of surprise, he was utterly unmoved by their bad moods. "Sorry to interrupt. Master Rothai is awake—he asked me to fetch you. He said you'd planned to meet this morning?"

Alyx stood and shoved her chair back against the table with more force than was necessary and stalked from the room. Finn followed silently.

The constant waves of Hunters coming at her made it nigh impossible for Alyx's group to gain strength or plan strategically. It was beyond frustrating that Shakar's assassins were able to find them no matter where they went outside of the mine, and despite Tarrick, Finn and Rothai's reasoned arguments, Alyx was beginning to suspect there was more than just Shakar's telepathy at play.

While she didn't claim to be a master at that aspect of her magic, she was not convinced she'd be able to track down a single group of minds over an entire continent so consistently. Particularly given how disciplined their mental shielding was. He'd have to be watching at one of the infrequent instances where one of them lost concentration and dropped their shield momentarily.

She would talk to Dawn about it next time they spoke. Whenever that was. A pang tugged at her. She missed her friend, currently in Alistriem with Cario. At least Cayr would have them at his side—the thought made her gladder than ever she'd left them behind to help fight back the Shiven in her absence.

Tarrick stood as she and Finn ducked under a low entrance way to enter the room they used to hold meetings. It had once been a storage area for sacks of food, judging from some mouldering supplies they'd found on first arriving. Rothai leaned against a half-cracked beam holding the roof upright. She gave it a dubious look, glad she wasn't claustrophobic.

"Magor-lier!" Tarrick greeted her brightly.

Oh for...! "Damn it, Tarrick, how many times do I have to tell you to stop calling me that!"

"It's your title."

"No, it's the title that you insist on giving me." She tried for calm. "I'm not anybody's leader, not hiding in here wrapped up in twenty layers of protection."

He cleared his throat, clearly struggling for patience. "Magor-lier, there are good reasons for—"

"Stop calling me that!"

A stack of rolled up maps on the table went flying in all directions, one smacking Finn's shoulder as it flew past. Another landed precariously close to one of the few lanterns providing light. Rothai gave Alyx a look of reproach at the evidence of her lack of control over her magic. Nobody said anything. She abruptly felt like a child all the adults were disapproving of.

She took a deep breath. "I'm sorry for shouting. Tarrick, you're one of my best friends. Please can you just call me by my name?"

Finn smiled slightly, then jerked a finger at Rothai. "I enjoy how you don't have a problem with him calling you by your title."

Tarrick chuckled, and even Rothai's severe expression softened, breaking the tension in the room. Alyx smiled too.

"I know you wish to talk to us, Magor-lier, but before we start, a message from Lord-Mage Astor arrived while we were away." Rothai held up a small piece of curling parchment.

Her heart thudded. Astor. He wouldn't know about Darien's death yet, but he would grieve the king's loss deeply. "What did he have to say?"

"That he was leaving Alistriem on a trip to meet with the Mage Council—apparently they requested it. He asked that we meet him in Racc if we get this message in time and are close enough to travel there."

"That's good," she said firmly. "Racc is not far out of the way if we're heading north to Zandia."

A moment's silence. She tried not to be furious at the glances the three men threw each other. Tarrick let out a breath. "I concede that the situation has changed. Rionn's new vulnerability could be dangerous—if Shakar's Shiven pressed harder now... an alliance with Zandia might make Shakar more cautious. But the danger to you hasn't changed. I propose that Finn and I travel to Sandira to speak with the emperor."

Alyx lifted an eyebrow. "And what will I do while you're off enjoying the emperor's hospitality?"

"Continue your training," Rothai said smoothly.

Spending weeks cooped up in the mine doing nothing but practicing magic was an unbearable thought. Not with how helpless she felt, how desperate she was to do something, anything. "No, I'm coming with you."

Finn cleared his throat. "This is a very public trip to Sandira, or at least it will be once we've arrived. If Shakar gets wind of where you are, he'll send his Hunters after you."

"Have you considered that the Zandian emperor will be much more likely to listen to our request if I'm there in person?" she countered, arching an eyebrow. "Tarrick, you're the one that told me the Zandians have a great deal of respect for mages of the higher order, that they remember the days of the Magor-lier. What makes you think he's even going to grant an audience to a motley collection of non-council mages, no matter your family connections?"

Tarrick's jaw clenched and he looked away.

Rothai opened his mouth. "Magor-lier—"

She summoned as much granite into her voice as she could muster. "I'm going, and that's final."

"Please, think it through," Finn urged. "There's a good chance Shakar will find out that you're in Sandira. If he does, we can't protect you."

"I think we can mitigate the risk." Reason was all that would convince them. "If we limit our time there, say to a week or two, no more, Shakar won't have enough time to get his Hunters so far north even if he learns of our presence as soon as we arrive in Sandira."

"He might have Hunters already there," Finn pointed out.

She raised a hand to forestall the inevitable agreement with Finn. "I'm going. You won't change my mind."

Rothai straightened from the wall and shrugged. "Then I'm coming too."

Relief flooded through her, leaving her almost lightheaded. Finally, she was going to be able to do something, and maybe even make a real difference to this war.

CHAPTER 3

Tarrick took the lead as they left the mine and headed east and slightly north, Rothai bringing up the rear. It was hard to tell which of the two was more focused. Alyx's gaze drifted over the rest of the party—it was a small group, but Rothai preferred that. It helped them avoid attention.

Apart from Tarrick, Finn, and Rothai, there were three other warrior mages, all handpicked and well-drilled in erecting their mental shields anytime they were outside the caves, and most particularly when they were near Alyx.

Of the three, she was most familiar with Jayn. The small, dark-haired mage was skilled with her staff and wielded a powerful magical shield. Perennially good-tempered, Jayn had been a member of Third Patrol when they were apprentices together back at DarkSkull Hall.

Adahn was another mage Alyx had met at DarkSkull, though she didn't know him as well. He'd passed his trials after her first year. Tari was an older mage, close to Rothai's age, with black hair always pulled back in a long plait that fell down her back. She was a quiet woman, and Alyx wasn't quite sure what to make of her yet.

Finn rode up beside her. "You look more relaxed already."

She smiled, giving another firm tug on the reins to hold in a restive Tingo. "Is it that obvious?"

He gave her a wry look, dark green eyes glinting with humour.

"I'm sorry I'm not better at this." She sighed, hands fiddling with her reins.

"Better at what?"

"Being the Magor-lier. Doing what you all need me to do."

He was quiet for a moment, thinking that over. She thought she'd surprised him, as if he hadn't realised that was the source of her discontent. "There's no manual on how to be the perfect Magor-lier," he said eventually. "Just like there's no manual on how to follow one. We're all doing our best."

"I know."

He arched an eyebrow. "Maybe remember that before you snap at Tarrick or me next time?"

She huffed a breath. "I'll try."

"Don't bother about Rothai, though. Snap at him all you like."

Alyx chuckled and returned Finn's grin, abruptly feeling better. She hated fighting with her friends, and despite their frequent disagreements, Finn was one of her oldest and dearest.

"We'll be okay," he said as if he could read her thoughts. "We just have to keep muddling through, and we'll get there in the end."

"It's not me that I'm worried about," she said, trying to keep the tears from her eyes. "It's Cayr, my best friend who has to become king in the middle of war, and everyone else I love who is in danger every moment and I can't help." Her hands tightened painfully on the reins.

He said nothing for a long moment, then he reached out to lightly touch her hand. "Me too," he whispered.

Two days later, Tarrick, Rothai, and Alyx left the others encamped on the outskirts of the bustling town of Racc. Clothed as travellers, they made straight for a specific inn on a secluded side street. Rothai spoke briefly to the innkeeper before directing them upstairs to a room on the top floor. A delighted smile spread over Alyx's face as the door opened to reveal her godfather. "Astor!"

Beaming himself, he stood back to let them in. "I must admit I'm surprised you managed to make it, though I am delighted you could. I was sure you'd have not long left Carhall."

Alyx's heart plummeted. "You haven't heard."

"Haven't heard what, Aly-girl?" His gaze sharpened on hers, penetrating and insistent.

Tarrick cleared his throat. "We'll leave you both a moment to catch up. Rothai and I should keep an eye outside anyway, just in case."

Alyx's gaze tracked the door closing, then fell to the floor. Astor said nothing, waiting for her to straighten her shoulders and meet his eyes. "There was a Hunter attack while we were in Carhall. The king... the stress of the escape... his heart was..." She stumbled, angry at herself for not being able to say the words. "He died. Cayr is now king."

Astor was still, unblinking, hands resting lightly in his lap. It was impossible to tell what he was thinking or feeling. After a long moment he gave himself a little shake. "Oh, Darien," he murmured.

"I'm sorry, Astor." She reached out to lay a hand over his. "I know you've been friends for many years."

He nodded absently, pale eyes settling on hers. "I suppose this news explains why you look so pale and drawn. Was anyone else hurt?"

"I'm not certain, but I don't think so. We had to leave so quickly." She swallowed. "I had to walk away and leave Cayr when his father had just died. He has to be king now, and I want to be there to help him, support him, but I can't. It's hard, running away all the time." Bitterness leaked into her voice despite her best efforts. "I hate every second of it."

"I know," he said softly, almost as if talking to himself. "And your news pales in comparison to the reason I asked to meet, though I'm glad I did. Darien's loss... I'm glad to know sooner rather than later."

She straightened, unable to dwell on their loss any longer. "I'm going to Zandia to ask the emperor for an alliance. I'd like your help. I want you to come with us. A representative of the Rionnan crown will only help our cause."

Astor sat back in his chair, letting her rush of words wash over him. "I hope you're not doing something reckless merely because you feel like you have to do *something*."

"It's risky," she admitted. "But necessary. You know as well as I do how vulnerable Cayr is going to be until he can assert his authority."

"I do." His eyes narrowed in thought. "And for what it's worth, I agree that an alliance with Zandia will forestall any perceived weakness in Rionn on Shivasa's part. But I can't come." He raised a hand to forestall her protests. "The council has officially requested my presence, and to flout such a direct request would only add to Rionn's precarious position. I'll send a bird to King Cayr today recommending he send someone immediately via ship to Sandira. If you're travelling overland, the timing should match up well enough."

She frowned at his mention of the Mage Council. While for all intents and purposes the council functioned as it always had, the masters hadn't ventured out of Carhall since the attack on DarkSkull. In the first days after the attack, Rothai had urged her to go north and join them in the formidable walled city. She'd flatly refused.

Over time, as Rothai learned through old contacts that the council's reach had diminished, along with their activities, he'd stopped trying to convince her. It wasn't only Alyx and those who followed her that Shakar's Hunters went after. Council mages were dying too.

Part of Alyx yearned to do more, to show leadership where the council hadn't, but all she could promise mages following her was the high chance of death. "What does the council want to see you about?"

He lifted his hands, giving her a little shrug.

She sighed. "I don't trust them, Astor. They murdered innocent children. Besides, it's not like they're doing much beyond hiding behind the walls of Carhall."

"Even so, is there anything else you need from me in Carhall?"

She hesitated, fighting through her gut-level hatred of the council. "Yes. I intended to speak with them while in Carhall, but the unexpected attack meant I couldn't. Would you please tell them of my trip, and offer that they send a representative to join us? The emperor is likely to respond more favourably to a request for alliance if the council and I appear unified."

"I agree." Astor smiled at her sympathetically. "I will pass on your offer and let them know that a representative from Rionn will attend."

"Can you also find out about Galien? Despite his murderous hatred of me, he's always claimed loyalty to the council. I want to know if that's still the case, and if so, what they have him doing."

Astor's gaze narrowed thoughtfully, though she got the distinct impression his mind was far away. "Yes of course, the other mage of the higher order." He blinked, eyes settling on hers. "I'll deal with that for you."

"And another thing. You know that before I fled Alistriem, Ladan and I found out that Shakar is probably a mage my mother knew personally?" She shook her head in frustration. "Tarrick and Finn and I have discussed it endlessly ever since, but we can't think of any good candidates. Could you do some sniffing around for us?"

"Of course I'll do anything I can to help. But you know I'm dubious about your theory. Even if Shakar could disguise himself so well that he could re-enter the mage world after them all thinking him dead... it would be arrogance in the extreme. And I'm not sure what he'd be hoping to achieve by it."

"Thank you." She sighed, leaned over to hug him. "I wish we had more time. It's so nice to see a familiar face from home."

"Maybe after you meet with the emperor you should consider going back to Alistriem, even if only for a few days," Astor suggested. "It might help if you could go home and see your family again. I know your father and brother miss you very much, and Cayr especially so after what's happened."

"I miss them too. I'd really like to do that," she said wistfully.

"Then give it some serious thought." He stood, beginning to usher her out. "Now, we both know you shouldn't linger. Keep safe in Sandira, Alyx."

She hugged him tightly. "You too. I hope to see you soon."

Alyx and her escort were well-accustomed to travelling light and fast, and in just over a week they approached Tregaya's northern border with Zandia. The Tregayan countryside had become more rugged as they moved north, less forested and green, but she saw no immediate difference when they crossed the border.

"Don't worry." Tarrick brought his horse up alongside Tingo, white teeth flashing against his dark skin. "You'll see desert soon enough."

"You must be happy to be going home." After all, he'd been away from his home far longer than she had hers. A good reminder she wasn't the only one affected by Shakar's existence.

His smile widened. "I can't wait to show it to you."

She returned his smile, touched by his uncharacteristic show of feeling. "Thanks, Tarrick. I suppose it's only fair, after you've spent so much time in my home city."

"I like Alistriem," Tarrick said. "It's got nothing on Sandira, though. You'll see."

"Is it really that different?"

"You remember the first time you saw Carhall? You and Dawn spoke about how much grander it seemed than your home."

"Yes."

"Well, you'll find the same with Sandira, only in a whole different way."

A little frisson of excitement tingled through her as he kicked his horse ahead. For the first time in a long time, she was excited by what lay ahead of her.

Later that night, Alyx lay staring up at the stars, wide-awake and unable to sleep. Finn snored softly beside her. Tarrick stood some distance from the dying embers of the fire, his back to the camp as he kept watch. Rothai slept soundly on Finn's other side. Alyx shifted in her blankets so that she could see the sleeping forms of the other mages with them.

Adahn was the closest. He slept sprawled out, one arm tucked under his head, his too-long chestnut hair covering half his face. He'd been a cocky, handsome apprentice during Alyx's first year at DarkSkull, well-liked and a member of the pure mage-blooded popular students.

Tari slept on Adahn's other side. A retired council warrior mage who'd been in Rothai's study group at DarkSkull, he had actively sought her out several months earlier. Alyx wished she knew how Rothai had convinced

Tari to join them—an old friendship surely couldn't be all there was to it. And she got the distinct sense Tari continued to reserve her judgment on Alyx's worth. Jayn, lying barely a handspan from her, muttered in her sleep and turned over. Alyx smiled. She'd been with them since the destruction of DarkSkull.

Tarrick shifted his stance and then relaxed. Alyx turned back to her other side, trying to get comfortable. Sleep remained frustratingly elusive for her. Her thoughts shifted to her recent fight with Finn and what seemed like her constant irritation with him, Tarrick, and Rothai.

She didn't want to be angry with them all the time, didn't want to be bitter and sharp. But managing the misery and frustration that had been building inside her for months was proving more and more difficult. The death of Cayr's father had been too much—Cayr was hurting and she couldn't help. Worse, she didn't know what to do about the situation. She missed home. She hated being so magically powerful yet so useless at the same time. She was terrified for those she loved.

And underlying all of that was a heavy dose of guilt. Her friends would be horrified to learn that she hadn't ended her relationship with a Taliath, that she and Dashan loved each other fiercely despite the distance between them. The fact they hadn't become lovers wouldn't matter—just the possibility of her absorbing his invulnerability was too great a threat. One Shakar in the world was bad enough. Two would wreak utter destruction. There was no doubt the Mage Council would turn all their resources to killing her and Dashan if they found out.

Her thoughts turned to Cario and Dawn in Alistriem. She'd sent them there because she couldn't go herself and they were the next best thing. Dawn's ability to read the thoughts of those around her had made Cayr's father far more effective at dealing with the Shiven incursions than he would otherwise have been. Cario's skill with diplomacy only added to that.

She missed them terribly, missed the way Cario would simply raise his eyebrow at her when she snapped at him, then wait patiently until she calmed down enough to talk rationally. More, she missed Dawn's quiet friendship and support. At least they would be there now to support Cayr. That gave her some comfort.

"You can't sleep either?"

Alyx shifted again as Finn's voice whispered in the darkness. "No. I was just lying here wishing Cario and Dawn were with us."

Finn let out a soft sigh. "You can't miss Dawn as much as I do. Part of me hopes King Cayr will send her to Sandira, but it would be almost as good if Cario came."

"What's keeping you from sleep?"

A hesitation, then, "I was thinking about Brynn, actually."

"Oh." Another pang of aching sadness shot through her, and she bit her lip. Sometimes it felt like she was never going to stop missing those she loved. Brynn was alive, or at least he had been eight months earlier when they'd received a message containing only greetings and an indication he was well, but none of them knew where he was or what he was doing.

Rothai told them Brynn had been and gone right before the attack on DarkSkull, sent on Mage Council business he wasn't aware of, just like Galien. She often wondered if the two absences had been connected, and each time the thought made her shiver.

"Why didn't he say more in his message?" Finn sounded frustrated, but underlying that was the same worry Alyx felt. Brynn was one of them, one of the original group that had bonded so fiercely during their first year at DarkSkull when they'd had nothing but each other to survive.

"I don't know. Maybe he couldn't." She sighed. "Brynn always has a reason for what he does."

"If he had enough time to write that he was alive and well, surely he had enough time to tell us what he was doing and explain why he hasn't come to us."

"I wish he had," Alyx admitted softly.

"Yeah, me too. He always makes me feel cheerful, you know? It's that smile of his, like nothing can bring him down." Rustling sounded as Finn settled into a different position. "I guess there's no point dwelling on it. We should try and get at least a little bit of sleep."

Soon after, his breathing evened. Alyx stared at Finn's back, thinking. The trip to Zandia was so important. If she could take an alliance back to Cayr, surely that would help him establish his rule and avert Shivasa taking advantage of a new king. Maybe it would even make her mages more open to letting her do something other than run and hide.

She hoped so. One thing had become a certainty—she couldn't keep running. Enough was enough.

As the days passed, the landscape gradually changed from dry, scrubby terrain with a few trees, to desert tundra. On the afternoon of the third day since crossing the border, Alyx realised with a start she hadn't seen a tree or bush since the previous afternoon.

"Have you ever been to Zandia?" Jayn spoke up. They'd been riding together in comfortable silence for a while.

Alyx shook her head. "You?"

"I've never been further north than Carhall, where I was born." The young woman laughed, her dark hair glinting in the bright sun. "This should be interesting."

"And hot," Tarrick called back to them.

"How long until we reach Sandira?" Jayn asked.

"If we travelled through the sands, it would take weeks. But since the stoneways were built, crossing Zandia is much easier. It shouldn't take us longer than a week. There are waystations along the stoneways, so we'll be able to get provisions at those."

"What are stoneways?" Alyx asked.

Tarrick was silent for a few seconds, then pointed out in front of him. "See for yourself."

They'd come to the top of a shallow rise. Below them, a long, wide road curved through the golden desert. As they rode closer, horses slipping slightly in the sand, the road became clearer. Constructed entirely of smoothly paved stone, it was swept free of sand and completely flat.

"That goes all the way to Sandira?" Adahn asked in interest, raising a hand to sweep chestnut hair from his eyes and peer ahead. Alyx glanced at him. He'd joined them months earlier, walking away from the council to do it. Outwardly, his lively and overly self-assured personality hadn't changed from what she remembered as an initiate at DarkSkull. She wondered what it hid. If anything.

"It certainly does," Tarrick answered. "And work crews travel through on a steady rotation every few months keeping them swept clean of debris."

"That's amazing!" Finn and Adahn said together.

Jayn chuckled and shared an amused glance with Tari. Alyx was equally impressed. Rothai was still watching their back-trail, wondrous sights paling in comparison to his obsession with keeping Alyx safe.

"Is this the only one?" Tari asked.

"No. Several of them crisscross Zandia, linking all the major cities. My father told me they took almost fifty years to complete," Tarrick said.

"They would allow the emperor to move his army south quickly if needed," Finn noted.

"Indeed," Alyx murmured, her gaze half on the stoneway, half on a future where Zandia helped them defeat Shivasa and they were free to face an isolated Shakar and finish this once and for all.

"What are you thinking that has you frowning like that?" Adahn asked. He'd ridden his horse up without her realising. As always, there was an amused glint in his eyes, robbing any real seriousness from his words.

"Why are you with us?" The words came out without thinking, and he lifted his eyebrows in surprise.

"I already told you that. The council wasn't doing anything to hunt Shakar. They sit in Carhall and do nothing more than increase the numbers of mage warriors sent out on assignment." Frustration edged his voice. "When I asked what their plan was to defeat Shakar, they told me to mind my business and follow orders like a good little warrior mage."

She considered him. "It's not like we're actively hunting Shakar either. All we do is run."

"Which you hate," he murmured. "I see you, Magor-lier. One day you're going to go at him, and I want to be there when that happens. Of any mage alive, you're the only one with any hope of beating him."

His words were low, intense, taking her by surprise. As if equally uncomfortable, he cleared his throat and then gave her a little nod before kicking his horse forward. Her eyes lingered on his back.

One more person to let down if she couldn't do what they all desperately hoped she could. The weight of that made it hard to breathe.

CHAPTER 4

M age robes were packed away one by one as they travelled deeper
into the seemingly endless desert. Even the horses felt the
oppressive heat; Tingo was much less eager to run than usual, and the
insects that buzzed around at night made the horses, and people, extremely
irritable.

Alyx's initial excitement about the new landscape faded as days passed
with no change to the unending sand around them. The stoneways and
the occasional waystation were all that broke up the monotony of the
flat, waterless landscape. When they finally reached Sandira, however, her
first sight of the wondrous city was worth all the long days of heat and
monotony.

Built along the turquoise northern ocean, the capital city of Zandia
sprawled out for miles into the desert. While Alistriem was all stately
homes and bustling markets, and Carhall wide, tree-lined avenues and
marble halls, this city was an exotic riot of coloured tents and sandstone
buildings. She couldn't do anything but gape in wonder, Tingo shifting
restlessly under her as they sat on their horses staring down at the city laid
out below them.

"How is there enough drinking water to support such a massive city?"
Finn asked.

"Really? That's your first question after seeing all... that!" Jayn lifted her
eyebrows at him.

Finn gave a sheepish shrug. "I'm curious."

Tarrick barely smothered a smile. "Underground lakes," he said. "They're scattered around the coastline of Zandia. Most of our towns were built along the coast for that reason, and of course for the ease of access to shipping."

"I've never seen anything like it," Alyx said in awe. He'd left all this to come with her to Alistriem? The thought humbled her.

"There's the emperor's palace." Tarrick pointed.

In the middle of all the bright chaos, situated on a section of raised ground, was a building surrounded on all four sides by high sandstone walls mounted with steel spikes. Her mind boggled at the sheer size of it. At least three miles long, and two wide, the palace looked like a small city unto itself.

Green gardens—astonishing for a desert city—littered the interior of the palace grounds, interspersed between tall buildings, the lowest of which had to be at least seven stories high.

"What does he need all that space for?" Tari asked.

"It looks like they have an entire barracks in there," Adahn said thoughtfully. "Look, where the soldiers are drilling? But that only takes up a small part of the overall size."

Tarrick grinned at their astonished faces. "See that whole eastern third, the buildings separated by a garden running the length of the walls? That's the emperor's harem. No man is allowed inside those walls except for the emperor himself. That wing is heavily guarded by the Leopards."

"How many wives does he have?" Jayn asked incredulously.

"Last I knew, he had twenty wives and at least double that number of concubines."

"Busy man," Adahn said, straight-faced. Finn snorted, then the rest of them burst into laughter.

"We should keep moving," Rothai interrupted the chuckles. Reluctantly, they tore their eyes from the wonderful sight below them and urged their horses on.

"Where in the city does your family live?" Alyx asked Tarrick.

He looked pleased she'd asked. "The Tylender home is in the sea quarter—you might have seen the cluster of bigger houses down by the water? Both of my brothers live in the Leopards' barracks inside the palace though."

"Your brothers are Leopards?" Jayn asked.

"Yes, they're both mage-trained and Leopard trained," Tarrick said. "They used to serve as bodyguards to the eldest prince, who was a mage of the higher order. When he disappeared, they became the strongest warrior mages serving the emperor."

"How many warrior mages does the emperor have at his disposal?" Alyx asked in interest.

"Only about twenty or so. Most Zandian mages join the council after graduating DarkSkull. The emperor likes having a ceremonial mage guard, but the Leopards are so well-trained and skilful, there's really no need for so many mage warriors."

The city was as bustling and crowded as Alistriem, but on a much grander scale. Vendors shouted their wares over and above each other, their cries blending with dogs barking, chickens squawking, and the general chatter of the populace. Overlaying all of it was the enticing scent of strange spices Alyx had never encountered before.

Their group got a few curious glances. They stood out with their fair skin and lighter hair, and the black robes rolled up behind their saddles marked them instantly as mages.

A wide square sat before the main gates to the palace, a beautifully carved stone statue of a leaping leopard at its centre. Water fountained from the top of the statue and splashed into a pool surrounding it. People crowded around the sparkling water, resting in the shade from the hot glare of the sun.

Market stalls lined the edges of the square, their awnings reflecting all the colours of the rainbow, selling goods ranging from caged ferrets to fresh fruit. Birds fluttered amongst the bustle, picking up fallen crumbs of food and screeching loudly whenever they encountered competition for the scraps. Alyx drank it in with delight—she'd never been anywhere so vibrant before.

"Those are the Leopards," Tarrick murmured, pointing to six guards standing in a perfectly straight line before the palace gates. "Let's hope my messages to my brothers were received and they have warned the palace of our arrival."

She eyed them curiously. All men, they wore a black wrap around their waists that hung to their knees, trimmed in gold thread, and that was all. Curved sabres hung at their belts, and their black hair was long, plaited neatly and falling almost to their hips. Their gazes were hard, steady and unblinking. In the full minute she watched them, none visibly moved, although she got the distinct impression those sharp gazes missed nothing.

"It's against the law for any Zandian male but the Leopards to wear their hair long and braided in such a way," Tarrick explained. "It's a mark of honour."

"So no female Leopards then?" Alyx lifted an eyebrow.

Tarrick cleared his throat, glancing away sheepishly. "No. There's a law against that, too."

"What if your brothers didn't receive your messages?" Jayn asked.

"Then we won't be getting anywhere near the inside of that palace."

One of the Leopards stepped forward to intercept them once it became obvious Alyx's party was making for the gates. He moved with an easy grace that brought to mind her Taliath brother and father. She refused to let herself think about Dashan.

"I am Mage Warrior Tarrick Tylender." Tarrick bowed his head politely. "I travel with Magor-lier Alyx Egalion. We are here to see the emperor."

The soldier's hard expression softened marginally. "Mage Tylender, we have been informed of your arrival. Come through, and I will send a runner to alert the emperor's aide."

Tarrick's shoulders relaxed at their words. Two Leopards moved gracefully to open the gates. The last horse was barely through before they were swung shut, immediately cutting out most of the noise of the city.

A circular courtyard faced them—it was easily three times the size of the one at the palace back in Alistriem. A tranquil pond sat in its centre, white lilies floating on the surface. Most of the yard was walled in, but greenery was visible beyond.

For a moment they sat there in the sudden quiet, alone in the massive space. But then, as if timed to perfection, several young boys came padding through a nearby gate, surrounding them and offering to take the horses. Despite their youth, they handled the highly-strung mage mounts with casual skill.

A servant wearing flowing white robes appeared to greet them, speaking flawlessly in the language shared by Tregaya and Rionn. "Welcome to Sandira. Please, follow me."

Tarrick didn't hesitate, and the rest fell in behind him. Alyx relished the coolness as they followed the servant into a high-ceilinged reception hall. A long walk followed, during which she caught glimpses of gardens, open-aired hallways and other sprawling buildings. The sandstone walls gleamed in the afternoon sun, the dry heat of the day tangible in the sluggish breeze that flowed through the halls. By the time they reached their destination, she was thoroughly disoriented.

Their servant guide came to a halt in a wide hallway with closed doors to the left and right. The hall ended in thick sandstone. "This wing has been set aside for your stay, Magor-lier, Mage Tylender. The servants who have access to the area have been thoroughly vetted by the Leopards and there will be a guard set at every possible entrance throughout your stay. The emperor wishes you to feel safe here."

"Your hospitality is appreciated. Nevertheless, we would appreciate the chance to speak with the Leopard captain in charge of the guard rotation," Tarrick said politely, speaking slowly enough Alyx could follow his fluent Zandian.

A smooth nod. "I will arrange it. If there is anything else you require, please use the bell by your doors and a servant will come immediately. My name is Iman. I ask that you call for me at once if you encounter any problems. The emperor has set aside some time in his schedule later today to receive you."

"Thank you, Iman," Alyx said before either Tarrick or Rothai could make any more potentially offensive remarks about her protection. Her Zandian was only a little stilted, and for the first time ever she was grateful for Master Prajana's excruciating language classes. "You have clearly made an effort on our behalf, and we truly appreciate it."

She caught Tarrick's look of approval from the corner of her eye, and Iman's mask of politeness softened discernibly at her use of Zandian. He gave her a little bow. "Magor-lier, this room is yours." He pointed each of them to a room, his gaze shifting to Tarrick once he was done. "I will organise for the Leopard captain to be here to speak with you shortly."

She arched an eyebrow at Tarrick as Iman left. "I take it your message to your brothers made it sound like I'm being hunted by a veritable army of assassins?"

"You are," he replied bluntly.

She fought against rolling her eyes. "Can we assume it's a good sign the emperor has taken such pains with our safety?"

"Yes and no." Tarrick cocked his head. "Honour is crucial in Zandian culture, and to have a guest harmed under your roof is a great personal dishonour. But the fact the emperor was willing to host you is a sign he at least intends to listen to what we have to say."

"So we should all be on our best behaviour and match our Magor-lier's exemplary use of Zandian?" A grin tugged at Adahn's mouth. "Noted. Good ol' Prajana, never thought I'd be grateful for those classes at DarkSkull."

She laughed at his exact echoing of her thoughts, and the others chuckled too.

"We should discuss how to arrange the Magor-lier's guard." Rothai was the only one not to laugh. Of course.

Alyx left them to it, curious to see the room assigned to her. She stopped only a few paces inside the door, delighted. It was a stunning space, reminiscent of the luxury she'd enjoyed growing up in Alistriem. Across from her, a wide balcony looked out over the city to the ocean. A bed shrouded in filmy white curtains sat in one corner near the balcony, with a green bathing pool opposite it. A plush lounge sat before an open window.

She clicked the door closed, shutting off Tarrick's and Rothai's voices as they discussed a guard rotation. Finally, a moment to herself!

Shoulders relaxing, she wandered out onto the balcony and took a deep breath of the hot Zandian air. It was sweeter than back home, smelling of spices and something else she couldn't name. Below the balcony was a small garden. She quickly picked out the two Leopard guards at opposite ends of the greenery watching her room with the same fixed gaze those guarding the palace gates had worn.

After a while, the heat grew oppressive, and she returned inside. The quiet was soothing, and she stripped her dusty, sweaty travel clothes off and spent a luxurious period bathing in the fragrant pool. Once she was clean and scrubbed dry, she dug through her saddlebag and drew out her mage robe with a heavy sigh—meeting the emperor without looking the part of Magor-lier wasn't a good idea, but she was going to swelter.

She was just brushing out her drying hair when there came a soft knock at the door. Tarrick stood there, black hair still damp from his own wash, mage robe stretched across his broad shoulders. He didn't even look a little bit hot, and she made a face at him. "How are you not stifling in that?"

His grin flashed bright against his dark skin. "This is nothing. We're technically in the middle of winter. You haven't experienced heat until you've lived through a Zandian summer."

"This is not winter," she grumbled good-naturedly. "Did you come by to check my room for hidden assassins?"

"Better, the emperor has called for us," he explained. "It's best not to keep him waiting."

The emperor's audience chamber was on the top floor of a circular building in the centre of the palace compound. It was surrounded by floor-to-ceiling glass windows, most of which were open to let in a faint breeze coming off the ocean. The view over the city was stunning, and Alyx had to fight not to let her attention be caught by it.

Iman led them into the room, bowing low before a man lounging on a plush divan. Four Leopards stood still and silent behind him. "Your Imperial Majesty, may I present Magor-lier Alyx Egalion and her retinue."

Dismissing Iman with a sharp gesture, the emperor stood to greet them, displaying a leonine grace, and a tall, muscular body. Tarrick had told Alyx the man was in his late forties, but he looked ten years younger, with a face too hard to be handsome and sharp eyes that took them in in a single, searching glance. "Magor-lier," he spoke in a deep, gravelly voice. "It is an honour to host you in my country."

"Your Majesty." Alyx bowed low, dropping to her knees as she'd been instructed. The other mages followed suit with varying degrees of grace. She winced inwardly when Finn almost rolled forward onto his face, but it didn't appear as if the emperor noticed.

"Please stand." He waved a hand. "I trust your accommodations are comfortable?"

Alyx rose, allowing her years of training in court etiquette to take over and make it easier to concentrate on speaking correctly in Zandian. "They are lovely, thank you. You have a beautiful home, and Sandira is a vibrant city. We are honoured to be here, Your Majesty, and I thank you for receiving us at such short notice."

He accepted that with a nod. "I have taken the liberty of increasing the Leopard guard surrounding the guest wing where you are staying. I mean no disrespect to your mage guards, but I know of the Hunters that Shakar sends after you. While learning of their existence was... disturbing... I am nonetheless grateful to you for uncovering the likely truth behind my son's death. For that alone I would receive you in my city at any time, Magor-lier."

"Your Leopards impress me as powerful warriors, Your Majesty." Alyx chose her words carefully; she had to win this man's support. "I appreciate your concern. The extra guard is welcome."

"My Leopards are unparalleled." He smiled, but there was nothing warm or soft in it. "They are modelled on the Taliath of old, did you know? Of course, my men have no Taliath ability, but they are fearsome all the same."

Alyx nodded, inwardly debating whether to raise Darien Llancarvan's death. It was impossible to know whether the emperor yet knew, and normally these things were better handled through formal diplomatic channels. Yet, she didn't want the emperor to find out later and think she and her retinue had been keeping something important from him.

"Your Majesty, I also have some grave news to share with you."

"Ah, yes." Surprisingly the tall, fierce man bowed his head. "I received the message from Alistriem yesterday. King Darien was a good man. I only met him on a handful of occasions, but he had my respect. You have my condolences, and those of my court, Magor-lier."

"Thank you."

"A young and untested king is not ideal in these times," he said bluntly.

"I have known King Cayr all my life, Your Majesty, and I believe he will make a strong king," she said firmly. "But I agree that there are those who may see Rionn as more vulnerable now. That is a large part of the reason I am here."

They all turned as a man entered. He wore a deep red sleeveless tunic, beautifully tooled belt and light sandals over matching breeches. From the body language of the servants in the room, Alyx judged this man as important, despite his simple clothing. An advisor, perhaps? The cropped hair ruled him out as a Leopard despite his muscular arms. He bowed low and waited for the emperor to acknowledge him.

"What is it, Hennan?"

"A ship bearing the flag of Rionn has entered the harbour, Your Majesty. They have been cleared and are docking as we speak."

"King Cayr's representative, I take it?"

"Yes, Your Majesty."

"Very good. Send a unit of Leopards to escort the king's representative here." The emperor turned back to Alyx while Hennan crossed the room to speak with the servants by the door. "I will have refreshments brought in while you wait if that suits?"

"That sounds lovely. Thank you," Alyx said graciously.

"Then please relax." With no further preamble, he strode to the opposite end of the chamber to speak in a sharp undertone with Hennan. Alyx and her mages were left to sit on the couches and be served cold drinks.

Despite her best efforts, she kept glancing towards the door, as if she could summon the Rionnan representative with sheer willpower. Anticipation filled her at the thought it might be Dawn or Cario. Even if not them, it would be *someone* from home. A familiar face that might ease some of her longing.

"You're doing well," Tarrick said in a murmur. "He was impressed by your use of Zandian."

She made a face. "I wish you or Finn had to do the talking. I fear I sound stilted, I keep having to search for the limited number of words I know."

"It's an expression of respect that you even try." Tarrick's mouth quirked. "And you're actually not bad."

Finn joined them. "It's a good sign that Cayr received Astor's message and was able to send someone. Things can't be too unstable in Alistriem."

"A united front from the beginning will be useful," Alyx agreed, ignoring the stab of worry at Finn's reference to what Cayr was facing. "And if this goes well, I'm sure we'll be able to convince King Mastaran to attend a summit."

"These sherbets are delicious," Jayn said brightly, offering one to Alyx.

"I'm more partial to these sweets, myself." Adahn spoke with a mouth full of some bright orange-coloured candy.

They weren't left waiting too long before a servant announced the arrival of the Rionnan representative.

"Should we get up?" Alyx asked Tarrick in an undertone.

"Yes. If you're eating, swallow quickly," Tarrick murmured back.

Alyx placed her glass down and rose to her feet. The emperor left Hennan to greet the man being escorted through the door by two Leopards. For a long moment the room fell silent. For the emperor and other Zandians, the sight of a revered Taliath in the flesh stunned them all. For Alyx, the sight of Dashan so unexpectedly here rendered her frozen, and then suddenly unable to breathe.

He was a head taller than any of them as he strode forward to bow low to the emperor, not seeming to have noticed there were others in the room. Her eyes drank him in—he wore his dark hair cut severely short, and his face looked even harder than she remembered, his expression guarded and watchful. Something was wrong. She knew it instantly, and it took everything she had not to run across the room and launch herself into his arms. Her heart pounded.

Dashan straightened. "Your Majesty. I am Dashan Caverlock, Taliath and formal representative of King Cayr of Rionn."

"Welcome, Lord-Taliath," the emperor said graciously, using a term Alyx had never heard before and switching easily to speak in Rionnan. "Your presence in Sandira is more welcome than I can express. And your timing is good. The Magor-lier and her retinue arrived earlier today. Perhaps you'd like to take a moment to greet them?"

Dashan froze for a moment at his words, and then he turned, brown eyes going straight to Alyx. The flash of pure joy in his gaze was quickly masked, but it sent her heart thundering even harder. The urge to run to him was close to overwhelming and she had to tear her eyes from his in order to hold back.

In the few steps it took to reach them, the watchful guardedness had returned to his features. "Alyx, it's been a while." His voice was warm with delight—if nothing else they were old friends greeting each other after a long time. Taking a deep breath, she lifted her head and smiled.

"Too long. I didn't expect to see you here, Dash."

"Me either." His smile widened a little, then he turned his attention to the others. "Tarrick, Finn. I was hoping you'd both be here. It's good to see you."

It was hard to gauge Tarrick's and Finn's true reaction to seeing Dashan. Neither of them had spoken to him since learning he was a Taliath, but in the presence of the emperor, they seemed genuinely pleased to see him. As they greeted each other, Alyx turned her gaze to the other mages. Rothai's expression was rigid. Adahn and Jayn seemed awkward, then stiltedly polite when Finn introduced them. Tari's face was a blank mask, impossible to read.

Greetings over, Dashan came to stand beside Alyx. His arms hung loosely at his side, his hand just barely brushing her arm. The closeness was bittersweet torture.

"I must ask a boon, Lord-Taliath." The emperor spoke. "As you might know; we Zandians hold a great fascination for those of your blood. I would love to see a demonstration while you stay with us in Sandira."

Dashan gave his typical rakish grin, and for a moment all traces of the reserved man faded. "I'd love nothing better, Your Majesty."

"Thank you, Lord-Taliath, I will look forward to it." He clapped his hands. "Once again, I welcome you all to my city. Tonight you will dine with me, and you may be assured I will make time soon to discuss the issues which bring you here."

"Thank you, Your Majesty." Alyx spoke politely. "We appreciate your hospitality."

He nodded and was gone, striding out of the room with Hennan and six Leopards flanking him. Iman appeared, offering to direct them back to their rooms. Alyx accepted this offer with alacrity, having no idea how they'd make it back without assistance.

"Dash, we had no idea King Cayr would send you," Tarrick said as they followed Iman. "Lord-Mage Astor thought it would most likely be Cario."

Dashan nodded. "I'd just come across the border from Shivasa when Cayr received Astor's message. He thought I needed a break, and so he sent me."

Iman brought them back to the guest wing and pointed Dashan to a room in the same corridor. Alyx had followed approximately the first third of the journey before becoming utterly lost again. She hoped Tarrick had a better sense of direction or they would never be able to leave this wing on their own.

The moment they came to a halt, a thick tension descended over the group. Dashan spoke into it, determinedly oblivious. "If you all don't mind, I'm going to take the opportunity for a change of clothes and sleep. Proper rest has been hard to come by recently."

"Of course." Tarrick spoke when nobody else did. "I hope we can catch up at dinner this evening."

"I look forward to it." Dashan nodded and raised a hand in farewell before disappearing into his room. Her gaze lingered on the door and she tore her eyes away before it became obvious.

Jayn cleared her throat. "Adahn and I are on duty, so I think we might go and check on the Leopards stationed outside."

Adahn followed with alacrity.

"Tari and I have an appointment with the Leopard commander," Rothai said. "He offered us a tour of their barracks. We'll see you at dinner."

That left the three of them alone in the hall. Alyx scrambled for something to say that would head off their inevitable lecture about her being too close to a Taliath, but surprisingly Finn spoke before she could.

"Shall we spend the afternoon investigating Sandira's inns? I know you're dying to show us around your city, Tarrick," he said. "Rothai can't complain if Tarrick and I are with you, Alyx, surely."

Alyx bit her lip. Finn was making a gesture—Rothai most definitely *wouldn't* approve of her wandering the city without a full mage guard. But she couldn't go out, not now. "Uh, actually, I should spend some time practicing this afternoon. It's probably a good idea to take advantage of the free time."

Tarrick looked surprised at her willingness to train. "Would you like me to practice with you?"

"No. Rothai set me some meditation exercises to help improve my focus, so I'll work on those." She gave a little laugh, ignoring the guilt that curled in her gut as she lied to them. "Find the best spots for me, will you? And try to remember I'm a noblewoman—no pungent dives, please."

Both young men laughed. "We'll do our best." Finn winked.

"No promises," Tarrick added before they disappeared around a corner.

Alyx opened the door to her room, closed it behind her, and went straight over to draw the filmy curtains across the balcony window to ensure the Leopards in the garden couldn't see into the room. Then she began pacing, her stomach twisting into knots. Sweat had begun beading on her forehead when a discreet knock came at the door. The moment she opened it, Dashan slipped inside.

"Did anyone see you?" she asked.

"Not a soul, ma'am," he promised, hand on heart.

They stared at each other for a long moment. She could scarcely believe that after thinking of him and wanting him for so long he was standing right before her.

"Alyx." He took a step towards her.

She let out a sob and moved, running straight to him. He pulled her into his arms, holding her so fiercely her ribs ached. She buried her face in his neck, sinking into his embrace as the loneliness and desperation of the past year finally began to drain out of her.

"You're really here," she whispered.

"Too long, Alyx," he murmured into her hair. "Too long."

They stood there for a long time, holding tightly to each other, neither wanting to let go until they were both certain the other was there.

Eventually Alyx mumbled into his chest, "Was it difficult to get in here?"

"They've got at least four Leopards in that garden outside, so I couldn't come in through the balcony, at least not in broad daylight," Dashan murmured. "Oh, Alyx, I've missed you." He crushed her more tightly in his arms and she pressed herself against his warm body. After so long without him, it was intoxicating to be so close again.

After a moment, she forced herself to step back, her gaze searching his face. "How's Cayr? I've been so worried about him, about both of you."

He smiled a little. "You'd be so proud of him. He's hurting, you know how much he loved his father, but he's strong. He's working hard to bring the lords into line, and he's picked up where his father left off in terms of managing the kingdom. Rionn is stable."

"And Papa?"

"I didn't see much of him, but I think he was hit hard by the king's death. You know your father, though. He's standing firm at Cayr's side, invaluable in influencing the other lords."

Her eyes slipped closed in pain. "I hated leaving Cayr. I had to watch his father die and then walk away from him." She swallowed. "And as desperately happy as I am to see you here, part of me wishes you hadn't come, that you were in Alistriem with Cayr so he at least has one of us with him."

"I would have stayed." Dashan tugged her back into his arms. "He insisted I come. He knows how much the emperor reveres the Taliath, and... well, he refused to let me stay."

Nodding, she allowed herself to sink into the happiness of having him so close again, and began dropping small kisses along his collarbone. He smiled against her forehead before he picked her up and in two strides carried her to the bed. He dropped her onto the soft mattress, then leaned down to kiss her. Instantly it was as if every nerve ending in her body was on fire, her world narrowing to the feel of Dashan's mouth on hers.

She freed her hands so she could pull him closer. When she was almost completely lost in pure sensation, he pulled back, his forehead touching hers. They were both breathing hard, and she'd be groaning in frustration if she wasn't so glad to have him there with her.

"So that's how much you missed me?" she teased.

"Even more." He kissed her again, a long slow kiss that turned the world to warmth and joy and a rising tide of wanting. When it ended, he shifted, lying down at her side and tugging her against him. "Talk to me, Alyx. Tell me everything I've missed."

"I don't want to talk about that," she mumbled, closing her eyes and snuggling into his chest.

His fingers reached out to trace the fine bracelet on her wrist, and she glanced up to see his dark eyes molten with affection. "You kept it."

"I touch it every night before I go to sleep, it's the only time I allow myself to think about you. It's too hard otherwise," she admitted.

He swallowed, the misery returning to his face. She curled further into him, trying to get as close as possible. "What's wrong, Dash?"

"I don't want to talk about it either."

She nodded against his chest, allowing her eyes to fall closed again and taking in a deep breath of his warmth and scent. "Let's just lie here for a while."

CHAPTER 5

"The Taliath seems different from the few times I saw him back at DarkSkull. Older. Harder, somehow, but not at all imposing," Jayn mused later, as she and Alyx prepared for the dinner.

Alyx tensed. While the council policy of hunting Taliath potentials remained a well-kept secret, all students at DarkSkull were taught the same thing she had been—that Taliath were a serious threat if allowed too close to a mage of the higher order. Their invulnerability was the reason Shakar, an uncommonly powerful mage of the higher order, had been impossible to stop the first time. Hundreds of mages dead. Thousands more innocents.

With Taliath all but gone—the only publicly declared Taliath were Alyx's father and brother and Dashan, as Jenna remained a secret—it was difficult to judge how most mages truly felt about them, though there were definitely those who aligned strongly with the council's view.

"You're not uncomfortable in the presence of a Taliath?" she asked eventually.

Jayn raised an eyebrow. "You mean because at DarkSkull we're basically indoctrinated with the view that Taliath are to be avoided like an infectious rash on the off chance one of them could contribute to creating another Shakar?"

Alyx steeled herself. "Yes."

"Well, the logic behind why they teach us that is clear enough." Jayn gave her a look. "But like with most of the council's teaching, it's too black and white. Personally, I don't think we should behave as if every mage of the higher order is a budding psychopath just waiting to inherit a Taliath's invulnerability so they can take over the world."

Alyx nodded, relaxing slightly. "I couldn't agree more."

"There's far more going on here than you've told any of us. Rothai looked like he was about to have an apoplexy at the sight of Dashan. Adahn and Tari weren't happy about it either." She lifted a hand when Alyx opened her mouth. "And that's fine. I'm perfectly happy not having to grapple with complicated issues like that. It's why *I'm* not Magor-lier."

A spark of Alyx's anger returned at Jayn's words, though it wasn't directed at her fellow mage. "I'm no Magor-lier, Jayn."

"Of course you are." Jayn sounded puzzled.

In name only. But Alyx didn't want to sound petulant, so she just smiled and nodded.

Once dressed, Alyx was escorted to dinner by Jayn, Tari, and Adahn, with Iman leading the way. The latter two mages were dressed in their robes, dragooned by Rothai into protection detail for the evening.

"Where's Rothai?" Alyx asked as they walked.

Tari smiled faintly. "Patrolling. I don't think he trusts the Leopards, despite the fact we were assured there would be at least twenty of them guarding this dinner tonight, and that's not including those in the gardens outside."

"Alyx?" Tarrick waited at the entrance to a large room, dressed in formal Zandian attire of a silken maroon hip wrap with gold thread edging it, sandals, and nothing else. He looked handsome and exotic, and Alyx stared a little; she'd never seen him dressed traditionally before. Tarrick Tylender had grown into an impressive man.

"You look very... good," she said, unable to find an appropriate word.

"You look good also." He smiled, offering his arm.

She took it, and they strolled inside together. The room was easily as big as Cayr's formal dining room in Alistriem, but airy and bright. Multi-coloured rugs covered the floor, a chaotic riot of colour that somehow worked.

The sun was setting outside, and its orange glow slanted through the windows, alighting on the deep red tablecloths and glittering silverware. A row of opened glass doorways let in a cool evening breeze that was rich with the scent of spices and flowers.

Abruptly, Tarrick straightened and began leading Alyx towards two young men wearing the Leopard black and gold wrap; both wore swords at their hips and a mage's staff hanging down their muscular backs.

"Hinga, Loren!" Tarrick called eagerly.

"Tarrick!" Both men spoke at the same time, delighted grins crossing their faces. Tarrick let go of Alyx's arm to embrace them warmly. All three closely resembled each other, with only slight differences in height and build to set them apart.

"Alyx, these are my brothers. Hinga, Loren, this is Magor-lier Alyx Egalion."

Both men bowed low, and she shifted uncomfortably. She'd once loved bearing the title of Lady Alyx Egalion until she'd realised how empty the title was. This new one she carried was just as empty, despite Rothai and Tarrick's arguments otherwise.

"Tarrick has told me a lot about you," she said. "It's an honour to meet you both."

"All good things, I hope?" Loren winked at Tarrick.

"Mostly." She nodded. "Apart for some childhood incident involving a toy carriage?"

All three brothers laughed heartily at that. Tarrick's eyes shone—he'd always spoken of his brothers with an equal mix of adoration and awe, and she was pleased this trip meant he could see his family again.

"Don't tell me I've missed a good joke!" Dashan's cheerful voice sounded. He wore a fitted silken shirt in deep violet above loose black pants and polished boots. His hair was cropped far too short to be as messy as Alyx remembered. The sword at his hip was unfamiliar but beautiful, its bone hilt and grip intricately carved and dyed the colour of Bluecoat royal blue, the sheath tooled from expensive leather.

"A gift from Cayr," Dashan murmured, catching her looking at it.

"Brothers, this is Dashan Caverlock. He is the Taliath representative of King Cayr Llancarvan." Tarrick introduced them.

There was a slight hesitation before both brothers bowed. Alyx inadvertently picked up a surface thought from Hinga indicating he was torn between his Zandian reverence for the Taliath, and the mage unease around one.

"It is an honour to meet you, Taliath Caverlock," Loren said politely.

Dashan smiled, his guarded expression showing that he had picked up on their hesitation. "Thank you. I'm glad to finally meet Tarrick's brothers. He speaks about you often."

"Only good things, or so the Magor-lier tells us." Hinga smiled.

"And the Magor-lier speaks only the truth, of course." Warmth lit her up from the inside out at the teasing sparkle in Dashan's eyes.

"Tarrick, these are your brothers?" Finn asked eagerly as he joined them. He wore similar attire to Dashan, and though he was shorter and leaner, there was no mistaking the strong young man Finn had become. Alyx struggled to remember the skinny youth with untameable hair she'd once known.

"Our brother has indeed been talking about us." Hinga laughed, Loren joining in. "I am Hinga, this is Loren. Judging from Tarrick's descriptions in his letters home from DarkSkull, you must be Finn, the clever one?"

"That's me." Chuckling, Finn offered his hand to Hinga, then Loren. "It's a pleasure to meet you."

Loren shook Finn's hand warmly. "We have too few healers in the mage order. Welcome to Sandira, Finn."

A gong sounded. Servants appeared from all directions, silently ushering the guests to their seats. There was a flurry at the doorway that heralded the emperor's arrival, flanked by Hennan and two Leopards. Alyx and Dashan were seated directly across from the emperor, with Tarrick, Jayn, and Finn arrayed on either side. Hennan sat at the emperor's right, and his other senior advisors filled the remaining seats. Hinga and Loren remained on guard at the main entrance.

"How are you finding my beautiful country?" the emperor asked, glancing between Alyx and Dashan. Servants were already placing steaming platters of food on the table. Her stomach grumbled.

"It's hot, and dry." Alyx smiled. "But beautiful in its own way."

"I haven't seen much of Zandia yet, but I look forward to exploring more while I'm here," Dashan added.

"You'll have to tell me more about Alistriem," the emperor said graciously. "I have not had a chance to visit since childhood."

"Rionn's beauty is very different from the open desert, Your Majesty," Tarrick said.

"You must see the waterfall that cascades down from the palace on a sunny day," Alyx said. "The water glitters in the sunlight like a rainbow. It's one of the most beautiful sights I've ever seen."

Dashan agreed with a nod. "Our harbor area is full of life and colour, too. You can buy freshly caught and buttered fish from the street stalls at any time of day. There is nothing more delicious."

Conversation fell silent for a little while as they began to eat. The meat dish had been treated with spices completely unfamiliar to Alyx—nor could she have said with certainty which animal the meat had come from—but it was rich with flavour and the meat moist and succulent. Large glasses of chilled wine helped diffuse the hot spices.

Her gaze darted between Tarrick and Finn, trying to get a read on how they felt about Dashan's presence. They'd seemed happy to see him earlier, but the last time they'd all been together both men had advocated for Dashan to flee Alistriem for his—and Alyx's—safety.

While she had confessed to her friends that she and Dashan had been in a brief relationship, she was confident she'd convinced them it had been nothing more than a casual fling. Even so, the mere presence of a Taliath so close to her was undoubtedly going to make them uneasy.

Her hand curled tightly around her fork at the surge of anger that caused. The metal began cutting into her skin, and she forced herself to relax. Both Tarrick and Finn seemed fine, talking as happily with Dashan as they did with all those around them. Maybe the fact they were only here for a short time discouraged any concerns they held. She hoped so.

Once the main courses were over, Alyx and Tarrick made several attempts to turn the conversation to more serious matters, but were politely rebuffed each time by either Hennan or the emperor. It was clear the emperor wasn't going to engage in more than light small talk this evening. Accepting that, she fell back on her court training and talked and laughed easily with those around her over dessert and then glasses of sweet wine.

As soon as was polite, she made her farewells to the emperor and left. Jayn and Tari accompanied her back to her rooms, but said goodbye at the door. Tarrick and Finn had remained behind to spend time with Hinga and Loren.

"Rothai will be on guard at the end of the corridor if you require anything, Magor-lier." Tari pointed. "Adahn will relieve him in a few hours."

"Thank you." Alyx injected warmth into her voice, trying to break down some of Tari's reserve with her. "You should get some rest. I think the Leopards have us well protected."

"Yes, Magor-lier." Tari bowed her head and walked away. Alyx sighed. She got the distinct sense there was something about her that Tari didn't like. It was frustrating. Shrugging it off, she stepped into her room and closed the door firmly behind her.

A cool night breeze was blowing in through the open balcony doorway. Breathing deeply of the delightfully scented Sandiran air, she tried to let the beautiful view relax the seemingly constant tension that built inside her. It worked, the sharp knock at her door startling her from a pleasant daze.

Her heart leapt as it always did at the sight of Dashan, and after closing the curtains she went straight into his arms.

"Let me light a lamp," she said, pulling back eventually. He touched her cheek with a gentle smile before heading over to the sofa. She busied herself lighting two of the room's many lamps before joining him, sitting as close to him as she could get. The memory of his face when she'd first seen him earlier floated into her mind, and she reached out for his hand.

"Things haven't been easy for you," she murmured. "Did something happen?"

His face closed over, a classic sign he was retreating into himself. "I'm fine."

"No, you're not." She shifted to face him.

"You aren't either," he said stubbornly.

She smiled a little. "I asked first. Come on, talk to me. I know you're not talking to anyone else."

His jaw clenched. "There's nothing to talk about."

Her heart dropped—it was worse than she'd thought. He was wary and guarded, like he would run if she made the slightest wrong move. He'd never been this closed off, not even before they'd fallen for each other.

She took a deep breath, entangling their fingers. "I've been snapping at everyone constantly. I can't even control my magic properly when I'm training with Rothai. I feel so helpless, because everyone is off fighting and I'm being kept safe, and that frustration turns to anger and it just keeps getting worse. I don't know what to do."

At the utter misery in her voice, Dashan turned. In a second his arms were around her and he was pulling her tightly against him. "I'm so sorry I wasn't there."

"That's how I feel." She pushed him gently away so she could meet his eyes. "My worry and fear for you only compounds my helplessness. And now you won't even talk to me. How can I believe you really love me if you won't let me help you?"

His eyes darkened. "Alyx, I love you. I love you more than anything else in this world. You're the most beautiful thing in my life."

"Then let me in," she whispered.

He let go of her, shifting away slightly and running a hand over his short hair. "I told you I wanted to stay in Alistriem, to be there for Cayr, to help him. But he insisted I come here, and not just because I'm a Taliath. He said he was doing it for my sanity. He thought the only thing that could help me was you."

Her chest tightened unbearably at the thought of Cayr sacrificing the support of his best friend in the world for her. It made it worse that she'd had to abandon him too. And Dashan... he looked in so much pain now that he wasn't trying to hide it from her. Her eyes searched his face. "It's that bad?"

"I've been living and fighting with a group of the Shiven rebels; it's a rabble really, but their leader—Tarian Astohar—he's a good man, and he truly wants a better life for the poorer Shiven. No matter that they look different, that their army is trying to invade Rionn, they're just people like us, you know? Trying to make a living and look after their families."

"I know," she murmured, letting him tell the story at his own pace.

"I'm doing what I can to help them. A month ago we came across a small Shiven village close to the southeast coast." His voice dropped until it was barely audible. "The whole thing was a charred ruin—every home, every building, everything had been burnt to the ground."

Shock flared, followed quickly by deeper concern. Whatever had happened, Dashan was clearly blaming himself, and he never coped well when he did that. "By who?"

He shook his head. "The Shiven army. We found most of the villagers a half mile out of town, bodies that had been tortured then left in a pile to burn. The Shiven soldiers thought they'd been helping the rebels."

"Oh, Dash." Her eyes filled with tears at his pain. Knowing him so well, she understood how badly something like this would tear at him.

"The children too." His voice hitched. "They'd been butchered... they did that to their own people. We were too late."

"What do you mean?"

He swallowed. "The villagers had sent a message asking for our help. We were supposed to get them onto boats to sail over to Rionn—to safety. It was something we started doing soon after I went to join the rebels, and word had gotten around. I was too late, and because I was too late, they all died the most horrible death imaginable."

She kept her voice gentle, but firm, taking his hand again. "Dash, you did your best. It was the Shiven soldiers who killed them, not you."

"That doesn't matter. They needed my help, and I failed them."

"It's not your fault," she said fiercely, reaching up to frame his cheek with her hand. "I went back to DarkSkull Hall a year ago and they were all dead, my friends, my master, the cream of the next mage generation." It was a grief that still hadn't left her, that still woke her some nights in tears, her heart breaking all over again. "I could have saved them, maybe, if I'd been there. But Shakar killed them, not me."

"I hate him." Dashan's face crumpled, tears running down his cheeks. "I hate him."

"Shush." Alyx reached for him, cradling him in her arms as tightly as she could. "I'm here, and I love you."

His tears soaked into her dress as he cried silent, heaving sobs, his whole body shaking with the force of his emotion. Alyx held on as tightly as she could, projecting all the love and reassurance she could muster.

Eventually he reached for her hand, grabbing it and holding on tightly. "Your turn, Alyx. Tell me."

"I don't know what to do," she whispered. "I'm no Magor-lier, no matter what they claim. They make me hide and run, and I understand why, but I feel so trapped and alone. I can't help *anyone*, not even myself."

He bought her hand to his mouth and kissed it gently, murmuring for her to continue.

"I feel like I'll never be ready to face Shakar, like I'm never going to get to go home again." She turned her face into his neck. "And the worst thing is my fear that I'll never have the chance to just be with you and not have to always miss you so badly it physically hurts."

"We're quite a pair, aren't we?" he murmured.

She chuckled at his attempt at levity, sitting back and scrubbing at her eyes. *We certainly are.*

He looked at her, eyes dark and still wet with tears. "I love you more than anything else in this world, Alyx."

Feeling so much she thought she might burst with it, she kissed him. His mouth was warm on hers, and the emotion they were both feeling sparked powerfully. He pushed her backwards, lips trailing along her jaw and then down her neck as he moved over her. His hand blazed a trail of burning sweetness as it slid over the silk of her dress. Her fingers fumbled at the buttons of his shirt.

"Dash..." She arched into him, delighting in the feel of his warm skin under her touch. Wanting more, she pulled him closer. His mouth returned to hers, harder, more urgently, and his hands roamed her body with abandon. Her mind and body were a haze of sensation and she knew nothing but the intoxicating sweetness of his mouth and his touch, the scent and feel of him all around her.

"Alyx..." He stilled above her, his eyes darker than she'd ever seen them. They were pressed close together, his shirt was gone completely, and her dress covered much less than it had moments earlier. "What are we doing?"

Her eyes slid shut as his forehead rested against hers. "We have to stop."

He nodded. "Yes."

"I *really* don't want to."

He laughed, and with a groan of reluctance, moved off her to sit on the opposite side of the sofa. "Just stay where you are for a minute."

She nodded, sitting up and trying to rearrange her dress back into position. Her skin still buzzed from his touch, her heartbeat reluctant to slow while he was still so near.

"Are you all right?" he asked, voice husky.

"Other than being extremely frustrated?" She flushed hotly at her own words, then cleared her throat, offering a smile. "Maybe your skills aren't so overrated after all."

He laughed aloud, and some of the tension faded. "Come here."

Grinning, she crawled over to lean against his side. He wrapped an arm around her and pulled her close. She tried to ignore the desire still humming through her and focus on just how good it felt to be close to him again. Her gaze fell on his sword where he'd propped it against the side of the couch.

"Did you name it?"

Dashan made a face. "Cayr insisted. He said your father named his, and that all Taliath swords should have names."

"And?" she asked eagerly.

He reached out to run his fingers over the hilt, gaze turning distant. "*Kingsbrother.*"

"You named it for Cayr." She swallowed around the sudden lump in her throat. "It's perfect."

"Alyx?" He shifted away a little so he could see her. "We need to talk about telling Tarrick and the other mages about us. I also want to discuss the possibility of us becoming lovers."

She swallowed, trying not to let the hope leap in her chest. "Dash, I want you, please don't ever think I don't. You have no idea how much I... but this fear the council has, of you, of me? It's powerful."

"I know," he murmured. "And I'm not saying it's going to be possible. But let's at least start with telling our friends. Finn's a genius—maybe he'll be able to come up with something."

"They'll be furious with us, and... they'll be scared too. Finn especially."

"They're our friends. You trust them with your life," Dashan said gently. "As angry as they'll be, they'd never do anything to hurt you. I think we should both trust that."

Alyx nodded slowly. "Astor suggested a trip home after this. There, with Dawn and Cario, we could talk to them?"

He smiled gently. "Sounds like a plan."

CHAPTER 6

"Where's the emperor?" Alyx entered an audience chamber that was empty apart from Tarrick, Finn, and Rothai. A hastily written message from Tarrick—passed by Iman—had dragged her from the most restful sleep she'd had in a long time.

"He'll be here. The meeting isn't for a little while," Tarrick said.

She stared at him. "Your note said I should hurry."

"We wanted to talk to you about Dash beforehand," Finn said.

Her mouth tightened. *Damn.* It seemed her worry during dinner the previous night hadn't been unwarranted after all. "You really think that's necessary?" she asked, a pleading note to her voice.

"You know that if we'd been aware King Cayr was sending Dashan, you wouldn't have been able to come on this trip." Tarrick kept his voice gentle, and that was probably the only reason she was able to hold her temper at his words.

"What I *know* is that we've had this conversation before." She fought to keep her voice even, eyes landing on Finn. "Dashan and I are not lovers, and I am not invulnerable." It was technically true, but she couldn't help her twinge of guilt at what she and Dashan had been discussing only the night before.

"That's not the point," Tarrick said. "You're aware of what the Mage Council would do to both you and Dashan if they knew you were near each other. He's lucky to have survived this long after Casovar outed him as a Taliath."

"He's still alive because there are now three declared Taliath in Alistriem, and the council doesn't dare risk losing a potential ally against Shakar by attempting to assassinate men so close to Rionn's king," Alyx retorted.

"They would throw the entire mage order at you if they thought there was a chance you could become another Shakar." Tarrick's voice took on a pleading quality. It checked her anger briefly, the realisation that his true concern was her safety, not fear of another Shakar. "You know how paranoid they are. You're not under their control, and we all know how much that scares them. There's nothing they wouldn't do to prevent you from becoming a threat instead of an ally."

"And how am I supposed to absorb his invulnerability, Tarrick?"

"We don't know the fine details of how it works." Rothai weighed into the discussion. "Perhaps close proximity—"

"We *do* know how it worked in the two instances it ever has happened. Shakar and my mother both became invulnerable only after taking a Taliath lover," she snapped, rounding on him. "And don't remind me of what you've done. You hunted and *murdered* young children."

"That was at the order of the Mage Council, and for good reason."

"They were children!" she snapped. "Tarrick, do you really think what he did was right?"

"Tarrick's point remains," Finn said calmly into the tension. "Perception can be more important than reality. Whether you are invulnerable or not is immaterial. If the council knew you were together, then—"

"Fine," Alyx cut him off, utterly sick of the conversation. She had been lying to them long enough, she could keep it up for a while longer. She would simply pretend to avoid Dashan. Then, once they were in Alistriem, and it was just them, no Rothai, she and Dashan would tell them the truth.

"Really?" Finn frowned at her sudden capitulation.

She nodded. "Is there anything else? Because if not, I'd like to get some breakfast before this meeting."

Alyx managed a sweet pastry and half a cup of steaming tea before Iman appeared to summon her and Tarrick through to the emperor's private meeting chamber. He was there already, seated at a table with Dashan, Hennan and three other men, all of whom looked older. As usual, four Leopards stood guard behind the Emperor's chair.

"There is no need for further pleasantries or preamble," the emperor said once they seated themselves, his tone brisk and direct. "I know why you have come to me, Magor-lier, Lord-Taliath. Your country is under threat from the Shiven, even more so now that a new king sits the throne, and you need help to defend your borders."

"Your Majesty, while I was born in Rionn and am deeply concerned about its welfare, I am also here on behalf of the mage order," Alyx politely corrected him. "The threat we *all* face is more serious than Shivasa's territorial ambitions."

"You're speaking of Shakar?" Hennan asked.

"Yes."

The emperor leaned back in his chair. "You must see things from my perspective, Magor-lier. Zandia's army is large and powerful. Our deserts are a significant obstacle for any army intending to invade. We are protected here. I am not willing to risk my country's sovereign integrity by involving myself in matters that do not concern us."

Dashan sat forward. "Your Majesty, Shakar is a mage of the higher order with Taliath invulnerability. Everybody here knows what happened last time he challenged the Mage Council. He will not find your deserts an insurmountable burden. If you help us to nullify the threat he poses now, it will benefit you in the long term."

The emperor glanced at Hennan, then back at Alyx. But it was another man who spoke. He was much older, with grey at his temples and a lined face. He'd been introduced earlier as the overall commander of the Zandian army. "What is it exactly that you are asking of us, Magor-lier?"

"General Yurin," she acknowledged politely. "I ask that you attend a summit meeting with King Cayr of Rionn and King Mastaran of Tregaya to form an alliance against Shivasa and Shakar. The mage order wants to destroy him, but we can't do that alone."

"You speak of the mage order, yet you are not here on behalf of the Mage Council," Yurin challenged.

"That is true," Alyx acknowledged. "I will not swear loyalty to the council, but they are not my enemy. All mages will have to work together if we are to defeat Shakar. The council will of course be invited to the summit I am proposing."

The emperor and Yurin shared a glance before Yurin spoke. "We will consider your request. You understand we need some time to discuss this privately?"

"I do," Alyx said.

"Then we will end our meeting here for now." The emperor rose to his feet, dismissal in his face and voice. "I will send Iman to you once we are ready to continue discussions."

"Thank you, Your Majesty," Alyx said. "We appreciate your time."

They rose to their feet, filing out of the room slowly. Her heart sank as Tarrick gave her a little shake of his head. The emperor was brushing them off. Resolutely, she took firm hold of her optimism. This was just the first meeting. They had more time.

Concentrating carefully, Alyx reached for her magic and summoned a ball of green flame, carefully using it to light the candles placed before her on the table. The wicks on the candles caught alight, but nothing else was touched by the flame.

"Well done, Magor-lier." Rothai looked surprised.

She shrugged and smiled. "I suppose all those hours of practice paid off."

Finn wandered in, eating a piece of fruit. "Maybe next you could come up with a way to persuade the emperor to agree to the summit?"

She sobered. Three days had passed since their first meeting without him agreeing to another one. Hinga had privately told Tarrick that while the emperor acknowledged it was important to destroy Shakar, he didn't believe the threat to Zandia was sufficient to risk bringing war to their doorstep. The emperor also felt that Zandia's army, its mages, and its Leopards could handle Shakar's forces on their own.

He's probably right. Zandian military prowess and capability far outstripped that of large but under-resourced Tregaya, and capable but tiny Rionn. The optimism she'd been clinging to was eroding rapidly.

"You need to speak to him again," Rothai said.

"I can't force him to meet with us." Alyx sighed. "Whenever I speak to Iman about talking to the Emperor again, he puts me off."

"I'll try again today," Tarrick offered. "Maybe I can get my brothers to help."

"What we need is for Dash to talk to the emperor," Alyx said. "He seems obsessed with everything Taliath related."

"He spoke to Dash after the demonstration fight yesterday," Tarrick pointed out. "But apparently the emperor kept turning the conversation back to his Taliath training."

Tarrick and Finn had shared dinner with Dashan the previous night. In the spirit of their agreement, Alyx had excused herself, content with the knowledge Dashan would come to her rooms afterward.

Finn echoed Alyx's earlier sigh. "Dashan can't do it alone. We need something to convince the emperor that if he doesn't ally with Rionn and Tregaya, Zandia will be at risk."

"Did I hear my name?" Dashan entered the room with a characteristic burst of energy, raising his eyebrows at them all. Like Alyx, over the past few days his grim demeanor had lightened considerably, and he almost seemed back to his old self. *Amazing none of them have figured things out.*

"You did." Alyx smiled. "But you probably don't want to know what we were saying about you."

He cocked his head in amusement. "Oh, we're being funny this morning, are we?"

"I'm always witty, Dashan."

"Ha! You don't compare to my sparkling wit, Egalion."

"Magor-lier!" Rothai's sharp voice broke through their banter. "Perhaps he shouldn't be here."

Alyx's smile died as she registered agreement on Tarrick and Finn's faces. Dashan's expression darkened as he glanced between them, picking up on

Alyx's change in mood as always. Before he could say anything, she gave him a little shake of her head. It wasn't worth the argument, and she would see him later anyway.

"I was getting some practice in, Dash. Do you mind leaving Rothai and me to it for a while?"

His eyes rested on Rothai for a long moment, hard and almost challenging, but eventually he nodded and gave them all a flash of his easy smile. "Not at all."

"We thought we might take a walk through the city while Alyx trains if you want to come with us, Dashan?" Finn offered cheerfully.

"Oh, I think I've had enough of foolish stupidity for the day, actually." Dashan shrugged. "You enjoy yourselves though."

He walked out without another word, leaving a stunned room behind. Well, Rothai didn't seem to have noticed the pointed ice in Dashan's voice, but poor Tarrick and Finn looked completely shocked.

"You should leave us to it," Alyx broke the silence. "It seems like I'm making progress today."

"Alyx, I—"

"Leave it, Tarrick. We're never going to agree, and I don't want another argument with you," she said.

"I suppose there's no doubt on which side of the argument Dashan sits," Finn remarked bleakly.

The door closed behind them and Alyx turned back to Rothai, putting Finn and Tarrick to the back of her mind. She just needed to wait until Alistriem—she could fix everything with them then.

CHAPTER 7

"What do you think our chances are of the emperor ever agreeing to a summit?" Finn asked, swallowing the last of his spiced wine. They were in one of Sandira's bars, a delightful place with opened windows, strong drinks and a permanent scent of grilled meat drifting from the spit behind the bar.

Alyx suspected Finn and Tarrick had talked after the previous morning's incident with Dashan, because he'd been included in the invitation to come out for drinks, and in Rothai's absence, they seemed happy enough with Alyx and Dashan seated on opposite sides of the table. The relief was intense, and she desperately hoped it was an indication they would be willing to talk once they reached Alistriem.

Tarrick considered Finn's question. A second meeting with the emperor had finally been granted earlier in the day, but hadn't lasted long before an urgent matter had taken his attention. "Small. For the moment Zandia is safe, especially this far to the north. He's just not convinced enough of the threat Shakar poses."

"Then we need to find a way to convince him," Dashan said.

"How?" Finn asked.

"It may just be a matter of time," Dashan said. "Shakar's influence will continue to grow, and the emperor isn't a fool—even if he was, his advisors aren't. He'll eventually understand that Zandia is under threat too."

"Time is a luxury we can't afford," Tarrick said. "I'm uncomfortable with the length of time we've stayed already. Shakar could know we're here by now."

"Obtaining the emperor's agreement to this summit is important," Alyx said. "I think it's worth the risk to stay."

"Only if there's a chance he'll agree, and I don't honestly think there is," Finn said. "Particularly after what just happened in Carhall. If he's not convinced of the utility of having talks, then we'll never convince him to risk his safety by travelling out of Zandia to attend a summit."

Alyx sighed. As much as she didn't want to, she agreed with Finn. "I'll speak with Iman tomorrow morning and let him know we plan to leave soon. Hopefully the emperor will agree to meet with us before we leave. That will give us a final opportunity to convince him."

Dashan nodded. "Cayr will be disappointed, but I agree with your assessment of the emperor's thinking."

"Do you need assistance booking passage on a ship home, Dash?" Tarrick asked. "I'm sure my brothers could help."

Alyx and Dashan shared a quick look—she hadn't discussed her intentions yet, but they really couldn't leave it any longer.

"Actually, I think the three of us should go with Dashan back to Alistriem," she suggested.

"Why?" Tarrick frowned.

"I want to go home," she said honestly. "I want to see how Cayr is, and I want to see my father and my brother, as well as Dawn and Cario. Finn, surely you want to see your sister too?"

"It's not safe—" Tarrick began, but she cut him off.

"I'm not being foolhardy, I promise you. I'll only stay in Alistriem for a couple of days, no more, and then we'll leave. If we go with Dash via ship, Rothai can leave along the stoneways with Tari, Adahn, and Jayn. If there are spies watching us, they won't be certain which way I went."

Finn glanced at Tarrick. "I really would like to see my sister."

Tarrick stared down at his ale for a long moment. "Two days in Alistriem only."

"Agreed," Alyx said.

"Rothai isn't going to like this." He sighed.

"Good thing then that Rothai doesn't lead the mage order." Dashan spoke with an edge in his voice. Alyx smothered her smile.

"I'll speak to my brothers in the morning. We'll book passage for Dashan only, to make it appear as if we're leaving the way we came," Tarrick said. "They can organise berths for us under different names."

Relief swamped her. Maybe this would all work out okay after all. "Thank you."

"It's getting late, should we head back?" Finn asked.

Alyx smiled, her mood vastly improved. "I suppose. Much more of this spiced wine, and I'll be swinging from the rafters."

"I'd pay money to see you swinging from the rafters." Dashan chuckled.

"Not tonight." She stood and took a moment to get her balance. She wasn't drunk, but a pleasant buzz seeped through her.

"Need a hand?" Dashan asked mock-innocently, coming around the table to lay a steadying hand on her shoulder.

She shoved him playfully. "Keep your hands off."

"All right, let's go before you two start a brawl." Finn stewarded Dashan towards the door while Alyx made a face at him.

"Slow walk back to the palace or a carriage ride?" Tarrick asked.

"A walk!" Finn pleaded. "Or I'll never sober up."

"You mages need to learn how to hold your liquor." Dashan needled them, walking easily in a straight line to demonstrate his sobriety.

"Not all of us have Taliath blood," Finn said mildly. "I've read all about your magical ability to handle alcohol, so don't try to pretend."

"Besides, Dashan's had a lot of practice holding his liquor," Alyx said sweetly. "How many times did Cayr have to send his valet down to the Alistriem inns to fish you out of some awful dive?"

"Hey!" he complained. "That all happened back in my young, wild days. I'm much more responsible now."

Comfortable silence reigned for most of the walk back. The Leopards on the palace gates let them through without a word and—after much teasing from Alyx—Tarrick managed to successfully lead them through the labyrinth of corridors back to their rooms. The guest wing stood empty and quiet. Tari, Adahn, and Jayn had the night off, and no doubt they were down enjoying themselves in the city. She had no clue where Rothai was.

"I'm for bed." Dashan yawned, stretching his arms above his head. Alyx shot him a look—he was overdoing it *just* a little.

Finn didn't seem to notice. "Me too."

"I'll speak to my brothers first thing tomorrow about us leaving, and ask them if they can get us a final meeting with the emperor," Tarrick promised. "Alyx, *you* can tell Rothai about our changed travel plans."

"I suppose that's fair." She sighed.

They dispersed towards their doors. A pleasant sleepiness was descending on Alyx after the glasses of wine and long walk back from the city and she looked forward to her bed. Hopefully it wouldn't take Dashan long to sneak in. Despite the physical frustrations that would inevitably bring—frustrations that were only increasing the more they saw of each other—they were unlikely to manage any alone time in the cramped quarters of a ship journey to Alistriem.

Her hand was on the door handle when her peripheral vision caught Dashan stopping dead in the hall. His entire posture had stiffened, one hand dropping to the hilt of *Kingsbrother*.

"What?" Alyx asked. Both Tarrick and Finn stopped in their tracks, eyes jumping from Alyx to Dashan. She wondered if both were remembering exactly what she was remembering—the Taliath ability to sense approaching danger.

Dashan turned a full circle, face focused in concentration. "We've got trouble."

"From where?" Tarrick demanded.

Alyx sent her telepathic magic reaching outwards, listening for the thoughts of anyone nearby. Nothing. A shiver ran down her spine. There should at least have been Leopards on guard.

"You can't sense them?" Dashan was tense and alert, all traces of his previous smile vanished.

"No. There's nobody nearby... the guards are gone." Alyx tried again, using more power. This time she caught something on the very edges of her range, but it was wispy and insubstantial. The only thing she could really grasp was an intent, and that was instantly familiar. "Wait... damn. Hunters."

"You're sure?" Finn asked, already drawing his staff.

"I'm certain." Her eyes flicked open. "The sensation is too familiar."

"We'll be fine," Dashan said calmly. "Can you contact Rothai?"

She concentrated. The Hunters hadn't come close enough yet to stifle her magic, so she drew on it and scanned her immediate surroundings. All the guest rooms were empty. *Damn.* Once sure of that, she sent her magic out wider. Fear uncurled in her chest when it hit a barrier and dissolved. The blankness surrounded them—the Hunters must be encircling them in order to form a bubble that her magic couldn't penetrate. Dimly, she was aware of Dashan drawing his sword. The ring of steel echoed through the hall.

She let her magic die away—it wouldn't be any use for the moment, and instinct warned her to conserve her strength. "He's not in his room, that's all I can tell you. I can't reach him. The others aren't here either."

Finn paled. "That means we're surrounded."

"Yes, but inside a fairly large circle for now," she said, deliberately keeping her voice calm. "Dash, how fast are they approaching?"

His eyes narrowed in concentration. "It's hard to tell exactly, but they're moving with purpose. I think they know where you are."

Tarrick shook his head impatiently. "We can't just stand here."

"No." Dashan's gaze searched around them, as if seeing the approaching enemy coming from all directions. "But we shouldn't just run blindly either."

Finn said, "Tarrick, what is the shortest route to as many Leopards as possible? No number of Hunters are going to be able to get to us if the palace Leopards are roused."

Fear was beginning to flicker in her chest, a low flame she tried to ignore. This was her fault—she'd insisted on this trip and now the Hunters had found them.

Tarrick didn't waste any time. "Follow me," he barked, breaking into a run. They barrelled around a corner and ran for the door at the end. He pushed through and they ran into a small garden they'd walked through earlier—where there had been four Leopards on guard. Now it was empty.

"Where are the Leopards?" Finn asked, looking in all directions.

"I don't know." Tarrick sounded lost.

Everyone spun as the door opened behind them, but it was only Rothai. His staff was out and his eyes glittered with magic. Relief flooded Alyx at the sight of him.

"Magor-lier! I returned from a patrol and found the guards on this wing gone."

"We need to keep moving," Dashan said tersely. "I have a sense of where the fewest Hunters are—we'll fight through there."

"Wait!" Rothai snapped. "Where are Adahn, Jayn, and Tari? We have a much better chance of fighting our way out as a group."

"There are enough Hunters encircling us to create a barrier for my telepathy," Alyx explained. "They're not in their rooms and I can't reach them. They're probably down in the city for the night."

The grim look on Rothai's face deepened. "This was well planned."

"We can talk about that later. Come on!" Tarrick urged.

And so they ran.

Dashan was a step ahead, Rothai at his shoulder, when they came running around a corner to find the hall ahead blocked by darkly-clad Hunters, waiting. Dashan didn't pause—he ran straight at them, *Kingsbrother* slashing in a flash of light. He moved faster than they could see, cutting and hacking, a blur of movement.

"Stay with Alyx!" Rothai bellowed before moving forward to help Dashan.

Alyx spun her staff, tried for a concussion blast, and wasn't surprised when it failed to ignite. Instead, she hovered a few paces away from the fight, staff spinning in her hands in readiness. Tarrick stood half in front of her. Finn ran back to keep an eye on their rear.

For a few intense minutes Rothai and Dashan were neck deep in black-clad swordsmen. They fought bitterly, the number of Hunters slowly dwindling.

"We have to move!" Finn came running. "There's a pack of them right behind us."

Having heard Finn's shout, Rothai and Dashan stepped forward to take the brunt of the attack while Finn shepherded Alyx through and Tarrick covered them. By the time they were clear, Dashan had killed the last Hunter and they were all free.

They sprinted. Hunters rounded the corner behind them, the lead warrior shouting as he caught sight of his quarry. Alyx's heart pounded in her chest. Running hard, she almost overshot when Dashan took a sudden turn to the right.

"I can sense them around us," he said quickly. "I'm trying to see a way clear, so we can get to the Leopards."

"Something is wrong," Finn muttered, glancing back. "We should have run into Leopards by now. At the very least they should have heard us fighting."

Alyx agreed. It was on the tip of her tongue to stop, demand they think about what they were doing, but the Hunters were close on their heels, and there was no time for thinking.

Dashan led them a short distance down the hall, and then took another left turn. Alyx tugged on Tarrick's sleeve. "Where are we?" she asked, panting. Her breath was beginning to burn in her lungs.

"We're in the old servants' wing," he said. "It's been boarded up for years. There's nothing for the Leopards to guard down here, that's why we haven't seen any."

Uneasiness crept through her at his words, but she couldn't focus long enough to get a grip on why. She glanced back—the Hunters were closing the distance. At a quick count, there were more than ten of them. Not necessarily an insurmountable number, except for the fact Dashan could sense more of them all around. Stopping to fight them would only give the rest time to arrive.

"Here!" Dashan pushed through another set of open doors.

They ran through into a spacious chamber lit only by a few flickering wall sconces. There were windows set high up in the walls to their left and right—all barred—and no obvious exits.

Now what?

CHAPTER 8

"We need to hold those doors," Finn called, seeing as quickly as Alyx that there was no obvious way out.

"The chest!" Rothai snapped, and he and Tarrick ran towards an ornamental wooden chest that sat against the wall. Alyx and Finn helped and together they heaved it up against the doors. Dashan prowled the room behind them, looking for an exit.

"Is there anything else that could help barricade?" Tarrick looked around.

"Nothing," Finn said tightly.

"Where are we, Tarrick?" Alyx asked.

"One of the emperor's old audience chambers. My brothers showed me through here once. See the raised dais down there, opposite the doors?"

"There's another old chest over here!" Rothai called. "Help me move it."

"Where are these cursed Leopards?" Dashan swore, wiping the blood from *Kingsbrother* on the carpet. His shoulders were rigid with tension and for the first time he looked worried. Alyx's heart sank. While the others were concentrating on barricading the door, she went over and touched his shoulder. His eyes met hers, dark and opaque.

"How many beyond that door?" she asked.

His mouth tightened. "Too many for us to fight. Some are on the roof above us, but most of them are behind that door. They know we're in here and more are coming. Shakar has sent an army."

She swore in frustration. "How did he know I was here so quickly? Organising a well-planned assault like this takes time. And how have the Leopards not noticed?"

"I don't know. But I'm going to get you out of here, I promise. No matter what it takes." His hand came up to touch her cheek.

His eyes were intense, too intense, and worry trumped her fear the others might see. She took his hand, entangling their fingers and stepping closer to him. "Dash, I—"

"Alyx?"

She spun. Finn's voice was soft, his face stricken as he took in how close she was standing to Dashan, their joined hands. "What have you done?" he whispered.

"Nothing." She shook her head. "I've done nothing but—"

A large cracking sound reverberated through the hall, cutting off her words. An axe-head speared through one side of the wooden doors. Everything but the immediate threat forgotten, they backed away.

"It's not going to take long for them to break though those doors." Rothai was terse. "Minutes maybe."

"Is there another way out?" Alyx asked. "Tarrick?"

Tarrick paced up and down. "I'm trying to think."

Alyx considered her options. She could still summon her magic, but not use it over any distance. Hunters on the roof meant she couldn't melt or destroy the bars on the windows, or even rely on her flying magic to get them out.

"There has to be another way out." Dashan shook his head, his eyes closed as he frowned in concentration. "While we stand here, they're congregating on the other side of that door. They know they've got us trapped in here."

"They do!" Finn paled with sudden realisation. "Dash, they must have known you could sense them. They herded us in here."

Alyx stared at the healer, fear slamming into her chest so fiercely she had to catch her breath. They were in trouble. Serious trouble. This attack had been well thought out and perfectly executed. And there were only five of them, four mages who couldn't access their magic and a single Taliath.

"We shouldn't have let you come here," Rothai muttered, almost to himself. And even though she'd been thinking the same thing only minutes earlier, his words sparked the fear sweeping through her into bright hot anger.

"Damn you, Rothai!" she shouted. "You and the council and your stupid, idiotic fear of the Taliath. If I had more Taliath protection right now, we might have a chance of getting out. Instead I'm stuck with three protectors who can't touch their magic."

"Alyx, I—"

"No!" She cut over Finn. "This is what happened to the disappeared mages. The most powerful ones. The other mages of the higher order. Those who might have helped us actually stand a chance against Shakar. Instead they're all gone because of a bunch of spineless old men afraid of losing their power."

Rothai's face hardened to stone, but he said nothing. Dashan spoke into the ensuing silence. "We'll have to hope the door holds until one of the Leopards works out what's going on. This many Hunters in the palace can't stay hidden from them forever."

"Even if they do, they'll have to fight through the Hunters to get to us," Rothai said.

"Wait." Tarrick stopped pacing, hope brightening his face. "This is an old audience chamber. There is no way the Leopards would have allowed the emperor in here if there was only one way in and out. There has to be another exit, a secret one, in case he was ever attacked, so they could get him out quickly."

"Good. Where would it be?" Dashan asked calmly.

"If there's an exit, it will be near the back wall, where the dais is." Tarrick spoke quickly.

As a group, they sprinted for the wall. Alyx ran her eyes over the sandstone brick, most of it covered by thick, dusty tapestries. Nothing jumped out to her that looked like a door or any other kind of exit. She tried to stifle the growing panic in her chest with little success. Her fingers trembled as they brushed the rough surface of the wall, her heart pounding, throat dry. It was suddenly difficult to swallow.

"Get these down," Tarrick shouted, pulling at the tapestry nearest to him and sending a cloud of dust raining over them. "Start pushing against the bricks. Spread out. You're looking for a brick that pushes inwards, or swivels, like a key."

They lined up before the wall, frantically running their hands over the bricks, looking for one that would open a secret exit.

"Are you sure there are too many to fight?" Finn asked as seconds passed without any luck. There was a note of helplessness in his voice that sent Alyx's panic plunging into despair. She pushed it away, focused ruthlessly on the wall in front of her.

Dashan nodded tersely. "Too many even for me."

A high-pitched screech sounded as the cabinet blocking the door was shoved forward an inch. The axe smashed through the door again, making them all jump. Alyx yanked at another tapestry, coughing when dust flew into her lungs. She ran her hands over the section of wall revealed, ignoring their shaking, inwardly pushing back her terror. The Hunters were only moments away from coming through the door.

She tried again and again to summon her magic, but the Hunters were too close and she couldn't do it. A large grouping like this seemed to extend the range of the medallions they wore—making it effectively like a large bubble within which magic couldn't exist.

The axe came through the door for a fifth time with a loud splintering sound. Soon the ragged opening would be large enough for the Hunters to push inside. Hands reached through the gap to push at the cabinet and it screeched forward another inch.

As she glanced away from the ever-widening crack in the door, she caught Dashan exchanging a look with Finn and Tarrick. Tarrick nodded, and a nameless dread opened in the pit of her stomach.

"What?" she snapped.

"Nothing." Dashan turned back to the wall. He wouldn't meet her gaze. "Keep looking. We'll find it."

She opened her mouth to demand they tell her what that look meant, but Rothai spoke before she could. "Are you sure it exists, Tarrick?" he asked, frustration filling his voice.

"No," the mage snapped. "But if it doesn't, we're all going to die here."

"I think I've got it!" Finn shouted suddenly.

Another axe-strike slammed into the door. It split the wood even further, and then hands appeared to tear the splintered wood away from the ever-widening hole.

"Finn!" Alyx shouted. "They're coming through!"

"It's stuck," he called back. "Give me a second."

Alyx tensed, anticipation making her hands sweaty. The first Hunter appeared, shouldering his way through the crack and making it wider. Her eyes flickered between Finn, working desperately to turn the swivel brick he'd found, and the Hunters pushing through the gap in the broken doors. Tarrick joined Finn, lending his strength to the effort.

Another Hunter came through the gap, then another. Then, with a screeching, groaning sound, they moved the chest away from the door and kicked the shattered remnants of the door open.

"Nearly there," Finn said.

"Cover the Magor-lier!" Rothai cried out.

Dashan was suddenly at her side, leaning down to kiss her forehead, a hand coming up to cradle her cheek. "Love you, mage-girl," he murmured.

And then he was moving, too quickly for her to reach out and stop him. He ran, bloodied sword raised, to meet the Hunters just past the door, slamming into the wave of black-clad warriors with a shout of anger.

"Got it!" Finn's shout of triumph was almost swallowed up by the ring of clashing blades sweeping through the room. Alyx's gaze was fixed on Dashan, worry and fear flooding her, as he single-handedly kept the Hunters from progressing further into the chamber. Tarrick grabbed her arm, shouting something in her ear. She tore her eyes away as a door in the brick wall slid sideways, revealing a dim hallway leading upwards.

"Go!" she shouted, gripping her staff with the intention of going to help Dashan get clear. But Tarrick didn't let go of her arm, his strength yanking her sharply backwards.

"What are you doing?" she demanded, trying to shake him off. He wouldn't budge. There was an expression on his face she'd never seen before. A resolute intentness that terrified her.

"Dash is giving us time to get out. Your safety is our priority," he said, then began to tug her towards the tunnel. With stunned horror, she abruptly realised what the look she'd seen between him and Dashan had meant.

"No!" She shoved him as hard as she could. "Let go of me!"

The force of her movement dislodged his grip on her, but before she could even take a step, another pair of arms grabbed her, wrapping firmly around her middle. Rothai.

"Alyx, come on, please!" It was Finn from the exit, waving urgently at her.

But Dashan was still fighting, the Hunters trying desperately to get past him but so far failing. *Kingsbrother* slashed down over and over again but there were too many. Dashan would be swamped any moment.

"Rothai, let go of me!" she demanded.

Instead of obeying, he began dragging her towards Finn. Shock at what he was doing froze her utterly. And then her gaze fell on Dashan. A Hunter slipped around him, and he had to lean out too far to engage him—another Hunter snuck in on his other side, his sword opening up a bloody gash along Dashan's left arm. Alyx began to fight then, kicking and struggling with everything she had.

But it did no good. Tarrick joined Rothai and their combined grip on Alyx was immovable, no matter how fiercely she fought them. "Tarrick, let go!" she screamed, throwing herself to the side and attempting to dislodge their grip. "That's an order. LET GO OF ME!"

"I'm sorry," he grunted, not letting up.

"You can't just leave Dash behind to die," she yelled. "What are you doing?"

"He's holding them off, giving us time to get out," Finn shouted, eyes wild. "If we don't go now, they'll get ahead of us and surround us again. Please, Alyx, just come with us."

"Tarrick, get off me!" Alyx struggled as fiercely as she knew how. Desperation swamped her, overtaking any rational thought. She had to get free.

"I'm sorry," Tarrick insisted. Sweat poured down his face with the effort of holding her.

Alyx found herself inexorably dragged up the corridor towards a moonlit garden. No matter how desperately she fought, the distance between her and Dashan increased, inch by inch. Dashan was gradually swallowed up by the Hunters, moving like a true Taliath despite several bleeding wounds, keeping them with him, preventing them from breaking away to follow her.

Alyx dug deep for her magic. It was there but she couldn't grab it. Again and again she tried. Desperation made her wild, uncontrolled, but she still couldn't find it.

"LET GO OF ME!" she screamed at the top of her lungs, beginning to panic as the realisation sunk in that she wasn't going to be able to break free. Dashan. She had to get to him. Had to help him.

"No," Rothai said, his voice as iron-hard as his grip on her.

The audience chamber grew further away. Dashan appeared for a second out of the throng of Hunters surrounding him. Blood dripped down his side from a slash across his ribs, and he was sweating freely. He saw Alyx and their eyes met for a brief second. Unbelievably, he gave her his rakish grin, full of warmth and life, then gestured for her to go.

"Dashan, NO!" She fought with renewed vigour, but to no avail. Why wasn't he coming after them? He should be breaking free, following.

They had dragged her almost all the way along the corridor now, picking up speed as her strength started to fail. She almost dislocated an arm in her frenzied attempts to get free. She didn't care if she hurt herself, she just knew she had to reach Dashan before...

"No. Please no!" she begged as loudly as she could, but they kept dragging her away. "DASHAN!!"

Before her horrified eyes, Shakar's assassins began to overwhelm Dashan. One of the wall sconces had tipped over in the fighting and several of the fallen tapestries were alight. Smoke swirled through the room, giving the fight an eerie, hazy glow.

One of the Hunters hit Dashan hard across the back of his head. Dashan stumbled and fell to his knees. In an instant, they were swarming all over him.

"DASHAN!" She lost sight of him as Tarrick and Rothai successfully managed to drag her out into the garden outside, Finn leading the way. Her eyes fixated on the entrance to the corridor where smoke now billowed.

A second later her magic returned with a vengeance—they'd broken through the bubble.

All her grief and fear exploded out of her; she let loose with a panicked surge of magic, tearing Rothai and Tarrick off. They hit the ground hard a few meters away, rolling several paces with the force of their fall.

Breath sobbing in her chest, Alyx ran back towards the chamber, dodging Finn as he reached out to try and stop her. She was two steps away from the entrance when a concussion burst slammed into the sandstone inches ahead of her. The force of the blast sent her flying backwards. She was frenzied, not thinking quickly enough to use her flying magic, and she landed hard, the breath whooshing from her lungs.

"They brought mages!"

Alyx thought the voice was Rothai's and vaguely registered what he was saying, but all her thoughts were consumed with getting to Dashan. He had to be all right, he had to be; she could still save him. Staggering to her knees, lungs burning, she was almost felled again as more concussion blasts exploded around the garden.

A quick glance backwards showed Rothai and Tarrick battling with two mages, trying to get back to her, and then there were more concussion bursts coming at her. She raised her shield and they bounced harmlessly off it. Frustration seared through her—she needed to get back inside!

Fury and panic coalesced in a white-hot surge of emotion that brought with it a tide of hungry magic—raising her staff, she flung it all outwards.

Concussion power exploded through the garden, forcing everyone, mage or Hunter, flat to the ground. For a moment after the concussive boom of her blast faded, there was utter silence.

Into that silence rang the palace alarm bells.

Shouts followed. Leopards came running from every direction. Turning, almost falling, Alyx ran back for the audience chamber, only to be immediately enveloped by flame and smoke.

"Magor-lier!"

Adahn's voice, somewhere behind her. Ignoring him, she ran down the hallway, gasping through the smoke and heat. She made it into the chamber, lungs protesting the lack of air. Smoke was thick, the fire burning almost out of control as more tapestries caught alight. She stumbled blindly, watery eyes searching desperately for Dashan.

Another blast sounded behind her, and she hit the ground hard. Hunters came running through the broken doors, their medallions blanking her magic again so that when the next concussion blast came, she couldn't shield. It hit the ground inches from her right foot. She dived and rolled to try and avoid it, felt a sharp pain in her leg as a piece of flying wood slashed open her calf. Blood immediately began flowing down her leg, soaking into her sandals.

"Magor-lier!" Adahn appeared, soot mixing with the sweat running in rivulets down his face. He helped her up, turned to face the Hunters coming at them. A loud challenge rang out—from a group of Leopards running to intercept.

As soon as the Hunters turned to face the new threat, Alyx took her opportunity and slipped around them, limping heavily. Fiery pain shot through her left leg with every step. Finally she reached the broken doors, shouldering them open and staggering through.

There was a flash of steel in the corner of her eye. She ducked, but was too slow to avoid the attack entirely. A line of fire erupted along her ribs, and someone shoved her backwards. She hit the wall hard, landing awkwardly.

Blackness threatened her vision, and she fought with everything she had to stay awake. Adahn came running, fending off her attacker and dropping him with a well-placed blow to the head.

"Is she all right?" Finn's voice was dim, as if from a great distance, but it sounded desperate.

"She's alive. Help me lift her." This from Adahn.

"No..." she whispered, her throat too hoarse to shout anymore. "Please, no..."

Pain lanced through her ribs as rough hands picked her up, agonising enough to send her mind straight down into the blackness waiting to claim it.

Dashan.

CHAPTER 9

There was a faint, throbbing pain in her left leg, and an echoing ache across her abdomen and ribs. She cracked open her eyes, raising a hand to wipe the grittiness from them. Sun shone through the large window to the right of the bed she was in, and from its warmth she guessed it was late morning. Lifting the covers, she found both her ribs and left calf bandaged. Blood had seeped through the bandaging on her leg, though it didn't look fresh.

Her heart thudded. *What happened?*

She shook her head, trying to remember. And then it came, the memory of the attack flooding back in a rush, bringing with it a panicked sweat. She fought to control her breathing and force away the urgent pull of utter fear. *Dashan!*

The last thing she could recall was the sight of him dropping to his knees, surrounded by Hunters. Sobs welled up in her throat, and when she tried to hold them back, she couldn't breathe properly. Terror for Dashan roped through her veins, the thought of his loss more than she could bear.

"Calm down, Magor-lier." An unfamiliar voice broke her out of the panic she'd been descending into. "You're safe here."

"Where...?" she managed, her eyes focusing on a tall Zandian standing by the bed.

"You're in your room. My name is Nidra, and I am one of His Majesty's personal healers. You've been hurt, Magor-lier."

"What about the others with me? The Taliath—is he okay?"

Before he could respond, a sharp knocking came at the door. Nidra frowned but went to open it. Adahn stood there, Iman at his side. Alyx instantly struggled upwards, pushing off the covers. Pain shot through her chest, sharp enough to make her gasp.

"You're needed, Magor-lier," Adahn said, hesitating when he saw her wince. "Are you well enough to join the emperor?"

"She's not—"

"I'm fine." She gritted her teeth through the pain. "Dashan?" She managed the word.

"I'm sorry, I don't know." Adahn looked more uncomfortable than she'd ever seen him. "But you really should come."

"Magor-lier..." Nidra began to protest again, but stopped when he saw the look on her face. "You'll need a crutch, you can't put weight on that leg. I'll organise for one at once."

The emperor was waiting for them in his main audience chamber as Alyx limped slowly in, trying her best to ignore what was now a morass of pain throbbing through her body. The walk hadn't been a short one. But there was no time for weakness—she had to know what had happened to Dashan.

Surprise flickered across the emperor's hawk-like face at the sight of her, and he hesitated. "My deepest apologies for summoning you, Magor-lier. I had not realised how hurt you were."

"I'm fine." She managed enough strength to stand up straight. "I..."

A door opened to the right to admit Tarrick, Finn, and Rothai. Her mouth opened to say something—she had no idea what—but closed sharply when a tall figure in black mage robes strode in behind them.

Galien.

The shock of seeing him after so long was like a fist to the stomach. Abruptly some of the strength went out of her legs and she leaned heavily on her crutch, the only thing stopping her from falling to the floor. He was bigger than she remembered, broad shouldered and muscular, but with the same pale skin and dark eyes. Her attention was so completely captured by the potency of his presence she barely noticed the two other council mages that followed him through the door.

Galien bowed low to the emperor before turning to face her, his stance relaxed, his power neatly coiled around him.

"Egalion," he said flatly.

Her glance flickered to Tarrick and Finn—they'd remained off to the side. It was almost like they were trying to avoid what was coming. But that would be strange, why would they... she couldn't read either of their expressions, and although her first instinct was to reach out to them for help, the memory of what they'd done flooded her, and she suddenly felt ill.

Taking a deep breath, she turned instead to the emperor. "Dashan? What happened? Is he...?"

"Dead." Galien spoke the word, using a touch of telepathic magic to share the honesty of his statement. Tarrick flinched, taking a half step back as it reverberated about the room. Finn stiffened as Galien continued. "Somehow he survived the Hunter attack—at least thirty dead around him, very impressive—but it didn't take much for me to finish him off."

The only thing that kept her standing in that moment was Galien's presence. She'd never backed down to him before, and never, *ever,* would, but inside she was shattering into a million tiny pieces. There was no physical pain any more, just grief, an unending void of grief that threatened to swallow her whole. She clung to her crutch with a desperate, white-knuckled grip. *No. Please no. Not Dashan...*

"You still haven't explained why *you're* here," Tarrick spoke. His voice was rough, almost hopeless. All of them seemed to have forgotten the presence of the emperor.

"The council received your invitation from Lord-Mage Astor. They told him no, initially, but then one of our spies brought us information that our rogue mage of the higher order had become the lover of a Taliath, and that both would be here."

Rothai started in surprise. "Your spies are wrong. There's no relationship."

A cold smile curled at Galien's mouth. "Is he right, Egalion? There was no relationship? No sailboat ride from Alistriem to Ester a year ago? No stolen moments hidden away from your friends?"

They knew. How could they know? Her mind was broken, thoughts flickering in and out. Dashan, dead?

"Alyx?" Tarrick asked, sounding uncertain.

Finn was glancing rapidly between Galien and Alyx, with the familiar look he wore when his brilliant mind was rapidly putting pieces together. Bitter knowledge filled his voice as his gaze finally fixed on Galien. "You didn't come to join us in petitioning the emperor. They sent you here to kill her."

"Not her...yet." Galien's dark eyes watched her intensely. He knew how she was feeling—no doubt he was picking it all up with his magic—and he was *delighting* in it. "But the Taliath most definitely. Shakar made it easy for us in the end."

"Yet?" Tarrick asked sharply.

For a moment her thoughts turned clear and bright. "He wants to know if I'm invulnerable first. I'm not. We loved each other but we were never lovers."

Rothai's shocked gasp echoed clear throughout the room, but Galien's entire focus was on Alyx. "Can you prove it?"

She shrugged, not caring anymore. "Prove it any way you like."

Galien's hand flicked quicker than thought, quicker than either Tarrick or Finn could react. His telekinetic magic sent her flying across the room and into a wall. Something snapped as she hit the hard surface—another rib, if the stabbing pain was anything to go by—and she slid down to the floor, dazed.

"Disappointing," Galien drawled. "If Shakar wasn't still alive, I'd kill you without hesitation, but even as weak as you are the council thinks you might still be of some use to us."

"Enough!" The emperor's voice cracked through the room, drawing everyone's instant attention. His voice held an intimidating mix of disgust and anger. Alyx shook her head. Her thoughts had muddled again. There was emotion, too, flickering in and out like a torch in a breeze—sometimes so strong she couldn't breathe.

"If this is how mages behave toward each other I have no desire to ally myself or my country with you against Shakar." His words had the firm ring of finality. "Magor-lier, you may stay until you have recovered, but there will be no more discussions between us."

Leopards fell in behind him as he strode from the room, and the door slammed shut behind them. The echoes of it drifted through the silence left behind. Rothai moved first, placing himself in front of Galien. "Leave, now."

Amusement curled at Galien's mouth and he looked his old master up and down in contempt. "You don't give me orders anymore, *Master*."

"You've done what you came here to do." Rothai didn't rise to the taunt. He said something else, but the words weren't clear—her hearing was fading out. She needed to get up, to get out of this room. Using the wall for balance, she dragged herself upwards, tears of pain welling in her eyes. It all hurt so much.

Tarrick and Finn moved as if to come and help her, but she waved them off, instead grabbing at her crutch. "Don't," she warned them. "I can't even look at you." Her voice broke, and she swayed on her feet.

"Alyx, please," Finn whispered.

She shook her head, managed to stagger to the door. Adahn was waiting outside, mouth tightening at her appearance. Was he furious at her? Or just worried about the state she was in? He helped her back to her room, but she wouldn't let him inside, essentially closing the door in his face. Thankfully Nidra wasn't there either.

Alone in the darkness, Galien's words finally hit home. Grief flooded through her, so powerful it washed away any other feeling.

Dashan. Gone.

Gasping for breath, tears streaking her cheeks, Alyx stumbled out onto the balcony, clutching the railing to keep herself upright. A short distance away, the two nearest Leopard guards saw her movement and began heading in her direction. She ignored them.

She had to escape, had to flee the pain, had to leave it behind or she'd go mad. Her magic could save her. Letting go, she sank down into the glorious strength of it. They could break her bones and bruise her skin, but they couldn't touch this.

In a moment she was lifting into the air, soaring into the bright afternoon sky. The higher she went, the better she felt, until she was speeding away from Sandira with every inch of speed her magic allowed her.

She wasn't sure, but thought it took her three days to reach the border of Tregaya. She kept going when the reserves of her power began to drain, kept going as magic burned like fire through her body, forced herself to go on and on, eventually crossing over the sliver of Shiven territory and into Widow Falls.

By then her entire body alternately shivered and trembled, her magic burning like fire with nothing but itself to feed on. Sheer determination had brought her so far, but as she reached Ladan's home, her resolve died and her magic gave out.

She dropped out of the sky into his courtyard, hitting the ground hard. There was more pain then, and she whimpered. It was dark, and cold. She drifted in and out of consciousness, her mind focusing dazedly on the cold flakes of snow pressing into her feverishly hot skin.

"Lady Egalion!" Booted feet ran across the yard, then blackness overtook her completely.

CHAPTER 10

Alyx awoke once, briefly, with no conception of how much time had passed. Everything hurt, and she had no strength to move. Her thoughts were foggy. She had never been so weak or sick, and it would have scared her if she'd been lucid enough to think about it.

Somewhere nearby her brother was speaking softly to someone. She couldn't open her eyes, or even turn her head, but just the sound of his familiar voice made her feel better. Ladan would keep her safe.

She strained to move, say something, but her voice wasn't working, and the words she wanted came out as an incoherent mumble. Feet scuffed against the floor and then a weight settled on the soft surface she was lying on.

"Aly-girl, you're awake?"

Alyx took a breath and opened her eyes, struggling to speak. "Ladan...I..."

His expression hardened with worry as he saw how weak she was, and he gently touched her shoulder. "What is it, what happened?"

"Attack... Sandira." She fought to stay awake, to explain. "Dashan... they... he's dead. I can't..."

He flinched, and his hand on her shoulder tightened painfully. "Rest, Aly-girl, you're badly hurt. It's going to be okay, I promise. I'm going to take you home."

"I..." Tears streaked unbidden down her face, and she tried to speak, to tell him more, but the effort was too much and she sank into blackness again.

Most of the trip to Alistriem passed in a haze of sickness. Sometimes she was aware of Ladan's arms wrapped tightly around her as he rode, and the pain of being lifted down from the saddle each time they stopped usually served to wake her from whatever fever dream she was lost in.

Rarely, she managed to stay conscious long enough to manage a mouthful or two of the food and water that Ladan tried to get into her. Whenever she was awake, she couldn't stop shaking, or properly catch her breath. Her body alternately felt like it was burning up with heat or shaking with cold.

Sometimes in the worst of her fever, she wondered if she was dying. That might have bothered her, but thinking took too much effort, and mostly she just drifted.

One day, her eyes flickered open to the glow of early morning sun lighting up the distant spires of the Alistriem palace. Shivers racked her body despite the thick cloak she wore and the warmth of Ladan's arms around her. It was winter, wasn't it? Maybe her cold wasn't all fever.

"It's all right, Aly-girl," Ladan murmured—he was frantic but trying to hide it. She didn't want to hurt her brother like that and tried to hold onto consciousness for his sake. "Just hold on a little longer. It's going to be all right."

Despite her best efforts, she drifted off again soon after. The firm challenge from the Bluecoats on guard at the palace entrance woke her. Ladan's voice announced them, and she forced her eyes open as they rode through. They'd barely gotten past the gate when a familiar magic touched in her mind—Dawn, sensing her approach and wanting to know what was happening.

Alyx tried to respond, even if only to get Dawn's increasingly panicked questions to stop, but she couldn't. Her magic had completely burned out. It was gone, just like Dashan.

The horses' hooves clattered loudly into the cobblestoned courtyard. Grooms appeared, but Ladan halted them with a sharp word and sent them scurrying back into the stables. Romney said something, voice lilting in question.

"I don't want anyone seeing Alyx here," Ladan murmured. As he spoke, he tugged the hood of her cloak further down over her face.

"Sir!" Another rider called for Ladan, pointing towards the steps leading to the main entrance. Two figures appeared at the front doors, taking the steps two at a time in their haste.

Cayr and Dawn.

"Romney, sort the horses and the men," Ladan said. "I'll come and find you later."

"Yes, sir."

"What's happened?" Cayr was heedless of Romney's men as he pushed through the riders towards Ladan. Dawn was at his shoulder, faced pinched with worry. Ladan shifted, hefting Alyx in his arms.

"Alyx is hurt badly," he said in a low voice. "She needs a mage healer. Please tell me Leanli is still here?"

"He is, Ladan. He's here," Cayr soothed, clearly reading the growing panic in her brother's voice. "Now give her to me."

She found herself being lifted down from the saddle and into Cayr's arms. As gentle as Ladan was, the pain of the jostling was intense, and her eyes slid closed with the force of it. A whimper escaped her.

"Alyx?"

Gentle hands stroked her hair back and she opened her eyes to Cayr's deeply worried face peering down at her. There were dark shadows under his eyes, and new lines around his mouth, but he looked strong, as if adversity had burned through him and left only the toughest parts untouched. He flinched as he read the pain in her eyes, but then his embrace tightened a little and he gave her a small, reassuring smile. Something that had been wound tightly inside began to relax. She was home.

"What's happened?" Dawn asked frantically.

"Dawn, go and fetch Leanli," Ladan said briskly. "She's badly hurt and there will be time for explanations later. Don't tell anyone she's here."

"Bring him to the room adjoining my private quarters," Cayr added as they began walking. "Nobody is using it. I'll take her there for now."

Dawn nodded and ran off. Ladan fell into step with Cayr, hovering worriedly.

"Tell me what happened," Cayr demanded. "How did she get like this?"

"As far as I can gather, there was an attack in Sandira and Dashan was killed," Ladan said. "Alyx was injured in the fight, but I think the real danger is that she's gone into shock from grief. I think... she must have used her magic to travel all the way from Zandia. It's too far, too much."

Something broke inside Alyx at Ladan's stark words and she sobbed aloud, her body curling in on itself despite the pain. Cayr's stride faltered, but he recovered, rocking her gently and murmuring in her ear as he walked. "I've got you, Alyx. It's me. I've always got you."

"Go and get your father, Lord Mirren. I saw him earlier—he should still be in his office." Cayr spoke firmly, grief only barely edging his words. "Alyx is going to need him."

"I won't be long," Ladan promised, striding away.

Cayr continued to murmur soothingly to Alyx as he walked, and she relaxed in his hold. Soon, he was placing her on a soft bed and arranging pillows under her head. Then he sat and took hold of her hand.

"Was Ladan speaking true?"

She nodded, fresh tears welling in her eyes. Matching grief flashed into Cayr's eyes and for a moment he looked like an old man, deep lines furrowed in his forehead and around his eyes. Their hands clung tightly, sharing their grief. Once again it swamped her, threatening to drown her completely.

"I'm sorry," she babbled, fever and grief taking over. "I walked away from you after your father died. I'm sorry, Cayr. I'm so sorry."

"Shush, Alyx." He leaned down, stroking her hair back from her face. "It's okay. Don't think about me right now. Just concentrate on yourself, on getting better. I can't lose you and Dashan both, please. Just be strong for me."

She allowed his voice and touch to calm her, subsiding onto the pillows. When the door clicked open, Cayr let go of her hand and stood, clearing his throat and scrubbing at his eyes. Fresh tears spilled down his cheeks anyway. Dawn was first inside, but she stopped dead as the emotions of the room hit her like a wall. A mage Alyx didn't recognise laid a steadying hand on her shoulder, but she brushed him off. "I'm fine, please see to Alyx."

"Alyx, this is Leanli. He's a healer mage who's been working here for the past few months," Cayr said, standing back to let him work.

The mage—he looked somewhere in his thirties maybe, with thinning brown hair and kind eyes—gave her a reassuring smile. "I don't believe we've met."

Alyx shook her head. "I'm—"

"Shush, no need to exert yourself," he murmured. He laid his hands on her forehead, and a soothing warmth swept through her, taking some of the edge off the pain and sickness. After a long time, he removed his hand and sat back, looking grave. "You've got three broken ribs, an infected leg wound and a bad fever. I think one of your broken ribs may have punctured a lung. Worse, you've overused your magic quite seriously and it almost killed you."

"Will she be all right?" Dawn asked.

"It's likely, but she's still in danger," Leanli said. "I've done what I can for now, magically. I'll go and prepare some herbal medicines which will bring down the fever and then I'll clean out her wounds and re-dress them. I'll be back soon."

Cayr gave him a hard look. "Not a word to anyone about her being here, do you understand me?"

"I understand the threat she faces from the Hunters as well as any mage, Your Highness," Leanli said. "You have nothing to fear from me."

"Very well, then. Hurry back."

At the king's gesture of dismissal, the mage gathered his things and left the room. Sleepiness was drifting over Alyx and her eyes were about to slide closed, when Ladan stormed in. "Father wasn't in the palace so I've sent a servant to his home with an urgent message. He'll be here soon. Is she okay?"

"Leanli's just been in," Cayr reassured him. "She's mostly awake."

It took everything she had, but she managed to lift a hand in a weak wave. His shoulders relaxed, but he remained standing by the door, every inch of his stance screaming protectiveness. Dawn came to sit gently on the edge of the bed, pale with worry.

"What happened, Alyx?" Dawn asked.

"Dashan died," Cayr said, voice rough.

Ladan flinched. Grief sagged Dawn's shoulders, and she lifted a hand to her mouth. "No! But... what about Finn?" Her voice turned frantic. "Are he and Tarrick okay? Why did you come here alone?"

Alyx swallowed, pushed back the encroaching grogginess long enough to find her voice. "They're fine. I left them in Zandia," she rasped.

"Then what is it? Why did you near kill yourself flying all the way from Zandia?" Dawn demanded, her worry unassuaged. "Dashan's death is tragic, but why would you leave Tarrick and Finn behind and almost kill yourself coming here? Rothai too, he would never have let you do this."

"I can't... you have to... my thoughts..." Alyx croaked out then subsided, unable to talk further. Dawn hesitated, but at a slight nod from Alyx, her magic reached out and sank gently into her mind. Alyx was too weak to maintain a shield, and everything was there for the telepath to see.

"Oh Alyx, no," she whispered in horrified realisation. Tears ran down the telepath's face as she felt Alyx's utter despair. Then all at once it was too much, the memories too fresh.

"Dawn, enough," Cayr said firmly, reading the distress on Alyx's face.

Immediately the touch of Dawn's magic left her mind. The telepath sat back, a hand over her mouth and cheeks wet with tears. The pull of sleep was becoming too strong, and Alyx's eyes began sliding closed.

Cayr leaned down to kiss her forehead. "I'll let you know when your father gets here," he murmured. "If you need anything, I'll be right outside with Ladan."

When she woke again, it was to the click of the door opening. Footsteps crossed the room and the bed dipped as someone sat beside her. A hand reached out to tuck a strand of hair behind her ear.

"Aly-girl?"

Her eyes flickered open and took in the familiar face of her father. Worry creased his handsome features.

"Papa." She sobbed and lunged forward into him, heedless of her sore ribs. His arms came around her with aching gentleness and he rocked her while she cried helplessly into his chest.

"It's all right, Aly-girl," he murmured in her ear, one hand rubbing her back. "I'm here now, it's all going to be okay. I'm here, and I love you."

"It's not," she managed between the sobs. "It's never going to be okay again."

CHAPTER 11

The injuries Alyx had sustained during the attack in Sandira were bad, but the infection that developed in her leg and the crippling weakness brought about by the overuse of magic were even worse. In the rare waking moments when she wasn't delirious with fever, but too weak to move, she wondered whether she might die.

Leanli's worried face told her it was a possibility. Dying would at least end the horrible grief that tore at her every moment she was lucid. And each time she glimpsed her father's face, or Cayr's, she could tell they feared she wanted to die. And maybe she did.

But then one day she woke, and her first thought wasn't of Dashan and his loss. It was the memory of what *else* had happened that night. Rothai and Tarrick dragging her away against her will. Shakar's Hunters relentlessly coming at them. Galien delighting in telling her he'd killed Dashan. And with those memories came anger, burning bright and hot—a fury that the aching depth of her grief had temporarily drowned.

But that anger hadn't ever gone away.

She'd been angry for so long. First at her father for sending her away, so unprepared, to DarkSkull Hall, then at what she'd learned about the council. Their corrupt nature and the murder of innocents. Then Casovar and his constant humiliation and bullying. And each time she'd handled that anger, bitten her tongue, forced herself to deal with it.

And at the source of everything, of the council's fear, the Hunters, Dashan's death? Shakar.

Dashan's loss was like a raw wound in her soul; she felt it every waking second, couldn't take a breath without wanting him near and knowing in the next second he never would be again.

But he would want her to live.

And *she* wanted to live. Not just for Dashan. She wanted to *destroy* Shakar and everything he stood for. She didn't know how. Had no clue how to pick up the pieces of what had been utterly destroyed in Sandira. But that could come later.

First she would grow strong again.

One day she woke—had she been in Alistriem one week, two?— to a familiar figure sitting in a plush chair by the door. The room was otherwise empty.

"Jenna?"

The young woman's gaze had been focused on the doorway to the adjoining garden, but now it swung sharply to Alyx, calculating and cool. "Are you well?"

Wincing, Alyx pushed herself up a little higher on her pillows. Her ribs felt much better than they had, still sore when she moved, but no longer a sharp, stabbing pain. "Some water would be nice."

"Then ring for a servant. I'm not your nursemaid."

The dismissive tone took Alyx aback. It had been a long time since anyone had spoken to her that way. It was almost refreshing. "What are you doing here then?"

Jenna rose to her feet, and in that single graceful movement was a Taliath. A Taliath wearing a beautiful silk dress and matching slippers.

"The king asked me to guard you. He's worried for your safety." A little shrug. "I do as my king commands."

Alyx raised an eyebrow, unable to help herself. "You're going to protect me wearing that? What happened to the delightful breeches I saw in Carhall?"

Amusement flashed across Jenna's face. "I see you *are* feeling better."

She sank back against the pillows. "I left you here to protect Cayr, not me."

"I got him back safely from Carhall, didn't I? And last I checked, he's alive and well." Jenna's arched eyebrow put Alyx's to shame.

Touché. "So everyone knows what you are?"

Another little shrug. "Some do, most are unsure. I don't make it obvious. Appearances can be deceiving."

Weariness washed over Alyx, the effort of sparring with Jenna taking what reserves of strength she'd built up. Her eyes slid closed, even though she fought to keep them open, hating the idea of showing weakness in front of Jenna. But the pull of exhaustion was relentless, and the last thing she saw was Jenna gracefully resuming her seat by the door.

"Not up for more visitors yet?" her father asked gently. She'd woken again at his arrival, Jenna nowhere to be seen. "Dawn would really like to see you."

A little shudder went through her at the idea, and she shifted, trying to hide her reaction from his sharp gaze. She'd missed Dawn and Cario so badly... but now whenever she thought of them, an irrational terror would sweep through her, fear that they might believe Tarrick and Finn had done the right thing that night in Sandira. Even the mere thought of it left her shaking and ill. She shook her head. At least Cario was away from the city helping in the north.

"Not yet, Papa."

He was silent for a moment, but there was nothing but concern and understanding on his face. "Talking isn't easy, I know that better than anyone. After your mother died I..." He took a breath. "Have you at least talked with Cayr?"

"I can't," she said simply. Like her father, Cayr hadn't pushed, simply focusing on keeping up her spirits and offering quiet, unconditional support. It was exactly what she'd needed.

He squeezed her hand. "It will be easier when you do, I promise you."

She nodded, changed the subject. "Have you heard from Ladan?"

Alyx's brother had left Alistriem soon after her arrival, traveling into Shivasa, his goal to contact the rebels Dashan had been working with and inform them of what had happened to him—Garan hoped Ladan could preserve the fragile relationships that Dashan had been building.

"He arrived safely, that's all we know for now."

She swallowed, fighting back a wave of weariness. "Do we need to be worried? I've been here over a week."

Relief flashed across her father's face so quickly she almost wasn't sure she'd seen it, but the grip he had on her hand tightened suddenly. "What is it, Papa?"

"Nothing." He smiled a little. "I just wasn't sure... you were so hurt, so upset, I'm just relieved that you're coming back to us, starting to think about your own safety."

Ah. "You thought I wanted to die."

"*I* did." He said simply. "After I heard about Temari. If not for you, Aly-girl, I'm not sure what I would have..."

Tears welled in her eyes as he broke off and it was her turn to clutch at his hand. "I'm sorry. I didn't mean to scare you."

He cleared his throat, regaining composure. "In answer to your question, Ladan thought quickly when he brought you here. Only a handful of people know—Dawn, myself, Leanli and Cayr. Astor was told, and I'm sure he's sent a coded message to Cario on the border by now. Ladan trusts his men implicitly, but they've all been sent back to Widow Falls after being told you'd left. You'll notice your food and drink has been left outside the door for Cayr, myself or Leanli to bring to you."

"Jenna knows too," Alyx grumbled.

Garan smiled in amusement, astonishing her. "If only you'd seen the look on her face when the king asked her to keep an eye on you."

"She's probably already sold me out to the Hunters six times over," she muttered.

"Jenna is not the most traditional of Taliath, I grant you, but I trained her. I've seen what she can do. I feel safer with her keeping an eye on you."

Alyx straightened, a jolt of fierceness running through her that she never thought she'd feel again. "I can look after myself. I don't need Jenna Aridlen's protection."

Garan chuckled, reaching out to wrap an arm around her and pull her close. "I'm aware of that."

His embrace relaxed her, and with that came another wave of overwhelming weariness. Her father sat by her, holding her hand, until she was fast asleep.

Wearing a cloak with its hood well down over her face, Alyx followed Cayr's careful instructions through a number of the less-frequented gardens. While she tried her best not to limp, it was an impossible task—the scar on her newly-healed calf pulled painfully with every step. Eventually she paused outside a rusted gate set deep into an ivy-covered wall. The cracking of wooden practice blades sounded from the other side, reassuring her she was in the right place. Even so, she hesitated before going through.

Could she do this?

It didn't matter, she had to do it. Resolute, she pushed through the gate—well-oiled despite the rust—then came to a shocked halt two paces beyond. Jenna Aridlen was sparring with two familiar Bluecoats in a dusty yard surrounded by high walls.

In breeches.

Unable to help herself, Alyx let out a laugh. "If only Mira and Lissa could see you now."

The sparring came to an abrupt halt, but despite her amusement over Jenna, Alyx's attention went straight to the Bluecoats.

"Lady Egalion!" Casta, the more relaxed of the two, came jogging over. A wide smile spread across his face and he gave her a jaunty salute.

"What a pleasant surprise!" Tijer's serious face had lightened several shades. "Did you come back from Sandira with Lieutenant Caverlock?"

Her grief was still raw enough that Tijer's question hit hard. Dashan's death hadn't been announced yet—Cayr had wanted to wait until Alyx was stronger and had decided the best way to do it.

"No," Alyx said quietly, forcing herself to speak past the acute pain sweeping through her. "I'm sorry... Dash died in Sandira."

Both young men's faces dropped, Tijer letting out a breath like he'd been sucker punched, and Casta lifting both hands as if to ward off her news. Part of Alyx was surprised at the strength of their reaction.

"My Lady..." Casta spoke first, hesitating. "It can't be true."

She glanced away, unsuccessfully fighting back tears. "It is. I'm sorry."

"We, I mean—we're sorry," Tijer stammered, stricken. "We didn't mean to upset you."

"You haven't." She cleared her throat. "Seeing you both again, is—it's good."

"Lady Egalion." Tijer paused. "Do you mind if we ask what happened—how Dashan died?"

Alyx took a steadying breath. These two men had been Dashan's friends, and they deserved to know what had happened. "We were attacked by a large force of Hunters. He died giving me time to escape." It was close enough to the truth, and she didn't have the strength to go into the full story. Even this much was tearing her up.

"I'm sorry, Lady Egalion," Casta said quietly.

She shook off her emotion, voice turning brisk. "I'd like to catch up properly, soon, but if you don't mind I have to speak to Jenna."

Casta and Tijer shared a glance. "You know where to find us. Do you mind if we let Nario and Roland know what happened? Josha too? We all loved the Lieutenant."

"Only them," Alyx said quietly. "There are reasons it needs to be kept quiet for now—the main one having to do with my safety. Nobody can know I'm here."

Tijer gave her a sad smile. "We're well practiced at ensuring your safety, Lady Egalion. You can rely on us."

"What brings you here?" Jenna asked as the two young men left. She was sweating lightly despite the cold day, but of course still looked gorgeous. "No offence, but you look a little... fragile."

Alyx scowled. Fragile indeed! "I once threatened to burn that pretty hair of yours to cinders. I can still do that, you know?"

"Charming. What do you want?"

She took a deep breath. "Right now I'm weak. I need to be strong again."

The scowl turned to surprise. "You want to spar with me?"

"That, and I want you to teach me to be a better fighter." Alyx raised a hand as Jenna opened her mouth. "Just think of it as an opportunity to hit me as often as you like. It's going to take a while for me to rebuild my strength."

Jenna gave her a considering look. "It's not going to help me any, spending time trying to teach you. You look like you'll barely last a minute before collapsing."

"I'll last longer than that," Alyx promised. She would make sure of it. She couldn't be weak anymore. Strength would allow her to do something about the anger burning inside. Shakar and the council had taken what she loved most and destroyed her friendships in the process. "And consider this—the sooner I'm fit again, the less time you'll have to spend guarding me."

She appeared to consider that for a moment, then shrugged. "I'm not going to take the blame if you keel over."

Alyx reached back to unhook her mage staff. Her arm trembled with the weight of it, but she ignored the weakness. Going after Shakar wouldn't allow weakness. "I'm not going to keel over, you can be sure of that."

CHAPTER 12

Water tinkled in the background as Alyx and Cayr sat peaceably on a bench by a small fountain. He'd had something on his mind all morning, but she was content to let him come to it in his own time. Besides, she was slightly distracted. Her ribs were aflame after her second session with Jenna, and her leg was now too sore to put her full weight on it. It hadn't been a great hour—her stamina had been worse than appalling, but she was resigned to the fact that recovering her strength would take time.

Eventually Cayr cleared his throat, running a hand through his curls. "You should know... Dawn told me what she saw in your thoughts. When you first came here."

Ah. So this was why nobody had pressured her to tell them what had happened. They already knew. She wasn't sure how she felt about that, although relief was definitely part of it. It meant she wasn't going to have to say it all aloud.

"What exactly did she see?" she asked. "Does she know about Dash and me?" The thought didn't bring with it the twinge of fear it always had. Whether her friends knew or not no longer mattered, not against the drowning tide of grief that still tugged at her every waking moment. As if sensing that—or feeling the same himself—Cayr absently reached out to take her hand.

"Yes. She also told me that you tried to help Dashan, and that Tarrick and Finn stopped you. That Galien killed Dashan after he'd held off all the Hunters." He paused. "Dawn is struggling. She's hurt that you don't want to see her, and none of us know what to think about what happened, not without the full story. You're not the only one who's been in a dark place."

"She's a good person," Alyx murmured. "To be so worried and yet not look for the answers with her magic. I know I've treated you all poorly, but I just couldn't..."

"Will you tell me now?" His gentle voice broke her from her thoughts.

Alyx took a deep breath. They all deserved better. She was working on getting her strength back, and this was part of it. She would start with her oldest and dearest friend.

She squeezed his hand, giving him a little nod. "The attack was well planned. There were too many of them to stand and fight, so we ran, but we didn't realise they were herding us. They trapped us in an old audience chamber. We found a way out, but by then they'd caught up to us. Dashan... he went to hold them off so that the rest of us had time to escape."

When tears began welling in her eyes, Cayr moved closer. She forced back the tears and scrubbed at her face. "When I realised what Dashan was doing, I tried to go back and help him, but Tarrick and Rothai grabbed hold of me and dragged me away. I couldn't use my magic because of the Hunters being so close, and they were simply too strong for me. As soon as I got free, I went back. But I got hurt and then knocked out." She swallowed. "I found out later that he'd survived the Hunters, but he must have been weak and hurt, and that's when the council showed up. Galien killed him."

Cayr stood suddenly, letting go her hand. Tension vibrated from him as he began to pace.

"Cayr..." She hesitated, screwing up her courage. "Do you agree with what they did? Tarrick and Rothai, I mean. Tell me the truth. Please."

"No!" He said it so decisively it could only be the truth, and the relief was so great she sagged against the bench seat. "You could have saved him. I have faith in your magic, in you. And even if you couldn't..." He shook his head.

"Then what?"

"You loved him," Cayr said simply. "It was your choice to make."

Alyx stood and threw her arms around him, heedless of her sore body. "Thank you," she said. "For always being someone I can trust. I'm not sure I deserve it, after what I did to you."

Cayr smiled. "It was painful at the time, but neither you nor Dash could help how you felt. And Dashan deserved something good to happen in his life, after everything he'd been through."

Tears sheened her eyes. "You truly think that?"

"We were the best of friends as children, and that became confusing for both of us as we grew up. I had no right to expect you to fall in love with me."

"I could have been more honest with you," she said softly. "I will always be sorry for that."

"Forgiven long ago." He dismissed her apology with a smile.

"It's not just that. Your father died, and I left you. You've been alone here trying to establish your rule while grieving your father. And then I show up here badly hurt and once again you've had to look after me."

"Oh, I won't deny I've wished for you to be here constantly." He smiled sadly. "But if you think for a second I blame you for walking away... I know the danger you're in, and the last thing I want would be to have you in more danger just to be here." He paused, taking her hands. "The three of us made each other strong. We gave each other a home and a place to belong. But *I* am king, and I must learn to be strong standing alone. My country needs that from me."

His words resonated with her, and she filed them away for later consideration, along with the surging pride she felt for him. "You're a better leader than I am." She cleared her throat, straightening her shoulders. "And I'm recovering quickly. I'll be strong again. And whatever I can give you, you have to know I will."

"I know." His mouth quirked in a smile, a genuine one, and it warmed her from head to toe. It didn't last, his face turning serious. "Now explain to me why the council showed up, and why Galien killed Dashan."

This was harder to tell, and she sat back down as she spoke, not confident her weary legs would hold her. When she finally came to a halt, he must have seen something of the simmering anger on her face, because he came to kneel before her, taking her hands in his. "Alyx, you can't go after Shakar *and* the Mage Council."

She huffed out a breath, head dropping to rest on his shoulder. "Oh, Cayr. I have absolutely no idea what I'm going to do next."

A week later, she returned to her room to find Cario seated in the chair by the crackling fire. She paused mid-stride, completely taken aback. Her father had implied Cario was on his way back to Alistriem, but she'd had no indication of his arrival.

He seemed relaxed, but Alyx had become familiar enough with him over the years to know that the slight tensing of his jaw signaled carefully concealed distress. And unlike Dawn, he'd seemingly decided not to give Alyx a choice about whether to see him. *What if he agrees with them?*

"Astor's message said you were close to death." He spoke before she could.

"I was." A cold breeze was flowing through the partially opened door to the garden, and she walked over to shut it. Another indicator that something was off with Cario; he abhorred discomfort of any kind.

"I spoke to Dawn. She told me what happened."

Alyx froze, hand on the door latch. "Tell me you wouldn't have made the same decision as Tarrick and Finn that night," she said quietly.

"I wouldn't," he said without hesitation. "Just as I know that you wouldn't do it to me. The level of trust we've built between us is something I've come to rely on, and something I will never break."

"Thank you." Exhaling in relief, she turned to face him. He was watching her, his blue eyes dark against the flickering flame that cast half of his face into shadow. Then, abruptly, he rose to his feet, as if unable to sit still any longer. She took a step back, surprised at such a sudden movement from a man who was deliberately languid in everything he did. "What's wrong?"

"I wouldn't have done what Tarrick and Finn did, but you should never have put them in that position."

Shock flared through her. "What?"

"You should have fled when Dashan gave you the opportunity. You should have run for your life, and you should have prioritised your survival over every single other person that was there."

"What are you talking about?" Anger rose unbidden. "I couldn't willingly leave Dashan behind to die. I could have—"

"You are the Magor-lier." He didn't raise his voice, but the words were more cutting for the sheer ice in them. "You don't get to make selfish decisions about your life."

Shocked, confused, she took a step back. She didn't know what to say.

He stepped closer. "You are a figurehead. I thought you understood that, but clearly you don't. Alyx, who is going to defeat Shakar if you die?"

"There are other mages of the higher order."

"Galien? Are you serious?" His eyebrows shot skywards. "Can you be so deluded you think that psychopath is *any better* than Shakar? Being loyal to the Mage Council doesn't make Galien a good guy. Even if by some crazy chance he could defeat Shakar, then what?"

Alyx had no counter to that and took another step back as Cario continued in his cold, rational voice.

"If you die, Shakar wins. Have you thought about that? How many people will die, do you think? What would life be like for those who survive? Dashan knew the answers to those questions, it's why he sacrificed himself to save your life."

"Shakar wins anyway!" she shouted, desperately trying to raise a shield against the words he was flinging at her. "I've been running and hiding and learning *nothing* for the past year. Shakar is years ahead of me in power, learning and experience. I'm not going to catch up by running away. I can't face him unless I get stronger."

Cario's face tightened. "You are the most powerful mage the world has seen since Shakar, and you have a very capable team of mages around you. You're the one who proved at DarkSkull that battles can be won with teamwork, no matter the individual power of your opponent. But you have to be *alive* to do it."

"That's all gone now," she said bitterly. "I can't work with them anymore."

Cario continued as if she hadn't spoken. "If you want to take that small chance to win, then you need to start thinking about who you are. You need to be a *real* leader. That means ignoring yourself and what you want, it means putting aside the person you are in order to become what we need to win this war. You need to stop being Alyx Egalion and start being the Magor-lier of the mage order."

"I've been trying to—"

"No, you haven't," he cut her off. "You've been angry and trapped and blaming everyone else for it. You hid a relationship with a Taliath from those who trust you, and all you've been thinking about is how hard things are for you."

"You've never said this to me before," she whispered, utterly stunned by how he'd just ripped into her.

"I should have. When I heard you were near death... I've never been more scared. Not just for me, because you're my closest friend in the world, but for everyone else. The council couldn't defeat him last time, Alyx, but they didn't have you back then."

She could do nothing but stare as he let out a heavy sigh, then walked to the door, pausing on the threshold. "I'm not here to be an ornamental assistant to the Magor-lier. There were truths you needed to hear, and it's my job to tell them to you."

He was gone before she could think of anything to say, shutting the door softly behind him and leaving her alone in the room, the only sound coming from the crackling flames in the fireplace.

CHAPTER 13

Cayr came to see her one afternoon as she returned from a session with Jenna. Despite sweating profusely and aching all over, she'd managed to hold her own for the first time. Even the aching in her ribs had mostly subsided, although she remained unhealthily thin. There was no more reason to be hiding out in this room anymore, but she still had no clue what to do next. Some days it was hard even getting out of bed. Thinking of Cario's words didn't help, especially because a tiny part of her had a sneaking suspicion he'd been right.

"You look troubled," Alyx said as he closed to the door. "What's wrong?"

"I've had word from a Blue Guard patrol that just returned to the city. Tarrick, Finn, Rothai and a group of mages are on their way here, travelling from the direction of Widow Falls. They asked the Bluecoats to let me know of their approach. They'll be here sometime today."

She froze. She should have expected this—of course they would guess where she'd gone and come for her—but she hadn't. And now they were here.

"What do you want me to do?" he asked.

The trembling in her tired muscles suddenly intensified, and she had to sit down. Breathing was difficult too, her heart racing in her chest. She'd been desperately trying to rebuild her strength, but she couldn't do this. Not yet.

"I can't, Cayr. I can't see them." She swallowed. "Keep them away from me."

"All right." He sounded like he wanted to say more, but she refused to look at him. Eventually he gave a little sigh and left, closing the door behind him.

Tears rushed to her eyes then, and through sheer effort of will she pushed them back. It took some time—sitting there and taking deep breaths—before she was in control of herself again.

A flash of joy from Dawn echoed unexpectedly through her telepathic magic—she and Cario were greeting Tarrick and Finn. The twins had missed each other terribly. Alyx tightened her shield, drowning out everything but her own thoughts.

Then she sat back in her chair, staring idly at her right forearm, allowing a touch of magic to light the skin with a green pearlescent glow. She felt more whole with her magic fully revived, as if her body was healthy again.

Her spirit was another matter, but only time would heal that. Until then, she would have to keep fighting to get through each moment.

Outside, dusk had fallen, shrouding the garden outside in shadows broken only by the tiny pinpricks of the lanterns scattered throughout the palace grounds. She sighed. It *was* good to be home in Alistriem, but it hurt too. She felt Dashan's presence here, as if he were still with her. At the same time, she was constantly reminded of his loss, of the fact she was never going to see him again. She didn't know what she wanted; should she stay, or leave? What was she going to do now?

She was saved from immediately having to answer that question by the arrival of Ladan, grim-faced and still dressed from the road. His hard look softened at the sight of her on her feet and he drew her into a warm hug.

"I'm getting better," she promised, surprise filling her voice. "When did you get in?"

"Just now." He hesitated, the grim look returning. "I ran into your friends. Aly-girl, I know you don't want to see them, but they have news you need to hear."

"Ladan, I don't think I can—"

"I'll be with you," he said steadily. "And unless you plan on spending the rest of your life in this room hiding, then you need to hear this."

Tarrick and Finn were there, with Rothai, Dawn, and Cario. Every single one of them turned to look at her when Ladan ushered her in. Emotionally, it was like being plunged back into that terrible night, and she couldn't look any of them in the eyes.

The tension rising in the room was palpable. Neither Tarrick nor Finn could conceal the shock that crossed their faces at Alyx's gaunt appearance, but Rothai remained expressionless. Dawn was pale and drawn.

"I'm glad to see you are well." Tarrick spoke first, his words stiffly formal. "Dawn has been telling us how ill you were."

"I *was* ill," Alyx said. "But I don't want to talk about that. I'm only here because Ladan said you have news I need to hear. What is it?"

Another silence fell. Alyx sensed Ladan's rigid stance beside her, and read the stern, hard faces of Tarrick and Rothai. Dawn and Finn were glancing between each other and their shoes. Cario moved away to go and sit in one of the chairs, hands crossed loosely in his lap, long legs spread before him. Whatever this news was, nobody wanted to speak it aloud.

"Well?" she pressed, impatience edging her voice.

Tarrick's jaw clenched. "We passed through Carhall on our way here—King Mastaran had grave news. The Tregayan port city of Tennan was attacked by Shakar just over a week ago."

"Tennan?" Alyx asked carefully. "The busiest hub of merchant shipping in Tregaya, and the port where all militia troop transports pass through?"

"The very same." Cario nodded.

She swore under her breath. "How bad?"

"A large part of the city was destroyed. The docks were razed, and hundreds of its inhabitants are reported killed," Finn said. His green eyes glittered, she wasn't sure whether it was anger or fear.

Alyx frowned. "Tregaya hasn't been invaded—yet that would have taken an entire army to accomplish."

"Or a supremely powerful mage," Rothai countered. "An army could never have approached Tennan without notice, and the city has defences. A full division of militia is based at the barracks just outside of the city. Shakar did this."

Tarrick threw a concerned glance in Alyx's direction. "We should get Alyx away from here as soon as possible. There could be another Hunter attack coming at any moment. The first wave failed, it only makes sense Shakar would send another."

Anger surged, and she used it to give her strength. "I'm not going anywhere, especially not with you."

Shock flared on Tarrick's face, but Dawn shot him a quelling look before he could say anything, then turned to Alyx. "I know how you must feel, but that is a big decision to make."

"You have no idea how I feel," she said, some of her pain leaking into her voice despite her best attempts otherwise. "No idea at all."

"We had no choice." Finn's voice was cold. "You forced us into what we did."

"You damn well *did* have a choice!" She rounded on him, her eyes and voice blazing with fury. "You betrayed me, and what's worse is that you think you were justified in doing it."

"Were we supposed to let you die?" Tarrick demanded, his temper sparking as hotly as hers.

"You should have had more faith in me!"

"If we had let you go, you would have died too. There were too many Hunters. Without your magic—"

"I could have saved him!" The words tore out, full of the grief sweeping through her. It was like a scab ripping off a wound, all the betrayal and heartache leaking out. "Damn you, Tarrick, I could have saved him."

They stared at each other, both unwilling to back down. Alyx's hands were trembling and with an effort she tried to rein in her emotions. It didn't work.

Rothai spoke calmly into the ensuing silence. "You are not invulnerable, Magor-lier, and your magic was useless against their medallions."

"And if I hadn't been so afraid of your reaction to Dash and I becoming lovers then I *would* have been invulnerable!" she yelled.

Rothai's expression was unyielding. "Then you would have become as much a threat to us as Shakar."

"You really think that?" Ladan broke in, voice angry.

"How can you know for certain that she wouldn't?" Finn demanded, clearly forgetting in his anger that he was addressing a lord. "Alyx, you would have the power to do whatever you wanted. Nothing could stop you. That sort of power corrupts even good people."

"I am so sick of that argument," Alyx said coldly, realisation and clarity coming far, far too late. "Dashan grounded me, kept me from giving in to my worst impulses. I was wrong to hold myself back from him, and I was wrong to ever fear being invulnerable. And you? *You* were wrong to have so little faith in who I am. You betrayed me and you doubted me, and I won't ever forget that."

Her words reverberated through the room. As their echoes faded, the familiar exhaustion began creeping through her. She wasn't ready for this.

Tarrick looked equally tired and beaten. He shook his head. "You say we betrayed you, but *you* betrayed us just as badly. It's clear now that you've been lying to us. You carried on a relationship with a Taliath, knowing full well what that could mean. Worse, you kept it secret."

"You took my free will away from me," Alyx said quietly. "And you kept me from doing something to save a man that I loved very much. You destroyed me."

Finn turned suddenly, anger vibrating from him. "Cario, do you plan to weigh in on this at all?" he demanded. "You *are* her favourite, yes? The one she trusts more than any of us."

Cario gave a little smile before reaching down to casually straighten the cuffs on his shirt. "I've already discussed my thoughts privately with Alyx."

"You're not surprised," Dawn said suddenly. "None of this is news to you."

"Alyx and I have an understanding," Cario said, his eyes narrowing. "And I'll thank you to stay out of my thoughts, Dawn. I know that you mean well, but my mind is private."

"You knew about Dashan," Tarrick said flatly, and it wasn't a question.

Cario smiled faintly but said nothing.

"Alyx—" Once again Dawn tried to talk to her, but Alyx raised a hand, the silver-green glow of her magic lighting the room.

"Thank you for your information, but I can't do this right now," she said. "Please, just let me be."

"Fine." Tarrick turned on his heel and stalked out of the room. With a final helpless look around, Finn followed him. Rothai's features were unreadable as he left.

"I would not have held you back." Dawn stepped forward, her tone fierce. "You can read my thoughts, use every ounce of power you have, but that is the truth."

"Dawn..." she sighed. "I'm sorry you're caught in the middle of this."

"I'm sorry too," she said, pausing a moment before turning and striding out of the room, slamming the door behind her. Cario stayed in the chair, blue eyes contemplative as he stared into the flames.

Ladan's hand settled on her shoulder. "I'll take you back to your room."

"No." She shook him off. She couldn't bear the thought of being alone in her room. "I'm going to take a walk."

Outside the winter air had grown far too cold for comfort, so instead she sought the palace kitchens. At the sight of Astor sitting by the great fire, something in her relaxed. Part of her had been hoping to find him down here, one of his favourite places to think. She hadn't seen him much during her convalescence and suspected he'd been trying to give her space.

He huffed in mock irritation when she settled on the bench beside him. "A man likes to have time alone with his thoughts."

She smiled a little. "I'm here to do the same."

He eyed her up and down. "You look better than the last time I saw you."

"I *am* better."

"But not ready to face your friends yet."

She didn't like his knowing tone, but didn't call him on it. She'd come for comfort, not another confrontation with someone she loved.

"So you and Dashan never decided to become lovers?" Curiosity crept into his voice.

The question was unexpected, startling Alyx from her drifting thoughts. "Were you eavesdropping at the door or something?"

Astor gave a slight shrug. "I'm the lord-mage. A little eavesdropping never did Rionn any harm."

She huffed out a laugh, sobering when he glanced at her, clearly waiting on a response to his question. "No, we didn't."

"Did you mean what you said—about regretting holding back from him?"

The fire crackled between them for a few moments, and then Alyx spoke. "Yes. I'm not even convinced becoming lovers would have made me invulnerable—it doesn't make sense that can be the only way. Our whole lives, Dashan and I were... physically close, more times than I can count. If I didn't absorb his invulnerability from that, I doubt it was going to happen from us becoming lovers."

"I suspect you might be wrong there."

"Why?" she asked sharply. There'd been something like certainty in his voice.

He shifted a little, gaze dropping away, clearly growing uncomfortable with the subject matter. "When you're with someone that you love and trust completely, the experience of becoming lovers... well, all the walls come down. You're not thinking about yourself separately from the other person, you're sharing the experience together. In that context, where there are no more barriers or walls, that's when your magic would have absorbed his invulnerability. Unless you consciously held back, which is almost impossible, there would have been no way to stop it."

Her head jerked up to stare at him, stunned. "You sound like you know what you're talking about."

"I *am* a mage, and I had a life before you knew me." He finally looked up, and there was old pain etched on his face, an almost exact echo of what flashed over her father's face when he talked about her mother. "I've loved. I lost the woman I loved more than anything."

"I'm sorry." She didn't know what else to say.

"It happened a long time ago." He shrugged, the sadness vanishing from his face in a blink of an eye, as if it had never been there.

Silence fell. Was she still going to miss Dashan so badly when she was Astor's age? No, she didn't want to hold on to that sort of pain, didn't want it to be there, alive inside her, for the rest of her life.

Astor shifted, moving so that he could more easily meet her gaze. "Aly-girl, there's something else we need to discuss."

She frowned. His expression had turned overly serious, and worry flared in her chest, only adding to the weight of exhaustion on her shoulders. Suddenly, she didn't want to hear whatever it was he was going to say. "Is there any chance we could talk about it tomorrow? I can barely keep my eyes open."

"No."

She hesitated, but there was enough grimness in her godfather's voice to momentarily bring clarity to her thoughts. "What's wrong?"

"The king spoke to me in detail—and in confidence, never fear—about what happened to you in Sandira," Astor said. "What he had to say concerned me greatly, though I haven't broached my concerns with anyone else."

Worry took a firm hold. "What are you talking about?"

"Cayr told me that Galien was in Sandira, that the council had sent him there. *Why* they sent him there."

She looked away. The *why* was branded on her soul, a constant torment of grief and pain. A shudder went through her. What she remembered most clearly from that encounter was Galien's enjoyment of her utter devastation.

"He came to kill Dashan." The words came out woodenly, and her weariness was the only thing keeping her from reacting more deeply to that memory.

"He came to kill *you* because the council was told about you and Dashan." Astor's gaze was fixed intently on hers. "How did they know?"

"That we were in Sandira?" She frowned. "I told you to invite them there to join us."

"Not that," he urged. "How did they know *about you and Dashan*? You were hiding it from everyone, you were even lying to your closest friends about it. So how did the council find out?"

Alyx opened her mouth, then hesitated—she had no answer for him. "I don't know."

Astor sighed, sitting back. "That's what I was afraid of. There was no way they could have known. Not unless..."

"Unless what?" she snapped.

"I think you have a spy. Someone close to you. Someone who is feeding information to the council."

She was shaking her head before he'd even finished speaking. "No, that can't be it."

"You hid your relationship from everyone because of the risk. Even *I* didn't know about it. Someone close to you knew, or they figured it out, and they told the council."

"The only people who knew..." *No, it's unthinkable.* "You're suggesting that one of my closest and most trusted friends betrayed me to the council?"

"Who knew?" he asked.

"I don't—"

"Who knew, Alyx?" Stubbornness filled his voice.

She rubbed a hand over her face, giving in. "Cario, Cayr, and Brynn. My father and Ladan."

"Then it's one of them."

She shook her head. "Tarrick and the twins knew I'd had a relationship with Dash, even though I lied about it ending. And I often thought those closest to me could have known. Sometimes it was just obvious the way Dash and I felt about each other." She glanced at him, and he caught the meaning of it.

"You think *I* could be a spy?" Astor looked horrified.

"You're accusing my closest friends of being one," she snapped. "Why not you?"

The words, spoken in the heat of the moment, hung heavily between them. Alyx regretted them as soon as she'd spoken, but it was too late. She'd hurt him.

"Someone told the council about you and Dashan, and only those you trust most could have known the details Galien did about your relationship," Astor said wearily. "And it's not just that. Have you ever wondered how the Hunters seem to always find you so quickly no matter how well you hide yourself? Someone is feeding Shakar and the council information on you, and it's someone you trust. You need to be careful."

He left her in a huff before she could say another word and she promised herself she'd make it up to him later. The fire seemed lonely once he was gone, though, so after a short time she went up to bed.

Sleep was elusive, her mind replaying everything that had happened throughout the day. Each time she circled back to the Hunters. Shakar would know, if he didn't already, that she was in Alistriem. The Hunters would come, and those around her would be in danger once again. She would have to run and hide. Again. The thought was sickening. And Astor believed one of her closest friends was a *spy*. There was no way it could be true, and yet if it was, the Hunters would be coming already.

There had to be a solution.

And there was. As she lay in bed so exhausted she was almost delirious with it, the answer came to her. Utterly insane, but so beautifully simple.

And with that realisation came sleep.

CHAPTER 14

"**Y**ou owe me a favour, and I'm here to call it in." Alyx squared her shoulders, forcing a confidence she didn't feel into her voice.

Jenna's eyes narrowed. "What do you want?"

Quickly and succinctly, Alyx explained the idea that had come to her in the early hours of the morning. She hadn't breathed a word of it to anyone else. Astor had been wrong, he *had* to be wrong. But if not... well, Jenna was one of the few people she could trust, purely because she wasn't amongst Alyx's close circle of friends.

Once she'd finished, Jenna considered for a long moment before replying. "There are so many things wrong with that idea, I don't even know where to begin. And what exactly do you want me to do?"

"Come with me. I need a Taliath."

"Then take your brother."

"He's busy. And *you're* the one who owes me a favour." Alyx paused. "If we succeed, Cayr will be safer."

Jenna flashed her a cool smile. "He's not the weak point you seem to think he is for me, Egalion. I'm not the same girl you knew."

"Neither am I," Alyx said flatly. "And you're a Taliath. Which means you've already worked out how my plan could deliver us a significant tactical victory."

"*If* we succeed. That seems unlikely."

Alyx cocked her head, gesturing to the training sword hanging from Jenna's left hand. "You say you're not doing this for Cayr. What exactly is it that you *do* want? Because you haven't spent the last year learning how to fight for no reason."

Her mouth tightened. "Who else knows about this insane idea of yours?"

"Nobody." A little smile crossed Alyx's face. "We leave tonight, late, once everyone is abed."

"And after this is done, I no longer owe you a thing?" Jenna's eyebrow lifted.

"Agreed."

"Then I'll see you in the stables at midnight, Lady Egalion."

Sneaking out of the palace with two horses and bulging saddlebags just after midnight proved relatively easy with the aid of telepathic magic. She'd left behind a note for Cayr to reassure him she and Jenna hadn't been kidnapped, but not telling him where they'd gone. Jenna, surprisingly, hadn't seemed bothered by the thought of disappearing without notice.

"Your father and brother are both in the city. The king will be safe enough while we're gone," was all she said.

In a week they were deep into the north of Rionn and closing in on the southern border of the disputed area. The number of Rionnans travelling on the same road had thinned to little but farmers who lived in the region and the occasional unit of marching Rionnan soldiers.

The surface of the road was well-maintained and lined by thick, snow-covered trees. As they travelled, the terrain grew wilder and the road began winding to avoid hills or large rocky outcroppings. Wildlife was scarce too; the occasional bird flew squawking from the trees around them, and every now and then they spotted deer tracks crossing the road, but otherwise there was nothing.

Eventually they reached the point where they were close enough to the disputed area that there was no good reason for them to be on the road heading north. They began travelling at night to avoid being seen, then eventually had to leave the road to strike out east, skirting the sprawling Rionnan army encampment. The going was harder then, the horses forced to scramble over rough, forested terrain.

Alyx used her magic with increasing frequency, employing it to guide them around the Rionnan army and then angle north towards the Shiven encampment. Ten days out of Alistriem found them trudging up a steep, thickly forested incline on the far eastern outskirts of the battle lines.

"The Shiven took Port Rantarin three months ago," Jenna said suddenly, the first time she'd spoken all day.

Alyx glanced back. "I heard."

The message had come just before they'd arrived in Carhall. It was a critical blow. Shivasa could now use the port to ferry supplies and soldiers directly into the disputed area rather than having to march overland. She huffed out a bitter laugh—not that it was really the disputed area any longer. It belonged firmly to the Shiven now.

"Cayr is worried," Jenna said quietly. "He hides it well, but... he's worried."

"I know that too," Alyx said just as quietly.

Jenna fell silent again as Alyx guided them as close to the Shiven army as she dared, stopping in a thick copse of trees that would hopefully keep them hidden from prying eyes.

"I need to concentrate for a while," Alyx murmured. "Will you keep watch?"

Nodding, Jenna took up a position in the shadows of a nearby tree, the fingers of her left hand resting on the hilt of her sword. Alyx settled cross-legged on the ground. She relaxed her shoulders and closed her eyes. Then, taking a deep breath, she sank into her magic.

Soon she sensed the chaotic tangle of the thoughts of hundreds of Shiven soldiers. A shudder went through her at the sheer size of their forces—the main bulk seemed to be based at Port Rantarin, but she could pick up the thoughts of soldiers stretching out through the disputed area, a wide front pushing down on the Rionnan lines.

Frowning in concentration, Alyx began trying to untangle the knot, sinking down into individual minds in slow, methodical fashion.

First she looked for the commanders, rifling through their thoughts for the information she needed. Success came on the sixth mind—an older man whose thoughts indicated he led an entire division of the force camped at Port Rantarin. Under his command fell those Alyx was looking for. Weariness tugged at her as she delved deeper into his mind, trying to see exactly which... and there it was.

Ignoring exhaustion, she left his mind and began roving again, focusing on an area of the encampment in the northwest. It took nearly an hour, but when she found what she was looking for, a fierce glow of satisfaction filled her. Amidst all the sleeping minds and busy thoughts of the awake guards there was a bubble... an area of utter nothing.

Guided by the commander's mind, she'd found a unit of Hunters. *Gotcha.*

Her eyes flickered open. A wave of weariness crashed down and she became quickly aware of the soreness in her cramped body. When she stood to stretch, the cold air bit deep, the kind of cold that presaged snow. Limping slightly, she crossed to her horse and dug out a blanket from her saddlebags.

"You found them?" Jenna called softly.

Shivering, Alyx crossed to join her, the blanket wrapped firmly around her shoulders. The cold set her newly healed ribs aching and it almost hurt to talk. "Yes."

"You're certain they're going where we want them to?"

"I pulled the knowledge from their commander's mind."

Jenna nodded and turned away. "It's still a few hours till dawn and you look exhausted. I'll take first watch. Get some sleep."

The blanket kept out the worst of the night's cold, but even so Alyx found it difficult to fall asleep. It was impossible to get properly warm without a fire, and the ground was hard beneath her. The lumpy bark of the tree she rested against didn't help, and she found herself shifting constantly, trying to get comfortable.

Eventually she fell into a fitful sleep, but almost immediately after was dragged into Shakar's nightmare. His torment of her was edged with a note of vicious triumph over Dashan's death, and her grief left her with little emotional strength to fight him off. Tonight she simply curled her consciousness into a tiny ball, whimpering helplessly as he drove his hooks deep into her mind and buffeted her with his dark power.

"The council killed him, Alyx, and they would have killed you too."

"You're the one that sent Hunters after us." She hated the weakness that trembled through her mental voice, but could do nothing to stop it.

"But THEY killed him."

He read her flash of anger with ease, just as easily reading how deeply she hated the council for what they'd done. That she burned with the need to hurt them the way they'd hurt her.

"Join me and it would be easy to destroy them. You could watch as the council burned to ashes. I know that's what you want." His voice turned almost soothing. *"Your friends betrayed you. Your allies are not who you thought they were. But you don't have to be alone. We both know the council needs to end. Help me do it."*

"Alyx!"

She came awake with a gasp, lashing out at the hand shaking her shoulder. Jenna's Taliath reflexes allowed her to dodge aside to avoid the hit, a scowl on her pretty face. "Quiet!" she hissed. "You were crying out in your sleep."

"Sorry," Alyx mumbled, straightening up as wakefulness hit her properly. "Nightmare."

"I don't care what it was, you were about to bring the whole Shiven army down on us," Jenna said flatly.

"I didn't do it deliberately," she snapped, defensive. "Anyway, I'm awake now. Get some rest and I'll take watch."

As the light of dawn crept through the trees, Alyx, shivering, forced herself to climb stiffly to her feet and send out enough magic to check on the Hunters she'd found the night before. The bubble of blankness created by the medallions was still there, but it was moving.

"Hey!" Alyx kicked Jenna's figure where it was curled up under three blankets. "Time to go."

The woman didn't say a word, but rose lithely to her feet and quickly stowed her blankets away before untethering her horse and swinging into the saddle. Alyx followed just as silently.

The cold had deepened through the night and snow was already beginning to fall. She wished she'd thought to bring gloves—her fingers were turning blue where they gripped the horse's reins.

Throughout the day, the bubble moved in a steady north-westerly direction, following the coast as it curved away from Port Rantarin. They moved quickly. Alyx cursed the delay as she and Jenna had to first head northeast to clear the heaviest cluster of Shiven army, then creep around behind on a straight line towards the coast.

She employed her magic without respite, keeping part of her awareness monitoring the Hunters, and the rest scanning for Shiven patrols. Her head throbbed. Every bit of focus she had was taken up, her strength draining as the Hunters drew further away and she had to expend more energy to reach them.

Eventually, though, they left the boundary of the disputed area and crossed into Shivasa proper. Once clear of the army, they were able to make faster time, pushing the horses harder through bleak, empty terrain.

The Hunters stopped moving just after dusk, presumably to make camp. By then, her headache had spread down into aching shoulders, awakening the pain of her newly-healed ribs. She hadn't used her telepathic ability to this extent before, and it was testing the limits of her still-recovering strength.

Jenna wasn't oblivious to this. Once they'd found a suitable place to camp, she tossed Alyx a blanket and told her in no-nonsense terms to sit down and eat something. "I'll deal with the horses."

By the time Jenna returned to settle nearby, tossing a second blanket to Alyx, she felt a little better. Silence held for a while as they both chewed through the remains of the stale bread in their supplies.

"It's going to take some serious luck for this to turn out the way you want it to," Jenna commented eventually.

"I'm aware of that."

Jenna hesitated. "Why did you bring *me*?"

"Because if I tried to bring Ladan or my father, they would have refused to come and then locked me in a room until I changed my mind. Tarrick and Finn... well, I can't even look at them anymore. Cario would have had the same reaction as my brother, and Dawn is the most powerful telepath mage alive, but doesn't have Taliath skill at fighting."

"You don't trust me though," she pointed out.

"No." Alyx shrugged. "But I couldn't do this alone, so I took a risk that maybe you are trustworthy."

Sleep was hard to come by again. She missed Dashan with a fierce ache, and was beginning to feel guilty for running off like she had. Ladan, Cayr, her father... they were going to be so worried. Her plan was foolish and dangerous, but Alyx clung to the resolve she'd felt ever since the thought had first occurred to her.

She had to do this. Moving beyond what had happened wouldn't be possible unless she did. If she survived, then perhaps she'd be able to breathe again.

And lingering, always, at the back of her mind were Shakar's words, his offer to her. *Together, we can bring down the council and watch it turn to ashes.* It was impossible to ignore now how badly she wanted that. It was like all the warmth and softness in her had been burned away by what happened in Sandira, leaving only hard scar tissue and a burning need to see everything that had caused her pain destroyed.

Once, her friends had brought her comfort from that, allowing her to let the anger go, but now thinking of them only made her angrier.

With a slow, deliberate breath, she tore her thoughts away from them and summoned a memory instead. Her seventh birthday, when she, Cayr and Dashan had snuck away from the party her father had arranged and spent the afternoon playing hide and seek in the gardens. A golden day of innocent happiness. She allowed the memory of Cayr's bright laughter, the sun shining on the colourful flowers and Dashan's mocking laugh when she couldn't catch him to surround her and fill her up.

And then she slept.

The next day passed much as the day before had. The Hunters angled further to the west, and by late afternoon, Alyx's magic warned her of the presence of many other people ahead. Lifting a hand to slow Jenna, who trailed behind, she did a thorough sweep of the area.

"There's a town ahead," she said eventually. "I'm guessing they're staying at an inn for the night."

Jenna nodded. "Wait here and make sure they're staying put. I'll find a place to camp."

By now Alyx had learned that either innate Taliath skill or simple intelligence led Jenna to pick campsites that offered excellent defence in case of attack, and she no longer protested the woman taking charge of that aspect of their trip.

While she waited, she continued sending out sweeps, but the Hunters stayed where they were. Jenna returned shortly, leading Alyx a short distance to a rocky overhang by a slow-moving stream. Together they unsaddled the horses before settling as comfortably as was possible underneath the overhang.

"The nightmare you were having the other night. It seemed pretty bad."

Alyx glanced up in surprise. Jenna had been essentially uncommunicative for the trip north from Alistriem—not that Alyx had minded—yet this was the second time in two days she'd initiated conversation. "Shakar likes to torture me with them."

"The one you were having seemed particularly intense." Jenna's voice was deliberately casual. "You were thrashing about like a madwoman."

"He was..." She shuddered. "He was preying on my weakness, trying to tempt me to join him. I don't want to talk about it."

There was a long silence, then, "I still remember the night my parents died."

Alyx's head shot up, all weariness and discomfort forgotten. Jenna was staring at the piece of dried meat in her hands, her fingers toying with it, her gaze distant.

"I was six years old. I remember flames, the smell of burning. My mother's screams... even now I can hear them with perfect clarity. I was hiding under my bed. My father had put me there, told me to stay and hide. But he never came back." She paused. "I started screaming too, convinced I was going to die. Then a man came. He wore black robes and he scooped me up, carried me out where the air was fresh and I could breathe again. He told me he'd tried to save my parents but he'd been too late. He said he would look after me."

Another silence fell. Alyx waited, enraptured. Jenna hadn't used Casovar's name once.

"We lived in Carhall for years. He wasn't around a lot, and he was generally aloof, but he did look out for me. He made sure I was educated and had nice clothes to wear. He paid for a kind old lady to look after me when he was away." Jenna cocked her head. "I *always* knew, even at a young age, that there was something he wanted from me. That he'd rescued me for a reason. Then we came to Alistriem, and it became clear. He wanted me to lure the prince, to marry him. Make him the father of the future queen." She shrugged. "And Cayr was handsome, and he was *nice*. So I thought to myself, this isn't so bad. I would rule the court, and have beautiful dresses, and my husband would treat me well. But Cayr could only see you."

Suddenly Jenna looked over, her baby blue eyes fastening on Alyx with a frustrated intensity. "And I couldn't understand why. You were so high and mighty, so impressed with yourself and so ridiculously naive at the same time."

Alyx huffed a laugh, unable to argue with that. "I was."

"You were different after you came back from DarkSkull though. And now... you're nothing like that girl I remember first meeting." Jenna shook her head. "Anyway, then one day you told me that the man who'd saved me was the man who killed my parents. That what he was really after was my invulnerability. That he was working for Shakar."

Aching mournfulness hit Alyx like a slap in the face, and it took her a second to realise that despite Jenna's cool exterior, Alyx's telepathic magic was picking up the emotion under her words. Emotion seemed to leak through Taliath invulnerability like nothing else did. Jenna's pain touched her own, still raw and fresh and too strong to hold back.

"The council killed Dashan." The words spilled out of Alyx, stark with grief. "The things they've done... and despite my hatred of it, I've always been able to ignore the anger, push it away. But they killed him, and I can't... I just want them all dead."

"What about defeating Shakar?" Jenna asked with her typical bluntness.

Alyx took a deep, shuddering breath. "I can't do it alone, and the council commands more resources and warrior mages than I ever could."

Jenna frowned. "How can you work with them after everything that has happened?"

"I don't have a choice." She whispered the bitter truth, hands clenching into white-knuckled fists. "I think about Dash, what he would want. I know he would tell me to do whatever it takes to destroy Shakar, prevent him from hurting more innocents. So I have to ignore how I feel. How I miss him so much it physically hurts, how it was the council that took him away from me. I have to put that aside and find a way to work with them."

Jenna had shifted closer without Alyx realising, and she reached out to lightly touch her knee. "The way I see it, Shakar is not only hurting and killing innocents, he's also the cause of the fear the council have of the Taliath. He's the reason Casovar killed my parents and stole me away. He's the reason they killed Dashan."

Alyx nodded, scrubbing the tears from her face. "Right."

"So the primary goal is destroying Shakar." Jenna met her gaze. "The council has resources needed for that, yes. But does it have to be a bunch of corrupt, cowardly old men leading those mages and resources?"

Alyx sniffed, considering. There was intelligence in the blue eyes boring into hers, a sharp awareness she'd seen frequently in both her father and Dashan. But in Jenna's there was fierceness too, a burning hunger to avenge her parents.

"No," she said quietly. "No, I suppose it doesn't."

CHAPTER 15

They followed the Hunters steadily west, deep into Shivasa. Their food supply began to run low and Alyx tired from her constant use of telepathic magic. Each day it was harder to drag herself to her feet and summon more magic.

She and Jenna didn't talk much, but the Taliath wordlessly took on the responsibility of finding camp, settling the horses, and ensuring Alyx had food and water each time they stopped. Part of her hated that her lingering weakness was so obvious. Another part was starting to think that maybe she didn't really dislike Jenna so much after all.

When the Hunters turned in a northerly direction one morning, hope sparked. For the previous two days they'd been moving into more heavily populated territory, and Alyx was beginning to worry they'd reach a point where staying hidden would be impossible. But as morning stretched towards midday, it was clear they were moving away from towns again, and her hope increased.

The sun began sinking low on the horizon, the cold deepening and new snowfall beginning to drift around them. And then Alyx's telepathic magic suddenly hit a wall of blankness. She'd been half-dozing in the saddle, but sat up abruptly at the sensation.

"What?" Jenna demanded.

Alyx waved her off, closing her eyes to focus her magic. Reaching out further, she sensed only nothingness ahead of the group of Hunters—a massive area of blank space. Despite how far she reached or how much power she used, Alyx's magic couldn't reach the other side of it.

A slow smile spread over her face, and she opened her eyes to meet Jenna's demanding gaze. "I think we found it."

Fierce light leapt into the Taliath's eyes. "Are you sure?"

"I'm sure."

Jenna convinced her to wait until well after nightfall to move, insisting Alyx needed rest. She managed a fitful couple of hours' sleep while Jenna kept watch and came awake to the sight of her companion crouched over a long, narrow blade, polishing it to a high sheen.

"Where did you get it?"

Jenna's eyes shot to hers. "Your father."

Alyx ran her eyes over the gleaming steel, and then the hilt—carved beautifully in the shape of a swan. It was smaller and narrower than the Taliath sword she'd seen at DarkSkull, smaller than her father's too, but there was no doubting what it was. "What did you name it?"

"Huntress."

"It's beautiful," she said, then, "it suits you."

"Thank you, Alyx," Jenna said, and they shared a smile.

Alyx stood and stretched before calling her staff with a touch of magic and slinging it over her back. "Let's do this."

Moonlight cloaked the two young women as they moved swiftly through the snowy landscape. Using the bubble as a guide, Alyx took the lead, her old nemesis running at her shoulder with *Huntress* belted at her hip.

It wasn't long before they crested a snow-covered rise. Alyx dropped instantly to the ground at a sharp gesture from Jenna, cold snow soaking into her clothes. The night air was cold, biting, and she tried not to shiver as it sank its tendrils into her.

The valley floor was mostly visible under the glow of a bright moon. In its centre was a dim, mostly rectangular shape marked by lantern lights set along what she guessed were the outer walls. Squinting hard, she could just make out movement along the top of the closest wall. In the centre, a large cluster of lanterns cast orange light over a pair of closed gates, illuminating broken snow where many horses had recently ridden through.

Alyx shivered violently. "We're going to die of cold if we keep lying in the snow like this."

"We'll also die shot full of arrows unless we work out the pattern of the guards patrolling up there," Jenna's caustic voice came back. "Though I can't believe they're foolish enough to light their walls up like that."

"They're not fools." Alyx shot Jenna a look that was lost in the darkness. "They're in a well-fortified base in the middle of their own country."

"Before we try and break in, how certain are you that this is their base?"

"The place is full of Hunters. I literally can't sense anything for miles but blankness."

Jenna paused a moment, eyes searching hers. "Our goal is to kill the mage whose magic is creating those Hunter medallions. There are no guarantees he or she is in there. We could be sneaking into a base full of skilled warriors for no reason."

"I know," Alyx acknowledged. "But I have to try. And even if the mage isn't there... well, we can at least take out some Hunters before we go. Besides, this is their base—someone in there has to know where the mage is."

A moment's consideration, then, "I hope you can climb, because we won't be getting in by strolling through those front gates."

She smiled. "I can climb."

A long silence fell. Jenna's attention was focused fully on the wall. Alyx could barely make out more than dim shadows of guards despite the moonlight, but she trusted in Jenna's Taliath vision. The cold ate deeper into her bones. She tried her best to ignore it.

"They're patrolling the closest wall too frequently," Jenna said eventually. "We wouldn't make the distance from here to the wall before the patrolling pair turned back and saw us. We need to hope for clouds to move in and cover up the moonlight. Then, the valley floor should be mostly darkness and the lanterns on the walls will blind the guards to our approach."

"Great," Alyx muttered. She huddled under her cloak, drawing her knees in and wrapping her arms around them. In silence they hunkered down, waiting, eyes trained on the fortress. Within an hour, a cold breeze kicked up and a light snowfall began drifting around them. Their breath frosted in the biting air. Nearby, an owl hooted. Alyx started losing feeling in her toes and fingers.

She was about to suggest to Jenna that they move—death from cold was becoming a greater possibility than arrows—when slowly, inexorably, the moonlight began to dim. Clouds from the north were spreading over the night sky. Relief loosened the knot of anxiety in her chest.

Darkness spread over the valley floor until Alyx could only see the pinpricks of lantern light at the top of the walls. At a nod from Jenna, they both stood, stretching stiffened limbs and summoning resolve.

"Ready?" Jenna asked.

Checking her staff and knife were secured, she took a deep breath and nodded. "Ready."

Within five paces, Alyx hit the wall of blankness and her magic vanished from existence. Ignoring the instinctive clutch of panic that roused, she focused on Jenna's back and kept running, head down and eyes trained on the wall looming ahead.

They reached it without any alarm sounding and pressed themselves against the icy stone. Her heart hammered in her chest. Glancing back, she saw a line of their footprints leading across the open space, but the snowfall was growing heavier and already the prints were filling in. As if in direct support of what she planned, the night darkened further, thick clouds drifting to shroud the moon.

"Follow me," Jenna said, then began climbing the wall.

It wasn't easy—the wall was high and the gaps in the stone weren't large—but she'd climbed enough trees and walls in her youth to manage it well enough, and Jenna had natural Taliath agility. By the time Alyx reached the top, her arms burned and weariness shuddered through her body. She rolled onto the flat surface and lay there, sucking in air and willing away the pain in her muscles.

It was dark in the shadows between the flickering lanterns, and there was no sign of guards. Urgency thrummed through her. They were somewhere on the wall and could be marching along any moment.

Jenna touched her arm, then pointed down the wall before making a questioning gesture. Was Alyx okay to climb down?

"I'm fine," she muttered, refusing to acknowledge her trembling limbs.

Together they knelt and edged themselves out and over the other side of the wall. Climbing down was easier than climbing up, and Alyx's boots soon thudded softly into a thick pile of snow at the bottom. Again, they crouched there for a few moments, looking for signs of life.

A dark and empty yard sat between them and the nearest building. A closed door led inside—there was no way to tell whether it was locked or what it led to. Footsteps echoed above and they both pressed themselves into the wall until the guards passed them and continued on.

Jenna moved then, ducking across the open space. She tried the handle, and finding it unlocked, cautiously eased it open. When no cries of alarm sounded, she waved Alyx over. Glancing above, Alyx took a breath and dashed across the yard.

The hall beyond the door was dark, but there was a faint glimmer of light down at the end. Heart thumping so loudly she was afraid it could be heard, Alyx crept down the corridor after Jenna and they peered around the corner. Lanterns lit this corridor, much wider than the one they were in. A guard stood at another cross-hallway a short distance away.

Jenna turned, raising a single eyebrow. Alyx tried to calm her nerves. They were inside, exactly where she'd hoped to be, and nobody knew they were there. So far, her plan was working out fine. At that thought, her nerves turned to a tangled churn of anticipation, anger, and bitterness. Doing her best to ignore it and focus on the next step, Alyx met Jenna's blue gaze, then nodded.

While Jenna quietly drew a knife, Alyx deliberately scraped her staff along the stone wall before backing into the shadows. The moment the guard appeared to investigate the noise, Jenna leapt at him. He didn't even have time to reach for his sword before he was being dragged back into the hall, Jenna's knife at his throat.

"Do as I say, or I kill you," she murmured in his ear.

He nodded, once, his body stiff with tension. Alyx emerged from the shadows and stepped up to him. His eyes were dilated with terror, sweat beading on his forehead. Jenna's knife pressed unwavering against his skin.

Ignoring the man's distress, Alyx summoned the iron resolve that had brought her this far, infusing her voice with it. "Tell me where the mage who creates your medallions is."

"I'm not—"

"Tell her." Jenna's blade bit into his throat. Blood welled and began to drip. "And I'll let you live. Lie, and I'll come back and kill you."

"One level above." Terror slurred the words as they poured out of him. "Take a... a right back into the main hall and head down... I don't know, uh... about fifty paces. There'll be a stairwell on your left. Take that up. After that you'll need to cross to the other side of the compound. She's in the northwestern corner. Her room is on the right at the end of a long hallway."

For a moment all Alyx could hear was the rushing of relief flooding through her. The gamble had paid off—the mage was here! Even Jenna's hard mask dropped for a moment as she turned to Alyx with a triumphant look.

Alyx leaned closer. "How will I know which is the right hallway?"

He swallowed, his fear overcoming his ability to think clearly. "I... uhm... there's a tapestry hanging on the wall, I think it's a picture of the ocean."

Quicker than thought, Jenna withdrew her knife, spun it, and slammed the hilt into the back of the guard's head. He slumped to the ground, out cold. Together, Alyx and Jenna dragged his limp body further back into the shadows of the hallway.

"They could find him at any moment." Jenna was completely calm.

"Or notice he's missing from his post," Alyx agreed. "Time to run."

They headed out into the main hall and found the stairwell. From there the guard's directions were easy enough to follow. They sacrificed stealth for speed, moving through the hallways at a run. At any moment Alyx expected to hear alarm bells ringing, or a guard challenging them, but most of the corridors they passed through were dark, the occupants of the keep presumably asleep. Nobody was expecting attack from inside the keep, not here in the middle of Shivasa.

Alyx's heart leapt when they came to the end of another corridor to see a large tapestry depicting an ocean hanging from the wall opposite. Jenna saw it at the same time she did and they slowed, pressing themselves close to the wall and inching forward to peer around the corner.

There were six guards lining the hallway to the left, confirming someone important was sleeping down there. All were Hunters. Alyx's eyes went straight to the last door on the right.

Her quarry was only metres away. The tangle of emotion was back, threatening her resolve, but she squashed it. This had to be done.

"That's a lot of guards," Jenna murmured.

Alyx hefted her staff. "We can take them."

"Without a doubt."

Jenna moved first, launching out into the hall at a graceful run. *Huntress* whistled through the air, biting into the neck of the closest Hunter before he knew what was coming. She ducked the next Hunter's swing, spun past him, and slashed her sword across the back of his neck before countering the blow of the third.

Alyx, two paces behind, dodged the second falling man to find Jenna had already killed the third and fourth and was advancing quickly on the last two. These had seen sense and were attacking as a pair. Even then Jenna defeated them with insulting ease, and Alyx found herself simply standing there and watching, admiring the Taliath speed and grace.

"You just going to stand there and stare all day?" Jenna snapped. Blood dripped from *Huntress* to the floor and there was a fierce look on the woman's face that Alyx had never seen before. "There's no way that went unheard. The third one screamed like a baby. More will come."

"Right!" Broken from her daze, Alyx ran past Jenna, heading for the door at the end of the hall.

"Do what you need to do," Jenna called after her. "I'll hold off any more Hunters that come."

Almost before the words were out of her mouth a loud bell started clanging. Urgency spurring her on, Alyx pushed open the door. Only her glance back to check that Jenna was okay saved her from the mage knife that came spinning out of the room beyond.

Heart pounding at the near miss, she kept moving through the doorway, fingers itching to summon her shield. No more knives came, and she found herself in a well-lit room facing an older woman. Another alarm bell pealed. The shrill sound reverberated painfully through her eardrums, but she barely noticed, her entire focus on the mage before her. Despite the late hour, the woman was fully dressed in black mage robes.

This was her target. Her presence sucked at Alyx's magic, voiding it, killing it. The sensation was terrible, like all the air was being pulled from her lungs, her chest compressing until it collapsed in on itself. She would have to do this quickly or she might pass out. Even then she hesitated, fingers curling at her sides.

The woman looked at Alyx with contempt. "You're her, aren't you, the Magor-lier? He told me about you. And now you've come here to what... get yourself killed?"

"I'm here to kill you," she said calmly.

"Even if you managed that, you'd never get out alive. Without your magic, you can't defeat enough Hunters to escape."

There was something twisted in the woman's eyes, a darkness Alyx hadn't seen before, not even in Galien. She'd come here not knowing what she'd do if she found a prisoner, an innocent victim of Shakar's. But this was no innocent. She allowed the anger to take over then, halting her constant fight to hold back the bitter need to destroy, let it fill her with purpose and strength.

"Alyx, hurry!" Jenna's voice shouted.

The mage's gaze snapped to the door before returning to Alyx, surprise flashing over her face.

"Didn't I mention?" Alyx lifted an eyebrow. "I brought a Taliath with me. Once you're dead, she's going to get me out of here."

Alyx leaped forward, tackling the woman and sending them both crashing to the ground. The mage fought bitterly, but Alyx was coldly determined, younger, and a better fighter. Holding the mage off with one arm and her body, she reached for her knife, pulled it from its sheath, and then drove it into the woman's chest.

The woman's struggles ceased instantly, her eyes glazing over until she slumped, lifeless, to the floor. Blood pooled on her chest and flowed to the ground. Alyx sat back, gasping, trying to catch her breath. The anger vanished as quickly as she'd allowed it to consume her. With trembling hands, she pulled her knife from the mage's chest and wiped it on the carpet before sheathing it in her boot.

The horrible sucking on her magic was gone. The mage was dead. Turning, she heaved, emptying her stomach onto the plush carpet. Sweat slicked her skin.

"Time to go!" Jenna bellowed. She ran into the room, sword dripping more blood. Her gaze took in the dead mage, and she paused, holding out her free hand. Alyx blinked, staring at it.

"Alyx!"

The alarm bells broke through her daze. She grabbed Jenna's hand, was hauled to her feet. The Taliath led her to the window, then threw a nearby chair through it, breaking the glass.

The drop was long, but a high drift of snow broke their fall. Running soldiers were everywhere, but nobody seemed to know what was happening or where the attackers were.

Jenna killed another four Hunters on their way back to the nearest outer wall, and once there they found the stairs to the top. She killed both guards that rushed them, leaving the top of the wall momentarily clear.

"Go, quickly!" Jenna urged, waiting for Alyx to begin climbing down before sheathing *Huntress* and doing the same.

It had stopped snowing and the sky was clear again, moonlight shining off the white surface. Together, they ran for the trees. Alyx's legs were like rubber and her heart pounded in her chest. She kept stumbling.

Glancing back, she saw lights along the top of the wall, and still heard the ringing bells. Halfway across the clear area her magic re-appeared, like a bubble had burst. She staggered with the relief of it, then righted herself, kept running hard. Moments later they reached the trees, then kept going until they reached the horses. Once there, Alyx dropped to her knees, lungs burning.

"You okay?" Jenna demanded.

"Fine. Just need a... second."

When she'd caught her breath, Alyx sat up, her gaze falling on her hands. They were covered in drying blood, the stuff having splattered all the way up her forearms. Ignoring the sick slide of nausea, she buried her arms in the snow and scrubbed at them, cleaning off as much blood as she could.

Her thoughts were too fast, scrambling, colliding with each other.

She had to go. They would be coming after her and Jenna. The tracks they'd left would bring the Hunters right to them. They had to go.

"Alyx!" Jenna's cold voice broke through her daze. "Tell me you had an escape plan."

Nodding, Alyx staggered to her feet. "Grab the saddlebags. We're leaving the horses."

Jenna seemed confused, but with a worried glance back towards the Hunter base, quickly unbuckled the saddlebags and crossed back to Alyx. She reached out and took Jenna's hand then drew upon her magic, and they shot up into the sky, the sheer thrill of flight dispelling all the exhaustion and horror for one blissful moment.

CHAPTER 16

It was late afternoon two days later when Alyx and Jenna landed in the middle of the Rionnan army camp. She'd been forced to stop twice to rest on the way back after the trembling weakness had returned to her limbs, almost causing her to drop them both from the sky.

Jenna hadn't commented on either occasion, merely standing watch until Alyx was strong enough to fly again. Now two soldiers standing a short distance away were staring at them in awe. More were running closer, coming to see if they were a threat.

Ignoring them, Alyx turned to Jenna. "Give me the saddlebags. Lord-General Isharan is still the commander up here, right? He'll know who you are and can organise a horse and supplies enough to get you back to Alistriem," she said quickly. "If you get there before me, let them know I'm okay and won't be long after you."

"Where are you going?" Jenna was looking at her like she'd lost her mind.

"I have something I need to do... to see."

"And who will protect you while you're off sightseeing?" Jenna demanded.

Alyx laughed. "Are you saying you actually care about my safety?"

She huffed an irritated breath. "Your insane mission just succeeded. Don't be a fool and risk yourself further."

"I'm not doing anything foolish." Alyx took a step back towards the young Taliath. Her feelings on Jenna had shifted over the past days, but she still wasn't sure what they were. "Go back to Cayr for me, keep him safe. He's going to need you in the days ahead."

Now it was Jenna's turn to laugh as she shoved the saddlebags into Alyx's outstretched hands. "I don't owe you any more favours, Alyx Egalion."

"Then do as you wish." Alyx turned and began walking away. "I'll see you around, Jenna Aridlen."

"Alyx?"

She stopped and looked back over her shoulder, one eyebrow raised.

"You don't need to destroy the Mage Council," Jenna said. "You just need to make them irrelevant."

Alyx smiled.

She spent two and half days flying northeast, stopping several times along the way to rest. Whenever she pushed herself too hard, the trembling in her limbs would start, and she'd be forced to drop to the ground and find somewhere to make a basic camp. Slowly, though, her rest stops grew shorter, the length of flying time longer.

She was growing strong again.

While she wasn't exactly sure of the location she was heading to, in the end it was easy to find Tennan. She'd been flying up the eastern coastline of Tregaya, and not long after midday, spotted what looked like a large town below her. Dropping lower, she saw that most of the town had been reduced to rubble.

For a long moment she simply hung there in the sky, staring down at the devastation. Hearing about it had been bad enough, but seeing the reality...

A cold wind was gusting up from the ocean when Alyx landed. She wrapped her cloak more tightly around herself and began walking along the empty road towards the city, trying to ignore the icy-cold tendrils creeping through the gaps in her clothing. Snow lay thick all around her—nobody had been out to clear the road recently.

The main gates lay scattered in several pieces across the road, and the wall to either side of where the gate had been was destroyed. Alyx paused by the rubble, taking in the broken stone pieces and evidence of concussion blasts and mage fire in the charred edges.

Nobody was around. She climbed up a broken edge of wall, going slowly because of how unstable it was, and eventually reached the top of a still-standing section.

Wind tugged at her as she made her way around to the coastal side of the city. A light snow began to fall, the cold flakes landing on her cheeks and eyelashes. Stopping, she sent out a wide burst of magic and located a large group of people to the west. Their thoughts revealed them to be survivors of the attack on Tennan, living in a corner of the city still left relatively untouched.

There were so few.

A shiver racked her, not entirely to do with the cold. Thousands of people had once lived in this city, and only a few hundred had survived Shakar's attack.

What had been the point of it? Why destroy an entire city and then vanish? She stared down at the destruction below her as if it held all the answers. Shakar had done this, all of it. No mage had helped him destroy this city, he'd done it all alone and with sheer might and power. But why? To get their attention?

The questions swirled around and around Alyx's mind, as they had for weeks, when she'd been recovering and had nothing to think about but this. She had no good answers. This city was dead now, ruined, destroyed by a single mage.

You are responsible for the mage order.

Cario's words flashed through Alyx's memory, and she shivered, acknowledging the truth she hadn't been able to accept at the time he'd spoken it.

You need to stop being Alyx Egalion and be the Magor-lier of the mage order.

Deep down, she knew what had brought down those walls. It wasn't purely magical strength. It was magic fuelled by the same anger and bitterness that simmered inside her, the sense of betrayal, the need to destroy. She'd let it take over and killed a mage with it, and it had been *easy*. And it had made her feel sick.

Alyx raised an arm, the green glow illuminating her skin as she summoned her magic. She could use the new hardness inside her, use it to give her clarity and the ability to make hard decisions. But she wouldn't let it control her. Not ever again.

Finn had been right and wrong at the same time. She could be another Shakar, it would be as easy as breathing. But it was also a choice. And she would choose against it. Every day for the rest of her life. Because she didn't want to be like Shakar. She wanted to be like Cayr and Dashan. Like her father and brother. Like her *mother*.

How many more people will die, Alyx?

Alyx let the light surrounding her hand die and took one final look at the fallen town of Tennan.

It was time to go.

It was late afternoon when she arrived back in Alistriem, dropping down out of the sky above her family home. She was tired, weary from several hours of flying—she'd pushed herself hard, needing to test the limits of her returning strength. It was likely she'd even beaten Jenna back.

She went inside long enough to learn from Safia that her father and Ladan were still over at the palace. After a brief wash and change of clothes, Alyx went looking for them.

She found Ladan first, leaning against the railing of the open-aired hallway outside the lord-mage offices. The sun was setting over the city, its orange glow illuminating the houses and the bay. A chill breeze swept up as the sun faded.

At the sight of her, relief crashed over his face, followed quickly by anger. "Where have you been?" he demanded. "We've all been worried sick."

"There was something I had to do," she said, as if that were a good enough excuse for sneaking off.

A muscle ticked in his jaw. "What does that mean? Where did you go?"

"It's a long story."

He regarded her furiously for a long moment, anger and worry turning his green eyes bright in the fading dusk. "Don't ever do that to me again, Aly-girl. I don't care who else you sneak away from, you tell me. Am I clear?"

"Yes." And she meant it.

He let out a long breath. "I'm glad you're back safe."

"I feel the same way." She stepped into his side, leaning into him for warmth and comfort. "Are things well in Shivasa?"

"Yes. I get the impression Dashan was crucial to their efforts—their leader sings his praises, although he seems an impressive man himself. I can't go there full time, but we'll continue helping them as much as we can."

"Is that what's bothering you?" She sensed he was upset by something.

Ladan's jaw clenched. "You know that I don't find it easy to control my anger, and it's easier to feel anger than..."

"Pain?" she asked softly.

"He was the only friend I've ever had."

Alyx's heart tore open anew, but she wouldn't let the tears fall. "I'm sorry, Ladan."

"It is me who should be sorry." He seemed to wrestle with himself, before reaching out tentatively to touch her arm. "You loved him very much."

Alyx nodded, not trusting herself to speak. She looked away from her brother, out over the city.

"Papa is furious with you," Ladan said, a smile quirking at his mouth. "I suspect he will try and keep you from leaving the house again for at least a month."

"I'm sure he'll try," Alyx dryly.

Silence fell between them again. Alyx sensed there was something her brother wanted to say, so she gave him time to find the words. She had an idea of what it was anyway.

"Alyx?" he said eventually. "I think both of us need to... our parents left us with a difficult legacy, but there is no point bemoaning something that is already done."

"What are you saying?" She turned back to face him.

He was silent for a long moment. Then, in a single, abrupt movement, he drew the sword belted at his waist, laying it out on the marble railing before them. Her eyes widened in surprise at the sight.

"I have been a poor Taliath," he said. "I went to train on ShadowFall Island, as you asked, but I never fully committed. I was scared to leave my home, where everything was familiar. Papa has urged me for months to get my own Taliath sword. I refused." He paused, his right hand coming to rest lightly on the blade. "I had this made while you were away."

Alyx said nothing as she studied the sword. Unusually, it had no pommel, it's grip a single cylindrical piece of wood fitting firmly into the hilt. In fact, it almost looked like a... her indrawn breath was loud in the silence around them, and her gaze shot to his. "Oh Ladan."

"I remember her mage staff so clearly, even after all these years." His fingers distantly traced the intricate carving on the wood. "She told me once these lines were designed to match the leaping flames on Papa's *Heartfire*."

She bit her lip in an effort to keep the tears at bay. "What have you named it?"

"*Mageson*," he said simply.

Some of the welling tears spilled down her cheeks. "You say you've been a poor Taliath, but I've been no better as a Magor-lier." She rubbed her eyes. "Everything is such a mess."

"A mess that needs fixing."

Alyx sighed. "Cario said some things to me before I left, and he was mostly right. The way things were... it wasn't possible for me to be what the mages needed." She paused. "I understand what I need to do now, and I'm willing to do it. I just hope it's not too late."

"It is the same for me. I will leave Widow Falls in Romney's capable hands, and I will be one of the last remaining Taliath with our father. I owe Dashan that much at least."

"I know what I have to do, but I'm not sure if I'm strong enough," she murmured. "Sometimes I find it so hard to even put one foot in front of the other."

"Then you can borrow my strength for a while." Slowly, Ladan's arm crept around her shoulders and settled there.

"All right." She gripped his shirt in her hands, buried her face in his chest, and allowed his strength to hold her.

"Are they here?" she asked eventually.

He nodded, gesturing to the offices behind them. "They've been working in there, helping Lord-Mage Astor. I don't think they know what to do with themselves."

She let out a breath and pulled away from him. "I'll go and speak to them."

"Do you want me to come?"

"No. I need to be strong. I'll go alone." She considered. "At least at first. But I want you to come and join us in a little while. We need to talk about mages and the Taliath."

He nodded, speaking fiercely. "Things will be different this time." His green eyes met hers. "Together we'll build a better mage and Taliath order."

A small smile crept over her face, stretching her cheeks. She wasn't alone in this. Her brother would stand at her side.

A touch of magic confirmed Dawn was inside, and that Tarrick, Finn, Cario, and Rothai were with her. They weren't working though. She frowned, concentrating—they were outside, in the private garden adjoining the mage offices. Astor wasn't anywhere nearby.

She paused at the door, glancing down at her hand to find it trembling. With a massive effort of will, she reached for that certainty of purpose she'd felt while standing on the ruined city walls of Tennan and drew it down over herself like a cloak. Ladan's unwavering gaze was almost tangible on her back, a welcome source of strength.

Steadied, she walked through the dark, empty rooms of the mage offices and out into a small, walled garden. Tarrick, Rothai, and the twins were sitting on bench seats under a tree that was bare of leaves. Cario stood some distance off, hands in his pockets, staring at his shoes. None of them were talking—each looked lost in their own thoughts. Alyx's magic told her they despaired.

Dawn picked up on Alyx's arrival first. She leaped to her feet, relief and pain warring on her face. "Alyx. You're back!"

All eyes shot to her and she nodded. "I am."

"What do you want?" Tarrick asked listlessly. The fact he wasn't angry with her for vanishing so suddenly told her the depth of his despair.

She took a deep breath. "I want to talk to you."

"What about?" Finn sighed. "I think we've said everything we wanted to say. It is how it is, Alyx. You're going to do whatever you want. You've made that abundantly clear."

Alyx nodded, her gaze moving over to Cario, who was watching intently but as usual expressionlessly, before returning to those sitting at the fountain.

"What happened between us before I left... they were harsh words, but I think we all needed to say them. You call me your Magor-lier," she told them, grateful that her voice sounded clear and calm. "And I'm willing to be that for you. But not like before."

"What does that mean?" Tarrick rose to his feet.

"If I'm the Magor-lier, then *I* am the mage leader. I don't take orders from you or Rothai, or the Mage Council. I am the one that gives the orders," she said. "Secondly, I will not be trapped and hidden for my own safety. I will lead the fight."

Finn's mouth had dropped open. "You want to claim leadership of the mage order?"

"Isn't that what a Magor-lier is?" she asked pointedly. "Or is it just an empty title you, Tarrick and Rothai have been using so that the effort against Shakar has a ceremonial figurehead to rally behind?"

"The Mage Council will never cede their power to you," Rothai said.

"I don't care. The council is corrupt and weak. I represent the future of the mage order." Alyx paused. "I'm going to build a new order. And if you accept this, I promise to consider *all* your advice and not take unnecessary risks. I promise to always act with the knowledge that my death removes all hope of destroying Shakar."

There was a brief moment of silence, and then,

"I accept," Dawn said without hesitation. "I trust you, and I trust that you won't become another Shakar."

"Dawn—" Finn went to speak but Tarrick interrupted him.

"Alyx, you are a mage of the higher order, the most powerful mage alive aside from Shakar. The position is yours by right," Tarrick said quietly. "I accept your terms."

"So do I," Cario added.

Alyx turned to Finn, who seemed to be struggling with himself. She kept her gaze unflinching—she wouldn't back down from him on this. He would have to have faith that she would listen to him.

And in the end, he did. He gave her a slow nod. "I accept."

"Rothai?"

His ice-blue eyes focused on her with startling intensity, but after a moment the fire in them faded, and he nodded. "I accept your terms, Magor-lier."

"Good." Alyx turned and gestured to Ladan, who had been waiting in the shadows. The simple nature of his clothing only served to enhance his Taliath grace and ability. Everyone's eyes went to him, then back to Alyx as he came to stand at her right shoulder.

"We're no longer treating Taliath as the enemy," she said. "If we want to defeat Shakar, then we're going to need all the help we can get. There will be no more killing of Taliath or potential Taliath, and at least officially, they will be trusted allies. This is non-negotiable."

"The Mage Council's position on the Taliath has never been strategically sound," Cario spoke smoothly into the silence. "While the threat of another Shakar cannot be discounted, treating the Taliath as a threat to mages is counter-productive and foolish. I support your position."

Cario's rational argument seemed to get through to the others. Tarrick and Finn both nodded, seemingly not willing to fight Alyx further on the issue.

"I agree with Cario," Dawn said.

"I agreed to your terms, Magor-lier, so if this is what you order, it is what I will support," Rothai said tersely.

"Thank you," Alyx said, not missing their reluctance, but sensing they meant what they said.

"I will leave the city within the next few days," Ladan spoke. "I intend to travel through Rionn and Tregaya and gather all those with Taliath potential I can find and take them to ShadowFall Island. Alyx and I both agree that this fight will not be won without the Taliath and the mages working together."

"That will take months," Finn said. "And the potentials will be extremely vulnerable once they're gathered on ShadowFall."

Alyx nodded. "I will send a permanent mage guard to the island to ensure the trainees stay safe."

"We could send one or two mages to travel with your brother, Magor-lier," Tarrick offered, surprising her. "They can help protect the potentials."

"Thank you, Tarrick," she said softly, though not without a touch of sadness. His use of her title reinforced his acceptance of her leadership but also represented the loss of part of the friendship they'd shared.

Rothai stood. "Magor-lier, we need to discuss what comes next."

"Tomorrow morning," Alyx said. "When we have all had a chance to sleep. Which mages are in the city with you?"

"Jayn, Tari, and Adahn, those who were in Sandira with us," Rothai said. "But we've been keeping in ad-hoc contact with the mages still in the mine."

"We'll need to do better than that." Alyx frowned. "Now, give me your mage robes."

Tarrick looked puzzled. "What?"

"Your mage robes." Alyx held out her hand. "Hand them over."

Sharing confused looks, each of them shrugged off their robes and slung them over Alyx's outstretched arm. Once they were done—Rothai being the last—Alyx dropped them into an untidy pile on the ground. Before any of them could say a word, she flicked her right hand and green flames lit up the pile with a whoosh.

"What are you doing!" Finn protested.

"The council is done," she said clearly and firmly. "The way they did things is done. *We* are the future."

"That's fine," he said. "But it's freezing out here."

Tarrick snorted. Dawn chuckled. Even Cario's face broke into a smile. Rothai heaved a sigh. "If there's nothing else, Magor-lier?"

She hid her smile. "You're dismissed, Rothai."

Dawn stepped forward and threw her arms around Alyx as the others began leaving the garden. "I'm so glad to have you back with us."

Alyx hugged her friend. "I'm sorry I've been gone."

"Don't be sorry," Dawn said. "I'll see you in the morning."

Alyx was left alone with Cario, and they began walking back towards the palace together.

She broke the silence. "You were right, what you said to me before I left."

"Yes, I was." He smiled faintly. "You were also right though—it had to be your choice."

"I am truly glad of the trust we share, Cario. Thank you for staying."

He stopped as they reached a pair of doors leading inside. "I never imagined I would ever find a mage leader I wanted to follow. You've given me a purpose, despite how reluctantly I accepted it."

"Somehow I think I'm going to keep needing your advice." She smiled and opened the door. "Good night."

"Alyx?"

"Yes?" She turned back.

"I'm so sorry about Dashan." His hand reached out to squeeze her shoulder, and what she read in his eyes was empathy, not pity. "I should have told you that night instead of just yelling at you."

"Thank you," she said, and meant it.

CHAPTER 17

B y the time she made it home and up to her dark bedroom, her hands were trembling again, and this time she couldn't stop them. She ached for Dashan so badly that her chest hurt. Slowly, tiredly, she lay out on the bed, pulled the covers up around herself, and shifted so that she could stare out at the stars through her window.

She was still awake when the big knocker at the front door sounded. Safia was making his way towards the stairs when she emerged from her room, but she waved him off.

"Cayr!" she said in surprise as she opened the door, then winced as she registered the look on his face. Angry Cayr rarely made an appearance, but when it did, it was never fun.

He didn't bother with pleasantries. "We've been worried sick!"

She sighed, too weary to raise much of a defence. "I'm sorry. There was something I had to do, and... it won't happen again. I promise."

His gaze was fierce on hers. "That's not good enough. I get that you're still grieving, but that just makes it worse. It means you're not acting rationally. You need to let people help you."

"You couldn't help with this," she murmured. "Are you really here this late just to tell me off?"

His mouth tightened, but after a moment he let out a sigh, seemingly accepting he wasn't going to get any further apology. "No. I came to make sure you were okay and–I wanted to give you something."

She stepped outside, the brisk night air refreshing on her skin. Ten Bluecoats sat their horses just out of hearing distance.

"I suppose you can't just give your guard the slip anymore," she said ruefully.

Cayr chuckled. "Responsibility takes a lot of the fun out of things."

Alyx let out a breath, more guilt curling through her. "I've been whining and complaining all this time about how hard things have been for me, while you've had it just as bad, if not worse."

He was silent a moment, then, "Do you ever wish we were born the baker's son and the smith's daughter?"

Alyx laughed. "No, never. Ugh, have you *seen* the soot that gets everywhere in a smithy?"

"Hey, a laugh! It's been a while since I've seen you smile."

She reached out and took his hand. "Thanks."

"You're welcome. Now." Cayr bent to pick up a paper-wrapped package at his feet, hesitating briefly before passing it to her. "This is for you."

Curious, she carefully unwrapped the paper, peering into the contents in the light from the lanterns on either side of the door. Lying neatly folded inside the brown paper was a thick cloak of royal blue.

"A Bluecoat cloak?"

"Dashan's," Cayr said gently.

Emotion hit hard, tears instantly filling her eyes. She reached out a trembling hand to touch the soft fabric. Cayr's hand settled on her shoulder.

"If it's too much, I understand, I'll take it away," he murmured. "I just thought maybe you'd like to have it. I know he would have wanted you to have it."

Alyx looked up at her childhood friend, swallowing back her tears. "You still know me better than anyone."

He smiled softly. "I think he knew you even better than I do, but thank you."

"Thank you, Cayr." Alyx reached up with her free arm to hug him tightly. "Thank you so much."

"I'd do anything for you. Don't forget that."

"Same goes," she said, touching the thick fabric again, before covering it back up and clearing her throat. "I've called a meeting with the mages tomorrow morning. Can you be there?"

Sadness filled his face. "I suppose even the death of a beloved friend doesn't allow us to keep the world from going on around us."

"No, it doesn't."

A watery sun rose slowly above the horizon as Alyx readied herself the next morning. Winter was almost gone. With spring would come Dashan's birthday, then hers and Cayr's in quick succession. Twenty years old and she was about to take the first steps in leading the entire mage order.

She hesitated by the neatly folded pile of clothes atop her chest of drawers—her mage attire. She hadn't touched it since Sandira, and while there would be a comforting sense of familiarity in donning those clothes again she'd meant her words to the others the previous night.

She was done with the council and their way of doing things.

Instead, she raided her closet, pushing aside silk dresses that hadn't been worn in years to find a comfortable pair of breeches and light tunic, both in a light shade of blue. She was untangling herself from the dresses when she almost stumbled over a pair of beautifully tooled grey leather boots sitting neatly on the floor of the closet. A smile tugged at her mouth—they were the ones she'd had custom made before returning to DarkSkull as an apprentice mage. Dashan had teased her to no end about how fancy they were. Her smile widening, she grabbed them too.

Once dressed, she sat on her bed to lace up the boots. They still fit her perfectly, well-worn but delightfully soft. The paper wrapped package Cayr had given her rested nearby. With trembling fingers she unfolded the thick, fine blue cloak that had belonged to Dashan.

Standing, she slung it over her shoulders, closing her eyes as she was enveloped by his smell and the warmth of his presence. Tears spilled down over her cheeks, but she quickly scrubbed them away and opened her eyes.

The cloak was too big for her, but that could be fixed. She had at least an hour before the meeting, and Alyx had always been Sorin's favourite customer.

The tailor's delight at seeing her plunged to a frantic fluster when she told him what she needed. He shouted for his assistants, snapping orders at them as they gathered like hens around her, taking measurements as fast as they could.

Armed with her new sizes—apparently she was both taller and leaner since the last time she'd been in—he vanished to his workroom out back. Alyx was left waiting in his comfortable office, a cup of steaming tea in hand and several parchments depicting the latest court styles in her lap.

He stuck his head around the door at one point, eyebrow raised in question. "If this is to be your new mage cloak, Lady Egalion, do you wish me to stitch a sigil into it?"

It was on the tip of her tongue to say no—council mage robes had no sigil—but then the memory of their arrival at DarkSkull after the attack flooded into her mind. The sharp scent of smoke and charred flesh filled her nose as clearly as if it had been yesterday.

They'd spent hours carrying the dead bodies from the main hall and surrounds, reverently placing them together out by the green lake. As night fell they'd lit a funeral pyre to honour the dead, bright orange flames reaching up into the starlit sky. The sight had called to mind her father's Taliath sword. *Heartfire.* It had felt like that too, the apprentices and initiates she'd known. Mika. Howell. All burning together.

"Lady Egalion?" Sorin prompted.

She blinked, nodding. "Actually, I have an idea about that."

When she finally entered the lord-mage offices, Tarrick and the twins were already there. Dashan's blue cloak hung from her shoulders. Sorin had altered it to fit her slighter form, but it wasn't the cloak that drew the gaze of those already in the room, it was the emblem he'd stitched out in scarlet thread over the left side of her chest.

A leaping flame.

Dawn's eyes went straight to the cloak, and a little smile flickered over her beautiful features.

"The funeral pyre after DarkSkull," Tarrick murmured, eyes dark with memory.

Alyx nodded. "I don't want us to ever forget them, or what Shakar did."

"It looks good on you," Finn said quietly. "It looks right."

Recognising the peace offering for what it was, Alyx accepted it with a smile. "Thank you, Finn."

The door swung open then to admit Cario. His approval of the cloak was obvious from the sweeping glance he gave her, but he didn't comment on it. "I just spoke with the kitchens. They're sending up some food for us. His Highness sent a message to say he won't be long, but requested we not start without him."

"And in the least surprising news of all time, Rothai is out checking the guard detail," Finn said dryly.

So they had a little time. Alyx's heart thudded nervously. After Cayr's visit the previous night, she'd lain awake the rest of the night thinking. She'd known that she couldn't come to this meeting without resolving what to do about Astor's suspicion—that someone was passing information to Shakar and the council on her. But even now she remained undecided, and she didn't have long. Once Cayr walked in, it was time to move forward.

Her father and Ladan she'd ruled out entirely. That it could be one of them was unthinkable. Cayr too. But from what Galien had said, the spy knew she'd fled Alistriem with Dashan after killing Casovar. That was a specific detail that further limited the pool of suspects.

That left the twins, Tarrick, Cario, and Brynn, all but one in this room. Of them, only Cario knew for a fact she'd been with Dashan—but Finn had suspected it, and the others could have guessed. She could secretly read their minds in a heartbeat, and possibly only Dawn would notice. Better, she could tell them outright that she needed to read their minds. If they were innocent, surely they'd be more than happy to let her do it. But it would also tell them that she doubted them. It could ruin any attempt to re-build the trust between all of them.

The sound of the twins' laughter had her looking up. They were clustered with Tarrick, who was grinning, relaxed, hands in his pockets. All at once another memory flashed, their second day at DarkSkull after spending hours in the cold cutting themselves a mage staff. Dawn's words from the past echoed through her mind: *'The three innocents from Rionn, we're a team? We get through this year together?'*

And they had. Ever since that moment they'd stuck together. Finn had doubted her and betrayed her, but his intentions had always been to protect her. She knew that with as much certainty as she knew her hair was brown.

The laughter broke out again, this time from Tarrick, his white teeth gleaming against his dark Zandian skin. He'd given up so much to stay with them, his honour demanding he stay at Alyx's side to keep her safe despite it taking him so far away from home and his family.

"Is something wrong?" Cario had dropped into the seat beside her, making her start.

"No, I..." Her voice drifted. "I have a difficult choice to make."

"Can I help?"

Cario had spied on her once before, and for the council too, but she believed he truly regretted that. And Brynn was a council spy. Brynn with his constant impertinent questions and a smile that could cheer her in her worst moments.

"Alyx?" Cario prompted, a hint of concern in his voice.

She took a long, deep breath, her decision made. "If we're going to rebuild the trust between all of us, then we need to start somewhere."

"I... agree?" He frowned. "Are you talking about something in particular?"

"Just something I've been wrestling with." She smiled and squeezed his shoulder as she stood. "Where is that food? I'm starved."

It wasn't any of them. She was going to have faith in her friends, in what they'd built together at DarkSkull. There was another explanation, and eventually she would find it.

CHAPTER 18

Alyx was finishing off the last mouthful of a deliciously buttery pastry when Cayr, Ladan, and Astor walked in together. A step behind came Garan Egalion, *Heartfire* hanging at his hip, stride loose and graceful.

"Papa." Alyx opened her arms as he came towards her and enveloped her in a warm hug. Behind them, the door opened a final time to admit Rothai.

"Ladan told me you were well again, but I am so glad to see it with my own eyes, Aly-girl." He stepped back to look over her, reassuring himself she was okay. "You and I will discuss your abrupt departure later. When we're alone."

She couldn't help but smile at the stern look on his face. "Yes, Papa. I'm glad you're here."

"Good morning." Cayr instantly commanded the attention of the room. He sat down at the head of the table, Astor taking the chair to his left. Garan Egalion took the one to the king's right. "I apologise for being late."

"Has Jenna returned?" Alyx asked him while everyone else busied themselves taking seats.

Cayr nodded. "Late last night. She's on guard just outside."

"She should be a part of this meeting," Alyx said. "If it's all right with you."

He gave her an odd look, but nonetheless rose to go and open the door, murmuring a few words she couldn't quite make out. Jenna strode in a moment later, her watchful gaze taking in the room in a glance. When it landed on Alyx, a little smile curled at her mouth. "Lady Egalion. You wanted me?"

"Take a seat." Alyx waved her to the remaining free chair. Slowly, conversation died and the room's attention turned to her. With Dashan's cloak around her shoulders, she faced them confidently.

"Thank you all for being here. Your time is precious, so I won't waste it. Your Highness, Lord-Mage, Papa, you should know that I no longer recognise the Mage Council as representing the mage order. I am Magor-lier and I am going to build a new order. *I* am going to lead the mage fight against Shakar."

Her father looked utterly floored, but after a moment he frowned. "You can't fight the council and Shakar at the same time."

"I don't intend to fight the council." She glanced at Jenna, giving her a little smile. "I'm just going to make them irrelevant. In time, their mages—and their resources—will become mine."

"That sounds very... dramatic," Astor said dryly. "But what do you actually mean?"

"I mean that while the council hides behind the walls of Carhall and does nothing to hunt Shakar, *I'm* going to lead the fight against the Darkmage. They have resources we need, and fighting them directly would only waste those resources, but eventually, by virtue of their inaction, their mages will become mine," she said clearly. "The council's corruption and fear will bring about their demise. I just need to be patient and let them destroy themselves."

"I think you're aware of Rionn's position on the Mage Council," Cayr spoke. "Officially, I welcome your proposed changes. Personally, you know I have faith in you, Alyx."

Alyx nodded. "The mages in this room have already agreed to my plans. Astor, I love you. You may choose as your loyalty dictates."

"He may," Cayr said. "But if he chooses to remain with the council, he will be relieved of his position and provided a second comfortable retirement. Rionn's lord-mage will be chosen from amongst *your* mages, Alyx."

"No need for all this youthful posturing." Astor appeared to be going to great effort not to roll his eyes. "I am with my god-daughter, of course. I do recommend you remain on good terms with the council, Magor-lier, at least until you grow stronger in numbers."

"I agree." Alyx's shoulders relaxed in relief. Pulling out the chair beside Ladan's, she sat, her legs shaking a little now as the adrenalin wore off. "Thank you."

"Your Highness, Magor-lier, if I may?" Rothai spoke up.

Cayr nodded. "Go ahead."

"We've agreed that you will no longer hide as before, Magor-lier, but there is still the issue of the Hunters. It is imperative we have a plan to either move you or deal with an attack when it comes."

"I agree, and that is the main reason I called this meeting," Alyx said. "I'm pleased to inform you the Hunters are now a manageable problem."

Tarrick frowned. "What do you mean?"

"The reason I went away—Jenna and I went into Shivasa and tracked down the mage who was creating the Hunter medallions. I killed her," Alyx said calmly.

Stunned silence filled the room. Expressions ranged from horror at the danger Alyx had put herself in to reluctant admiration and shocked surprise. Cayr was glancing between Alyx and Jenna in astonishment, as if he couldn't believe they'd managed to get along for more than two minutes, let alone succeed in a dangerous mission together.

"You went alone into Shivasa?" Rothai's mouth had thinned until it was almost invisible.

"No." An edge sharpened her voice. "I took a Taliath for protection. Just as things used to be in the old days. Like they will be going forward."

"None of you could fight properly against Shakar while Hunters remained a renewable resource for him." Jenna's cool voice spoke before Rothai could respond. "The situation was untenable, and Lady Egalion and I solved it. Recriminations are a waste of breath. You would be better served turning discussion to what comes next."

Biting back a smile, Alyx continued, "Of course, Hunters will continue to come for me and other mages, but Shakar can no longer create new medallions. The more we kill or capture, the fewer there will be."

A low hum of conversation broke out. Alyx let them talk—it allowed her a moment to recharge. Rothai clearly still wasn't happy, but he remained silent. Finn wore his thinking look, probably already considering ways to take advantage of the situation. Cayr had leaned over to Jenna and the two were conversing quietly; Alyx's eyes narrowed at that, but her attention was drawn away when Ladan cleared his throat, quieting the room.

"Most of you already know I intend to leave Alistriem to search for Taliath potentials that have survived the Mage Council hunt," Ladan said. "It's time they were found, protected and trained properly."

Finn raised a hand. "Despite the re-emergence of Shakar, I don't imagine the Mage Council's desire to kill Taliath has faded—it may even have strengthened. You and any potentials you find will be vulnerable, particularly if Galien is still the one hunting them."

"Agreed," Ladan said. "But now that we know where the danger is coming from, we will be better able to protect them."

"My mages will help with protection." Alyx infused her words with how strongly she felt, moving her gaze between all mages present to ensure they received the message. "From now on, we work together."

Rothai astonished her when he spoke. "I will organise that if you like, Magor-lier? It will likely take the council some time to learn what is happening if we are careful with the information."

"Thank you." She hesitated, then firmed her voice. "I will trust you with it."

"With your permission, Your Highness, I will go to ShadowFall Island to conduct the training and help protect the potentials in case of attack," Garan said, looking at Cayr.

"Your valuable counsel will be a loss, Lord Egalion, but I can see the greater good in what you're suggesting." Cayr looked troubled, despite his words.

"You have a very capable Taliath at your side, Your Highness, despite her youth," Garan said.

Alyx wasn't sure who was more astonished by her father's endorsement, her or Jenna, but Cayr's worried expression eased. "Thank you, Lord Egalion."

"I'd like to go with Ladan." Dawn said. "I think a telepath could be useful in finding Taliath."

Most of the room, Alyx included, looked over at her in surprise. Ladan's expression was as hard to read as always.

"If it's what you want, of course you can go," Alyx said to her friend. "My telepathic magic was instrumental in tracking the Hunters through Shivasa, and Taliath present with a similar sort of blankness to our magic. Ladan, I assume you have no objections?"

"None. You are welcome, Dawn." Ladan inclined his head.

"And what will you do next?" Cayr asked Alyx.

Alyx sat back. "Tarrick? You've thought about this since last night, I presume?"

He looked pleased she'd asked him. "I have, yes. If you're not willing to continue hiding from Shakar until you grow stronger, then I suggest we go on the offensive. We attack the Hunters when and where we can and destroy their medals. If we can nullify the threat they pose sooner rather than later–"

"Then less mages will die in Hunter attacks," Finn said, following the train of thought instantly.

Tarrick nodded. "Mages we'll need, along with the Taliath, to fight Shakar."

"We'll need to do more than that." Cario spoke for the first time. "If you're establishing an alternative mage order, Alyx, then you need to provide protection, stability and structure to the mages under you."

"I agree. What would you suggest?"

"First, the implementation of a formal command structure and a series of covert communication methods," Cario said. "Without that we will be scattered and ineffective. Secondly, you need to be visible. A commanding leader that mages want to follow."

"We could set up safe houses, or bases. Knowledge of those locations can be restricted to only those mages who need to know, like the mine in Tregaya," Tarrick said, and Cario nodded.

"Before we can do any of that, we need to find all the mages out there that aren't already sworn to us or hiding in Carhall," Alyx said. "If possible, I'd like to speak to as many of them as possible in one group."

"A single event with all the mages gathered?" Rothai looked sceptical. "That would leave us and them dangerously vulnerable."

"Then we'll figure out a way to keep them safe. Cario's right, I need to show them I'm in charge, and we need to give them a plan, a reason to join us. We need to offer them hope." She thought on that for a moment. "Cario, Finn, you're in charge of coming up with ideas for protecting a single gathering of mages for a short period of time. No more than a couple of hours should be necessary."

"I believe I could help with that," Garan offered. "I have some thoughts already."

"We would definitely welcome your ideas," Finn said.

"Good, then can we move on to Rionn's increasingly dire situation?" Astor asked. "Alyx, I'd like to discuss what mage resources you could provide us."

"Of course." Alyx nodded. "But before we move on, there is one more thing that I need to establish."

"What is it?" Tarrick asked.

"Cario spoke of the need for formal structure. I am the leader of the mages, but beyond me there is no clarity about position or leadership," she said steadily. "I have promised to be a more responsible leader, and part of that means having capable mages under me who can carry out my commands but also provide me with advice."

A little smile curled at Finn's mouth. "Go ahead and name Cario your second. It's fine."

She risked a glance at Tarrick, but he shrugged equably. "Very well. Cario will be my second. Now, Astor, how many mages do you want?"

"Alyx, do you have a moment?" Cario walked up after the meeting had finally ended. She was exhausted, but for the first time since Dashan's death the miasma of depression around her heart had lifted a little. It wasn't gone, not even close, but deep down what she was doing felt right in a way nothing had for a very long time.

"If you're going to complain about being my second, I don't want to hear it," she said, rising from her chair.

"I live to serve." He gave her a sweeping bow, overdoing it until she snorted in amusement.

"What do you want, then?"

"I'd like to discuss reaching out to the Mage Council. They have access to resources that we don't, and they have another mage of the higher order. Galien, despite his faults, could be a significant help when fighting Shakar."

She made a face. "I don't want to give them the impression that we're in any way subordinate to them," she said.

"One step at a time," Cario said. "I'm not even sure the council would agree to help us—especially once they learn you've claimed leadership of the mage order—or what concessions we'd have to make. But it's something we need to at least explore."

"You're right." Alyx let out a breath. "Go on then, reach out. You're my second now, you have the authority to act on my behalf."

A faint smile crossed his face. "Very well, Magor-lier."

When she stepped outside the following morning, five showy cavalry mounts were grazing on the lawn beyond the pebbled drive. Casta and Tijer stood at the base of the steps, Nario, Josha, and Roland lingering just behind them.

The famous five. The thought gave her a flicker of amusement.

"Lady Egalion," Tijer greeted her.

"Tijer." She raised an eyebrow, running her eyes over the group of young men. "Good to see you all again."

"Lady Egalion." Roland grinned, tipping his hat. The others followed suit. "Long time since we stole the king from his palace."

"Indeed." A smile curled at her mouth. "To what do I owe this unexpected visit?"

"Tarrick and Finn came to the barracks last night. They wanted to know if we had any spare cloaks we would be willing to give them," Tijer said. "Like yours."

"Did you show them the way to the storage room, Nario?" Roland asked.

"I did not," Nario said seriously. "I didn't see Josha give them the key for it, either."

Tijer cleared his throat. "Tarrick mentioned you were planning to leave Alistriem. He said you're now the proper leader of the mages. We'd like to come with you."

Surprise flashed through her. "You would?"

"Yes. Lieutenant Caverlock was very serious about your protection, and he was our brother," Tijer said. "We're no Taliath, of course, but we've protected you before, and we know how it works. We can fight with and against mages, and Shakar doesn't scare us."

"Besides," Josha added. "The head of the mage order needs to look the part—we Bluecoats are well trained in filling the role of flashy ceremonial guard."

"We're also the five best looking Bluecoats in Alistriem," Roland added, managing a straight face.

She bit her lip, trying to hold back the sobbing laugh that desperately wanted to escape. "You have permission from your commander?"

"No, Magor-lier," Casta said sheepishly. "But we're hoping you might square it with Lord-General Caverlock."

Great. A conversation with Dashan's father. Alyx couldn't stand him. It sounded like she was also going to have to explain how a pile of blue cloaks had gone missing from the barracks' stores. But she also couldn't deny the idea of having these Bluecoats with her gave her a sense of comfort she hadn't had for a long time.

"I'll talk to him. We're leaving tomorrow. Be packed up and waiting here at dawn." She fought a smile. "And make sure your tack is gleaming and there isn't a button out of place on those uniforms."

"Consider it done!" Tijer saluted snappily, and all four others followed suit before spinning and striding back over to their mounts. Her gaze lingered on them until they faded from sight.

"Dashan had many more friends than he thought," she mused, wishing with every fibre of her being in that moment that he was still alive and with her.

The door to the Caverlock mansion was opened by their sober-faced steward, who gravely assured Alyx he would fetch the lord-general straight away. Dashan's father appeared shortly after, boots rapping sharply on the tiled floor. His eyes flickered over her new cloak, but betrayed nothing of how he was feeling.

"Lady Egalion." He was polite, his gruff voice a sound familiar to her since childhood. "What brings you here?"

"Lord-General Caverlock," she spoke just as politely, but didn't bow her head. "Firstly, I wanted to pass on my condolences on the death of your son. You know that he has been a friend of mine for a long time."

She thought his hands, resting at his sides, might have flickered slightly at her words, but he showed no other emotion. "Thank you, Lady Egalion. Your father has passed on similar condolences."

"I would have married him, if he'd lived." The words came out before she'd realised she was going to say them, but she didn't regret it. There had been a challenge in her voice—part of her wanted to see some sign that Caverlock mourned his son. Dashan deserved that, at least. "He was a good man, a man any father should be proud to have as a son."

Caverlock's face tightened, both in surprise at her words and repressed anger at her implied accusation. She waited in silence, meeting his gaze steadily, while he searched for a response. Eventually a look of resignation swept over his face, as if maintaining anger was suddenly too much effort. "Lady Egalion, I had no idea."

"That seems to have been a theme with you and Dashan, sir," she said, unable to help herself, before gentling her tone. "I wish you'd known him like I did. If you'd taken the time to do that... you would have loved him too."

"Regan has said something similar." Caverlock cleared his throat. His shoulders were no longer ramrod straight. "He has taken the death of his brother hard. Harder than Dashan would have thought, I think."

"That is very sad, sir." Before he could say anything, she kept going. "I'd like your permission to take five of your Bluecoats with me when I leave Alistriem. They've been part of my protective detail before and I trust them."

He blinked, frowning a little. "If what you say is true, Lady Egalion... if you were to be my daughter in law... my Bluecoats are as much yours as they are mine. Pass their names to my steward and I will sign the orders today."

"Thank you, Lord-General."

She turned to go, but his voice called her back. His eyes were on the ground, but he looked up slowly as she waited for him to speak. "He died a good death, my son?"

"He died to save my life, and those of my friends." Somehow, some way, she managed to keep her voice even. "Good night, Lord-General Caverlock."

CHAPTER 19

S hakar went to ground after the destruction of Tennan. It was confusing and frustrating. Alyx had made it a priority to learn more about him; where he based himself, how many mages followed him, what exactly his plans were. Yet two months on and they'd had no success on any of those fronts. She was gnawing over the problem as she rode back into Alistriem late one evening.

"Cheer up," Cario said from where he rode at her side. "Shakar remains as elusive as ever, but we're making strides in our other goals."

"That's true." If things had gone well there she would shortly be leaving Alistriem again to undertake the next step of her plan. And only a week earlier they'd turned the tables on a large group of Hunters who'd sought to ambush her, killing them all and taking their medallions.

"Magor-lier?" Tijer rode up as they passed through the city gates. "Casta and Nario will escort you home. The rest of us will take the medallions to the usual place."

"Thanks, Tijer." She shuddered. "Make sure you store those blasted things well away from me and the other mages." Even when not touching them, they made her skin crawl. The location they were being stored was a secret even to Alyx—known only to a select few including Tijer, Finn and her father.

"Consider it done," he said with a smile and a salute before riding off. Roland and Josha peeled off to follow him, leaving her with Casta, Nario, and the mages. Tarrick turned back to look at her, a hopeful look on his face. "Join us for a drink in the party district before going home?"

Her chest tightened fractionally. "Thanks, but I'm feeling pretty tired. I'll see you in the morning."

"Come on, we're all tired," Finn said. "Have a drink with us."

She paused, trying to find the words to explain—reluctant to tell them that the inns in the party district reminded her too much of Dashan, of his laughing and high spirits. "I don't feel like drinking tonight. Next time."

"All right," he said reluctantly. "See you tomorrow then."

"Shall I ride back with you?" Cario murmured as Finn and Tarrick began moving away.

"No, you should join them, take the opportunity to relax," she told him. "If things have gone to plan, we'll be on our way again tomorrow morning."

"Then I'll see you first thing. Oh, and I'll bring the fritters you like from the morning markets," he promised with a smile before riding off to join the other mages.

The two Bluecoats were a silent but reassuring presence around her as she rode through the gates of her home. Her decision not to join her friends in the city played on her mind, and she was unsure she'd done the right thing. They were all working hard to put the events of the night in Sandira behind them, but she sometimes wondered if they were trying to make something happen that just wasn't possible.

It was more difficult with Dawn gone. Alyx hadn't had word from either her or Ladan since they'd left. She wondered whether they'd found any Taliath yet.

"Do you need anything more this evening, Magor-lier?" Casta asked as she dismounted by the front steps.

Alyx glanced at the young man fondly. She'd endured a certain amount of puzzlement from the mages as to why she needed five Bluecoat bodyguards without any mage power or Taliath ability, but so far had ignored it. Their presence comforted her.

"No thank you, Casta. Why don't you and Nario take the night off? I'll just be going up to bed."

"All right. I'll check in on the guards at the gates, make sure they know you're home, before I leave." He tipped his hat. "Sleep well."

"You too."

Warned of her arrival back in the city, two warrior mages waited at the base of the steps to take over her protection detail. Adahn was one of them, and he gave her a jaunty wave. She waved back, waiting until a groom came to take Tingo. The stallion snuffled affectionately in her hair before allowing himself to be led away.

"Magor-lier." Adahn's bow was a touch too casual to be seriously meant. When he straightened he gestured to the broad-shouldered, bearded man beside him. Neither of them wore mage robes, she noted with approval. "Have you met Chestin?"

"You look familiar." She frowned, trying to recall. It took a few moments to come to her. "Carhall! You were on guard when Cario gave us a tour of the Hub all those years ago."

"That's right, Magor-lier." Much more formal than Adahn, Chestin was trained council mage through and through. She wondered what had brought him over to her side.

"It's nice to see you again," she said warmly, then turned to Adahn. "I assume my father has already gone?"

"Yes, he left yesterday."

"And King Cayr? He's in residence?"

"Yes, my lady," Safia answered for Adahn as she walked in the door. He gave her a quick smile of welcome, taking her riding gloves and cloak. "You have a visitor in the study."

Surprise speared through her. "Who? Nobody knew I was coming back tonight."

"We only just got here." Adahn frowned when she looked at him questioningly.

"He didn't give a name, but he's a mage," Safia said. "He arrived yesterday and said he'd wait for you. I told him I didn't know when you were expected back, but he insisted. I had the servants set up a room for him, but I've barely seen him since."

It was unlikely that Shakar had decided to wait in her study, and any other mage she could handle, even if their intentions weren't good. Still, she couldn't imagine which of her mages would have come to see her at her residence and then have the audacity to insist on staying. Curiosity niggled at her.

"Wait here," she told Adahn and Chestin. "If I scream, you have my permission to come running."

"We'll stay close," Adahn promised.

She crossed the cavernous foyer towards her father's study. The room went largely unused in her father's absences, but it was a good place to meet guests.

The mage standing at the fireplace turned at her entrance, and she stopped dead in the doorway. Brynn's boyishly handsome face was drawn and pale, and there were dark circles under his eyes. It had been well over a year since she'd seen him, and for a long moment she couldn't quite believe he was standing there in her father's study.

"Alyx," he said, voice raspy as if he held back strong emotion so that he wouldn't upset her. "I heard what happened to Dashan. I came straight away... I..."

His voice trailed off as if he didn't know what to say. Alyx was getting better and better at managing her grief, and she swallowed back the rush of emotion, even managing a smile at the sight of him.

"I can't believe you're standing here." Her smile widened to a genuine one. "Where have you been all this time? We've been worried sick!"

"That doesn't matter." He dismissed her words, taking a step towards her. "I'm so sorry, I had no idea what had happened to Dash, and when I heard, I—"

"It's okay, Brynn."

"It's not, it's not okay." He stopped his forward movement. "Will you tell me what happened?"

Alyx let out a breath—going through everything was the last thing she wanted to do, but Brynn deserved to know. Slowly, haltingly, she relayed everything that had occurred that night, and all the developments since.

When she was done, Brynn looked even more tired than he had, and his eyes were dark with emotion. Alyx gestured him to one of the chairs by the fire and she sat in the one beside it. They sat in silence for a while, not needing to talk.

"Where have you been?" she asked eventually.

"That's a long, tiring story." He sighed. "In short, I've been spying for the council, working against Shakar."

"Why didn't you come to us, to me?"

"At first I couldn't find you. I didn't know what had happened or where you'd gone after DarkSkull was destroyed. Then, when I did learn where you were, I couldn't leave. I had worked my way into a key position with a group of mages allied to Shakar."

"What happened?" she asked.

"The council killed them," he replied.

"I'm sorry," she said, squeezing his arm.

"Don't be. They weren't good people. I just hate the killing, you know?"

"I know," she said softly.

"Safia told me that you're establishing a new mage order." Brynn sat forward, face eager. "If you truly have become Magor-lier, then I don't work for the council anymore."

"Really?"

"Really." He spoke so emphatically, she almost laughed.

"Oh Brynn." She sank back in the chair, taking in his familiar features and feeling some of her tension drain away. "I'm glad to have you with me, finally."

"The council's worried about you, Alyx. They wouldn't say much to me because they know how close we are, but you're scaring them. When they hear you're setting yourself up as an alternative—"

"They *murdered* Dashan," she gritted out, hands curling into the arms of the chair. "They don't scare me."

"They should. At least be aware that they'll be watching you closely." He sighed when she refused to look at him, then reached over to squeeze her hand. "You look exhausted. Why don't you head up to bed, and we can talk more in the morning?"

"Sounds good." She smiled. "But how do you feel about talking while we ride instead?"

"Where are we going?"

She waggled her eyebrows. "It's a secret."

Brynn laughed. "Count me in."

CHAPTER 20

Tingo moved at a swift gallop, his hooves thundering over the flat surface. Tarrick and Finn rode close behind, Brynn a little further back with the other mages of her protective detail.

The hazy outline of Tennan appeared in the distance, and then was hidden again as the road took them through a forested area. Rothai and Jayn, also mounted, waited for them just before the trees ended and the road continued towards the city. Alyx reined Tingo in sharply. Clouds of dust rose into the sky as horses milled around on the dry road.

"Magor-lier," Rothai greeted her. "I assume you had no issues on your way here?"

"None. Is everything in place?" She hoped so. They couldn't afford to linger.

Her old sparring master actually smiled. "Yes. They've been gathered about an hour already. Lord Egalion is overseeing them."

She matched his smile. "In that case, we'd best get to it."

Alyx urged Tingo back into a gallop along the road, hooves thundering as mages fell in behind her. It took them through the open fields surrounding Tennan before straightening into a line towards the southern entrance to the city. A group of people were gathered before the destroyed city gates, most standing in the shade cast by the half-ruined wall. Though still early morning, the sun was warm and bright in the sky above.

A jolt of surprise went through her at how large the crowd was—at a glance she estimated well over fifty mages. Many more than she'd expected.

Not one of them looked comfortable. Most shifted restlessly, while some even had their staffs drawn. Moments later, the reason for that became clear as her magic suddenly winked out of existence. Even though she'd been expecting it, she winced. Behind her, several curses were uttered, and there were a couple of gasps.

Those at the back of the crowd caught sight of the approaching riders and started moving aside, creating a passage down the middle of the road leading to the gates.

Alyx reined Tingo in and dismounted. Casting a single glance back to check that Cario, Finn, and Tarrick were behind her, she straightened her shoulders and began walking with long, loose strides down the road.

There were many things reflected in the faces of those she passed, from curiosity to fear, and in one older man, a focused attention, like he was assessing her already. All of them had a medallion hanging from their necks. All stared at the scarlet sigil on her chest.

Her father waited at the base of the wall, standing alert but relaxed. *Heartfire* was sheathed at his side. He inclined his head in greeting but made no move to approach her. She gave him a quick smile as she passed him and began climbing the rubble towards the top.

Now she was alone. Cario, Tarrick, and Finn remained at the bottom, taking up positions beside her father. A cool ocean breeze whipped at her blue cloak and tugged free loose tendrils of her braided hair. At the top, she paused a moment, facing the waiting crowd of mages below.

Rothai and Jayn had spent the past months tracking down every mage they could find, council mage or not, asking them to be present in Tennan on this particular day. Those that agreed to come had been given a medallion and strict instructions about timing their arrival so they wouldn't be there long. None of them had been told what the meeting was for, only that it had to do with the destruction of Shakar.

Alyx raised a hand. Slowly the shuffling and hum of conversation silenced. The weight of their attention on her was palpable, as if close to a hundred pairs of eyes were boring into her soul.

Swallowing, she closed her eyes and summoned every bit of strength she'd managed to cobble together in the months since Dashan's death. Then, letting out a low breath, she straightened her shoulders and let her gaze run over the crowd below.

"I am Alyx Egalion." She made her voice loud and clear, filling it with confidence. "I have assumed the position of Magor-lier of the mage order. That is my right as the most powerful mage alive in time of war."

Muttering broke out at her words, and she raised her hand again to quiet them.

"I went to DarkSkull Hall just like all of you. I survived through dawn breakfasts, Master Rothai's sparring sessions," she paused for the brief chuckle, "and long nights of watchtower duty in the middle of freezing winter snows. I learned the same things you did. I am one of you. But I am not a creature of the Mage Council." She paused again to let that sink in.

"The council wants Shakar dead too, I know. Council mages do good work across all countries you come from, I know that as well. But the council is also afraid. They are terrified of Shakar, and more than that, they are terrified of losing the power they hold. That fear has led them to hunting and killing every Taliath potential they could find over the past decade." The shocked outbreak of chatter was loud and intense, forcing Alyx to stop. Without using telepathic magic it was impossible to tell whether the outrage she saw on some faces was directed at her or the council. Eventually she raised her hand again and slowly they quieted. "The council's fear makes them prize the most powerful and pure-blooded mages over all others. 'Lesser' mages are treated as worthless." When more talking broke out this time, Alyx raised her voice, silencing them all.

"*I* am not afraid! I am not afraid of the Taliath, I am not afraid of having or losing power, and I believe there is no such thing as a lesser mage." Her words rippled over them, ringing with conviction. "I am here today to ask for your loyalty, to help me build a new and better mage order. If you choose to follow me, you will be working alongside mages *and* Taliath. In return, I offer you protection and the chance to destroy Shakar. The Mage Council cannot defeat Shakar, but *I* can. *I* will. It won't be soon, but it will happen. I promise you that."

Alyx let those words settle for a long moment then,

"That is all I have to say. We shouldn't linger here or we risk detection. Those who wish to join with me, please remain and speak to myself or one of the mages you see standing below. You will need to temporarily take off your medallions, lower your mental shields and allow either myself or one of my telepath mages to verify your honesty. That is for your protection as well as mine. You'll be provided details about the safe house and code system we've set up. If you choose not to join me, then you're free to leave. Thank you."

Without any further fanfare, Alyx began stepping back down the rubble towards the ground. After three steps, someone started clapping. Two steps further and it sounded like at least half the crowd had broken into applause. Soon there were whistles and cheers too.

By the time she reached the ground, almost all the mages who'd been gathered were lining up into rough rows before Tarrick, Cario, Finn, and Rothai. She spotted only a handful leaving.

Cario's intense blue gaze snagged hers. "Well done, Magor-lier," he said quietly. "That was exactly right."

Once all the mages had been spoken to and then dispatched to various safe houses already set up across Rionn, Tregaya, and Zandia, Alyx went looking for Finn. He was digging through his saddlebags.

"Tarrick's found a good campsite and your father has promised us a decent stew with a rabbit he caught if I can find the flask in my..." Finn muttered, then "There it is!"

"Before we join them, can we talk?" she asked.

Finn successfully tugged the flask from his saddlebag, then turned to look at her in surprise. "Is something wrong?"

"No." She smiled a little. "I just want to borrow that genius brain of yours for a little while."

It was late when she and Finn joined the others at the campsite. The stew was long cooked, the remnants bubbling over a fire waiting for them. Rothai had disappeared, unsurprisingly, to patrol. When Tarrick asked where they'd been, Alyx shrugged it off. "My ribs have been sore recently, I wanted Finn to take a look."

Her father lifted an eyebrow as if he sensed the lie, but didn't push her on it. "Once you've had a rest and something to eat, you should get moving," Garan said.

"She's fine, Tarrick." Finn chuckled when Tarrick opened his mouth. "Promise."

Alyx ignored them, looking at her father. "Will you be going straight to ShadowFall?"

He nodded, face brightening. "I had a message from Ladan two days ago. He and Dawn have found three potentials already. Ladan wants to take them to ShadowFall to start learning before expanding his search into northern Tregaya and Zandia."

She was pleased, and not just at the idea of potentials being found. The idea of rebuilding the Taliath had given her father a purpose and life she had never seen in him before. "I will send three warrior mages with you."

"What's next for you, Alyx?" Brynn asked, mouth full of bread and cheese.

"It will take time to establish my leadership, and to ensure the safe house and communication systems are working smoothly. We also need to keep tracking and killing Hunters. After that..." She let out a breath. "We haven't gotten anywhere in terms of learning more about Shakar. We can't begin working on a plan to defeat him unless we understand him better."

Tarrick nodded. "I couldn't agree more. What do you think of giving the job to Rothai? He has extensive contacts within the mage world and he's still the most powerful warrior mage alive outside you, so he can look after himself. Let Rothai loose and tell him to learn everything he can about Shakar for us."

"It's a better idea than you realise," Brynn said quietly. "Rothai burns for Shakar's destruction."

"Why?" Alyx asked.

"Shakar murdered his family when he was a young child. Only he and his elder sister survived. Many in his village were killed in the same attack," Brynn said.

Alyx paled. "I had no idea."

"*That's* why he was so against you and Dashan, Alyx, and why he is so protective of your safety," Finn said in realisation. "Rothai has firsthand knowledge of what Shakar does to those he perceives to be a threat."

Alyx glanced down, fingering the blue cloak still slung around her shoulders.

"Alyx?" Brynn said. "You did nothing wrong."

"I made mistakes." She looked up at him. "But all I can do now is learn from them."

"I think I know exactly how you feel," Tarrick said, meeting her eyes across the table. A flicker of understanding passed between them, a true and honest one.

"Send me after the Hunters," Brynn volunteered. "I am trained for tracking, after all. Shakar might withdraw them once he realises your strategy. This is the best way I can serve you."

She nodded slowly. For a long moment they were silent, all occupied with their thoughts as the fire crackled between them.

Eventually, Brynn rose to his feet, drawing their attention. "Well then, shall we go and try to destroy Shakar, one step at a time?"

"I'm free." Cario carefully straightened his tunic as he, too, stood.

Finn shrugged. "I can probably fit it in."

Alyx touched her cloak again, then looked up. "Yes, let's. I'd like to keep the promise I made to those mages today."

PART 2

CHAPTER 21

A lyx's boots whispered through the grass, quick strides bringing her closer to the farmhouse in the distance. A watery moon cast a dim glow over the empty fields surrounding it. Nothing moved in the open space around the house, which stood shrouded in shadows.

"I have a bad feeling about this," Adahn spoke at her side. A royal blue cloak hung from his shoulders, the scarlet stitching over his chest glinting bright when it caught the moonlight. Alyx couldn't help a little smile at the sight. *Heartfire.* No longer just the name of her father's Taliath sword, but a word and symbol that represented everything she was trying to build with her new mage order. Adahn had told her, years ago when he'd first donned the cloak, that he wore the leaping flame emblem for his cousin, an apprentice mage who'd died in the attack on DarkSkull. Each of her mages wore it in honour of someone who'd been lost that day.

"I'd like to second that," Nario piped in from behind.

Alyx glanced back to where Casta and Nario walked behind them. Both Bluecoats rested their hands on the hilts of their swords. "Nario, you and Adahn always have a bad feeling about these meetings."

Adahn's mouth quirked in a smile. "For good reason, Magor-lier. We don't trust those you're meeting with."

"To defeat Shakar, we need the council. For now, at least." Alyx spoke the same tired old words she'd been saying for years. Until she could make all their resources hers, she needed to work *with* the council. And while she drew more and more mages to her every month, most of the order remained loyal to the old ways. If she fought them for control, it would only dilute the effort against Shakar, and for now it seemed the council agreed. Despite fury over her claim to the Magor-lier title, they hadn't actively moved against her. A fragile truce lingered.

"The problem is, we're not united," Adahn said.

"Three years ago they wouldn't even meet with me. Now we're about to attend our fifth meeting over the past eighteen months. I call that progress," she said.

"I'd term the information sharing as limited," he said pointedly.

"We have to build on something." Alyx stifled her flash of irritation with Adahn. It wasn't him she was truly angry with—his sentiments merely echoed her own. It didn't help that even the very idea of working in concert with the council made her insides twist with bitterness. After everything they'd done to her...*Focus. Shakar is the goal. Whatever that takes.*

"I can't argue with you when you're being so reasonable about it." His smile flashed in the dim light.

"I'm the mage leader, it's my job to be reasonable." No matter how exhausting that was sometimes.

"And a fine leader you are too, if I may say so." His eyes lingered on her, warm and appreciative. She ignored the look, and the deliberate flattery, turning away to employ her telepathic ability to do a sweep of the area for potential danger. The mages in the house they were heading towards had their minds shielded, of course, but she picked up nothing to make her worry.

"Good," Casta said once she passed this on. "The smoother this goes the better. We'll have to ride quickly if we're going to make it to the mine to pick up Tarrick and the others and get to Alistriem in time for the wedding."

Of the five Bluecoats assigned to her, Casta was the most disposed to worrying about Alyx's schedule—he was like a mother hen at times. She loved him for it.

She smiled. "Don't worry, I'm not going to miss the wedding."

Nario made a face at Casta. "I don't know why you're so eager. Guard detail for an event as elaborate as an Egalion wedding is the most boring post possible. Hours of standing there watching rich, ridiculously-dressed people talking, eating, and drinking."

"Heads up," Adahn said. His flirtatious demeanour was gone, replaced by the keenly focused attention of a mage warrior. It was often like that with Adahn—his light and amused nature could turn in a blink to that of an alert and passionate fighter. "Keep your eyes peeled."

Two mages stood guard at the top of stairs leading to a verandah surrounding the house. As arranged, Nario and Casta walked forward to converse in low tones with the guards, exchanging previously agreed upon passwords.

Alyx and Adahn waited some distance off. If there was any cause for alarm, Alyx could grab Adahn and fly quickly away. The idea of leaving Casta and Nario behind to die was close to unthinkable, but she had forced herself to accept the bitter possibility. She was Magor-lier. They wouldn't hesitate to give their lives for her.

After a few moments, Casta raised a hand, signalling all was well. He and Nario remained with the two mage guards while Adahn and Alyx walked through the front door. Flickering torches lit the way down a staircase into a small, rectangular underground cellar.

A rickety table and chairs had been set up in the centre of the room. Three mages sat at the table, all familiar. Alyx's gaze went to the young man in the middle. The insolent look on his face had never changed, despite him growing older and more experienced. "Hello, Parja."

"Alyx, glad you could make it."

It never failed to irritate her that Parja was usually chosen as the lead council representative sent to these meetings. No doubt a deliberate choice. Amongst Galien's close friends at DarkSkull, he'd been one of her main tormentors.

"You forgot to address her by her proper title," Adahn said, eyes glittering with poorly concealed anger.

"My apologies, *Lady* Egalion," Parja spoke with equally fake civility. "I'm unsurprised to see you haven't lost your airs and graces in all these years."

Adahn tensed, muscles bunching under his cloak, but Alyx hushed him with a quick telepathic nudge. The council mages refused to acknowledge her as Magor-lier, but trying to force them to do it would only make her seem petty. She knew what she was and didn't need validation by a group of people she neither respected nor trusted. All she needed was their help to kill Shakar.

So she gave them a polite nod of greeting. "You remember Adahn?"

"I do," Parja said, and gestured to the two other mages at the table. "And you know Dustan and Tomas."

"It's nice to see you both again," Alyx said politely. Both were older warrior mages with years of experience. They stayed loyal to the council because they'd been council mages their whole lives and had never known anything different. They still clung to the old mage traditions, ones Alyx was doing her best to change, but she respected their experience and knowledge, and they'd never been anything but reasonable at previous meetings. "Where's Galien?"

It was something she always asked. Part of it was a desire to know exactly what he was up to. Then there was the deeper part of her that truly feared to see him. That night in Sandira was seared in her heart, no matter how much time had passed. He'd broken her that night. They both knew it, and it gave him power over her.

"He's busy on council business. We do have more important things to do than meet with an upstart mage and her rabble." Parja frowned.

"I'm sure you do." Alyx accepted that without comment, the knot in her chest relaxing. She hated it, hated both Galien and herself, and even now she felt only shame that she was relieved he wasn't coming.

"Shall we get down to it?" Parja asked.

She brushed aside thoughts of Galien as she and Adahn took the seats opposite. "We've just come from Sandira," she said. "The emperor remains uncommitted to a formal alliance with Tregaya and Rionn, but he is keeping a close eye on events as they develop. I sense he is becoming concerned with the inroads Shakar and the Shiven army are making into both our countries."

"You've been trying to get the emperor to join an alliance for years. Maybe it's time to accept he isn't interested and look at other options," Parja said.

"If you've thought of some other options, I'd love to hear them," Alyx said coolly.

"What do you think it will take to convince the emperor to commit to a formal alliance?" Dustan asked, giving Parja a warning glance. The council wanted the alliance with Zandia as much as she did, and for the same reasons. If nothing else, the council could always be relied upon to try and protect itself.

"We're not sure," Adahn said. "Zandia is powerful and well protected by both its geography and strong army. Last time Shakar was a problem, it was contained in Tregaya before his influence spread to Zandia. It will take a lot to convince the emperor that his country is in danger from Shakar and the Shiven army."

"It will be no use him allying with us if we're already destroyed," Parja snapped. "Surely the fool can see that?"

"I did suggest that to him in more diplomatic terms," Alyx said dryly. "The emperor does not see the situation as we do, and he is a stubborn man." Not to mention he hadn't forgotten the disaster of Galien's appearance in Sandira all those years ago either. Subsequently learning about the council hunting Taliath potentials—a piece of information Alyx and her people had made deliberately public—had the undesirable effect of Zandia cutting all formal ties with the council and treating even Alyx's mages with cold disdain.

Parja nodded reluctantly. "The emperor refuses to receive us in Sandira, as you know, but if you identify any way we might help you gain the alliance, we are open to considering it."

"Thank you."

He cleared his throat. The genuine offer had clearly pained him, and he moved on quickly. "We would like to suggest coordinating our efforts against the Shiven in Tregaya."

"How so?" Alyx asked.

Tomas rose to gather a roll of maps and lay one out on the table. He spent a few minutes outlining areas in which the Tregayan border was under pressure from the invading army. None of it was new to Alyx, but she was pleased to note her information was as good as the council's.

"As you can see, Tregayan forces—including the mage assistance the council has provided—are stretched thin. We've lost nearly a third of our territory to the Shiven."

"How much mage assistance are you providing exactly?" Alyx asked bluntly. "Until the Shiven army can put more resources into attacking Tregaya, which won't happen until Rionn falls, you should be able to provide enough help to the militia for them to hold Shivasa back."

"You are not providing any help to Tregaya," Parja said. "So it is not for you to judge the council's deployment of mages."

"My warrior mages have been integral in holding the Rionnan borders and protecting the training Taliath on ShadowFall from Shakar and your mages," Alyx shot back. "I haven't seen a hair of council help in Rionn, yet if it falls, you'll be in significantly more trouble."

"You mean you're wasting critical resources protecting the next generation of those who could create another Shakar." Parja sneered. "Yes, very noble indeed."

At her side, Adahn tensed. She glanced at him, but his face was unreadable, eyes focused on Parja.

"Parja, enough," Dustan said firmly. "We are not here to focus on our differences, but on where we can help each other against Shakar."

"Mage Dustan is right." Alyx gave him a grateful nod. "Are you officially asking for our help in Tregaya?"

The three men shared a brief look, too quick for Alyx to interpret. It made her uneasy.

"What we are suggesting is a mutually beneficial coordination of deployments," Tomas said.

Whatever that means. She tried not to roll her eyes at the double-speak. "What exactly do you want? I understand the council is concerned that if

Tregaya falls they will lose their safe haven in Carhall, but protecting them is not my responsibility."

Parja scowled at Alyx's blunt words, but Tomas and Dustan looked discomfited. Again, they shared a look. Her gaze narrowed. Something else was going on here. The urge to use telepathy rose strongly, but logic stopped her—these were trained mages who would be paying close attention to their shielding with her in the room. Being caught out would end any cooperation instantly.

"The council is not afraid," Parja said coldly. "King Mastaran has a skilled commander running the defence of Carhall."

"I'm very happy for them," Alyx said dryly. "But you're not exactly convincing me why I should help you."

Parja smiled, and Alyx frowned as she detected a hint of triumph in it. "You are declining our offer, then?"

Another quick look between the three and she'd had enough. Levelling a glare at Parja, she lifted her eyebrows. "There's something you're not telling us. What is it?"

"Are you reading our thoughts?" Parja demanded, anger clouding his face.

"No, but I have instincts, and I don't trust you. What aren't you telling us?"

Parja didn't respond. Alyx flicked her gaze to Tomas and Dustan—both men looked away from her gaze, clearly uncomfortable.

"Is it Shakar? Have you finally gotten a lead on where he is?" Her heart leapt with hope. Every time Rothai had gotten close over the past years, Shakar had disappeared without a trace.

'No," Dustan said heavily, sincerity in his dejected tone. "We assist Master Rothai where we can, but nothing new yet."

Alyx glanced between them. She was confident they were hiding something from her. If not Shakar, then what? Whatever it was had prompted this meeting tonight, she was sure of it. But why not just come out and tell her the real reason for being there? They had to have known she would turn down their request—it made no sense.

"Gentlemen, if you're not going to tell us why we're really here, this meeting is over." Alyx rose to her feet, Adahn following suit. "We can discuss *coordinating* our efforts again once you decide to be honest with us."

"Alyx!" Parja's voice cracked across the basement as she and Adahn reached the steps.

"What?"

"The council is willing to work with you. I advise you not to let them regret that decision."

She gave him a cool smile, her patience gone. "I'm the Magor-lier of the mage order, Parja. I think you'll find that refusing to work with me is something *you* will regret." She paused. "I'm not a fool, and I'm not an apprentice they can bully anymore. Send word when you're willing to meet again. In the meantime, when we come across information that may help your efforts in Tregaya, we will send it to you as a priority."

None of the three council mages said anything further as Alyx and Adahn left, climbing up to the main level.

"That went well," Adahn said in an undertone as they exited the house. Casta and Nario emerged from the shadows of the verandah and fell into step with them.

"Everything all right?" Casta asked.

"The council is keeping something from us," Alyx said as they began crossing the field.

"Are you sure?" Nario asked. "Why even meet with us if they're going to hide their true purpose?

"No idea, but they were hiding something," Adahn said, then hesitated. "Alyx, maybe we should consider giving them help. The council isn't worth our time, I agree, but there *are* good mages that work for them. Aren't we abandoning them?"

She didn't like it when he dropped her title, something he felt entitled to given he'd become a close advisor, but she never called him on it. Particularly since she wasn't sure why it irritated her so much. "All mages have a choice to either join me or stay with the council. I can't make that decision for them."

"It's more complex than that and you know it. Especially since what you offer them is such a radical change from everything they've ever been taught."

She knew instantly what he was getting at, and it infuriated her. "If they're so scared of me becoming another Shakar because I'm letting Taliath live and train, then they're no better than the council. They'll get what they deserve."

His jaw hardened, and she winced—she hadn't meant to sound so blunt and unforgiving. It was her anger talking. Whatever he was about to say was forestalled by the sound of galloping hooves from across the other side of the field. In the dim moonlight, Alyx could just make out a group of riders approaching the farmhouse. The lead rider dismounted and walked forward to speak to the mages emerging from the front door.

"Do you think that's the militia commander Parja spoke about?" Adahn asked, his anger seeming to have faded.

"Maybe, we're not far from Carhall," Alyx murmured. "If it is though, why wasn't he at the meeting?"

"We've been mostly out of touch since leaving Sandira," Adahn said as they continued walking. "Maybe Tarrick will have news that might explain what Parja was hiding."

"I hope so," she murmured.

Moments later they reached the horses and mounted quickly. Nario took the lead as they moved into a swift gallop southeast. Alyx put her annoyance with the council mages to the back of her mind and concentrated on what was ahead. It had been months since she'd seen Tarrick and she missed her old friend. And after that—a wedding! Too-rare happiness bubbled up in her at the thought, and a smile spread helplessly across her face.

The mine had become one of Alyx's main bases, with another in the southwest of Zandia and a third in the far south of Rionn. All were underground and had so far remained secret from Shakar and the Mage

Council, largely due to Tarrick's and Rothai's careful planning and strict security practices.

Tarrick came striding out to meet them as they clattered into the ground level entrance. A wide smile spread across his face. "You made it."

"It's been a long, tiring ride, but an uneventful one, fortunately." She flashed him a warm smile in greeting. "I think Shakar is finally running thin on Hunters."

"Or is holding them back for a different purpose," Adahn said darkly.

She shot him a sharp look. It was a thought that rose often in the back of her mind. Once Alyx had actively begun going after the Hunters, Shakar had withdrawn them. Brynn's tracking had been invaluable in finding nests hidden in various locations, but none of them could go into the heart of Shivasa. Shakar was no fool—he would be holding Hunters in reserve. But for what? The thought made a shiver go down her back.

"Let's hope not," Tarrick said, meeting her eyes with a look that indicated he shared her fears. "I'm glad to see you safe and well. I don't like you having only one mage warrior guard for these meetings, although I understand the council's insistence on it. We have to build trust somewhere, I suppose."

Alyx only nodded, well aware of Tarrick's views about her safety at such meetings. At all other times, she moved around with a constant guard of at least five warrior mages plus her five Bluecoats. It made for a crowded retinue.

"We've been expecting you. I've gathered warrior mages to fill out your escort and of course the rest of your Bluecoats have been waiting impatiently too. We're ready to ride out for Alistriem as soon as you like," Tarrick continued.

"Tomorrow morning," she said. "If we have to sneak around Shiven patrols, it could add a few days onto the journey."

He nodded. "Come down. We'll get you something to eat and drink."

Between mouthfuls of grilled bread and cheese, Alyx relayed what had happened at the meeting. Tarrick frowned when she and Adahn spoke about the mages hiding something.

"We haven't had any news of the council recently," he said. "But I think I know at least part of what they weren't saying."

"Do tell?" Adahn mumbled around a large bite of bread.

"The Tregayans are in worse trouble than Parja let on. About four weeks ago, not long after you left for Sandira, the Shiven army breached the Tregayan border near the southwest coast. The Tregayans haven't been able to close the breach, and now Shiven warriors are marching northeast, taking towns as they go."

"What?" Shock flared, and she forgot about her meal. "How could the Shiven army make such a push into Tregaya when they've got so many forces committed to the Rionnan border? What are the Tregayans doing about it?"

Tarrick held his hand up to stem her flow of questions. "I only learned of this two days ago in a message from Brynn—and his message was sent over two weeks ago after running into Rothai in the west somewhere. Apparently Rothai thinks they're heading straight for Carhall," Tarrick said grimly. "Their strategy might be to take the capital first."

Alyx stared at him. "How close to Carhall are they?"

"It's unclear. Ladan should have more information when we get to Alistriem if we haven't heard from our scouts by then."

Casta shook his head. "Shiven soldiers aren't mounted, and even if they force the pace, it will take them weeks to reach Carhall."

"They probably won't force the pace," Nario added. "They'll want to be rested and ready to fight once they get there. The city has never been breached before."

"If you're right about them taking towns as they go, that will slow them up too," Casta said. "And that's the smart thing for them to do. They don't want to end up isolated and vulnerable in the middle of Tregaya. Without protected supply lines, they can't mount an effective attack on such a fortified city."

"Then why aren't the militia attacking the supply lines, keeping them from moving further forward?" Alyx demanded.

"I don't know." Tarrick seemed as mystified as she was. "Maybe they're stretched too thin."

"But Shivasa has to be stretched thin too," she murmured, mostly to herself. To be pushing so hard into Tregaya while still fighting in Rionn...

"What about council mages? A group of powerful warrior mages should be able to do it without much militia support," Casta said.

Adahn frowned. "Maybe they don't have the resources? Hunters were killing council mages too, don't forget, and we've lured even more over to our side."

"Lured?" Alyx lifted an eyebrow. "I gave them a choice."

"I know." He flashed her a smile. "A much better choice. But I still think we should help them if we can."

She wasn't reassured by his smile or light words, and rose from her chair. "The council murdered the man I loved and wants me and those closest to me dead too. Stop asking me to bend over backwards to help them or their mages, Adahn!"

"Alyx, I'm sorry." He looked genuinely upset, but she turned on her heel and stalked out of the room, climbing up the ladder that led to the level where her room was. The rusted ladder creaked alarmingly under her angry steps. Tarrick caught up to her before she'd gone too far, giving her a little smile.

"Sorry," she said. "I know you probably want to help them too. But there's only so much I can do. I'm trying as hard as I can."

"I know you are," he said simply.

They walked companionably through the narrow walkway, at one point passing a much larger space filled with a handful of young mages. Alyx stopped when she saw who stood at the head of the group, talking intensely about the importance of focus when using mage power.

"I didn't know Alaria was here."

"He arrived a few months ago. We needed another teacher for the apprentices, and this is where we do most of the training."

"They're all apprentices?" Alyx asked.

"Yes. Unfortunately we can't offer the level of training that was provided at DarkSkull, but what we give them is better than nothing. In fact, I swore in an apprentice as a new warrior mage last week."

"I'm glad," Alyx said quietly. "I wish we could do more."

"Like you said, we do the best we can, Alyx." Tarrick smiled suddenly. "Prajana is still here, you know. Did you want to go and say hello?"

"I think I'll pass, thanks." Alyx chuckled. "I'm glad she's here though. She's a good teacher. I'm still surprised she and Alaria chose to leave the council to join us."

Tarrick shrugged as they came to a stop outside her small room. "They both taught you at DarkSkull. They remember you."

"That's very nice of you to say," Alyx said softly.

He cleared his throat in discomfort and turned away. "I'll let you get some rest."

Before he could leave, she reached out to touch the leaping flame on his chest. "Who do you wear yours for?"

His dark eyes turned solemn. "For the patrol member I lost. For Mika."

Memories of that day flooded through her as Tarrick walked away. The pain and grief was still as fresh as if it had only happened yesterday. Dashan's death on top of that, along with the mages she'd lost since... she wanted so desperately for this to be over. For those she loved to be safe. But even more than that she wanted a life. A life without fear or fighting. A life where she could just be Alyx again—she yearned for that so badly it physically hurt.

But that was never going to happen. Not until Shakar was dead.

CHAPTER 22

After another eight days of hard riding, Alyx and her escort rode through the gates of her family home. Bluecoats from her father's private detail were posted at the front gates, and a quick touch of magic told her several more were scattered throughout the gardens and fields of the property. Delight leapt in her at this discovery—her father was home!

All of the estate's grooms emerged from the stables at the arrival of eight mages and five Bluecoats. Henri came straight over to Alyx and Tingo, as always.

"Magor-lier, welcome home." He took the stallion's reins once Alyx had dismounted, calming the high-strung horse with a light touch and an affectionate word. "You should know me by now old man, so stop your fussing."

"It's good to see you, Henri. Can I assume from all the guards about that my father is here?"

"Yes, he is. Go on inside, I'll take good care of Tingo for you."

The mage warriors of her detail apart from Tarrick and Adahn dispersed to join the Bluecoats guarding the property. Tarrick would arrange for mages stationed in the city to replace them so they could get some rest, but in the meantime, her safety was the priority. Well-practiced, Alyx ignored the unease that caused. It didn't matter how deeply she hated it. *It is necessary.*

"We'll report in at the barracks, Magor-lier." Casta saluted.

"Do that, and while you're at it, take a few days off," she told him and Nario. "You deserve a break, and I'll have plenty of guards while I'm in the city."

Nario grinned. "See you at the wedding. We'll be the ones trying not to look bored."

Her legs and back ached from days in the saddle, and she was glad to reach the door and be greeted by Safia.

"Lady Alyx." The old man's face creased in pleasure. "We've been looking forward to your arrival. Your father is in his study. Can I take your cloak?"

She gave him a warm smile in greeting. "Thank you, Safia."

"You've been riding a long way—I'm sure you could do with a mug of cook's cold apple cider?"

"That sounds perfect, thank you." Alyx turned to Tarrick and Adahn as Safia left. "You two check the house or whatever you need to do. I plan to stay in for the evening, so you can stay here or head into the city to check on things, it's up to you."

Tarrick smiled. "I'm bushed, so I think I'll stay here once I organise a fresh mage detail for you. I'll ask Safia to set up a room for me. See you in the morning."

"I'll do the same," Adahn added. "Good night, Magor-lier."

Alyx found her father sitting in a chair by the fire, reading a book and sipping on his own mug of cider. At fifty-three years old, he was getting too old to be travelling constantly back and forth from ShadowFall Island, but he disagreed. A nasty fall while training potentials earlier in the year had left him with two broken ribs, forcing him to stop for a while.

He chafed at the lack of activity, but had regained full health after some months of proper rest. When he wasn't on the island he spent time in Alistriem, contributing heavily to all their strategic planning. Alyx wasn't sure what any of them would have done without his steady, sharp mind helping them run things and keep Rionn whole. Sadness and guilt twinged whenever she thought about it—all those years while she grew up he'd had to hide what he was, the finest Taliath of his generation. And all for her.

"Aly-girl." He smiled and placed the book down so he could rise to wrap her in a warm hug. "You made it."

"I did. I've been riding for what feels like forever. How long has it been since I was here last? Six months?" She dropped into a chair with an exhausted sigh. "I feel old."

"You're only twenty-four." He laughed.

"Right at this moment, I feel much older than that, Papa." She let her head fall back against the chair and closed her eyes. Rest, finally.

When she opened her eyes again, it was to study her father carefully—the rest of her relaxing fully when she saw that his gaze was sharp and his physique had filled out again. "How are those ribs?"

"They're fine," he said pointedly. "They've been fine for months. In fact, I'll be heading back to ShadowFall soon."

"Papa—"

"Save it," he said. "It will only be a short trip, but I'm a Taliath. I need to do more than just sit here and advise the king."

"You do an excellent job of advising," she said. "And sometimes that's more valuable to us than training Taliath, especially now there are others to help."

He gave her a look. "You remember how you felt that year you were hiding from Shakar, cooped up and unable to go out and do anything. It's no different for me. Being older doesn't change that."

"I do remember." Alyx sighed. "I just don't want to see you get hurt again."

"I won't."

Changing the subject, she moved to her next priority. "Is Ladan back yet?"

"No, but I had word from him today. He should be here later tonight, if not tomorrow sometime."

There was an unmistakable note of pride in Garan's voice and Alyx eyed him, a little smile curling at her mouth. "Should I be experiencing sibling jealousy?"

Garan laughed again, genuine amusement rippling through it. "One child the head of the mage order, the other head of the Taliath. I think you're about on a par, Aly-girl."

Her smile widened. "Yeah, he's done good, my big brother."

"As have you."

"I try. Sometimes I feel like everything is just one step forwards and two backwards, but I'll keep trying."

Garan nodded soberly. The Shiven army had finally breached Rionn's northern border almost a year previously, and now every month they inched further and further south. The Rionnans fought back with everything they had, taking advantage of the naturally difficult terrain of forest and mountain, but still they lost ground with each passing month. That wasn't even the biggest problem they faced, it was merely a symptom of the true issue—Shakar's existence.

The darkmage had proven a wily quarry. For reasons Alyx didn't fully understand, he had avoided direct battle with the mages, either the council's or hers, and remained behind the scenes in Shivasa, helping their army progressively invade the rest of the continent. Any time they got an inkling of where he might be, he moved. It was frustrating beyond measure, because until Shakar was found and destroyed, the war wouldn't end.

Even the occasional nightmare he tormented her with failed to help. He continued to alternate between tempting her to join his side and outright enjoyment of his power over her. He never gave her an indication of where he was or what he was doing, and every time she tried to subtly use magic to find out, he would effortlessly quash her. All the nightmares succeeded in doing was reinforcing how unlikely it was she could ever defeat him in a mage battle.

Still, Rothai hadn't given up, his determination stronger every day. She had faith he would eventually get there. And the other information he came across in their hunt was usually extremely valuable—like the breaching of the Tregayan borders.

They also now knew the likely strength of Shakar's mages. While he had the full Shiven army at his disposal—Alyx often wondered if he'd done to the Shiven leader what Casovar had done to Cayr's father—Rothai was confident his mages didn't number much more than seventy or so. A not inconsiderable number, but one that could be matched with her own army of mages if it came down to a straight-out fight.

"How did things go in Sandira?" Garan asked.

"About as we expected."

"Hmm," he said thoughtfully. "Maybe Ladan or I should travel there to speak with the emperor. You said that he holds a lot of respect for the Taliath?"

"That's true, but I don't think anything short of an invasion of Zandia is going to change his mind, unfortunately. It doesn't help that he distrusts mages so strongly." Alyx sighed and rubbed tiredly at her eyes. "We should discuss it with Cayr, though. It might be worth trying."

"The news from Tregaya isn't good either," Garan said. "I assume you've heard of the rapid advances the Shiven army has made?"

"I did. What is the latest on that?"

"We're waiting on further information—it's hard to get anything through from Tregaya these days. For the moment I believe Carhall is still safe, but the Shiven army is inching closer every day."

She sighed. "Slowly but surely, Shakar is getting what he wants."

"He hasn't got it yet, and he won't." Her father squeezed her hand. "Because of you, and your brother, and everyone who fights with you."

She found a smile for him. "We're certainly doing our best."

A comfortable silence fell, and Alyx allowed her eyes to slip closed again, relaxing into the soft crackle of the fire and the warmth and comfort of the room. The knocker at the front entrance echoing through the house had both father and daughter sitting up straight.

Sore muscles protesting, Alyx leaped up from her chair and strode through to the entrance foyer just as Ladan came through the front doors. The smile that spread over her face was unreserved, and her father's recent words of pride echoed through her thoughts.

Both Alyx and her brother had worked long and hard to bring the mage and Taliath orders back together to fight Shakar. There were now ten trained Taliath under Ladan's command, and another seven in various stages of training on ShadowFall Island. Not one had been killed by the Mage Council or Shakar—Alyx, Ladan, and their father had seen to that.

"Aly-girl." Ladan's hard face softened in a smile as they met in the middle of the foyer. He picked her up and hugged her tightly, spinning her around in the air before setting her down gently.

"I missed you, big brother." She beamed up at him.

"Me too. I'm glad you could make it."

"You were almost late," she pointed out.

He shrugged. "Nobody would have noticed."

"I think someone might have noticed that you were late for your own wedding."

Ladan's smile widened, and Alyx was still astonished by the happiness in her brother's eyes on the rare occasion she saw him these days. Her heart almost burst with joy for him. She still remembered a time when he'd barely smiled, let alone laughed or looked joyous.

"Dawn's good for you," Alyx said, hugging him again. "I'm happy for you both."

"Speaking of whom, is she here?" he asked. "I haven't seen her in two weeks."

"Not here, I'm afraid. But I'm sure as soon she hears that you're back in the city, she'll come running."

His mouth twitched. "I suppose I'll have to make do with you, then, little sister."

"Make do, is it?" She raised eyebrows at him.

"That's right." He slung an arm around her shoulders. "Don't you know how annoying little sisters can be?"

"Not as annoying as big brothers, I'm sure."

"Ladan!"

Their father appeared, and, Alyx noted with relief, walked easily and gracefully without a trace of pain. Ladan smiled a genuine welcome and the two men hugged tightly.

"Safe trip?" Garan asked.

"More or less. I came straight from ShadowFall Island."

"I'm glad. Alyx just arrived, too. Why don't we have an early dinner, and you both can relax for the evening?"

"Sounds good to me." Alyx linked her arm through Ladan's, the hilt of *Mageson* poking her in the ribs as they walked to the dining room together.

Alyx sat up far too late with her brother and father that night, talking and sipping at steaming glasses of potent cider. At some point after midnight she realised that she was far too comfortable and inebriated to move from the chair to go to bed.

They left her there asleep, and she woke in the morning curled in the chair with a blanket draped over her. Stretching, she groaned at the stiffness of her muscles, and tossed off the blanket so she could rise and stagger upstairs to the bathing room.

A warm bath helped her aching head and sore limbs, and when she stepped outside she was met with a rising sun and warm breeze. She smiled at the evidence of summer in Alistriem, and some of her inherent weariness dissipated.

The mage guard by the door greeted her, brisk warmth in her voice. "Good morning, Magor-lier."

"Tari." Alyx smiled. "How are you, it's been a while?"

"I've been well. Back in Alistriem after two months up north near the border. It's nice to have a break."

"I'm sure it is," Alyx said in sympathy. "Are the other guards around? I'm going to walk over to the palace."

"Won't be a moment." Tari raised her fingers to her mouth to give a short whistle. Mages quickly appeared from nearby, all offering a cheerful greeting—it seemed the weather had lifted everyone's mood. Apart from Tari, Alyx didn't know any of them very well, but answered their greetings warmly. Once they started walking, however, only Tari remained at her side.

The palace hallways were mostly empty so early in the morning, and Alyx and her detail didn't run into anyone as she made her way to the office of Rionn's lord-mage.

In the brief times she made it back to Alistriem, there was always far too much work that had piled up while she was away. Being the head of a disparate group of mages brought with it far more administrative work than she'd ever imagined possible. Then she often had to travel into Tregaya or Zandia to meet with her mages there, or attend meetings with the council. Her trip to Sandira, although important, had taken valuable months of her time.

It was a good thing she never slept much. As it was she never had time for anything in her life but the duties that came with being Magor-lier. It made her doubt the endless cycle of moving and fighting would ever end. The weariness that thought brought was quickly dispelled by the sight of Dawn working at one of the tables by the window.

"Well, if it isn't the bride to be!"

Dawn looked up, a wide smile breaking out over her face. "Alyx! I was worried you might not make it."

"You didn't think I would have missed your wedding?" Alyx said, hugging her best friend fiercely.

Dawn laughed. "I never thought in those first days at DarkSkull when we were dreaming about your royal wedding to Cayr, that *I'd* be the first to have a court wedding."

"I don't think *any* of us did." Alyx chuckled.

Dawn mock-frowned. "And why hasn't there been a wedding for you, Magor-lier? Don't you have a responsibility to pass on the line or something?"

Alyx looked away, keeping the smile pasted on her face. "I think I'll let Ladan take care of continuing the family line."

"Thank you." Dawn rolled her eyes. "Seriously though, Adahn absolutely adores you, and I know you like him."

"And how could you know that?" Alyx scoffed. "I haven't seen you in months, and that was only for a few days. Before that it was three months between visits."

Ladan scowled as he entered the room. "Adahn is a sheep's brain."

"Thank you, brother dearest." Alyx smirked at Dawn and dropped into a chair with her coffee. She was suddenly overwhelmingly grateful for her brother's arrival.

"He's not a sheep's brain, Ladan. He's a powerful warrior mage," Dawn said, serious in the face of their frivolity. "He's a good man, Alyx. I think he could make you happy if you'd let him."

Silently urging her brother to jump in again, Alyx tried to brush her off. "He's my subordinate. It's not appropriate."

"Rubbish. He's one of your senior mages. How is that inappropriate?"

"Did Tarrick come with you yesterday?" Ladan asked, neatly changing the subject. Alyx leaped on his assistance with alacrity.

"You think he'd let me travel here alone?" She snorted. "Yes, he came with me. He was still sleeping when I left this morning, but I'm sure he'll be here the moment he wakes up and realises I'm not there. Adahn and the Bluecoats came too, though I've given them some well-deserved time off."

Laughter rang out from the hallway, heralding the arrival of Tarrick, Cario, and Jayn. Jayn had become somewhat of a personal assistant to Cario, who held Alyx's authority when she was gone and ran things on her behalf.

"Alyx." Jayn beamed. "Welcome back."

"Thank you." Alyx gave them quick hugs. "Are you both well?"

"Busy but good." Cario gave his characteristic shrug. "Glad to have you back, Magor-lier."

"Magor-lier, Lord-Taliath, it's good to have you both back." General Sparkish appeared at the door. "The king asked me to pass on his apologies. He promises he'll be back in the city by this evening."

"Good." Tarrick clapped his hands together. "Now, should we get down to business?"

Alyx nodded and they gathered around the table in the centre of the room. The surface was covered with a map of Rionn, Tregaya, Zandia, and Shivasa.

Small red pins outlined the ever-shrinking borders of Rionn, and blue pins did the same in Tregaya.

"He still hasn't moved against Zandia?" Tarrick asked.

"No," Sparky replied. "Not even close."

"If he's smart, he'll wait until he has Rionn and Tregaya firmly under his control before he tries for Zandia," Ladan said.

"Which doesn't help in trying to get the Zandians to join us," Alyx said, relaying her lack of success with the emperor.

"I'm sure Shakar is as aware of that as we are," Adahn pointed out.

"You'd think that would make the emperor more willing to help us," Sparky grumbled, not for the first time.

"Look who I found wondering the halls." Garan's voice addressed them from the doorway.

"Finn!" Dawn squealed in excitement before rushing over to the wiry mage and throwing her arms around him.

"It's good to see you too, sis." Finn grinned. "I wouldn't have missed your wedding for the world."

"Join the party." Tarrick waved Finn and Garan over.

A few boisterous moments passed as everyone greeted each other and quickly caught up. Even Ladan smiled as he slapped Finn on the back. Alyx hugged the healer mage tightly, beyond glad that all her friends were together for the first time in so long.

"How are things going in Tregaya?" Ladan eventually brought them back on topic. "The last I heard before leaving ShadowFall was that the Shiven had breached the border and were marching on Carhall."

Sparky looked up from the map. "The latest scouting reports came in yesterday. The Shiven are moving slowly, and being careful to shore up their rear. We estimate they're still some weeks away from reaching the capital."

Alyx sighed. "I can't believe things changed so rapidly while I was in Sandira."

Cario's eyes narrowed. "That's not as much progress as I would have suspected from the last scouting report."

"The militia defences are proving tougher the closer the Shiven get to Carhall," Sparky said.

"That might have something to do with the new commander Parja mentioned," Alyx said. "He seemed confident this person would hold the city against the Shiven. It might even be a warrior mage, with the success he seems to be having."

"Should we send aid?" Tarrick asked.

Adahn opened his mouth, but Alyx spoke before he could, shaking her head. "I rejected the council's request at the meeting. I'm not willing to trust them until they're honest with us. They were hiding more than the fact that Carhall is under direct threat."

"Like what?" Dawn asked.

"I don't know," she said, frowning. "But there was something..."

"There is little we could do to help even if we wanted to," Sparky said. "We don't have enough soldiers to spare more than a token force to assist."

"I could send them a couple of Taliath?" Ladan offered. "That might help them hold out a little longer."

Alyx looked at her brother. "I don't trust having Taliath anywhere near the council. The Tregayans have always been allies, and I hate to abandon them to defeat, but it's too risky."

"Magor-lier, I know you're already aware of my views on this, but there's something else you need to consider," Adahn spoke up firmly. "The mages that follow you have friends and family who still work for the council. It's not only me that thinks we should help them. Leave them to their fate, and you risk losing *your* mages."

She considered that, sharing a look with Tarrick. Adahn was popular amongst her mages, his easy charm and pureblood family making many ex-council mages inherently comfortable with him, and by extension, more comfortable following her. If he said this was how they felt, he was likely right.

"Adahn, even if I wanted to, there's not much I can do. Our warrior mages are on ShadowFall or the north of Rionn. I can't afford to recall enough of them to make any difference to the situation in Tregaya. Those in the mine in Tregaya are teachers or too young or old—I won't send them out to fight."

"You could recall the mages from ShadowFall. The Taliath are back in the world, you've done what you set out to do. If they are true allies of ours, they should be able to look after themselves."

"He has a point," Ladan spoke, clearly reading the look on her face and trying to forestall her temper.

"You forget that I'm trying to build a new mage order, not just survive this war with Shakar," she told Adahn coldly, ignoring her brother. "The Taliath potentials deserve our protection, and they will have it."

"At the expense of the lives of mages?" he pushed.

"Yes," she said clearly. "Because mages are no more important than anybody else that lives in this world, Adahn. If I haven't made that clear to you by now, then I don't know why you still follow me."

"You've made it clear, Magor-lier," he said steadily, blue eyes meeting hers. "But it's going to take more than a handful of years to change thinking that is generations old."

Finn unexpectedly came to her defence. "I agree with you, Adahn, but change has to start somewhere. As the leaders of the new way of doing things, we have to set an example with our behaviour and actions. We have to think beyond just winning this war."

"All right." Adahn smiled, the intensity vanishing from him in a flash. "My piece is said, and I accept your words."

"On that cheerful note." Alyx matched his smile, hoping he truly meant it. "Unless there is anything further that we urgently need to discuss, I suggest we break until after the wedding. I think all of us could do with some time to rest and not think about war and Shakar."

Her suggestion was taken up with alacrity. While the others rose to their feet and milled around, making plans for catching up before the wedding, Alyx caught Finn's eye. He gave her a little nod.

"Will you come home with me, Alyx?" Dawn asked, eyes shining. "I can't wait to show you my dress."

"I have a couple of things to do, but I'll be over soon," Alyx promised, excited by the thought. She wondered what wonderful creation Sorin had come up with.

Eventually all but Finn had gone. He stood, stretching, before walking over to stand by the window that looked out over the garden. Alyx went to join him.

"Your shield's up?" she murmured.

"Always," he replied, then gave her a little smile. "He's moving on Carhall—just like we hoped."

"A lot earlier than expected," she pointed out.

"This was never an exact science. There are going to be other miscalculations."

She nodded, unable to help the little smile on her face. "You know what this means?"

His green eyes flashed. "It means we can start implementing our plan. Now we just need..." His voice trailed off, there was no need to say it aloud. They both knew. He frowned a little. "We need to be careful of what Adahn was saying—our mages will be crucial to success. Even if our crazy plan works, if we lost them, it would all be for nothing. With his mages, Shakar can rebuild."

"They've made a choice to join me, knowing everything I stand for. And if the council doesn't do something to help themselves, well, all their mages might soon be mine anyway. There will be no alternative for them."

Finn nodded agreement. Sometimes it seemed as if the destruction of Shakar was such a mammoth task it could never be done. Sometimes she wondered if the road she was on would ever end. But sometimes, just once in a while, she thought about the little steps they were taking, and she had hope.

CHAPTER 23

Being both lord of Widow Falls and now-acknowledged heir to Garan Egalion, there was no avoiding a sumptuous court wedding for Ladan when he'd announced his betrothal. Still, he and Dawn had managed to limit the guest list for the actual ceremony to those that could fit in the smaller of the two palace halls.

Alyx admitted that Nario wasn't wrong—the thing did drag on—but she was so happy for her brother that she barely noticed. He looked so tall and handsome in his finery, so much like their father, and Dawn was more beautiful than any bride Alyx had ever seen.

The celebration following the wedding was a much more exciting affair. The great ballroom of the palace in addition to all four lesser ball rooms were opened wide for everyone in the nobility to attend.

"I remember a time when you couldn't wait to be standing up there yourself," Cayr said later, as they sat watching the dancing together. Her gaze had been on Ladan and Dawn dancing—Ladan tilted his head close to his new wife to hear something she was saying, before smiling and whispering something in reply. Whatever it was, Dawn's face lit up—but Alyx shifted her attention away from them to give Cayr a sheepish smile.

"I think I was more excited about the dress I would wear and the perfect shoes and the fact everyone would be watching me," she admitted. "It's been a long time since I've had those fantasies."

"They look happy, don't they?" he said, a touch of wistfulness in his voice.

"They do." Alyx smiled. "We haven't had a chance to talk since I got back. I missed you."

His blue eyes brightened a little at her words. "I missed you too. Sorry I couldn't make it to the meeting yesterday morning. Sparky tells me the emperor wouldn't agree to your latest request for alliance?"

"No, and I don't think he's going to change his mind anytime soon," she said. "However, this is a wedding, and we should leave talk of Rionn's impending doom until tomorrow."

"Impending doom?" Cayr raised an eyebrow. "Perhaps we could put that off until next week?"

Alyx chuckled. "I do as my king commands."

A comfortable silence fell between them as they idly watched the dancers. Even Alyx's father was up dancing with Sparky's wife. She took a sip of her wine, an amused grin spreading over her face when she spotted Nario, standing at attention with another Bluecoat at the main entrance. He looked horribly bored.

"I've been thinking of marrying recently," Cayr mused.

Startled, Alyx almost spat out her mouthful of wine. She hadn't even known he was courting anyone, let alone thinking of marriage. "Really?"

"Really." He nodded, the look on his face telling her how serious he was.

She cleared her throat, putting down the glass and giving him her full attention. "Do you have a particular candidate in mind, or is this just a general desire that has come upon you?"

Cayr's gaze was back to the dancing, his hands toying with the edge of the silk tablecloth. Eventually he took a breath and turned to meet her eyes.

"I'm going to marry Jenna, Alyx."

It took her a full moment to register that her mouth was hanging open as she stared at him in slack-jawed astonishment. "Excuse me?"

"Which part didn't you hear properly?" he asked dryly.

She flashed him a scowl. "To be clear then, you're talking about Jenna Aridlen? Adopted daughter of one Lord-Mage Casovar?"

"Jenna has changed a lot, you know that," he said patiently. "She's done her best to make up for her father's mistakes, even though she's not to blame. All these years she's protected me, never once asking for recognition."

"That's because it was safer for her that nobody know she's a Taliath."

"No." There was a note of finality in Cayr's voice. "She's become a close friend. I trust her, and I'm asking you to trust me."

She frowned. "That hardly sounds like a declaration of undying love."

Cayr's face clouded over. "Well, undying love seems to me to cause much more pain than it's worth."

Alyx flinched, heart sinking. She'd never stopped feeling guilty for what she'd done to him. "I'm sorry, I didn't mean to—"

"No, I wasn't aiming that at you." He sat forward earnestly. "I told you years ago that I accepted what happened between us, and I meant it."

She studied him, trying to tell if he was being honest. "But Jenna of all people? You'll face mutiny from your court—and not just because she's the adopted daughter of a traitor. She has no noble blood, no standing. You're the king of Rionn, you need to think about marrying for strategic advantage. Doesn't Mastaran have a niece our age?"

"Says the young noblewoman who would have married an illegitimate, half-Shiven Bluecoat captain!" Cayr countered.

She gasped as if hit, and remorse flooded his face. "I'm sorry, I didn't mean to—"

"He's been gone three years." She waved off his concern, quickly and neatly shoving her emotions back into their box. "And while you are correct, I am not the king of Rionn. The court would have been scandalized and probably ostracized me, but that's the worst that would have happened. You could face unrest amongst your nobles."

"So? We might not even survive the next year. I'll fight tooth and nail to protect Rionn, but the odds are against us. We've already lost people we love. Marrying Mastaran's niece won't help us defeat Shakar or Shivasa, and while I would give anything for my country, I want my own little piece of happiness."

Alyx stared at him. "You love her."

"There is a reason I chose her to marry." He huffed in irritation.

"Have you asked her yet?"

"No." A troubled look crossed his face. "We are close, but I don't think she's aware that I... and I'm not even sure that she—"

"She does." Alyx didn't even hesitate. Whatever her personal feelings on Jenna, Cayr's happiness was all that mattered.

His head shot up. "How do you know that?"

"Women's intuition." She grinned at his scowl, but then sobered. "She burns to avenge her parents, Cayr, and she places the blame for their deaths squarely at Shakar's feet. And she's a Taliath, a powerful warrior."

"I know all that. So what?"

"So she chose to stay here, with you, for the past three years. Doing nothing but ensuring your safety. She could have been out fighting with me, taking her revenge. But she stayed." She smiled a little. "You don't do something like that for a friend, or even a king."

A wondering smile spread across his face as he processed her words, joy lighting up his eyes. "Thank you. You didn't have to do that."

"Of course I did. You're my dearest friend and I want you to be happy."

Cayr leaned closer. "I want you to be happy too."

"I'm happy enough, thank you."

"Oh, Alyx," he said, and his voice ached with sadness. "I know you. You still grieve his death. Deep down, you haven't moved on, you haven't stopped loving him, not for one second."

She stared at him, utterly torn open by his words. *Too much.* "Why would you say that?" she whispered.

"Because it's the same for me." His voice broke, and he cleared his throat before continuing. "He was a part of me, just like you are. We *belonged* to each other in a way that nobody else ever can or will."

She swallowed, pushing aside his words and what they made her feel. Unable to sit any longer, she rose from her seat. "I think I'd like to dance. I'll see you later."

He didn't try to stop her.

Adahn looked up as Alyx approached, one eyebrow raised in query. He looked handsome and debonair in his court finery—as at ease amongst the nobility as he was amongst the mages.

"Dance with me?" She held her hand out to him.

His lips quirked in a smile and he took it. "I wasn't afraid to ask you."

"Is that right?" she asked, allowing herself to be led onto the dance floor.

"I was, however, a little afraid to approach the king of Rionn and ask his best friend to dance." Adahn's smile widened. "I thought there was a definite chance of being imprisoned in the palace dungeons."

She raised an eyebrow. "I wasn't worth risking the palace dungeons?"

"Well... to be honest no."

They both laughed. It felt good to laugh. "At least I know where I stand."

"There are, however, circumstances where I might be encouraged to risk the palace dungeons for you."

"And what might those be?"

He pulled her a little closer. "I know you're the Magor-lier, but... I more than just like you, and I think we could be good together. I would never hurt you."

His face was uncharacteristically earnest as he waited for her response, his hand warm where it rested on her hip. He *really* was handsome. It was on the tip of her tongue to refuse him, but then Cayr's words came back to her. They weren't true. He was wrong. "Adahn, we—"

She broke off as a servant materialised discreetly at her side, bowing slightly before offering a folded note. The writing on it was unmistakably Brynn's, though it was messy and the paper was crumpled. Was that *blood* splotched on one corner? Worry swamped her.

"What is it?" Adahn asked

"Brynn. He needs to meet with me. He's on his way to my house."

"Do you want me to come with you? At the very least, you should have a guard."

She shook her head. "The city is so heavily protected tonight I don't think I need a protection detail just to walk across the palace gardens home, and there's no use both of us missing the party. Stay here and I'll find you when I get back."

"I'll hold you to that." His gaze was warm and concerned, affection filling his voice. Impulsively, she leaned up and pressed her mouth to his in a soft kiss. He started in surprise, and she smiled as she pulled away and left him staring after her.

Worry for Brynn replaced her uncertainty over kissing Adahn as she left the ballroom. Not sure what she would be facing, she ran for the mage offices to change out of her ballgown.

Once changed, she briefly debated contacting Tarrick to ask him to come with her, but didn't want to interrupt anybody else's fun, and if Brynn's news was urgent, she could spoil their evening then.

"Alyx!"

Alyx turned as a voice hailed her from behind, a smile lighting up her face at the sight of her godfather. Astor spent a lot of time riding between Alistriem and the border on Cayr and Alyx's behalf and she'd been disappointed he hadn't been back in time for the wedding. He still wore his travelling clothes and his jaw showed a few days' worth of silver stubble. "You made it!"

"Just barely." He returned her hug. "As you can see, I'm not quite dressed for a party."

"I'm sure nobody will notice," she assured him. "Plenty of wine has been consumed."

"Then I'd best get in there before it runs out. What's your excuse?" He gestured to her lack of formal clothes.

"I've just had word from one of my mages arriving in the city. It sounded important. I'll try and come back before the party is over."

"All right, I'll let you go. I need to go back to the border in a few days, but try and find some time for your godfather before you leave Alistriem, will you?"

"Absolutely. Now go and have some fun." She smiled as he kissed her cheek before continuing into the ballroom.

Safia met her at the front door, offering to bring drinks when she explained that Brynn was coming. As with most people Brynn ever met, Safia adored the young man and always blanketed him with food and attention when he came.

"It's late, Safia, go back to bed. Brynn and I can look after ourselves."

"Yes, Lady Egalion." He bowed.

The house was dark, the entrance foyer lit only by two wall sconces either side of the front doors. Alyx went to the kitchens to get a jug of cider and some mugs and was just re-entering the foyer when the door opened and a cloaked figure entered. Smiling, she placed the tray on a small table and walked over into the pool of light cast by the flickering sconces.

"Brynn, I hate to tell you, but you didn't quite make it in time for the wedding," she teased. "I don't think Dawn plans to forgive you anytime soon."

He didn't reply immediately, and Alyx frowned as he reached out a hand to lean against the door while using the other to pull back the hood of his cloak.

"Brynn? What happened?" she demanded as soon as she caught sight of his face. His eyes were sunken and a dark bruise coloured the left side of his jaw. Now that she was closer she could see that there was a gash in the right arm of his tunic, caked in dried blood. Her heart leapt in her chest.

"Alyx," he rasped. "I had to... they tried to stop me..." He shook his head, swayed alarmingly on his feet.

"Calm down." She took his arm to steady him, worry flooding her. "You need to sit and rest."

He shook his head. "Need to tell you."

"Tell me what?" Fear made her voice sharp.

"It's..." He coughed and almost fell. Alyx caught him and they both staggered. Panic started seeping through her. Brynn looked in bad shape, and clearly he was desperately trying to tell her something.

"Brynn, please, what's wrong, what happened?"

"I..." he mumbled, then his eyes flickered closed. "So tired."

There was a blinding flash and both front doors flew inwards. Both she and Brynn were thrown across the floor. Brynn landed hard, his head cracking on the marble. Alyx summoned enough magic to soften her fall and instantly rolled towards Brynn, who was out cold.

A shadow flickered over her and she turned to face it, magic flaring to life, but she was too slow. Something heavy came crashing down on her head and blackness claimed her.

CHAPTER 24

Alyx opened her eyes with a start.

Her heart thudded in her chest as if she'd been in the middle of a nightmare that was now forgotten. The cold, bumpy surface she lay on was most definitely *not* her bed in Alistriem. Adrenalin surging, she rolled quickly to her feet, hands flaring with a green shimmer. The glow punched through the otherwise dim light, revealing that she was in a cell.

Rocky walls surrounded her on three sides and a barred opening stood before her. The air was cold and dank, smelling of damp and something else she probably didn't want to know the source of.

Closing her eyes, she tried to remember what exactly had happened. It was useless. She'd been at the wedding. She'd gone to meet Brynn, and then... whatever faint recollection she had was blurred and intangible, and there was a lingering grogginess in her mind that indicated she'd probably been drugged. Which meant she could be anywhere. Panic closed over her chest—how much time had passed?

Whoever had taken her had left her in the clothes she'd changed into after leaving the wedding, but her mage staff was gone. Her heart lurched when she realised her cloak was gone too. Had she worn it back to her house to meet Brynn? Her memory teased her, offering wisps of recall, but nothing substantial enough to grasp.

Fear was useless, so she pushed it away and allowed anger to take its place. Raising an arm, she loosed a concussion ball at the bars of her cell. Instead of destroying the metal, however, her magic hit a shimmery wall and winked out of existence. Frowning, she tried again, a stronger blast this time. The same thing happened.

Switching to her telekinetic magic, she reached out to try and yank the bars from their foundations. Try as she might, however, she couldn't grab hold of them. Something was blocking her.

"Dammit!' Alyx let loose with a burst of temper, and her third concussion ball gouged out a chunk in the wall, spraying chips of stone all over the cell. The subsequent concussive burst inside the small space was deafening and Alyx winced and covered her ears, riding out the squeezing sensation in her chest.

Once the reverberations had subsided, she tentatively reached out to touch the bars. Cold metal slid under her fingertips—there was nothing tangible she could feel that could be inhibiting magic. Frowning, she tried extending her telepathic ability beyond the bars to see if anyone was nearby. Nothing.

There must be some type of mage shield surrounding the bars which was impervious to her magic. Deciding on a more practical approach, Alyx gripped the bars and gave them a good shake.

Nothing.

Unsurprised, she peered out into the corridor beyond. It looked just like the palace dungeon in Alistriem, a long corridor with cells just like hers on either side, a handful of flickering torches providing the only light. The floor was hard-packed earth, suggesting she was underground.

Who had taken her? Shakar? But why would he imprison her instead of just killing her outright? She closed her eyes and focused the way Howell had taught them when learning to erect their mental shields, running her mind back through the hazy flashes that remained of her memory.

There! Brynn had been knocked out. Someone had leaned over—she'd hadn't caught sight of their face, they'd hit her before she could focus on... a flash of black fabric swirling around a pair of leather boots.

A mage. The Mage Council.

Alyx groaned and allowed her head to fall forward against the bars. The council had taken her.

A stab of worry hit her—Brynn. He'd been trying to tell her something, but her abductors had interrupted. Whatever it was, it must have been important, possibly the reason that she'd been taken.

A door banged down the hall, and she backed away from the bars, preparing herself for whoever was coming. Her fingers twitched, searching uselessly for the reassurance of her mage staff.

When the tall, broad shouldered figure stopped in front of her cell, the momentary cheeriness she'd felt at realising it wasn't Shakar who'd taken her vanished in a heartbeat. Instead, she was plunged back into the Sandiran palace the night Dashan had died, her heart shattering into a thousand pieces, Galien's triumph and delight tearing her apart.

This man had killed Dashan and then lorded it over her. Was she burning with the desperate desire for revenge, or utterly torn apart by the grief that had never gone away? It was impossible to tell. Everything was so tangled up inside her chest.

"Well," he drawled. "I never thought it would be so many years before I saw you again."

She said nothing. It took everything she had to keep her shoulders straight and meet his dark Shiven gaze as the emotion churned within her.

He stepped closer to the bars. "I heard your attempt to escape earlier. You didn't really think we'd put you in a cell you could just blow your way out of, did you?"

"I never took you for being particularly clever," she managed. Her hands were white-knuckled fists at her side, nails cutting into her skin. The pain helped her focus. "Not that stupidity completely explains your odd loyalty to the council."

His smile faded and a flash of something almost like emotion flickered in his eyes. "They took me in when my parents abandoned me. They cared for me, they fed and clothed me, and they taught me how to become the most powerful mage alive. I will never forget what they've done for me."

Her shoulders relaxed a little. No matter what had happened, this was still Galien. The same cruel bully who'd known her at DarkSkull. Who'd tried and failed to best her a number of times. And as her fear began to fade, a cold anger grew in its place. This man had killed Dashan.

She flashed his mocking smile back at him. "Shakar is the most powerful mage alive."

"I'm sure he likes to think so. There will come a time when he will learn different."

Delusional as well as arrogant. "Well, your precious council decided it would be better to kidnap me instead of kill me. Why am I here, Galien? Where's Brynn—did you take him too? Is he okay?"

He shrugged. "They think you're useful, for now. As for Brynn, he was alive last I checked."

Alyx pushed away her worry for Brynn, since showing it would only give Galien satisfaction, and instead smirked. "Oh I see. You're not powerful enough for their liking. They want two mages of the higher order, just to be safe."

It had been a guess, thrown out as much to taunt Galien as anything, but he flinched. It was miniscule, but the reaction was there. The council *did* want her as protection. Which meant there was only one place she could be. Her mind raced to try and piece it together, but Galien's presence distracted her and she wanted to push her advantage.

"We're in Carhall, aren't we, and the city is close to falling?" she said. "And you aren't enough to stop it. That's why the council wants me."

"I'm plenty enough," he snarled, leaning closer. "And as soon as I drive back the Shiven army surrounding this city, they will see your uselessness and have you killed."

Alyx stepped away from the bars and crossed her arms. "Off you go, then. You picked the wrong side, Galien. They might not have realised it yet, but *I'm* the future of the mage order. They're quickly becoming irrelevant. I'm looking forward to the time when those snivelling old men you call a Mage Council try to kill me."

"Oh, it won't be them. It will be me," he promised. "I'll gut you like the worm you are."

Satisfied with having the last word, Galien turned and strode away. Their conversation had restored some of her confidence—he was still too easy to bait, too arrogant. What he'd done to her in Sandira... she was different now. Older. Stronger. She was a leader. He remained a minion of the council.

She told herself all those things but the doubts crowded in, trying to break her confidence. He'd had the benefit of the past ten years of tutoring by the council. Her training had been ad hoc and not always successful.

Sighing, Alyx slid down the wall and drew her knees up to her chest, resting her head on them with the intent of sleeping. There wasn't much more she could do than rest and be ready for whatever came next.

Her sleep was restless, filled with dreams of men in green falling off horses and Shiven warriors swarming over the walls of Carhall. It was impossible to tell whether they were figments of her imagination or flashes from when she'd been drugged. When she woke, it was to what sounded like shift change amongst the guards at the end of the hall. A tray of food had been delivered, containing a bowl of oatmeal and mug of water. She ate hungrily, deciding the oatmeal likely meant it was morning.

Not long after she'd finished eating, Galien re-appeared, this time with six militia soldiers flanking him.

"What do you want?" She remained at the back of the cell, eyes running over the drawn swords of all six soldiers.

"We're going on a little trip," he told her, jangling a pair of metal cuffs. "I'm going to come in there, and you're going to allow me to put these on you."

She snorted. "I'd like to see you try."

"If you try to attack me in any way, we will kill your friend Brynn."

"Brynn's here?" Alyx stepped forward, a mixture of relief and concern flooding her. "Is he all right? Where is he?"

Galien's sneer deepened. "He's here, and we'll keep him alive as long as you cooperate."

Alyx stepped back, away from the door. "Come in, then, I won't attack you."

Galien gestured for the door to be unlocked, and once it was, he stepped inside. He approached Alyx warily, but she stood completely still while he secured the cuffs around her wrists. Brynn's life wasn't worth disobeying Galien, and if she allowed him to take her out of the cell, it would give her the opportunity to study her surroundings and identify potential escape methods.

As soon as the cuffs clicked shut, her access to her magic vanished. A bitter laugh escaped her. "I see you found a use for Shakar's medallions."

"You weren't the only ones clever enough to capture them for your own," he smirked. "Melted down they can be used to make pretty much anything."

The soldiers closed around them as Galien took a firm grasp of Alyx's arm and marched her upstairs. They climbed enough stairs to confirm her supposition the cells were underground, and at the top they emerged onto the ground floor of the building she remembered clearly as the Carhall Town Hall.

People moved around them, most seeming intent on their own business, and none of them looked twice at Alyx or Galien. He led her out the front doors and down into Centre Square. She blinked, her eyes adjusting to the bright sunlight glinting off the marble paving.

The square was as impressive as she remembered, but she didn't have much time to admire the view. Galien hurried her into a waiting carriage. He closed the doors behind them, and as the carriage lurched into movement, he pulled the blinds down over the windows.

"I've been here before," Alyx told him. "I know where we are."

He made no response, so she sighed and settled back into her seat. They jolted along for some time before squeaking to a halt. Galien opened the door before grabbing her arm and pulling her out behind him. She stumbled on the step, and it took a moment to right herself. Once she did, she found herself standing at the base of one of the city's outer walls.

"This way," Galien said shortly, gesturing to a flight of steps leading up to the top of the wall.

He kept a firm grip on her shoulder as they climbed, and the militia followed closely behind, swords hovering in readiness. It was strangely amusing that they obviously considered her so dangerous. It made her wonder what they'd been told about her.

When they reached the top, an old mage and more militia soldiers waited for them. It took her a moment to place the mage, but the air of arrogance and authority that hung around him like a cloak was unmistakable. Cario's grandfather stood before her.

"Councillor Duneskal," she greeted him. "What a surprise."

"Alyx Egalion," he returned coolly. "It's been a while."

"Since I met you at the council meeting here in Carhall and heard you talk about murdering Taliath?" She raised an eyebrow. "Yes, I suppose it has been."

"Leave us, Galien," Duneskal said, and the younger mage bowed before walking away. Reluctance showed in every stiffened line of his body. He didn't like being dismissed. It made her smile.

"You always did have an unhealthy fascination for the Taliath," Duneskal commented, turning to stroll over and lean against the wall parapet.

"Because I don't condone murdering them out of hand?"

"Because you took one as a lover."

She froze. "He wasn't my lover."

"A mere technicality. It was inevitable. Fortunately for all of us, we removed that threat." He waved a hand. "That was years ago, and the past is the past."

Alyx looked away, wrestling viciously with her emotions until she had them under control. If she'd had access to her magic in that moment, she wasn't entirely sure she wouldn't have used it to kill Duneskal where he stood. "Why did you bring me here?"

"Look out there." He pointed. "See the camps, the soldiers? Shiven, all of them, and within miles of Carhall."

She stepped up to the parapet, staring out over the flat plains surrounding the city. Just over a mile to the south there was thick forest, but otherwise it was all open grass. Her heart thudded against her ribs in shock to see the encamped army filling the plains, just far enough distant to be out of the range of longbows or catapults. It was difficult to count the number of tents at such a distance, but there were at least several thousand.

"How did they get through Tregaya so quickly?" she asked.

"Mages." Duneskal pointed towards one grouping of tents right at the edge of Alyx's vision. "If it weren't for our own mages, that army would have been here weeks ago."

Alyx sucked in a breath. So many! She frowned as she stared at the distant tents, asking questions while she stalled for time to think. "If that's the case... why haven't they sent their mages against Rionn?"

"A good question."

"They want you," she murmured, feeling a stab of satisfaction despite the dire situation they were in. Finn had been right. "*He* wants you."

Duneskal nodded. "We've come to that view also."

"Why?" She rounded on him. "Why does he want to destroy the Mage Council so badly? Leaving Rionn undefeated behind him is a tactical error, and he doesn't make those."

"He's a madman." Duneskal shrugged. His words were casual, *too* casual. Once again he was lying to her. "I apologise for the manner in which you were brought here, but we gave you the chance to work with us and you refused. You left us no choice but to force your cooperation."

"You want me to save your city?" she asked.

"Carhall has never been breached. We simply need your assistance to help fight back the Shiven-trained mages."

"You have a mage of the higher order already. Why do you need me?"

"There are too many for Galien alone to defeat." Duneskal smiled.

"Where are your mages?"

"They've been deployed attacking the Shiven army as it progressed north and trying to limit the effect of the Shiven mages."

Alyx stared at him in shock. "You haven't recalled them into the city?"

"The Shiven progressed more quickly than we'd hoped." Duneskal looked slightly discomfited. "We lost our communication lines before we could recall them. Galien has contacted those still alive telepathically, but it's almost impossible for them to get back inside the city. We barely managed getting you in here. The militia are working on it."

"How many warrior mages do you have in here?"

"Just our personal guard. Maybe ten mages."

She let out a long breath. The council had severely miscalculated. No wonder they'd resorted to kidnapping her. "You need to start evacuating the city, Councillor Duneskal."

"Carhall isn't going to fall. Especially not if you agree to help us."

Swallowing, Alyx turned to survey the view from the walls. There were Shiven everywhere, camps only a mile or two from the city walls. "If those Shiven take this city, hundreds of the people living here will die. Militia will die. Do you want that on your conscience?"

"The city has never fallen, and it won't under our watch."

"I can't stop that," she said quietly. "There are too many. I suggest you start evacuating the city, save as many people as you can. Where is the king?"

"Taken north for his own safety. He left with his family a week ago."

At least there is that. "I can't stop what's out there, Duneskal. They will breach these walls," she said firmly.

"A disappointing attitude," Duneskal said. "Perhaps some time to think about it might change your mind. Galien?"

The mage reappeared at the top of the steps.

"Alyx needs some time to think. Please take her back to the cells."

She tried reasoning with Galien as they rode back through the city streets towards Centre Square. "Surely you can see the reality?" she asked him. "We both attended Master Renwick's strategy classes."

"The council knows what they're doing."

"Are you sure about that? They need to start evacuating this city before that army out there surrounds us completely."

"It is of little matter if they surround the city," Galien said. "They won't be able to breach the walls, not with a mage of the higher order defending them."

"Do you truly believe you can face down so many mages, not to mention an entire army, and win?"

"I do as I'm ordered," Galien said coolly. "I suggest you do the same."

"You're even more of a fool than I thought you were."

Nothing but silence greeted her words. Alyx looked out the window, watching the life of Carhall happening on the streets outside.

She wondered if they knew what was coming.

CHAPTER 25

Once back in her cell, Alyx paced its small confines restlessly. Duneskal's display had shaken her, but she pushed it to the back of her mind in favour of more practical thoughts—namely the likelihood of a rescue.

Ladan would be frantically trying to figure out what had happened to her, as would Tarrick and her mages. Guilt curdled in her stomach at the knowledge Ladan and Dawn's happiness had been marred so quickly.

Adahn and Astor had known she was going to meet with Brynn. But even armed with that information, Alyx wasn't confident they would work it out. They wouldn't necessarily tie Alyx's meeting with Brynn together with her abduction. And even if they did, it was likely they'd assume Shakar had taken her, and if that happened, none of them would know where to even start looking for her.

No, she was going to have to get herself out of this mess. Galien was the main obstacle to escape. If she could overcome him, she would have no trouble with any other mages in the city—especially if Duneskal had been telling the truth and there were only ten warrior mages inside the walls. Of course, if she managed to escape the cells, then she would have to get out of the city, sneak through—or fly over—the surrounding Shiven army, and get back to Rionn alone.

Leaving Carhall to its fate in the process.

Guilt niggled at her, but Alyx pushed it away. She hadn't been lying to Duneskal; she couldn't stop an entire army even if she wanted to. And even if she agreed to work with Galien, he'd never do it. Her thoughts raced around her head, too fast.

One step at a time.

The first step being her cell. Magically protected as it was, she couldn't blast her way out. The guards that delivered her food were careful not to open the doors. Maybe she could try talking to one, tell him who she was, bribe him in some way to let her out.

Her busy thoughts were interrupted when the door down the hall opened again. Stepping back from the bars, she braced herself for Galien. He appeared at the doors, the two guards behind him carrying something.

"You remember our deal?" he asked mildly.

She nodded once, sharply.

Chuckling at her forced compliance, he unlocked the door. The guards carried in an unconscious body and dumped it on the floor. Her attention was firmly on Galien in case he attempted anything, and so she didn't realise it was Brynn they'd carried in until the cell door was closed and Galien was walking away.

He lay prone where they'd dropped him, his clothes torn and dirty. She scrambled over and used her magic to help gently lift him and place him on the pallet.

"Brynn?" she asked, brushing dirty blonde hair from his eyes. There was a nasty gash on his forehead, blood clotted around it. His skin was deathly pale. He murmured and shifted slightly at her touch.

She laid a hand on his throat and used what little healing magic she had to try and help him. Despite years of working side by side with Finn, she'd only ever absorbed a fraction of his powerful healing talent—really all she could do was provide energy.

Brynn murmured again but after a while seemed to relax and fall into a more peaceful sleep. She sat back and watched him, worry and fear rising up in her like a vice. She hadn't felt this in a long time, not since... she clamped down on the emotion.

Brynn was her friend, she loved him, and he was going to be fine.

But at the same time, the anger inside her, her hatred of the council, burned even stronger.

It was dark when he finally woke, mumbling her name and opening his eyes.

"Brynn?" Alyx scrambled over to him. "How do you feel?"

"Alyx?" he murmured, blinking. "I feel terrible."

"You've got a head injury. I'm worried your skull might have been fractured. You really need to see a healer."

"I'm glad you're okay." He tried for a smile. "I thought they might have killed you."

"Did they torture you?" she asked softly.

"They questioned me." He smiled faintly.

"Why? What did they want to know?"

"There was someone there... I can't remember... he made them stop, I think." Brynn frowned again. "A mage–he took my memories."

Alyx sat back. "I'm so sorry."

"Not... your fault. I'm so tired."

"Sleep." She touched his forehead gently. "I'll watch over you."

"I really can't remember anything." It was the first thing he'd said in hours, and it broke the heavy silence that had fallen over the cell. Alyx had been half-dozing against the rough surface of the wall and jerked awake at Brynn's words.

"You look a little better." Some colour had returned to his skin, though he still looked gaunt and sickly.

"I feel a little less terrible than I did." He frowned, touching his head. "How did I get here?"

"We're in Carhall. We were kidnapped and brought here by the council. I don't remember much, and if a mage took your memories, it's unlikely you'll ever get them back. Don't tire yourself out trying to remember."

Brynn winced. "Did I imagine seeing Galien?"

"No. He's here."

His eyes wandered around the cell. "Did Duneskal tell you why he'd chosen this particular time to kidnap you?"

"Carhall is under attack." She told Brynn everything she'd seen and heard. "The council believes they can hold the city if I help Galien."

"But you can't?"

"I saw a glimpse of the Shiven army out there and he told me there are something like forty mages with the army. I can't stop that alone. I'm not even confident I could do it with Galien, even if he agreed to work with me."

"I think you're selling yourself short," he said softly.

She looked at him. "I may be powerful, but I can't save this city. The best I can hope for is to escape, and then try and help from the outside. Perhaps we can find a way to help the Tregayans flee, or at least shield them while they do."

"And the council can't be convinced to evacuate the city?"

"I tried, but Duneskal wouldn't listen. They haven't even considered the fact that Shakar might be out there with that army."

Brynn sighed and laid back down. "I'm glad you're planning on running things better when the entirety of the mage order is under your control."

"I'll make sure of it," she said quietly.

"I'm glad you plan to survive this." A smile ghosted over his face.

Exasperated, she tried not to snap. "Brynn, I'm not miserable, you know. Not like Cayr seems to think anyway. I'm just so tired. I wish this could all be over so that I could stop and try to build some sort of life for myself." Since going to DarkSkull, her life had been almost entirely dictated by the fact she was a mage of the higher order. It had restricted who she could love, what she could become. If she managed to destroy Shakar then maybe she could win herself freedom from that.

A brief silence fell between them. Brynn placed his head back down and closed his eyes. His voice, when he spoke, was so quiet that Alyx barely heard him.

"Being away from Sarah so often is a constant, unending struggle. It *hurts*. If she died, I can only imagine..."

Brynn's soft snores soon filled the room as he drifted into sleep. Alyx sat with her knees against her chest, arms wrapped tightly around them, staring into the darkness and fighting to hold on to her shield of numbness.

"How long have we been here?" Brynn asked as they ate their most recent meagre offering of food. He was sitting up, and looked a lot better than he had. Alyx hoped he was through the worst.

"I was awake for about two days before Galien dumped you in here, but I have no clue how long I was out before that. Judging from the meals, I think it's been almost another two days since then." Hopefully the council had seen sense and was evacuating the city. From what she'd seen on the walls, the Shiven would encircle Carhall soon, if they hadn't already.

Brynn nodded. "And why haven't you just blasted your way out of here already?"

She explained about the shield over the door.

"Oh," he said. "So how are we going to get out?"

"That's where you come in." She waggled her eyebrows at him.

He grinned. "I know that compared to most men, I am a giant of strength, but I don't think even I could rip out those bars."

"A giant of strength?" Alyx unsuccessfully hid her smile. "I think that 'vertically challenged' is a better description."

His mouth dropped open. "Did you just call me short?"

"I absolutely did."

He scowled at her. "How does this plan involve me?"

"You remember that Galien isn't exactly a thinker?"

"I do."

"He usually sends the guards with our food alone—he doesn't come with them."

"So, not a thinker, but a master of delegation?"

Now Alyx scowled. "I suggest that the next time a guard brings us food, you have a nice chat with him."

Brynn's smile widened as he caught on. "And perhaps ask him nicely to unlock the doors, with that useful mage talent I have?"

She shrugged. "It's a thought."

"And worth a try." Brynn chuckled. "Do you think Tarrick and the others will be on their way?"

She sighed. "If they've found our trail. Counting travel time, it has to have been at least two weeks since we were taken."

"But you're not hopeful."

"How would they have found our trail?"

Brynn shrugged. "I don't think we should underestimate them. They often get overshadowed by you, but Tarrick is pushing Rothai for strongest warrior mage alive, Cario is a master diplomat, Dawn has enough faith for all of us combined and Finn can think so logically and rationally it's scary. And that's not accounting for your Taliath brother and father."

Alyx looked over, smiled. "You're right. I've been very lucky."

"You've been very smart about who you've gathered around you." Brynn snorted. "What do we do once we're outside the cell?"

"Sneak out of the Town Hall. Sneak out of the city. Fly over the Shiven army and somehow try and find Tarrick and the others..."

"That's your plan?" Brynn's eyebrows shot skyward.

"Do you have a better one?"

"No, but I'm going to work really hard on trying to come up with one, because flying with you always makes me seasick."

"Plan away," she said, reaching out to shove him playfully in the shoulder.

CHAPTER 26

It was a long time before anyone came again with food—longer than the previous intervals, Alyx was certain. Brynn had managed several hours more sleep before a guard appeared carrying a tray with two bowls and a small jug of water.

Brynn was waiting at the bars, smiling widely. "Hello."

Even from the back corner of the cell, the sheer charisma of his magical voice washed over Alyx—he was using every inch of mage ability he had on the guard.

"Hello." The man smiled, uncertainly, as if he really wanted to, but didn't know why.

Brynn beamed back at him. "I could really use some fresh air. Do you think you could let me out for a walk?"

The guard hesitated. "Our orders are to make sure you stay in here."

"Surely a few minutes of fresh air won't hurt? I promise not to try and escape," Brynn said, a cajoling note filling his voice.

The guard's expression turned dazed. "I suppose it wouldn't matter," he muttered. "Just for a few minutes. It is pretty damp down here."

"That would be wonderful. I'll owe you one," Brynn said.

"It'll have to be quick." The guard pulled some keys off his belt and stepped forward to unlock the door. It swung open with a screech, and Alyx didn't hesitate. She leapt forward, slamming hard into the opening door and sending the poor guard stumbling backwards. Their tray of food clattered to the ground. Before he could reach for his sword she summoned her telekinetic power, ripping his sword belt from his waist and sending it flying up the corridor. It landed with a distant thump.

She used more magic to yank the dagger he wore at his belt and rap him smartly over the head with the hilt. His body crumpled to the floor.

"Heavy handed," Brynn noted. "But effective."

"At least I didn't promise not to try and escape."

"Couldn't you have saved our breakfast?" He stared mournfully at the remains of the oatmeal splattered all over the floor. "We haven't eaten since yesterday."

She was about to reply when a powerful shuddering swept through the corridor. Alyx gripped one of the bars for support as the walls rocked around them.

"What was that?" he asked.

"I have no idea. But I'm not waiting around to find out."

She set off down the corridor at a swift jog, Brynn at her heels, magic illuminating her arms as she held it ready. The other cells were empty, and they hit the stone steps leading upwards without running into anyone.

"There is a curious lack of guards around," Brynn muttered as they climbed, echoing Alyx's concerns aloud.

They'd just cleared the top step when another resounding shudder shook the ground under their feet. Alyx slapped a hand against the wall for balance, fear shooting through her. It would be beyond horrifying if the roof collapsed on them and they were trapped underground.

"That's not normal." Brynn's voice was heavy with dread.

"You don't say." She paused and closed her eyes, sending out her telepathic magic. She had to reach farther than expected before hitting a raucous cacophony of thoughts, most of them reflecting panic and chaos, and it took a while to find a mind calm enough to read what was happening. It wasn't good. Gritting her teeth, she expanded the reach of her magic.

Her eyes snapped open, fixing on Brynn's light green eyes in the dimness. "The city has been under siege since last night. Shiven soldiers have fully surrounded Carhall. The mages started their attack a few moments ago."

Brynn's eyes widened. "That's why the ground is shaking. The Shiven aren't going to breach the outer city walls without mage power."

Alyx shivered. "Everyone is so afraid. It's awful."

"Stop." Brynn laid a hand on her arm. "There's no need for you to keep picking up on all of that."

She nodded. "In better news, there were fewer minds than I expected outside Centre Square—they must have finally seen sense and evacuated most of the residents. From what I could tell, the militia are still deployed along the outer walls, but most of the minds I touched are expecting them to fall to the Shiven mages soon."

"And then they'll concentrate their defence here in Centre Square, which won't hold forever against magic either." Brynn shook his head. "The council were fools to think they could hold off Shakar's army."

She nodded. "At least we have a clear run out of the cells. All the guards have been sent to help man the inner walls around Centre Square."

"But then what?" he asked. "It's going to be almost impossible to get out of the city now unless you fly us. Can we really just leave everyone here behind?"

Alyx looked away, unable to help remembering the hundreds of thoughts filled with fear. *Damn.* "No, we can't."

"What do you want to do?"

She thought quickly. "I'll see if I can locate Galien. Maybe we can do something to hold the Shiven mages off, at least temporarily. If we can take them on together it might allow the militia left in the city to gather and fight a way through for Town Hall and the Hub to evacuate."

"The other council mages should be able to help too," Brynn added.

It might have been over eight years since she'd last been at DarkSkull, but Alyx had no difficulty telepathically locating Galien. It had been a survival mechanism, something she'd done far too often to ever forget.

She was on the verge of speaking to him when she caught one of his surface thoughts. Frowning, she delved deeper, surprised he wasn't shielding. What she saw sent any hope she had fading into oblivion. Cursing, she withdrew her magic. "Tarrick, Finn, and some of the others are in the city. Galien knows they're here and he's planning a trap. He wants to kill them."

Brynn frowned in puzzlement. "Why is he bothering with them while the city is under attack? And how did they get inside the walls in the first place?"

"I don't know!" Anxiety was creeping through her—standing still wasn't helping. "I didn't dare reach further into his thoughts in case he sensed me." She considered her options, a list that was becoming rapidly shorter. "I'm going to find Galien and deal with him before the others walk into his trap. I need you to go and find them and warn them."

"What about the attack on the city?"

"I can only do one thing at a time!" she snapped, overwrought with competing emotions. "Galien isn't going to work with me, not ever. The fact he is wasting time carrying out petty revenge when the city is about to fall... no, he's clearly lost perspective. I need to shut him down as quickly as possible, then we can do what we can for the Tregayans."

"You're sure this isn't about revenge for him killing Dashan?" Brynn raised his eyebrows.

For a moment she stared at him, unbelieving. "For the past three years I have done *everything* I can to make nice with the council and seek their help against Shakar. They tried to kill my father. They would have tried to kill my brother. They *did* kill Dashan. Yet I put aside my feelings every single time I met with them. You have no idea what that has been like, so don't you dare stand there and suggest I'm putting my personal feelings above what is best for all those people out there."

"I'm sorry, Alyx." He spoke quietly, but his face was stricken with guilt. "I spoke without thinking. Will you let me come with you?"

"Your talent will be of no use against Galien." Her voice was harsh. "I need you to find Tarrick and send them to help me. Then see if you can get to the council members and this commander of theirs. If we're going to try and help the city, we'll need to do it together."

Brynn hesitated, indecision in his green eyes, but then he nodded. "Where are they?"

She closed her eyes. Dawn was not difficult to find, and for a moment she hovered, debating whether to reach out. But no, she couldn't afford the time or energy to argue her plan.

"They're closing in on Centre Square. If you run, you might be able to catch them coming in the eastern gate."

Brynn sighed. "Tarrick's going to turn purple when I tell him you're fighting Galien alone."

Alyx found a smile for him. "Have fun with that."

"You made a promise to them. You said you would keep yourself safe."

"I've held to that promise, and I'm sending you to them now so that you can bring them to help me. I'm not being reckless. I'm the Magor-lier, and it's not Shakar I'm going to face."

Brynn hesitated a moment and then nodded. "I'll bring help as quickly as I can."

Alyx passed soldiers running down the halls as she headed to where her magic told her Galien was, but none of them seemed to take any notice of her. All looked afraid, and she didn't blame them. The mage attack on the walls was continuing, if the irregular shaking of the ground was anything to go by.

She ran lightly down a wide set of marble steps. An arched set of wooden doors stood closed at the bottom. Here she paused, taking a deep breath. Galien was on the other side waiting for the others to walk into the trap he'd set them. His shielding was down deliberately so they could find him—but it also meant *she* had been able to find him.

She was alone, with no mage staff. But she wasn't afraid. In fact she was relieved—it was finally time to end this enmity with Galien. Her magic glimmered inside her, and she reached for it, allowing it to sweep through her.

Then, she opened the door and walked through.

Another set of steps beyond led down into a cavernous militia exhibition hall. Galien stood in the centre of the sawdust-covered floor, surrounded by rows and rows of empty seating reaching up towards the roof high above.

Tall oak pillars lined the oval floor, the seating in wedges between each pillar. At the very top, a viewing gallery ran around the entire surrounds of the hall.

"Are you really going to abandon the city to the Shiven army?" Her voice rang out clearly. "What about your soldiers on the walls? The people still in Centre Square? The *council*?"

He spun, cat-like, at the sound of her voice. His eyes narrowed, but there was no surprise on his face. "I was hoping to keep you contained until I'd dealt with your friends."

"Unfortunately, they can't make it. You get me instead."

He shrugged. "I'll kill you first, then hunt the others down one by one."

She began walking down the steps to the arena. "You do realise how dire things are? Shiven mages are attacking, concentrating all their magic on the south wall around the gates—it won't hold much longer."

His head craned upwards, eyes focused as if staring through the roof up to Centre Square. "Yes, the city is under siege. There's nowhere for your friends to run, and once you're dead, nothing to protect them."

A retort was on the tip of her tongue, glib and cutting, but as she was about to utter it, she thought of those still trapped in the city. So, instead she swallowed the words and took a deep breath. "How about we put aside our differences for the next twelve hours. We fight together to push back the invading army, or at least hold them back long enough for those remaining to get out." She held out her hand, opening her thoughts to him to show her sincerity. "What do you say, Galien? After twelve hours has passed, you can try and kill me again."

His eyes narrowed, fixed on her hand, and he hesitated.

"If nothing else we could win time for your precious council to escape," she urged.

Time lengthened, stretched out, then snapped back into focus as Galien shook his head. "Nothing is going to stop the Shiven taking this city today, you were right about that," he said. "I just want to make sure you're all dead before I get out. *I* will be the Magor-lier. Once you're dead, the mages will have no choice but to follow me. Then I'll have an army to drive back the Shiven and defeat Shakar."

Damn. She was genuinely disappointed, surprising herself. But at least now she'd done everything she could. "That's supposing you kill me."

"Supposing?" He raised an eyebrow. "That's a foregone conclusion."

He struck quickly and powerfully. A gust of air swept down the hall towards her, pulling up all the sawdust from the floor into a spinning tornado. Just as quickly, she drew on her flying ability, using it to maintain control as Galien's wind swept her up towards the ceiling. At its apex, she increased the strength of her magic and broke free of the wind. It whistled shrilly in her ears as she dove towards him, eyes closed against the dust in the air, telepathic magic telling her exactly where he was.

But he had telepathic magic too. Just before she hit him, the wind died as suddenly as it had risen and in its place a wall of fire leapt into existence. Alyx dodged desperately to avoid it, almost losing control of her flight. Careening sideways, she stumbled to a landing seconds before hitting the low wall below the bottom tier of seating.

Galien let the fire die and stalked towards her. His staff was raised, the bright light of anticipation in his eyes. He wanted this. He wanted *her.* He was a fool. She summoned her magic, lifted her hands and sent concussion burst after concussion burst at his oncoming form. Green light flashed, but Galien's shield absorbed the blasts, robbing them of their concussive power. He kept moving, coming straight at her, and without a staff to defend herself, she raised her own magical shield.

He was moving too quickly to stop himself and the two shields crashed together, sending out a sonic boom. The pure visceral thrill of her power and his exploding together rushed through Alyx, and in that moment, she felt invincible.

This is what it is like when two mages of the higher order battle!

It was nothing like fighting Casovar. Then, she'd been hurt from his torture and scared—fighting him had been a desperate, instinctive affair. Galien was no Casovar. Excitement licked at her, born of adrenalin and the sweet rush of her magic flooding her body.

Alyx stepped back, flicked her wrist and yanked at his staff with her telepathic magic. It flew halfway to her before he recovered, yanking it back and attacking her mind with a vicious and unhesitating assault. But here she had the advantage—she'd defeated Casovar's attacks on her mind many years earlier, and Galien was not as accomplished in telepathy as Casovar had been. She thrust Galien from her head with every bit of strength she could muster, following him out with the intent to explode into *his* mind.

He felt her coming and launched a counter attack—two blue concussion bursts firing out from his staff. She raised a hand and matched him. Green and blue crashed together, the opposing forces enough to send another sonic boom ripping through the air. They were blown off their feet and across the open space. Alyx drew on her flying magic quickly enough to control her fall, and looked down the hall to see Galien land gently on a cushion of air.

Splinters of wood and dust rained down from above—one of the wooden beams supporting the roof had cracked almost all the way through. She spat sawdust from her mouth, then gathered her magic, shaped it, and reached out to tug hard at one half of the broken beam, tearing it free. With a roar of effort, she sent it spinning towards Galien. Flames leapt into life, burning white-hot, reducing the beam to cinders so that by the time it reached him it was a harmless pile of ash drifting to the floor.

"Is that all you've got, Egalion?" he taunted.

He called up his wind power again, this time stirring all the air in the hall into a frenzy so that Alyx's vision was obscured by flying debris. Closing her eyes, she located Galien's thoughts, then leapt upwards and flew unerringly through the gusting winds to where he stood.

She collided with him at full speed and they both went rolling along the floor, the gale still screaming around them. Galien grabbed at her, trying to get a hold on her throat. She fought as Dashan had once taught her to, moving quickly enough to keep free of his grasp while landing punches anywhere she could.

They rolled over and over. The wind shrieked, tugging at her clothes and hair, trying to distract her. She ignored it, ruthlessly drew upon her telekinetic magic to keep Galien's hands from getting too tight a hold on her. He retaliated by setting fire to her clothing. She rolled off him to douse the flame, glanced over when he didn't follow up. He crouched, watching her with a feral snarl twisting his handsome features. But he was sweating freely, chest heaving as he gasped for air. The wind had faded to nothing. He was starting to tire.

"Is that all you've got?" She threw the words back at him at the same time she launched herself towards him, using magic to increase the force and speed of her motion. Her knee slammed into his stomach, her palms shoving him down hard.

He roared in anger, the cries cutting off as she closed a hand around his throat, using the weight of her body to keep him pinned down. He threw his magic at her, but she was in a position of strength. Her fingers tightened, cutting off his breathing. He twisted and writhed, pale skin turning red as he gasped for air.

"Now you know what it's like to have someone choking *you*," she snarled at him. "And *I'm* not afraid of the DarkSkull masters catching me. This is what you were afraid of, wasn't it, the first time you saw me? You knew I was stronger, better, that one day we'd end up here! That's why you've always hated me so much."

All of Alyx's long-repressed hatred and anger swelled to life, everything she'd hidden and buried and refused to acknowledge. All the torture and bullying she'd endured from him. It gave her strength, enough to close her fingers more tightly around his throat. "You're done, Galien."

And Galien, the slow realisation of defeat dawning in his eyes, used the final card he had left to play.

"He's alive."

The thought crept into her mind, the touch of his telepathic magic sickening. She shuddered, not letting up on her steady attempt to choke the life out of him.

"Your Taliath. He's alive."

CHAPTER 27

W hat?

Her grip faltered, shock flooding her. Snarling, he used that briefest moment of distraction to hurl his body upwards, trying to break free.

She summoned magic, using pure strength to fight him off and hold him down. But her fingers loosened slightly on his throat, and her hesitation was enough. He gasped like a fish beneath her.

"I lied, and you believed me." He spat the words at her. "Your paltry magic couldn't even tell I was lying that night and you think you can defeat me. I never killed Dashan. The council took him—he's been here in Carhall all this time."

What? It couldn't be...he was lying to her again. Trying to save himself. But what if he wasn't? A gasp escaped her, a momentary slumping of her shoulders, but that was all Galien needed. She found herself flying sideways as he got the leverage he needed and used his magic to fling her away.

On instinct alone she staggered to her feet, barely avoiding the fireballs he tossed at her. Her roiling thoughts were a distraction, one she couldn't afford, but she didn't know how to still them. Galien came at her again, and she took to the air, flying up through his wind to perch on the railing of the gallery high above.

"Come down and face me," he roared. "Or I'll kill you where you are. And then I'll kill your friends. Including him."

She clung to the railing, fighting desperately to keep her focus amongst the emotion flooding her. No. Dashan. He couldn't be... it wasn't possible.

"Weak," Galien taunted.

She tasted blood on her lip from where he'd landed a punch, and her body was bruised and battered. It didn't matter—her magic was still strong inside her, and Galien hadn't been able to hide the weariness in his voice. He was taunting her because he needed to end this quickly.

She took another deep breath, fighting and clawing to bring back her focus. He'd used Dashan once before to break her. She wouldn't let it happen again. No matter the truth, all she had to do right now was concentrate on this fight. If she did that—she'd win. She'd seen the full extent of Galien's power now, and hers was greater.

Galien roared again. She remained still as he began drawing on an incredible amount of magic. Flame flew from his hands, controlled and shaped into an enormous wall of fire that stood at least six men high and ten across. He sent it at her, moulding it as it moved through the air, turning it from red hot to white hot flame. Alyx took a breath and summoned her shield.

The fire hit the shield and battered at it, flames licking hungrily over its surface, seeking entrance any way it could. Heat bled through and sweat slicked her skin. She steadily controlled the amount of power feeding into the shield, using more and more as Galien fed more of his own energy into the strength of the flames.

The shield was the weakest of Alyx's talents and the one that used the most energy. For the first time, her reserves began to drain. Fortunately, Galien didn't know that. He gave up as her shield held, the fire vanishing as if it had never been. The scent of charred wood filled her nose. The beams around her had blackened, in some places all the way through. Concern flickered in her. The roof might not hold much longer.

But the fire had taken up a considerable amount of Galien's strength. He was still standing but his shoulders had sagged and it looked like he was working hard not to sway on his feet.

Alyx dropped from the ceiling to land in front of him. They both raised their hands at the same moment. White flame flared from the tip of Galien's staff and silver-green concussive energy from Alyx's palms. Magic exploded through the room, encompassing everything in its path.

Her magic leaped and twisted with life as it poured out of her, meeting and countering the threat posed by Galien's magic. The air crackled with power too strong to be contained. The room began to disintegrate. Splinters tore from the walls and floor, spinning around in a frenzied dance. As she poured more and more power into the deadlock, another beam snapped above them and came crashing to the floor. Seats at the edge of the stadium were torn up and joined the spinning hurricane of debris filling the open space. Neither of them were holding back—they were throwing everything they had at each other.

This is the true power of a mage of the higher order. This is my power!

Dimly aware of the destruction around them, Alyx gritted her teeth and held on. They strained against each other for what seemed like hours, neither giving in, neither willing to be the first to break. Whoever broke now would die. Through the disintegration of the hall, and the flying destruction, Galien's face was clear—the familiar sneer marring his handsome features and the hate that had always been written in his Shiven eyes.

Alyx waited. She waited until she could sense that Galien had engaged every part of himself in their battle, until he had nothing left but to hold her off.

In that moment, she moved. As Howell had forced her to learn so long ago—the use of more than one ability concurrently—she reached for the one remaining whole beam in the roof above them. She almost couldn't do it. The strength required to rip the beam from the roof was close to impossible while holding off Galien. But she worked at it slowly, gritting her teeth and almost crying along with the effort, and then she had it.

Alyx focused her gaze on those dark eyes one last time. "Goodbye, Galien."

With every bit of strength she had left, Alyx brought the broken beam arrowing down on Galien's head. He didn't see it coming, didn't even know what was happening as it slammed into him and he dropped the ground, his neck broken and body crushed.

Alyx let go of her magic, staggered, nearly fell. Blackness dotted her vision as she took deep, gasping breaths. Unable to stand upright, she hunched over her knees.

Above her there was a loud, wrenching sound followed by an echoing crack. Without the final beam to hold it up, part of the roof spectacularly caved inwards, raining more splinters and flying debris onto the ground around Galien's body. Alyx dropped and curled into a ball, reaching wearily into her magic again to raise her shield. There she huddled until the crashing and tumbling stopped.

Soon there was only the faint rustling of debris that had been dragged off the floor by their battling magic settling back to the ground. After a few moments, she stood, groaning, trying to stretch her stiffened and sore body. Parts of fallen beams, stadium seating, and unrecognizable rubble were piled haphazardly all around her. A jagged hole in the roof let in bright sunlight.

"Alyx!"

The door at the far end of the hall opened and Tarrick's lanky form came running in, followed closely by Cario, Brynn and the twins. All five slid to a halt at the carnage before them, frantic gazes surveying the rubble until they landed on Alyx in relief.

She raised a hand in greeting, still too breathless to be able to muster speech. It took a few moments for them to clamber their way over to her. Tarrick was the first to get there, his eyebrows shooting skyward at the sight of Galien's crushed body.

"I told you she was doing fine," Dawn said, almost crossly.

"Yes, but..." He trailed to a halt.

"What the hell happened?" Finn asked, jaw slack as he took in the destruction around them.

"Magic," Cario said simply.

"You and Galien did all this?" Tarrick was staring, as wide-eyed as Finn.

"Yes," Alyx managed. "Was hoping... you might be here faster."

"I don't know why she just didn't sort him out like this seven years ago," Brynn offered.

"She could have," Cario remarked. "Galien was never the threat to her that he thought he was. The exhibition games showed that very clearly."

"Seems like if she had, she would have destroyed DarkSkull Hall along with him," Tarrick said in awe.

"Are you..." Alyx panted. "Everyone... okay?"

"We're all fine, but we can't say the same for Carhall," Cario said. "The Shiven had just broken through the south wall before we got here."

"I've been monitoring the thoughts of the militia commanders," Dawn said in response to Alyx's questioning look.

"How did you... find me?"

"That's a long story, and we'll tell you later." Tarrick looked at the others meaningfully. Alyx didn't miss the mutinous look that flashed across Brynn's face, but didn't have the breath or energy to demand he explain what he meant.

"Here, let me help." Finn stepped over to Alyx and laid a hand on her shoulder. Almost immediately she felt sweet energy flow through her body.

"Are you all right?" Dawn asked softly. "Did he hurt you?"

"I'm fine, just a little banged up," Alyx said. "I think I used most of my reserve of magic to kill him. Thanks, Finn, that's enough."

"We need to get up to the great hall," Tarrick said. "The Shiven army was heading straight for Centre Square—"

"—and is probably here by now..." Cario interjected.

"...and we agreed to meet the others in the Hall," Tarrick continued over him. "Ladan will bring them and meet us there."

"Ladan's here? What others?" Alyx was beginning to get her breath back and Finn's healing had helped with her energy and restoring some of her power. Clarity returned to her thoughts and she stood straighter, stretching weary muscles.

Dawn opened her mouth, then shut it again. "He'll meet us there," she repeated.

"What is going on?" Alyx demanded, before realisation flooded her. Galien's revelation, his attempt to distract her. It all fell into place in her head, like dominos in a perfect line. It was Dawn she looked to, voice pleading. "He's alive, isn't he? Dashan?"

"Yes," she said simply, reaching out to take her hand.

Alyx clung to Dawn's hand, swallowing, trying not to let the storm of emotion that was threatening to drown her come out. "He's here. He's the commander who's been running the defence of the city."

"Yes," Dawn said again.

"How did you..." Brynn ventured.

"Galien dropped that little gem in the middle of our fight. He did it to distract me, to try and save himself." Abruptly she was winded again, and it had nothing to do with physical exhaustion. Reeling, she wasn't even close to processing the news, what it meant. It was like there was some sort of block in her head, keeping her numb. She wondered if it was overuse of magic.

"Alyx." Tarrick said soberly, with the tone of voice he used when what he was saying was of utmost seriousness and gravity. "We will tell you everything, I promise, but not now. We need to move fast. While we came to get you, Ladan was fetching the council members and the remainder of the militia guard still here. We're going to get out together."

"All right," she said, accepting that. "Lead the way."

Cario was intimately familiar with the layout of the inter-connecting buildings of Town Hall and led them up from the destroyed exhibition hall into the main corridors. They were eerily empty, and Dawn explained that everyone who could fight was out trying to hold the Shiven back while non-fighters had already fled.

"Why are we meeting them in the hall?" Alyx asked.

"It was the one place all of us knew in case we got separated, and it's defensible," Cario said tersely.

They rounded a corner into a much narrower hallway, and Cario slid to a halt by a decorative copper statue. A narrow door was set into the stone beside the statue, and he reached out to yank it open.

"Back entrance," he said. "Go up, quickly!"

Alyx followed the others up a narrow staircase to emerge into the back of the hall. She stopped to catch her breath. On the opposite side of the hall, the great arched doors that marked the entrance were closed, but shaking on their hinges. The cavernous space was empty. Memories flooded back—long boring sessions of watching the council members talk, hiding up in the gallery above while they spoke of murdering Taliath potentials.

"Now what?" Alyx looked at Tarrick.

"We wait for Ladan," he said grimly.

"We didn't exactly expect the city to fall right in the middle of us rescuing you," Finn said.

"And then what?" she asked.

"There's an escape route to get the rest of the fighters out of the city. Dashan had it set up—once we're all together, he'll take us there." Cario said, then glowered at the look Tarrick shot him. "What? You think she's so fragile we can't even mention his name."

"I just—"

"Enough." She glared at them. "All our focus needs to be on this situation. Me included. All right?"

Terse nods followed, then Dawn spoke. "Shiven fighters are approaching the main doors. Their thoughts... they're using a marble statue to slam against the doors. I count maybe twenty. They think the council members are hiding in here."

"That's the way Ladan will be coming," Finn said tightly. "He won't know Cario's back entrance."

Dawn spoke again. "Centre Square is breached. It's hard to tell what is happening, so many chaotic thoughts."

"Dawn, withdraw!" Alyx said firmly, remembering what had happened to her earlier. "Restrict your magic to our immediate vicinity. Are there any mages out there?"

"No, I don't think so." The telepath's frown of concentration deepened.

Her words were punctuated by the sound of something heavy thudding into the hall doors. They shook violently, but held. Without needing to be told, Cario reached out a hand, using his telekinetic power to bolster the doors as they were hit again, harder this time.

"I've managed to distract those carrying the statue," Dawn said. "They've dropped it, but more are coming to help, and I can't hold off so many minds at once."

"What if we let them in?" Finn suggested. "Together we can take twenty or so."

"I can help," Alyx said instantly. "Maybe I could throw a shield over us."

Tarrick gave her a look. "You just fought and killed Galien, and your shielding is your weakest talent. Are you telling me you could do that and cover all of us?"

Alyx conceded with a shrug. "I still have some power left. If Finn helped me—"

"They're about to break through anyway." Brynn pointed at the ever-widening crack in the left door.

"What if we let them in, then I bring down the wall over the door?" Alyx asked Tarrick. "Then the way in will be blocked entirely and we can pick them off."

"Then how does Ladan get in?" Finn asked.

Alyx swore. "Dawn, where is that brother of mine?"

"He's coming." Her eyes snapped open. "The council members are with him, and whatever militia they could muster. Ladan thinks they were seen, and there are more Shiven soldiers on their trail. He and Dash are leading them straight here."

"Ok, let's do it. Cario, lift the bars from the doors. Let them in," Tarrick ordered, but his words were dim. All Alyx could hear was the echoes of what Dawn had said. *Dashan.* His name echoed over and over in the back of her mind.

"Alyx," Brynn said, his voice soft and gentle. Something in her face must have worried him. She shook her head, waving off his concern. *Concentrate, Alyx.*

"Heads up!" Tarrick bellowed.

Shiven soldiers came flooding into the room as one door slammed open. Cario stepped forward, using his power to divest the Shiven of their weapons one by one, sending swords and bows flying across the room and out of reach. Alyx raised her hands in preparation to launch a concussive burst.

"Alyx, wait!" Dawn shouted. "They're coming through behind."

Shuddering under the force of a mighty kick, the second door flew inwards. Then Alyx's brother, sword raised, came through the gap. Behind him huddled three men in mage robes surrounded by a handful of militia. One of the mages had telekinetic ability and was using it to help keep the Shiven away. The militia were bloodied, and all of them had wounds. But Alyx didn't register any of it.

Because running a step behind, bringing up the rear, was Dashan Caverlock.

Her numbness evaporated in a heartbeat and emotion flooded in to take its place. For a moment there was only pure, blinding joy. Then she took a step backwards, stumbling into Dawn and sending the telepath's staff dropping to the floor with a clatter she barely heard. Ladan laid into a Shiven warrior from behind, killing him before engaging two or three more warriors at once. Dashan matched him thrust for thrust. The mages ran for the relative safety of where Alyx and the others stood.

Her quick gaze recognised Duneskal, Walden, and Yirith—white faced from the effort of expending his magic—before snapping back to Dashan. He killed his last opponent and came to a stop. He turned and said something to Ladan, then his head came up as he scanned the room for any more threats. When his gaze fell on Alyx, his entire body stilled. His eyes widened, both in stunned recognition and a strange surprise, like she wasn't what he'd expected.

Then Ladan grabbed his shoulder, shouting, "There are more behind us, we have to go!"

As their eye contact broke, Alyx shuddered and turned towards Dawn, who was staring at her as if she didn't know what Alyx would do. Strangely, that gave her the ability to behave calmly.

She took a deep breath, not exactly sure what she was thinking or feeling, and right at that moment there was no time for either. "Can you sense a way out of here? If there are more Shiven behind those we just killed, we'll have to go back the way we came. Find us a path not filled with Shiven."

"I'll work it out." She nodded and closed her eyes.

"Tarrick, we need to go out the way you came in," Dashan yelled as he arrived with Ladan. The remains of the militia milled behind him.

Tarrick nodded. "Take them on ahead. Alyx and I will bring up the rear."

"Hold on and wait for Dawn to find a path!" Alyx ordered, stopping their forward progress. "There's no point rushing straight down and into an army of Shiven."

"Got it!" Dawn's eyes snapped open. "I'll lead the way."

"And once we're out of Centre Square? Then what?" Alyx asked.

"I had an escape route prepared," Dashan responded. "Whatever militia are left in Carhall will be gathering at a spot along the western wall. If we can get there, we'll break out of the city."

"What about those who couldn't make it to your rendezvous point?" Brynn asked. "Are we just going to leave them behind?"

"I've given the retreat order, most of them should be clear." Dashan spoke as if he hadn't been dead for three years, jaw clenched in familiar frustration as he snapped at Brynn. It was both maddening and perfect at the same time. There was no space for any distractions. "The council refused to budge from Centre Square because they believed it would hold. I can't save everyone. We have to go, now!"

"You're the Magor-lier. We need to get you out," Cario said, gaze firm on Alyx.

A bitter twist of nausea and guilt clenched her stomach at those words, but she accepted the truth of them with a nod. "All right, let's go."

Finn shook his head. "What about the army laying siege outside the walls?"

Dashan snapped, "we'll be relying on you mages to clear a path for us."

She refused to let her eyes linger on his face, instead turning to move as they finally headed for the stairs.

Duneskal's words brought them all to a halt. "We should stay here."

"Grandfather, this is not the time to—"

"We are mages." Duneskal cut across Cario as if his grandson hadn't spoken. "We can hold out here. We can't just let the city fall."

"There is an army of hundreds outside. You can't prevail against that," Ladan said.

Alyx stepped forward, channelling her frustration and anxiety into sharpness. "You should consider yourselves lucky I'm even bothering with you three after what you've done to me, so don't waste my time. Get moving, now."

"The Mage Council does not take orders from you," Master Walden said contemptuously.

Alyx stared at him. "Fine. Then stay."

"Alyx—" Dawn ventured but she cut her off.

"It's their choice. Go!"

Cario hesitated only briefly before following Tarrick. "You always were a fool, Grandfather."

"Mage Egalion!" Duneskal's voice thundered at her as she paused in the doorway.

Alyx stopped, turned back. "Come with me, or stay here and die. Your choice."

Duneskal hesitated further, and it was Walden who shouldered past him, looking suddenly haggard. Yirith followed suit. Contempt for both of them flashed over Duneskal's face, but eventually he too headed for the stairs.

CHAPTER 28

They clattered down the narrow stairwell and burst out into the hall at the bottom. Unlike earlier, it was now filled with running green-clad soldiers. Alyx almost collided with one of them as she exited the stairs, trying to keep up with the others. Tarrick took her arm from behind, steadying her, and then they were running again.

Dawn led the way, Ladan a step behind. Dashan hovered by the councillors, hurrying them and keeping a protective eye on their surroundings at the same time. Fighting sounded not far off. A woman screamed, her voice cutting off abruptly.

They crossed the wide hall and headed through another doorway that led into an empty room. Without hesitation, Dawn ran over to the sliding door opposite and hauled it open.

"The Shiven haven't reached this section of the building yet. We've got a clear run to the inner western wall," she said.

"Good, that's the way we need to go." Dashan shouldered past her. "Stay right behind me and let me know if we're about to run into any danger. Ladan, watch the old men."

He led the way across the small garden beyond the doorway, and from there it was a short distance to a narrow gate set into the inner wall. Then they were running through the city via a series of narrow, winding alleyways. Despite the flushed faces and staggering steps of the old men, Dashan refused to slow the pace. Dawn ran with eyes half-closed, Ladan's guiding hand on her shoulder, warning them if any Shiven approached.

The sounds of fighting filled the city around them. At one point they had to cross a main street filled with militia battling Shiven at both ends, but Dashan and Ladan merely shouted for them to keep running. Smoke billowed into the air to the south; something had caught fire and was burning strongly.

Eventually Dashan led them into a large courtyard that ran alongside the outer city wall. A small gate was set into the thick stone on the other side of the yard, though it was hard to see through the milling horses and riders—at least a hundred of them, all militia.

"The gate is camouflaged on the outside to make it look like part of the wall," Dashan explained. "My scouts have used it as a secret way to get in and out of the city."

A familiar young man emerged from the throng and saluted Dashan. "Commander!"

"Are they ready to move, Rodin?"

"Yes, sir. We were just waiting for you."

"How many got out?"

"Three full units just before the Shiven surrounded us completely. More have been trickling out at night since, as you instructed. Those still fighting in the city have orders to retreat as soon as the council members are out safely."

"Good. Send the retreat order at once. Then find some spare horses for the mages."

With that, Dashan was gone, disappearing into the mass of militia. Alyx dragged her eyes back to Rodin, suddenly realising he was speaking to her. *Focus!*

"Are your party all well enough to ride un-aided?" he asked.

"We're fine." She nodded.

"Good. If you'll wait here a moment." Rodin followed Dashan into the throng of horses and riders, returning a few moments later with horses for each of them.

Behind her, Duneskal was muttering some sort of complaint, but Ladan's terse words quieted him. Mechanically, Alyx hauled herself onto the back of a chestnut stallion. Despite her best efforts, Dashan's sudden appearance had completely thrown her, and she was struggling to keep her thoughts focused.

Dashan is alive.

The words screamed through her entire soul, but there was no time to react to that knowledge. They were trapped in a city surrounded by Shiven and facing the possibility nobody was speaking aloud—that Shakar was out there too.

Taking a deep breath, she straightened her shoulders and kicked her horse over to Tarrick. "If we're going to force our way out, I'll need to ride up front. You and Cario bring up the rear so that once I blast a path through, you can keep them from following too closely."

"And the rest of us?" Dawn asked.

"Stick as close together as you can. If things get too bad, I'll drop a shield over us, but then I'll need your strength to maintain it, Finn."

"Understood," Finn said. "I'll keep close to you."

"What if Shakar is out there?" Tarrick asked, saying aloud what had been hovering in the back of Alyx's mind.

She gave a little shrug. "We put our heads down and ride as fast and far as we can. I don't know what else we *can* do," she said.

Dashan reappeared, now mounted. "We need to go now, before they find us here and realise we're about to escape. Alyx, can you clear a path through the Shiven army once we're beyond the wall?"

She hesitated briefly before replying, his appearance once again throwing her thoughts into turmoil. *Stop this!*

"I should be able to." She explained her plan.

"Good. I'll ride up front with you, and Ladan can take the rear."

"*I'll* ride with Alyx," Ladan said firmly. "*You* watch the council members."

She glanced at her brother, startled by the suppressed anger in his voice—there was a glimpse of the old Ladan in the tautness of his features.

"Fine." Dashan wheeled his horse around and shouted an order to the gathered militia. "Everyone close up in tight formation and stick as close behind the Magor-lier as you can. Go!"

Without a word, Alyx kicked her horse out of the gate as it swung open before her. Ladan rode at her left, and the other mages and the militia followed, Dashan shouting orders for them to fall in line.

The Shiven army had completely encircled Carhall, and while many of their number had entered the city, it didn't take those still outside the walls long to spot the streaming line of riders trying to escape.

A horn blast rang through the morning air, then a second and a third as various Shiven units responded. Like a slow-moving stream, warriors began moving across the open grassy plain to cut them off. Sunlight glinted from their naked swords, their challenging shouts drifting in snatches on the breeze.

Taking a few seconds to get accustomed to the stride of the horse under her, Alyx waited until she could almost make out the features of the individual Shiven racing towards them. Then, sitting up straighter in the saddle, she took a breath, fought past her exhaustion, and let loose with her magic.

Her control suffered when she was this weary, and the concussion bursts that flew from her hand were nearly as large as the horse she was riding. They flew across the intervening distance in bright green flashes. When they struck, a massive tectonic boom exploded through the air. Shiven went flying like they were nothing but straw dolls, and Alyx had to erect her shield to prevent the backlash hitting those behind her.

As soon as the concussion wave had passed by them, she dropped the shield and sent another two bursts flying. It was enough to blow a large hole in the Shiven line. Even then, the left and right flanks reformed quickly to try and get in front of them. Gritting her teeth, Alyx dug deep for more strength, sending two more blasts to her left and right, destroying the closest of their pursuers. Behind them, more blasts went off as Tarrick waded into the defence of their rear.

Then they were through and racing south across the open plains towards the forest. Behind them, the Shiven massed in complete disarray, and relief edged her weariness. They probably wouldn't be able to pursue them immediately.

"Veer to the southeast," Dashan shouted from behind. "There's an escape route set up; supply camps, more soldiers and fresh horses."

Alyx glanced back, then reined in her horse, allowing Dashan to catch up. "Then take the lead."

He gave a quick nod as he flew past. She waited—Ladan sticking close by—while the hundred-odd militia raced by her, then urged her horse after them at the rear.

They rode as far and as fast as the horses could manage. Dashan took a handful of militia scouts and pushed ahead to ensure the route ahead of them remained clear. The rest followed more slowly to allow the injured soldiers to keep up.

Nobody talked. The relentless pace made it necessary to focus all their energy on simply staying awake and in the saddle. When they did stop to rest and water the horses, Alyx moved from her saddle to the softest place on the ground she could find to catch an hour or two of sleep before moving on again. They had a single purpose—get as far from Carhall as fast as possible.

Regular messages came back from Dashan, letting them know the best route to follow to avoid the Shiven lines. In his absence Rodin commanded the group in regular consultation with Tarrick. Exhaustion pressed down on her like a weight, and any scrap of strength and focus she had was used to help Dawn scan their surroundings for danger.

Almost a week later the terrain grew steeper, their pace slowing as they climbed what felt like an unending incline. When they finally reached the top, she was astonished to look down and see DarkSkull Hall in the valley far below them. In her haze of weariness, she hadn't even noticed they'd been climbing the northern valley wall.

Trying not to sway in the saddle, she followed the long line of horses down into the valley. Night fell as they rode, but as they emerged at the bottom, a large cluster of tents and horses grew visible. The flickering light of lanterns shone from the windows of the DarkSkull buildings that hadn't been completely destroyed in Shakar's attack.

Her tired horse stumbled to a halt behind the others in a cleared area before the steps leading up to the main hall. Someone was shouting orders, and around her everyone was dismounting. Trying, and almost failing, to keep her eyes open, Alyx threw a leg over the saddle and slid to the ground.

Her legs gave out, and she would have crumpled to the grass if she hadn't the presence of mind to grab hold of the stirrup. It took a moment for her to steady herself and then she stepped away from the horse, allowing it to be led away by an unfamiliar militia soldier.

"You okay?" Tarrick appeared, Finn hovering at his side. She waved off his wordless offer of healing energy. He looked as exhausted as she felt.

"I'm awake," she said wryly. "Which is something. Where are the others?"

"The whole group got here safely, and Dashan apparently rode in last night. I saw him and Ladan together just a few moments ago," Tarrick said. "They were heading into the old stables."

"So was Dawn," Finn added. "I gather it's being used as a meeting space."

"We're all exhausted." Tarrick looked dubious. "Maybe we should just…"

He trailed off, clearly uncertain. She was tempted to take the out he offered, to find somewhere to sleep and deal with what came next when she felt better, stronger. In all the fighting and running, there'd been no time to talk, no time for questions. But now they'd stopped running.

He was alive. He'd been alive and in Carhall for three years. She didn't even know where to begin with that. Questions crowded into her thoughts, bringing with them a tangle of conflicting emotion, a knot so confused she couldn't tell them apart.

"No," she said softly. She wasn't going to be able to rest until this was over. "We should at least take stock of our situation before getting some sleep. Come on."

The grassy area around the old DarkSkull stables was covered in orderly rows of tents. Fires had been lit outside several of these, and green-jacketed militia sat around them, talking and cooking food. The scent of grilling meat filled the air. Alyx's stomach grumbled—it had been days since she'd eaten anything more substantial than oatmeal or a hunk of stale bread.

She used a quick burst of telepathic magic as they tiredly picked their way between the rows of tents, tent ropes, horses, and people—there were sentries up in all the watchtowers and along the valley walls, mages included. No Shiven patrol would get near DarkSkull without them knowing about it.

After the magic she'd used in Carhall, even that effort left her with a dull ache at the back of her skull. Thoughts of the impending meeting sent the ache into overt throbbing.

Finn pushed through the door first, Alyx following behind Tarrick, eyes roving the interior. The open space between the rows of stalls had been filled with a long table and a scattering of crates, large pieces of rubble, and boxes that served as chairs. The surface of the table was covered with maps, and lanterns sat high on the wall above, giving the place a warm glow.

All at once she was edgy and restless, nervous energy filling her despite her weariness. There was no more battle to focus on. Nothing to use as an excuse to delay dealing with reality. Cario and Dawn sat at the table, Tarrick and Finn joining them with quick smiles of greeting that quickly faded in the sober atmosphere. Ladan leaned on one of the stall doors. Finally her gaze landed on Dashan, standing at the head of the table, one booted foot resting on a box.

Nobody was looking at the maps. Or each other.

"What comes next? Can we expect pursuit?" Tarrick spoke first, his voice determinedly casual. Alyx shot him an incredulous look—*that* was what he was going to start with?

Dashan glanced at him. "We have a good head start on the Shiven, and I had measures in place to divert any attempts to follow us. Plus, their army will be busy consolidating their hold on Carhall. I'd say we've got a couple days of safety here to rest horses and men."

"I—" Finn cleared his throat, but Ladan's patience snapped and he pushed off the stall door, angrily cutting him off.

"I'd like to know what the hell you've been doing these past three years, Dashan. Did you have a *reason* for making all of us think you were dead? Or did you just enjoy being the big man in charge in Carhall too much to let us know you were alive?"

Dashan's eyes flashed. "How about you back off and give me a second to explain. I don't need to stand here and be interrogated by you."

Ladan's face darkened with fury, and before any of them could stop it, he leapt over the table, crashing into Dashan full-force. Part of Alyx yelled at her to stop them, but the rest of her was frozen, slow to follow what was happening. Slow to react. The others at the table seemed equally uncertain.

"You bastard!" Ladan shouted as they hit the ground. "Do you have any idea—"

The rest of his words were muffled as he hauled Dashan to his feet and slammed him against the stable wall. Dashan shoved him back, but Ladan didn't loosen his grip. He slammed Dashan against the wall again.

"I didn't remember!" Dashan roared, shoving Ladan off him with enough force to send Alyx's brother staggering away. He turned to face the rest of them, chest heaving. "I didn't remember."

Alyx's eyes shot to his, because of course he was only looking at her, pleading written deep in his brown eyes. Shocked silence filled the room, but she barely noticed. She couldn't see anything but him.

"Everyone out," Alyx said into the silence. "Go. Dash and I need to talk."

"Alyx—" Tarrick began.

"Don't." She levelled him with her hardest stare. "Just go."

The mages filed out of the stables with varying degrees of reluctance. Ladan left last, the anger on his face fading a little as Dawn took his hand. When the door swung shut behind them, Dashan moved to pick up the crate that had fallen over during his scuffle with Ladan, breaking their stare.

"Dashan..." Alyx's voice broke on the word, and all of the energy that had been building up inside her suddenly drained away, leaving her limp and worn out.

He sat, smiling bitterly as he looked up at her. "Three years is a long time, isn't it?"

"Just tell me what happened. Please."

Something in her voice—the utter weariness or long held grief—registered with him, and he was up in a flash, moving with Taliath-quickness to gently take her arm. "You need to sit down. Come on, mage-girl."

The words brought tears straight to her eyes, and she allowed him to lead her over to the table and sit her down. She hadn't heard those words in so long. Had thought she would never hear them again. All at once she wanted to put her head down on the table and cry. Fighting that urge was almost impossible, and when she met his eyes, his face was equally stricken.

"You really thought I died?"

"In Sandira," she whispered. "Yes."

He nodded, pulled a box close to hers and sat down. "I woke up in Carhall three years ago as a guest of the council, and had no idea how I'd gotten there."

"You remembered nothing?"

"I knew my name, that I was a Bluecoat and that I came from Alistriem, but that was all," he said. "The council told me I was a Taliath, that I'd been badly hurt in a battle. I had a pretty nasty head injury." He pointed to a narrow white scar than ran along his hairline before disappearing into the dark brown curls of his hair. "The healers said that was what had caused the memory loss."

Her gaze lingered on his scar. Her emotions were churning, but a hint of anger was beginning to establish itself over the others. "Did you remember how you got hurt?"

"No," he said quietly, voice rich with pain. He couldn't look at her.

"You got hurt because you sacrificed yourself for me." Bitterness rang through her voice. "Because you decided all on your own that you needed to die so that I could live."

"I know." His gaze remained firmly fixed on the floor. "I remember that night. I remember everything now."

She frowned. "When did you remember?"

He finally lifted his head. "Just over a week ago, I rode out of Carhall leading a unit of scouts to explore the approach of the Shiven. We passed another unit of militia with two mages guarding a cart being led into the city—and a young woman lay bound and unconscious in the cart. It was you, Alyx." His jaw tightened, his eyes still on his hands. "And the sight of you... it all came back, all at once in a rush. I fell from my horse, and I was unconscious for hours. When I woke up, all my memories were there."

Her heart lurched. She believed him, and the thought of him remembering like that was awful. "That must have been terrible."

"The rage..." he whispered, and she glanced away as his body suddenly vibrated with it, his hands curling into white-knuckled fists on his lap. "I found them questioning Brynn, and I made them stop," he said, voice full of barely-controlled fury. This was a Dashan she'd never liked to see. "Then I got word that the Shiven were surrounding the city. I did what I could to get the residents out, defying the council's orders, and I set up this escape route."

"Tarrick and the others, they knew you were alive before I did."

"Not for long," Dashan said. "Brynn ran into me on his way to find them. They went to help you while Ladan and I went for the councillors."

At a loss, she let her gaze wander around the room. An awkward silence fell, a silence full of tension and energy and discomfort.

"You died," she said eventually. "I accepted that. It... it *stole* something from me, losing you, but it's been three years."

Dashan looked up, his dark gaze filled with despair. "I don't know why they didn't kill me, or let me die from my injuries, but I suppose by then they were growing scared and decided a Taliath might be useful to defend their city. And as long as they kept me away from you..."

Eventually she looked at him and gave a little shrug. "I don't know what to say, what to do next."

"Neither do I." He rose slowly from the chair. "Go, talk to the others. I don't think I can deal with them yet, but they'll want to know what happened. Then get some rest, mage-girl. You're going to need it."

They were waiting for her outside the barn in a worried huddle, as if in the past few minutes she might have suddenly absorbed Dashan's invulnerability. That made her simultaneously tired and sad. Everything in her longed for sleep, but they deserved to know the truth too.

"He lost his memories," she said, relating to them everything Dashan had told her. "And then Galien used his magic to convince us of Dashan's death. I was so weak after the fight in Sandira, so grief-stricken by what you and he had done, I didn't even think to..." She shook her head, voice trailing off.

"So what now?" Tarrick asked. He looked grim.

Her heart sank like a heavy stone in her chest. "I guess this is where we see how much you actually meant it when you agreed to follow me three years ago. Because I'm not changing my policy on working with the Taliath just because Dashan is back." The idea of it all falling apart again, after she'd worked *so* hard to build a new way of doing things... tears pricked at her eyes.

Their silence was a living thing, the thoughts racing through each of their heads almost tangible. Surprisingly, it was Finn who spoke first.

"I meant it, Alyx. When I agreed to the way you wanted to run the mages, I meant it. And that still stands. We'll find a way to work through this."

The healer mage was sent stumbling several steps backwards as his sister launched herself at him, throwing her arms fiercely around his neck. Alyx had to fight a similar urge, and the tears now flowed freely. She scrubbed at them.

"It's the same for me." Tarrick's face was drawn, the shadows under his eyes visible even with his dark skin, but he had a little smile on his face as Dawn finally let her brother go.

"Thank you." Alyx's voice shook with relief.

Ladan was still holding on to his anger—it must've been easier for him than the grief of learning he'd mistakenly believed his best friend was dead for so long. "You really believe him?"

"I do," she told him.

His shoulders relaxed fractionally, and he gave a little nod. Dawn took his arm and the two of them wandered away.

"The militia commanders have a tight watch set over the valley," Tarrick said. "We're safe enough here for now."

"Time for sleep." Alyx couldn't stifle the yawn that swept over her.

"Let me walk you," Cario offered. "One of the militia came by while you were talking to Dashan. I can show you where they've set us up."

She nodded, waving a farewell to Finn and Tarrick, who mumbled something about finding their own beds.

A comfortable silence fell as they made their way back through the camp. Cario led her inside the old boy's dormitory building and showed her to one of the rooms. What had once been a window was now a hole in the wall high above the bed. The stone around the edges of the hole was blackened and charred.

"Get some rest," Cario told her. "I'll find somewhere nearby if you need me."

"Thanks, Cario."

He hesitated before leaving. "I assume you know that you don't need to question my trust in you."

She gave him a tired smile. The one person she would never have to question, no matter if she bedded twenty Taliath. "I do."

Alyx slept the sound sleep of exhaustion, and when she awoke, it was to the glimmer of early dawn shining through the hole in the wall. Yawning, she sat up on the narrow pallet. Everything that had happened flooded back, and she let out a breath as if winded. Raising a trembling hand to her eyes, she rubbed the sleep out of them before hunting around for her boots.

A short exploratory walk found the old dormitory bathing room untouched and still functioning. It was temporarily empty, and Alyx took the chance to slide into a steaming bath of hot water.

The warmth soaked away some of the stiffness her body had accumulated in her fight with Galien and the long ride from Carhall. As she scrubbed her skin and hair with soap, she ruefully catalogued her myriad of bruises and scrapes—from the look of them, she was going to be sore for a few days yet.

As the blue light of early dawn turned to actual sunlight, Alyx rose from the bath and dressed quickly. Once clothed, she walked over to the doorway and lingered, a smile curling at the edges of her mouth as she spent a moment looking out at the sky and fields surrounding DarkSkull Hall.

It was the loveliest sunrise she'd seen in a long while.

CHAPTER 29

The camp was bustling when Alyx stepped outside, but what first caught her attention was the sheer number of mages in the vicinity. The first one she recognised was Adahn, hand lifted in greeting as he crossed to her. She smiled in genuine pleasure at the sight of him.

"The Magor-lier was kidnapped," he said in response to her unspoken question, easy grin firmly in place. "Tarrick gathered every mage in Alistriem to come after you. We've been on your tail since Carhall—we were waiting outside the city for Dawn to call us in if Tarrick needed more mages to get you out."

"I'm glad." She smiled. "If the city hadn't been falling, he might have needed you all to get me out of the council's clutches."

"Sounds like you managed that all on your own." Respect filled his voice, and there was a glitter of something in his eyes she couldn't read. "Everyone here already knows you bested Galien by yourself."

"It wasn't easy," she said ruefully.

"But you did it," he murmured. "I always wondered if that was why he hated you so much, if he sensed you were more powerful than him."

"Well, you knew him better than I did," she said pointedly, referencing Adahn's membership in Galien's group at DarkSkull.

He flashed his grin at her. "I'm reformed now." The smile faded to a look of affection. "I was worried about you, Alyx. I'm so glad that you're safe."

"Thank you for worrying." He had shifted closer to her, and the memory of kissing him flashed through her mind. She'd done it because she'd been trying to disprove Cayr's words and because, despite everything, she genuinely liked Adahn. In a world without Dashan, there might have been hope to build something with him, but now all of that was thrown back into confusion.

"Adahn..." She hesitated. "You've heard that Dashan is alive?"

He looked away, blue eyes flashing, and gave a sharp nod. "I heard. The council were using him to hold Carhall. And before you ask, of course I haven't forgotten why they came after him in Sandira." He let out a breath, turning back to her. "It's been three years, Alyx, and things are different now. I won't give up on you because he's back."

"Why?" she asked softly.

He shifted even closer, smiling, lifting a hand to sweep the chestnut hair from his eyes. "You and I make sense, Alyx. You're strong and brave and I'm reckless and brave. We're mages, we understand each other, we understand the same world. Together we could be an amazing team." He paused. "And we both know he is dangerous for you."

"If you think—"

He lifted his hands to ward off her quickly rising temper. "It's a reality. The council might be almost gone, but a lot of mages still think like they do. If you and he were together..."

His voice trailed off, and she didn't dispute his words. Even last night she'd been afraid her closest friends might change their minds about following her because of Dashan's reappearance. Still, Adahn pointing it out didn't warm her to him and she looked away. "I can't make decisions about any of this right now. Not in the middle of a war."

"I understand that." He shifted away from her, light mood reasserting itself. "How can I help?"

"Can you find the others? We need to talk through what happens next. Get them to make sure Dashan and Ladan are there too."

"I live to serve." The cocky smile flashed and he was off.

Alyx turned for the stables and almost ran into Dawn. A smile spread over her face and she hugged the telepath warmly. "I'm so sorry for ruining your wedding."

"Me too," Dawn said ruefully. "How are you?"

"Sore, still a little tired," Alyx said. "And my magic probably isn't quite back at full strength yet."

Dawn gave her a look mixing amusement and exasperation. "That is *not* what I was asking and you know it."

"Brynn!" Relief swamped through Alyx at the sight of him jogging towards them, and it wasn't entirely from the fact he looked much healthier than he had in Carhall. "You look good," she said, running her eyes over him with a smile.

He nodded, touching the bandage on his right temple. "After Finn worked on me, I pretty much slept straight through. I just woke."

"Good. You can join us for a meeting." Alyx cast an anxious look around the valley. "I don't want to linger here too long."

He nodded and fell into step with her and Dawn, asking, "How are you, anyway?"

She shrugged. "I overextended my magic, and I'm a little bruised, but I'll be fine."

Brynn blinked in surprise, then shared raised eyebrows with Dawn. "That's not what I meant."

Alyx tried not to roll her eyes—if people were going to be tip-toeing on eggshells around her for the foreseeable future she was going to get really annoyed *really* fast. "Did someone tell you Dash's story?"

"Cario told me as I was dressing just now. I can barely believe it."

"You and me both." She tipped her head towards the stables. "Everyone is inside. We'd best not keep them waiting."

Alyx and Brynn were the last to arrive. Everyone else was already hunched around the map table, staring at the lines and squiggles as if they held the answer to defeating Shakar and the entire Shiven army. All the windows and doors in the stables had been opened to allow in the sunlight, though it also let in the cool morning breeze. She wished she had her cloak.

"How are our honourable council members doing?" she asked.

Cario flashed an amused smile. "They're busy annoying their militia guard—I'm not sure the creature comforts here are quite up to their lofty standards."

Ladan looked over at her. He looked calmer than he had the previous night, all traces of anger gone. "What do you want to do with them?"

"Well, they're not my prisoners, but if they want my protection we'll need to take them back to Alistriem with us," she said. "I'm guessing the best way through will be via Widow Falls?"

"You've still got an armed outpost there?" Dashan asked Ladan. He was sitting at the head of the table, one booted foot propped up on its edge.

Ladan nodded.

"Good, but we need to stay here another day at least," he said. "The soldiers and horses all need rest."

Alyx glanced at him. "Will you bring the militia into Rionn?"

"No. None of them will be willing to hide out in Rionn while Tregaya is under attack. Besides, we can be useful, even if we're now cut off from the army in the north."

We? Did Dashan still consider himself the leader of the militia? She wasn't sure how she felt about that.

"Are you certain King Mastaran is safe?" Tarrick frowned.

"The king and his family are alive and in a safe location," Rodin answered. "Nobody knows where he is apart from Dashan and myself, and he has a heavy guard with him. Two council warrior mages are his personal bodyguards."

"It's worth pointing out that just because the Shiven have Carhall doesn't mean they have Tregaya," Cario spoke. "The entire northern half of the country, and much of the west, remains under militia control, and there are two or three other heavily fortified cities the Shiven will need to take before they'll control those areas. It will be some time before they have the resources to do that."

"He's right," Dashan said. "Tregaya is far from lost and contingency plans were set in place months ago. The king is actively controlling the militia in the north."

"What is your plan for the militia remaining under your command, Dash?" Alyx asked, taking a seat and leaning over to get a proper look at the map they were studying.

"We'll split into smaller, more mobile units and harry the Shiven army as they try and push north." He pointed to a few locations on the map. "If we can't stop their forward progress, we can certainly slow it up."

"That's a good idea," Adahn spoke. "Conducting a guerrilla war will create a continuous drain on the Shiven resources and delay them from pushing further north."

It was a statement of the obvious, something everyone in the room had grasped for themselves. Dashan's dark Shiven eyes landed on Adahn, a hint of amusement in them. "Right. And who are you?"

"Adahn Torse." He smiled easily. "I'm one of the Magor-lier's senior advisors. We met in Sandira, if you recall."

Alyx sighed inwardly, trying not to roll her eyes. The last thing she wanted was some sort of rivalry between Adahn and Dashan. She needed to nip this in the bud, and quickly.

"You're one of the *Magor-lier's* advisors?" Dashan clarified.

"That's right."

Dashan shifted his gaze to Alyx. She was close to certain she was the only one that could read the flicker of amusement in his voice. "That's the Alyx I remember, still insisting that people refer to her by title."

She gave him a look, leaving him in no doubt of what she thought of his teasing. "I'm the head of the mage order. My advisors give me the respect that position deserves. I demand it from them."

The amusement escaped into a quick grin. "Oh absolutely, I completely agree, your Magor-lier-ness."

Tarrick's head fell forward until it hit the table with a loud *thump*. Finn snorted. Dawn smacked her brother in the head. Alyx thought she might lift into the air, her heart was so light. Adahn said nothing, but his jaw was clenched, his gaze focused on the map.

"Back to the matter at hand," Cario said, trying but failing to hide his smirk. "Brynn, I assume the news you came to Alistriem with was related to Dashan's existence?"

"It has to be." Brynn nodded. "Rothai put me on the tail of one of Shakar's mages who was looking to infiltrate the council. Presumably I saw Dashan in Carhall and travelled to Alistriem to tell Alyx. They got to both of us before I could."

She looked at Tarrick. "What *I* want to know is how you found me?"

"Safia saw everything that happened," he explained. "He came straight to the palace to tell us that mages had taken both you and Brynn."

"Dawn did the rest," Finn said with a proud smile for his sister. "Safia got to us quickly enough that Dawn could just reach far enough to catch their thoughts heading north and work out they were council mages, not Shakar. Tarrick immediately rounded up every mage in Alistriem and we came after you."

"I didn't even think about Safia," Alyx mused, shooting her friend a grateful look. "Thank you, Dawn."

Ladan cleared his throat. "Back to the plans. We stay here another day to rest, then we head back to Alistriem as fast as we can. King Cayr needs to know about the fall of Carhall, and we need to plan how we're going to respond to it."

"I'll come with you," Dashan drawled. "I want to see Cayr, and the Bluecoats. I have capable captains here who can manage things until I return. Rodin will be in overall command."

Their eyes met, and she couldn't ignore how glad she was that he wasn't staying in Tregaya.

"The mages that came with me are well-rested," Adahn said suddenly. "It might be worthwhile if we ride out now and scout out the way head, make sure there aren't any nasty surprises in your path, like a second Shiven force following the first."

"Good idea." She smiled at him. "Do that, and we can maintain contact with telepathy. Either Dawn or I will check in with you every few hours."

Adahn's departure broke up the meeting. After a brief hesitation, plus a gentle nudge from his wife, Ladan joined Dashan to pour over the maps and discuss strategy in more detail. Tarrick pulled up a chair too. Alyx joined the twins in seeking more sleep.

She slept away most of the morning and early afternoon, allowing her body and magic to regain strength. As late afternoon settled over the valley, she took a walk to loosen still-sore muscles. Without conscious effort, her steps took her to the dome housing the Taliath sword she'd been so fascinated with during her time at DarkSkull.

She wasn't the only one. Councillor Yirith stood before the cracked dome, eyes on the empty casing inside that had held the sword.

"Someone stole it?" she asked, stopping beside him. "A looter, maybe?"

"No," Yirith said distantly. "It's why he attacked DarkSkull first. He wanted to strike a blow against the council, yes, but he also wanted his sword back."

A shocked gasp escaped her. "The sword you were keeping here was *Shakar's?*"

He nodded. "He had it made during his time on ShadowFall Island. We kept it here as a way to remind ourselves of what had happened. To keep alive the memory of all the mages he'd killed."

"More likely it was to remind yourselves how scared he made you," she countered. "Why does he hate you so much? I don't understand. It's not just about power—I've felt his bitter hatred, it's personal."

"It doesn't matter. It was a long time ago." Yirith gave himself a little shake, seemingly coming back to himself. "And if I told you, you would twist it all around to make us sound evil, just like you always do. You never learned how to think outside black and white terms, despite how hard Rothai and Romas tried."

"Oh I learned," she said, cold and cutting. "I'll see you later, Yirith."

After walking off her anger with Yirith and his condescension, she settled by a small campfire with Tarrick and Finn. Ladan and Dawn had been conspicuously absent all day, and Alyx was glad that amidst everything they could find some time just for themselves.

Tarrick eventually rose to walk a patrol, and Finn soon after to seek his bed, leaving her by the fire. She welcomed the opportunity to be alone and have some time to process recent events. It was a lot to accept. The council had been reduced to three old men and a scattering of surviving warrior mages, leaving her to lead the mage order and face down Shakar. But overriding all of that—Dashan was alive.

As if summoned by her thoughts, he appeared out of the darkness. For the first time since she'd learned he was alive, she felt as if she had enough control of herself to look at him properly as he walked towards her.

He was older, that was the first thing that popped into her mind—he would be twenty-seven now, given their age difference. His features were subtly different, his face was harder and there were faint lines around his eyes. The lines only added character though, and the touch of maturity in his features made him even more handsome. He walked with the grace of a Taliath, tall and muscular, his dark eyes watchful and rarely still. The aura of reserve he held close around him like a cloak hadn't changed.

"Scare everyone off?" he asked, taking a seat to her left, but leaving a comfortable distance between them.

"They're sleeping."

"And you're not?"

She shrugged. "I got some earlier."

"You look better than you did," he said, then hesitated. "Can I ask you something?"

She glanced at him. "Yes."

Dashan took his time, shifting slightly along the log they leaned against to get more comfortable. "Would you prefer that you never discovered I was alive?"

The answer came instantly, without any hesitation or doubt. "Not for a second," she said firmly, meeting his eyes for the first time since that moment in the Great Hall.

He smiled then, that tiny smile that curled up one edge of his mouth and lit up his eyes. She almost leaned into him, the response so instinctive it scared her. Instead she stayed where she was and tried not to feel cold.

"What sort of mages do you think would be most useful to you for this guerrilla war you're planning?" she asked, turning the conversation to business.

Surprise lifted his eyebrows. "You're going to help me?"

"Like Adahn said, your plan is a good one, and it will certainly help us in Rionn if you're harrying the Shiven in Tregaya."

"How is Rionn coping?" he asked soberly. "I would get regular reports over the past few years, but I usually left those for my captains to keep up with. I was too focused on Carhall and Tregaya."

"We're barely holding on. You'll see for yourself when we get back. I'm sure Ladan will be happy to give you an outline."

"He seems different," Dashan said. "I saw him laughing this morning. I think I can count on one hand the number of times I remember him even smiling."

Alyx chuckled. "He's changed a lot. He and Dawn married recently, and I think she makes him so happy he can't maintain that angry, stern exterior of his. I tease him about it all the time."

He nodded, accepting that, and his expression changed slightly, as if his thoughts were shifting. "You know, when I first saw you back in Carhall, it was... you've changed too. More than the rest of them, I think."

She gave a startled laugh. "You think so?"

"You've got such a presence about you now. Part of it is your magic, anyone near you can feel your power, but it's more than that. You command the attention of everyone around you without even thinking about it." Sadness crossed his face. "It will take some getting used to."

She didn't know what to say to that, and he didn't seem to expect a response. Silence fell, and Alyx listened dreamily to the crackling of the wood in the fire. It was a peaceful night. She grabbed on to that moment of peace and kept it close—it wasn't going to last.

"In answer to your original question, I could use any telepaths you could spare me, and some warrior mages," he said eventually.

"I'll discuss it with Tarrick." She looked over, trying to keep her voice casual. "How long will you stay in Alistriem?"

He turned to her, shifting slightly to bring them closer. She didn't move away. His gaze caught hers and held it. "Not long, Alyx. I think that's best for both of us. The last thing I want is to cause you more pain or unsettle the life you've built. And for me—" His voice dropped to a whisper. "It's like I only saw you yesterday in Sandira, and now I've woken up in a world where you're not mine anymore."

She bit her lip, the words spilling out of her. "Dash, I had to let go... to become the Magor-lier, I had to let go of me and what we were together. You were right, I'm not her anymore." And that was a good thing—she'd become what was needed to lead the fight against Shakar. But she also mourned the girl that had spent those magical weeks of an Alistriem summer with Dashan, free and in love. Before knowing he was a Taliath. Before Shakar's re-emergence and the destruction of DarkSkull.

He stood, brushed the soil and leaves from his breeches, and gave her another one of those sad smiles. "Give it time, mage-girl."

Her gaze tracked him as he left, her thoughts returning to her conversation with Adahn earlier that day and the realisation she would have to talk to him soon. Nothing had changed. Not in three years of thinking Dashan was gone. Because he'd been wrong. Maybe too much time had passed to go back, and maybe they could never be fully together because of what they were, but it didn't matter. She *was* his. Always.

CHAPTER 30

At the touch of familiar dark magic on her mind, Alyx woke with a gasp, sitting straight up on her pallet. Rain pattered against the stone wall outside but otherwise all was quiet. Her heart thundered in her chest—*nightmare or reality?* She threw out her telepathic power, withdrawing almost instantly when it brushed up against Shakar's familiar mind. She froze, heart continuing to pound as she sat still as stone. But his magic didn't follow her.

Tentatively, she reached out again. He wasn't looking for Alyx, but he was close enough for her to sense him, and his thoughts were less ordered than usual. Hesitating only a moment, she decided to take advantage of his distraction. As delicately as her skill allowed, she hovered over the surface of his thoughts. What she learned had her leaping from the blankets.

"Dawn!"

"Alyx?"

"Help me wake the others. Quickly! Are you all in the old boys' dormitory too?"

Dimly she sensed Dawn scrambling, untangling from Ladan's sleeping form and waking him in the process. *"Yes. Cario's on your floor, two doors down. Finn, Brynn, and Tarrick are near us on the ground floor. I'll get them. Ladan's already going for Dashan."*

"Meet in the foyer. Now!"

She yanked on boots, reached for her staff, cursed when she remembered it was gone, then pulled her door open and ran. Cario was fast asleep but thankfully fully dressed on top of the covers.

"Cario!" she hissed. "Up, quickly!"

As soon as she saw his bright blue eyes blinking awake she turned back for the door. His long strides caught up to her and they ran down the stairs, clattering out into the dormitory foyer. The single lamp lit by the door flickered wildly as it was shoved open—Ladan, with Dashan on his heels.

"What's going on?" Tarrick demanded, striding into the open space, Brynn and the twins flanking him.

"Shakar's on his way here. Right now," she said, trying to keep panic from her voice.

"How close?" Ladan demanded.

"I don't know. I was sleeping, and my magic snagged his unconsciously," she tried to explain. "I was able to read his intentions because he was distracted. He's after the councillors."

Dashan didn't hesitate. "I'll rouse the militia."

"Dawn, go with him," Alyx said tersely. "Your telepathy can help find and gather them all more quickly."

As they ran for the door, Cario turned back and started up the stairs. "I'll get the councillors and bring them to you."

"Tell them to hurry, but reassure them," Alyx called after him. "We'll do our best to protect them."

Finn stepped forward. "The focus needs to be on getting you out, Alyx, and well away from here before Shakar arrives. Not the council."

"We leave the council members behind," Ladan added. "If it's them he's after, hopefully he won't keep coming after us."

"No," Alyx said clearly. "I'm not leaving the masters to die."

Ladan's features went taut with anger. "You owe them nothing. Every moment we stand here arguing about it puts you in greater danger."

She stood firm. "They are mages, and that makes them my responsibility. I owe them my protection as much as I owe any other mage. There is no picking and choosing about who we do and don't like." This was directed at Tarrick, Brynn, and Finn. "We are not the council. Remember that."

Tarrick's jaw was clenched tightly. Her heart went out to him—he was clearly torn between duty to the council he'd been raised to respect and his desire to protect Alyx—but he gave a terse nod. Finn was looking at her oddly, like for the first time he truly understood something, "Then we all go together," he said simply.

"And then what?" Ladan demanded. "We keep running until he catches us or we run out of places to hide?"

"I—" Her words were drowned out in the resounding boom of a concussion burst rocking the valley. Orange light flashed through the windows followed seconds later by the ground shuddering beneath their feet.

For a moment they simply looked at each other in horror. Alyx swallowed. Shakar was here.

"Too late," Brynn spoke for all of them.

Ladan was already backing towards the door. "We go for the horses while Cario gathers the mages. Dash will be doing the same with the militia. Quickly now!"

It was still raining outside, but the valley floor was alive with activity as soldiers ran to bolster the perimeter defences. Alyx paused on the threshold, scanning their surroundings, trying to work out where Shakar was. Could there be some way to flee without him knowing they'd gone? It was certainly possible he was directing this attack from a distance.

"Let's go!" Tarrick shouted, grabbing Alyx's arm.

She yanked her arm away. "I can run on my own. *Dawn?*"

"We've roused the soldiers—they had contingency plans for the valley being attacked, so they've all got rendezvous points to head for. We're on our way to the stables. Dash says we don't have the numbers or defences in place to stand and fight Shakar—he wants to know if you agree?"

Alyx hesitated only briefly. Running wasn't a good solution, but she couldn't see how staying and fighting would lead to anything but death. *"No, he's right. We're headed for the stables to ready the horses while Cario gathers the council members. Can you send to Cario to meet us there too?"*

A pause, then, *"Done. I'm on my way to the stables. Dashan will be close behind."*

Shakar hadn't come alone. Two warrior mages and a stream of Shiven soldiers had cut off the open space between the dormitories and the stables. Another concussion burst went off, bathing the open space in bright orange. It lit up Dashan as he led a group of militia to intercept. One of the mages stood at the top of a large piece of fallen rubble, hands raised as he used his magic to attack every militia soldier in sight.

Unhesitating, Dashan went after him, leaping gracefully up the rock, sword raised and glinting in the light of magic. Ahead of Alyx, Ladan lengthened his stride, letting out a roar as he drew his sword and joined the militia fighting through to the stables.

Alyx and Tarrick, flanked protectively by Finn and Brynn, summoned magic and helped Ladan fight through, their green and pearlescent magic lighting up the night in a beautiful echo of their opponent mage.

Moments later they were clear and sprinting towards the stable door. Inside, Dawn was already working quickly and calmly to saddle the horses. Alyx glanced back when she realised the night had gone quiet and the flashes of concussive magic had temporarily ceased.

Dashan was still on the rock, but the Shiven mage lay crumpled at his feet. As he turned to go back down, the air shimmered and a cloaked figure flashed into existence behind him.

His power was like a slap, clear across the space to where Alyx stood. And it was instantly familiar. The magic of her nightmares.

"DASHAN!" she screamed.

He heard her and spun, sword raised, but the cloaked figure was too quick, knocking Dashan a hard blow. He dropped, rolling precariously close to the edge. Alyx took one step forward then launched into flight, magic burning through her as she used it desperately for speed. She hit the cloaked figure mid-air. They tumbled endlessly towards the ground. In such close contact the tendrils of his magic clung to her, winding around and through hers, dark and oh so familiar.

Her magic fought back instinctively, and then they slammed into the ground. She caught a flash of pale skin, the blink of an eye, and then her vision blurred and she slumped into the wet ground, almost eating a mouthful of mud. He'd vanished from underneath her as quickly as he had appeared.

That was a mage ability she hadn't seen before.

Alyx scrambled to her feet, breathing hard, trembling from head to toe at the knowledge she'd just faced Shakar in person for the first time.

"Dashan!"

She sprinted for the rock. A concussion burst hit the ground at her feet, lifting her bodily off the ground in a flash of blue light. Instinctively she reached for her flying power, using it to spin mid-air, and then to propel herself forward to where Dashan had been standing. As she flew she drew magic, located the mage with her telepathic ability, and sent two bright green concussion bursts at him.

They went off with a magnificent explosion of light and power. The moment she landed she summoned her shield just in case, but there was only silence. She'd hit her target and the second mage was dead.

"Dash?"

He was alive, moving, clambering to his feet. A moment later he was almost knocked off his feet again as she threw herself against him.

"Alyx, I'm all right!" he said. "I'm fine. Invulnerability, remember?"

She nodded, pressing her face into his neck and holding onto him as tightly as she could. His arms settled around her, holding on just as fiercely.

"I'm okay, Alyx." He eased her back from him, Shiven eyes alive and well as he watched her.

"Good," she said firmly. "Now, let's get out of here."

"Alyx!" It was Tarrick, shouting up at her.

"We're fine."

They dropped quickly to the ground and made straight for the stables. The open space was filled with stamping, snorting horses picking up on the anxiousness of their riders. Her mount tossed his head and backed up a step as Alyx approached, her gaze searching to make sure everyone was there. They weren't. "Where's Cario?"

"With his grandfather." Dawn looked grim. "They're in the main hall—I think Walden had the bright idea they could hole up and hide in there."

"What are they thinking? That Shakar will just give up and go away?" Dashan asked incredulously.

"Cario was trying to convince them to come with him and meet us here, but then his mind was cut off, like another telepathic mage was blocking me." Dawn didn't say any more. They all knew what that likely meant.

Alyx took a breath, bracing herself for the inevitable barrage. "We need to go back for him."

"Alyx, no!" Tarrick's response was quick and firm, brooking no argument.

"Tarrick, it's as simple as this," she said steadily. "I'm not leaving Cario to die. I won't deliberately engage Shakar, and I won't put myself in unnecessary danger, but I will not leave him to die any more than I would leave you. Is that clear?"

"I—"

"This is what you didn't understand that night in Sandira," she cut him off, trying to keep the remembered grief from her voice. "I won't walk away from those I love and leave them to die. I *can't*. I will avoid Shakar if I can, but I won't leave."

Tarrick took a deep breath, the air fraught with tension. She kept her gaze locked on his, willing him to decide differently this time. And after what seemed like an eternity, his hard expression softened and he slowly nodded his head. "All right."

"Thank you," she whispered, almost swaying with relief.

Finn glanced between them. "How can you avoid engaging him?"

"He's here for the councillors—the need to destroy them burns in him. I tried to protect them, but their choices have doomed them. I can't save them now. We just need to get Cario clear." It was brutal, what she was suggesting, and it felt like a failure—that at the first hurdle she was leaving her ideals behind, but what other choice did she have? *Damned foolish old men!*

"All right, Alyx," he said simply.

Tarrick straightened. "Ladan, you and Dashan will come with Alyx and me. Dawn, Finn, Brynn, you take an extra horse and ride hard and fast to get clear of the valley. Once we have Cario safe, Alyx will fly straight to you and the rest of us will find our own way out." He met Alyx's eyes. "That's the only way we're doing this."

She wanted to hug him. Instead she settled for a warm smile. "Deal."

Brynn swung himself into the saddle without preamble, reaching out to take the reins of the closest horse. Dawn went to Ladan, leaned up to kiss him hard, then joined her brother in mounting up. They rode out at a gallop. Ladan's expression was lost, like his entire life was riding out with them.

"She'll be fine, big brother." Alyx squeezed his arm. "Now let's get Cario and get out of here."

CHAPTER 31

With Tarrick in the lead, they walked cautiously up the steps and through the front doors of the hall. It was dark inside, the only light from the occasional flash of lightning coming through the windows.

Alyx's hair was plastered to her skull, and she was soaked through. Water ran in rivulets down her face and she took a second to wipe it away. She shivered, and not entirely from the cold. The last time she'd been here she'd walked into a hall full of dead mage students. Howell's body had been in the library lying alone amidst his beloved books. Her heart clenched. *Focus.*

"Tarrick, any thoughts on using my telepathic magic to find them? It could risk Shakar knowing I'm here," she murmured.

"No," Ladan answered quickly, Tarrick nodding agreement. "Right now Shakar's attention is on the councillors. Let's keep it that way."

"I'll take the lead. Ladan, you bring up the rear," Dashan breathed. "We head for the main hall but do nothing until we find out what's going on in there. Clear?"

They passed the deserted dining room and the hallway opposite where Alyx had once attended language classes. The place felt and sounded empty—Shakar hadn't brought any of his mages in here with him. *If* he was still here. Frustration niggled at being unable to use magic to sense ahead. Finding Cario was going to be difficult without it.

She opened her mouth to suggest a small, shielded burst of telepathic magic, but as she did a shudder swept through her and she stopped abruptly.

"Alyx?" Ladan stopped beside her. "What is it?"

She took a deep breath, tried to fight another shudder. "He's here."

"How close?" Tarrick hefted his staff, glancing around as if Shakar was about to leap out from the walls around them.

"I don't know. Close. Definitely in the hall. I can feel his magic." It was the same dark presence from her nightmares, unmistakable, and tinged with triumph. Nausea curled in her stomach. She fought to keep her shield up, to keep the darkness out of her head. "I think he's found the councillors. He can't hide his glee."

"Keep going," Dashan said.

They moved on, but now Alyx started every time she heard a noise, fear leaping in her each time they rounded a corner, expecting Shakar to appear any second. She was terrified for Cario, hoped he had the sense to distance himself from the councillors if Shakar had found them.

Tarrick waved them silently past the main doors into the hall and instead led them down a corridor which ran parallel to the length of the hall. Reaching a side entrance, they huddled low, straining their vision to try and see what was happening. The space beyond was dark—the storm outside had moved past the valley, taking the lightning with it.

"I'll have to use magic," Alyx murmured. "Just to find Cario. Otherwise we'll be stumbling around blind in there."

Tarrick gave a stiff nod. She closed her eyes and took a deep breath. First she summoned a tiny trickle of magic, keeping it as small as she could, then cautiously she reached out, seeking Cario's mind. Terror gripped her at the thought of Shakar picking up what she was doing, and the moment she found Cario's thoughts she let go of her magic completely.

"He's in there, down the end to our left." She swallowed. "He's scared, but uninjured."

"Shakar?" Ladan asked.

"I don't know."

"What's Cario doing, just standing there?"

"I don't know, Ladan. If you want me to risk Shakar sensing me by using more magic, I can find out," she hissed, irritation flaring to mask her worry.

"No, we can't risk it," Dashan said. "Best case, we get Cario and slip out while Shakar is busy with the councillors. If we hit trouble, Ladan, you get Alyx and Cario out. Tarrick, you and I will give them time to flee before following."

Dashan's eyes flicked to hers as he spoke. She wanted to scream at them both, to say no, to say she couldn't survive him dying again just to give her time to flee. But she'd learned from that night in Sandira that as much as she wanted her friends to respect her choices, she had to respect theirs in return. And her survival was critical.

"There's an exit at both ends of the hall, as well as this doorway," Tarrick added. "If we get separated, you all know the ways out of the valley. Get out as quickly as you can and keep moving. We'll trust Alyx and Dawn to contact everyone once we're clear. If you don't hear anything, make straight for Alistriem."

Alyx shivered at a scenario where both she and Dawn weren't able to contact anyone, but nodded agreement. It was a sound plan considering the circumstances, and she intended to hold up her end of the bargain. Once she got clear, she'd fly straight to safety. Even so, she reached out to grab Dashan's arm as they rose to move.

"No ridiculous heroics," she hissed. "Promise me!"

"I promise I'll do my best to get out," he said solemnly. "If you promise me the same thing."

She nodded, and he smiled at her. Even in the darkness it lit up her heart, and if the circumstances weren't so dire, she would have kissed him then and there, three years apart be damned.

They moved out into the dark space, Alyx and Dashan in the lead, Ladan and Tarrick close behind. Their breathing was frighteningly loud in the open space, though the darkness closed in around them like a blanket. Alyx held her magic ready—once they got closer to the opposite end of the hall she'd use another burst to pinpoint Cario. Though it was strange they couldn't hear anything—if he was there, where was Shakar? And where were the masters?

They stopped abruptly when a violet pearlescent glow lit up the darkness ahead—another mage was there, walking quickly towards them. It took a few moments for Alyx's eyes to adjust to the light, but when they did, she wasn't sure she was seeing right.

"Astor?" Puzzlement filled her, followed by a rush of relief. Her godfather's presence was welcome... but Astor didn't have concussive power, so how was it his staff glowed with the shimmer of a powerful warrior mage? She shook her head, wondering if her eyes were playing tricks. "How are you doing that? You're a..."

"Lesser mage?" he asked, arching an eyebrow.

Ice-cold tendrils wrapped around her chest in a grip so firm her breathing stopped for a moment.

No. Oh no. Not this.

"Alyx?" Dashan's glance was shifting quickly between her and Astor—as always he knew the instant something was wrong with her. "What is it? Astor, what are you doing here?"

She barely heard him. On the heels of her shock came a deep flood of bone-melting grief. Not Astor. Her godfather. The man she'd loved and admired her whole life.

"It's him," she whispered, somehow finding the power to speak, her eyes firmly fixed on her godfather despite the tears now blurring them. "All this time."

Clothing rustled as Ladan appeared at her side, hearing the distress in her voice even if not understanding yet what was happening.

"What's him?" Tarrick snapped out. "Lord-Mage, what are you doing here?"

Astor smiled slightly. "I came for the council, of course."

"Alyx!" Dashan cried out a warning.

Responding to his tone, Alyx raised her shield without thought. A concussion ball easily as powerful as hers slammed into it, shooting violet sparks in the air.

"What the hell...?" Ladan stared at Astor, where the attack on Alyx had originated.

"He's Shakar," Alyx shouted, the intensity of Astor's attack breaking through her grief. Anger rose now, hot and cleansing. She lifted her right hand, magic illuminating it in a bright green glow. "It's you."

"It is." Astor moved closer. She'd never felt such power radiating from a mage before; it was almost enough to burn her. All this time he had hidden it. She couldn't quite believe what she was seeing or hearing. The nightmares that tormented her, the endless waves of Hunters trying to kill her, the attack in Sandira that led to Dashan's 'death'... her beloved godfather the cause of it all? A man she thought loved her, who she loved and admired. All this time it had been *Astor*? It was only her terror for Cario that allowed her to scratch and claw her way to enough focus to function. "Where are the councillors?"

A wide, almost maniacal grin spread over Astor's face. It twisted the familiar features she'd grown up loving, turning them into something she only recognised from her nightmares. He moved the arm holding his staff and the violet light pulsed more brightly, showing the three dead bodies piled on the floor just behind him.

Walden, Yirith, and finally, Cario's grandfather.

"The council is finally gone, Alyx. I destroyed them. You should be happy, it was what you wanted too, wasn't it?"

She swallowed, gaze fixed on the bodies. Old men all, they looked so helpless and fragile lying there in a heap. She couldn't tear her eyes away. "Cario?" she whispered.

Astor shrugged a little, lifted his hand. A floating body emerged from the dimness to land at Alyx's feet. Cario's bright blue eyes stared up at her, alive but trapped, unable to move. Another magical ability she'd never seen before. Fear struck, threatening to overwhelm her—Shakar was so much more powerful than she could ever be.

"I have to admit, I planned to use the young man as a tool to torture his grandfather before killing him," Astor said. "Sadly, though, Councillor Duneskal seemed far more concerned with saving his own skin. But *you*... well, I didn't expect this level of stupidity from you, Aly-girl. And over a single mage."

She needed to play for time. Enough time for either Dashan or Ladan to come up with a way out of this. Even if it was only extending the time until he killed them. "You could have killed me when I was a little girl. You could have killed me a thousand times since. Why wait until now?"

"I have to admit to a certain... reluctance to hurt you." There was an odd softness to his voice that clashed with the contempt ripping over his face. For a heartrending moment she saw her godfather, the man that had loved and cared for her since childhood, but then the contempt won and harshness returned to his voice. "But mostly, there was never really a need. You're not a threat to me."

The words sank in, but distantly. She was thinking while he spoke, trying to come up with a plan. A thought came to her and she spun. "Dash, get Cario and the others clear. I'll be right behind you."

He met her gaze, hesitated for only the briefest of seconds, then gave her a sharp nod. Alyx stepped forward, covering them, as Dashan launched into movement. Her magic leapt out, quick as she could, to take hold of Cario and send him sailing towards Ladan.

"*Trust me, Tarrick!*" She flung the thought at him, and then Astor was on her.

He went for her mind and body at the same time but her mental and physical magical shields were firmly up and he couldn't get in. The force of energy he sent her way, however, battered her shield and sent her stumbling backwards several paces.

"Why?" she shouted, trying to keep his focus on her. Dashan and Ladan were lifting Cario's dead weight between them while Tarrick hovered protectively. Then they were moving, heading for the exit. "Why become a monster? Why destroy so many lives?"

He laughed and attacked again. Her shield held off the concussion bursts, but they were powerful. Maintaining the shield under such a barrage drained her energy. She summoned her own magic, throwing a few concussion bursts at him. She had no hope of damaging him, but all she needed was to keep his attention on her for a short while longer.

Her magic dissipated before hitting him, like sliding off an invisible shield. Even though she'd known that would be the outcome, she gasped. Taliath invulnerability in a powerful mage was a fearsome thing to behold.

"I'm no monster, Alyx. I assure you I am a completely sane and rational man."

She stepped forward. "Was it because you became invulnerable? You thought you could have whatever you wanted. Is that why you took a Taliath as a lover?"

Shakar's face twisted and madness flashed briefly in his eyes, belying his claim and erasing all traces of the loving godfather she'd grown up knowing. That loss hit her like a punch, and she bit her lip, refusing to be shaken. She had to focus or she'd die here.

"I loved her!" He screamed the words across the open space, and she flinched at the desperation in them. His magic exploded out of him, manifesting in a great wall of flame bearing down on her. She leapt into the air, flying above the crackling fire and landing on the other side.

"You're not capable of love," she shouted back.

"They killed her." His face was a mask of raw, aching grief. "I loved her and she died because they ordered it. I couldn't save her."

"Who killed her, Astor? Was it you? She gave you what you needed to become invincible so you murdered her?" Alyx gritted her teeth as he attacked her mind, as always unable to hold him off. But he wasn't as disciplined as usual, his emotion chaotic and uncontrolled. What she saw in his thoughts made her gasp in surprise. He withdrew with a scream of rage and she stumbled backwards with the suddenness of it.

"*Dawn, are you clear?*"

A moment's silence, then, "*We're out of the valley headed south.*"

"*Good, I'll be with you soon.*" Alyx expanded her magic, looking for Tarrick. His thoughts were frantic, torn between coming back to help and trusting her as she'd asked. But he was with Dashan and Ladan and they were mounted, riding hard for the valley exit. Cario was on Tarrick's horse. She used a touch of effort to reassure him. "*I'm fine. Keep moving!*"

Breaking off, she met Shakar's gaze, the gaze of her godfather, and some of the grief from earlier came back. "I'm glad I finally know who you are."

"You'll die happy then." He'd calmed, sanity reasserting itself. He was done playing with her.

"I'd prefer to leave that to another day," Alyx said, and took off at a run for the doors.

He came after her, loosing energy balls and firing at her fleeing back. She erected her shield, blow after blow slamming into it as she sprinted for the door. Then he used his telekinetic power.

Her feet came out from under her and she hit the stone floor hard. Gathering her strength, she leaped back to her feet and was immediately buffeted by another burst of his power.

"*Coward,*" he hissed into her mind.

Alyx ignored him, using her flying power with more control than she ever had before, using it to keep her balance against his power, to keep her feet moving towards the door.

Crying aloud with the effort, she spun, lifting her hands and sending bright green-silver concussion bursts flying directly at him. Carefully controlled, they exploded before hitting him, lighting up the cavernous space in a green glow and blinding Shakar for a precious few seconds.

Then she reached the exit and leaped into the sky

CHAPTER 32

O nce clear she hovered high in the dark skies over DarkSkull Hall. The
air outside the front entrance shimmered and he appeared out of
nothing, staring up at her. She tensed.

He couldn't fly.

She almost laughed at the frustration evident on his face—he had an
ability to move between particular, *specific* locations, but he mustn't be able
to fly. Dragging together what strength she had left, she erected her mental
shield. Then, she flew higher, so high into the dark sky that not even Taliath
vision would be able to see her. Once well away to the north, and confident
he hadn't been able to track her with his magic, she turned and wheeled
back south.

It took her less than an hour to find Dawn and Brynn, the extra horse
following behind with Brynn's hand firm on the reins. Alyx dropped wearily
into the saddle.

"Get your mental shields up!" she snapped. "He'll come after us if he can
find you and we're close enough." She explained what she'd learned about
his ability.

"I've been monitoring the others," Dawn called over. Exhaustion tinged
her voice. "The militia have splintered into several groups, all riding to
different rendezvous points throughout Tregaya. Rodin is in command.
Finn got separated from Brynn and I—we ran into a group of Shiven on the
way out—but he's clear and safe now."

"Great work," Alyx said, relieved. "Can you check in with Tarrick?"

Dawn closed her eyes for a few moments, Brynn reaching over to help guide her horse. When they snapped open a smile was creeping over her face. "They're following us as fast as they can. Cario is free of whatever magic Shakar had him trapped in—it must fade with distance."

"What happened back there?" Brynn demanded.

Relief swamped her so strongly at Dawn's words that it took Alyx a moment to collect her thoughts and respond. She had to lift her voice to be heard over the thundering of hooves.

"So the council is gone then," he said grimly.

"We're the council now," she said. A new confidence was trickling through Alyx—what she'd seen inside Shakar's mind the source of it. He was undoubtedly more skilled, possibly more powerful. But maybe, just maybe, there was a way to match him.

They didn't stop until the horses were floundering and the early light of morning lit up the sky. They'd unsaddled and watered the horses and were starting a fire when Tarrick, Ladan, and Dashan found them. Dawn beat Alyx to her brother by a few steps, so she turned to Tarrick instead.

"Thanks for trusting me."

He gave her a little smile. "Thanks for doing what you promised."

"Alyx!" Dashan was there then, shouldering past Tarrick to haul her into his arms. She didn't fight it, instead wrapping her arms around his waist in relief. He was solid and warm, the world disappearing for a moment as if three years had never been.

Cario's voice broke through her daze. "Hey, I'm alive too, you know?"

Alyx was out of Dashan's hug in a flash and running over to Cario. He smiled wearily at her, opening his arms.

"You shouldn't have come after me," he murmured in her ear.

She stepped away. "I'll always come after you, Cario."

He gave her a little bow, but there was nothing mocking in it. "My Magor-lier."

They rode hard for Alistriem, crossing through the narrow piece of Shivasa and stopping only briefly at Widow Falls for supplies and to change horses. They were three days out of Alistriem, encamped by a swiftly flowing stream just off the main road, when Ladan finally raised the spectre of what they'd left behind.

"There's a good chance he'll guess where we're going and come after us," he said as they chewed on strips of salty dried beef.

"He wanted the council and now they're dead. Maybe that will be enough for him," Cario suggested. "For now, at least."

"He truly didn't seem to consider me a threat," Alyx mused. "Although that could change now that I'm effectively the new council."

"Confrontation with Shakar is inevitable," Tarrick said, surprising them all. "And going back to running and hiding isn't the solution. We should be smart and cautious, but stand and fight if he comes."

"I'm probably in range of Rosa," Dawn said of the telepath stationed at the palace. "It might be worth checking in and warning them what's happened. Adahn and the others will be almost there too, I reached him a while ago and his thoughts indicated the way ahead is clear."

"You'd better get her to warn Cayr we're bringing an extra guest," Alyx said with a glance in Dashan's direction. There'd been no time for conversation in their ride from Tregaya, nor much time for figuring out what she was supposed to do now that he was suddenly back. Nonetheless, she had to fight back a smile every time her eyes fell on him. Cayr was going to be overjoyed.

Dawn settled back against her saddlebags, Ladan's arm draping around her shoulder in silent support. Brynn appeared with a half-loaf of bread and tossed a piece to Alyx before dropping beside her. She swapped him for some of the dried beef she was chewing on, chuckling when he made a face.

Dawn's gasp of shock caught them both by surprise, and Alyx was halfway to her feet before she realised there was no immediate physical danger.

"What is it?" Dashan demanded.

"Alyx, I... oh Ladan." Her hand shot out to take her husband's. He turned grim, and his shoulders stiffened as if he was bracing himself. "There was an attack on the palace last night—they were after Cayr. Hunters. So many."

Terror clutched at Alyx's chest. "Is Cayr okay? Dawn, tell me!"

"He's okay. Jenna was with him. She..." Dawn shook her head as if trying to process the information that had been given to her. "It's your father."

Alyx swayed on her feet. Brynn quickly reached out to take her arm and steady her. She leaned into him, needing his support. "He's... is he–?"

Dawn shook her head, tears glistening in her eyes. "I'm sorry. It doesn't sound good. Cayr was with Rosa when I reached her. He said you and Ladan should both come as quickly as you can."

Alyx nodded, meeting her brother's stricken gaze. "I'll go now. We'll fly. I can get us there in a few hours."

"He planned this." Ladan began pacing, shoulders rigid. "Hit the council and Carhall with his mages and use all remaining Hunters to take out the king of Rionn. Cut the legs out from the resistance against his Shiven army."

His words didn't help. She stared at him. *Not Papa.*

Dashan was there then, his hand gently squeezing her shoulder, gaze warm and reassuring. "Take a breath, Alyx. You go, we'll be right behind you."

She nodded, swallowed. She needed to be calm to use her magic. "Follow us as quickly as you can."

"We will," Brynn said steadily, still at her side. "Go, do what you need to do."

Alyx and Ladan landed inside the palace gates tired, aching, and filled with dread. She'd reached out to Rosa as they approached, and Cayr was coming out to meet them, his handsome face uncharacteristically grave. The strength suddenly went out of her legs, and Ladan reached out to steady her just in time. His shoulders were rigid, face a featureless mask.

"Alyx, Ladan, I'm so sorry." Cayr came to a halt before them. His blonde curls were tousled, as if he'd been running his hands through them over and over. Guilt shadowed his blue eyes, tiredness obvious from his wan appearance.

"How is he?" she managed to force the words out through the sudden lump in her throat.

"It's not good," he said, meeting her eyes. What she saw there almost made her burst into tears on the spot.

"I should go and... we should see him."

"I'll take you." He was hurting for her, but she couldn't acknowledge that. If she did, she might explode into a million pieces.

Together, she and Ladan pushed open the door of the room. Their father was unconscious on the bed, the peaceful expression on his face marred by the stitched wound down his left cheek.

Ladan took a single, heaving breath at the sight. "I want to hit something," he said tightly, his face grim with pain. "I should have been here. I should have—"

"This isn't your fault," Alyx murmured.

He nodded, but she sensed he didn't truly believe her words.

Cayr hesitated at the door, "He saved my life, you know? He and Jenna together. There were Hunters everywhere, and they..." Cayr smiled slightly, even though there was a sheen of tears in his eyes. "Your father was magnificent."

It was hard to summon anything but worry for her father, but she couldn't let the pain in Cayr's eyes go unacknowledged. "Is Jenna okay?"

"Some cuts and bruises, but nothing too serious," he said.

"I'm glad." She squeezed his hand. "I'm glad you're okay too."

He tried to smile but couldn't manage it. Instead he settled for squeezing her hand back before leaving the room and closing the door quietly behind him. Alyx moved over to sit on her father's bed. He was pale and gaunt, his breathing shallow.

The door opened to admit Leanli, and he and Ladan had a brief conversation. Once the healer had gone, Ladan pulled up a chair beside her.

"How bad?" she managed.

Ladan cleared his throat. "He sustained several deep wounds and lost too much blood. It weakened him." He paused. "He collapsed after the fight. Infection set in soon after and his body hasn't had the strength to fight it."

"What about Leanli's healing magic?"

Caged frustration filled her brother's voice. "His invulnerability limits the amount of magical help Leanli can give him."

When Alyx reached out to touch her father's face, his eyes flickered open. Pain echoed in them, but then he smiled when he saw them both.

"I thought Taliath were supposed to be invulnerable," she murmured.

"Almost..." His voice was faint. "Too many though."

"Don't talk," Alyx soothed when she saw how much effort it cost him. "You need to rest."

His eyes flickered closed again and she thought he'd lapsed into unconsciousness, but then he rallied. "You okay?"

Alyx huffed a laugh. "You're worried about *me* right now?"

"Love you... my girl."

"I love you too." She swallowed through the lump in her throat. "Papa, Dashan is alive. Surely you want to survive this so you can lecture me about how inappropriate a Bluecoat captain is for the daughter of Lord Egalion?"

Garan's eyes flashed with light at her words. "He's good for you, Aly-girl. Don't let them... don't let anyone tell you otherwise."

"I might," Ladan grumbled, making them all chuckle.

Garan's laugh turned into a choking cough. It took too long to subside, leaving his breathing harsher than it had been. He shook his head slightly, a wince crossing his face. "Ladan, Alyx. You're both so strong. You don't need me anymore."

"That's not true!" Ladan's voice was tight with pain. Alyx reached for her brother's hand and he took it in a vice-like grip.

A faint smile crossed their father's face. "Don't be sad for me. It's my time. This is how I was always meant to go... a fighting Taliath. I'm happier than I can ever express that I got to be that once again."

"Papa," Alyx whispered, her chest feeling like it was being torn asunder. "Please don't leave."

"I go to Temari now," he said heavily, eyes sliding closed. "Love you both. So much."

Alyx clung to her brother, tears streaming down their cheeks as their father's breathing slowed, and then came to a stop. One last breath escaped him and then he was still.

It was as if her heart was being literally torn from her chest. Her beloved father, the tall, strong, too-serious man who'd raised her and loved her and protected her. He was gone.

Goodbye, Papa.

"I wish—" Ladan's voice was ragged, rough. "I wish I hadn't missed all those years with him."

She turned and threw her arms around his neck, holding him as his shoulders shook and warm tears soaked into her skin.

CHAPTER 33

Three days later the others arrived. The time had passed mostly in a blur for Alyx, and, she suspected, for Ladan too. They kept to their father's home, spending the time sleeping when they could, and in silent companionship when they couldn't.

Dawn let her know of their approach to the city, and Alyx went over to the palace to greet them. As leaden with grief as she was, she couldn't miss Cayr's reunion with Dashan.

Alyx walked into the courtyard just as they were coming through the main gates. Cayr was there, hopping eagerly from foot to foot in anticipation, his own grief momentarily forgotten. Dashan let out a loud whoop of laughter when he saw the king, dismounting and crossing towards him in two strides. "Well, if it isn't my old friend Cayr!"

"Dashan Caverlock." Cayr shook his head, eyes wide with astonishment and joy. "I don't believe it."

"It's true," Dashan said. "I have become even more handsome since the last time you saw me."

Cayr laughed. "Oh, Dash, you have no idea..."

"I'm glad to see you too." Dashan clapped him on the back, before Cayr pulled him into a fierce hug. They clung to each other for a long time.

When they parted, Dashan's expression turned sober. "Alyx. Is she okay?"

Sadness filled Cayr's face. "She's—"

"I'm all right, Dashan." She walked over to join them. And for a brief moment, when he turned and smiled at her, it was true.

"Alyx." Dawn came over, throwing her arms around her tightly. Alyx fought tears, reinforcing her mental shield so that Dawn didn't have to deal with the strength of her grief. Eventually Dawn pulled back. "Where's Ladan?"

"He's at home," Alyx said softly. "Go to him—he could use you right now. I'll stay here for a bit, give you both some space."

Dawn nodded and squeezed her hand. "Reach out if you need anything at all."

Alyx glanced over at Cayr and Dashan, clearly waiting for her, and gave Dawn a little smile. "I think I'm going to be okay."

A matching smile curled at Dawn's mouth. "I think you will be too. See you soon, Alyx."

Cayr slung his arm around her as she re-joined them. Dashan shot her a look, eyebrows raised, and she gave him a little shake of her head. Cayr didn't know about Astor yet—she literally hadn't had the heart to tell him, her emotions too fragile.

They walked in silence together towards the king's private study, and for once nobody bothered him or needed his time. Jenna stood at the door. A stitched wound over her left eyebrow marred some of her beauty, but she looked stunning as always in silken dress and slippers.

"Magor-lier, may I have a word?" she asked.

Alyx nodded, waving Dashan and Cayr through into the study. Once the door closed, a silence descended. She waited for Jenna to speak, not sure what it was the woman wanted to talk to her about.

"I hope you know, Alyx, that I did everything I could. Your father, he told me to stay with Cayr." Astonishingly, tears glistened in Jenna's cool blue eyes. "He said that no matter what I had to protect him. And there were so many. When he was swamped, I couldn't get to him, not without leaving Cayr."

"Jenna, stop." Alyx surged forward, taking her arm. "My father's death isn't your fault. You did the right thing. You saved Cayr's life, and I will always be grateful to you for that."

"I wish I could have done more."

"They say you were magnificent. A true Taliath." Alyx smiled through her own tears. She missed her father with a deep, yearning ache, but the words were genuinely meant. "I'm glad you're on my side, Jenna Aridlen. I'm glad you're on *his* side."

She nodded once, then stepped back. "I should let you go."

Alyx paused in the doorway, glancing back. "You're nothing like Casovar, Jenna. I hope you know that."

"So you really had no memory at all?" Cayr marvelled. The fire had burned low in the grate, and Alyx was sure it was past midnight. She sat stretched out on a soft couch, sipping at a mug of cider, while Cayr sprawled on a sofa opposite her. Dashan sat on the floor between, back against a chair, long legs stretched out before him. They'd already finished three jugs of the cider.

Dashan shrugged. "I knew I was from Alistriem, but didn't know who my parents were, or remember anything about my life here."

"And you led the militia forces that whole time?"

"Not straight away, but once I recovered from my wounds, I started working with some of the militia—those I'd worked with at DarkSkull remembered me and we were very quickly successful. From there, it wasn't long before I found myself commanding the defences of the city. Even so, the council were careful to keep me out of public sight as much as they could. I finally understand why, now."

"Didn't Rodin and the others tell you who you were when they recognised you?" Alyx asked quietly.

Dashan looked up, replying just as quietly. "They told me I had been a Bluecoat captain, and that I'd led a unit sent to DarkSkull Hall as the escort for a noble Rionnan mage, a Lady Egalion."

"What did they say about me? Good things, I hope," Alyx said lightly, trying to break the sad tension suddenly filling the room.

"They liked you very much. They told me you were a powerful mage, and that when they had known you, you'd been betrothed to the prince of Rionn." Dashan shrugged. "I thought no more of it. I had no conception that if I was a mere Bluecoat captain, I would have had any association with someone like you beyond being your guard."

"Dashan, if you truly had no memory, and you were building a life for yourself in Carhall..." Cayr paused. "I just wonder if it's difficult now, if you still feel like you belong there."

Dashan studied the mug in his hands, a pensive look on his face. "I remember everything now; my childhood, everything. This is my home, where I belong. I didn't realise it at the time, but the past three years have been empty."

"Empty?" Alyx spoke without thinking—his words mirrored her feelings so well.

"I just mean... I thought I had a full life in Carhall, but I was only living part of my life, without even realising it."

Cayr chuckled, emulating Alyx's attempt to lighten the atmosphere. "Not a full life? So no blonde barmaid and illegitimate offspring tucked away somewhere?"

Silence dropped over the room like a blanket, and Cayr's face fell as he realised what he'd said. "I'm sorry. Blame the cider. That was a stupid question."

Alyx turned away, unable to decide whether she desperately wanted to hear Dashan's answer to the question or not.

"No blonde barmaid and no illegitimate children," he said quietly.

"I think we should talk about something different." Alyx put down her now-empty mug.

"I agree. I've told you everything about the past three years of my life," Dashan said. "I want to hear what's happened with the both of you."

"Well," Cayr smiled. "That's a story and a half."

"Before we do." Alyx swallowed, tears rising unbidden before flooding down her cheeks. Annoyed at herself—would these emotions never stop threatening to choke her?—she scrubbed at her face. "Cayr, there's something we have to tell you."

"Alyx, what is it, what's wrong?" Concern flooded his face and he sat forward.

"You know that Shakar followed us after Carhall fell." She sought for the words, struggled to find the right ones.

"Yes, yes." He waved her off impatiently, his worry growing. "I know he killed the council and you barely got away."

"Cayr." Dashan's voice was heavy with regret. "Shakar is someone we know. Someone close to you and Alyx."

Shock and puzzlement flooded the king's face. "What?"

"I'm so, so sorry." She took a breath. "All this time it was Astor."

CHAPTER 34

Alyx awoke with a sore neck, and she blinked, trying to work out where she was. Empty glasses and jugs littered the table directly in her eyeline. Soft light glimmered behind closed curtains.

Cayr's sitting room.

After the revelation about Astor, Cayr had changed the subject, his characteristic reluctance to deal with difficult issues shining through. For once it hadn't annoyed her, instead coming as a relief. They'd talked late into the night, telling Dashan everything that had happened during this absence. It had been close to dawn before they'd fallen asleep where they sat, exhausted and still slightly inebriated.

A soft snore broke her from her thoughts. Cayr was stretched out on the couch opposite, asleep, and Dashan lay flat on his back on the floor, the source of the snoring. She gazed down at his sleeping form for a long moment, unable to help herself after so long thinking she'd never see his face again. He looked more peaceful asleep, younger even.

Tearing her eyes away, she sat up, groaning softly as a pounding head added to her sore neck. Then, as on every morning since it had happened, she remembered her father had died. She bit down hard on her lip, tears rushing to her eyes.

She had to move. Distract herself from the grief.

Her intention had been to sneak out quietly and make her way home, but she opened the door to find Jenna still standing there, gaze alert and watchful. Not far away were three mage guards—Tari, Adahn, and Chestin.

"They found you on their own," Jenna spoke first, not sounding at all tired despite the fact she must have been up all night. "Don't blame me."

Alyx smiled at her. "Thanks for watching over us last night."

She said nothing to that, only inclined her head slightly. Alyx turned away, moving to join her guards. Adahn fell into step behind her while the other two went on ahead after she told them she was heading back to the mansion.

Outside, the air was cool and heavy clouds overhead promised rain at any moment.

"Is there anything I can do?" Adahn asked after a while.

"Thank you, but no. I'll be okay," she said softly.

"Because it was *him* that you needed." A trace of bitterness edged his voice, even though he clearly tried to hide it.

She sighed, slowing until they came to a stop. It took a few moments to muster the resolve she needed to look him in the eyes. He already knew what she was going to say, it was written in his hard blue gaze. "Yes. I'm sorry, Adahn."

"So that's it?" his voice was soft, almost pleading.

"I like you and I respect you more than I can say. You've become one of my closest friends," she said. "But I don't feel any more than that for you. I'm sorry."

He nodded, jaw clenching. "All right. I accept that."

She opened her mouth to respond, but despite her best intentions had no idea what to say to try and make things better. In the end he turned away, beginning to walk off. She fell into step with him and they walked in silence back to her home.

The house was quiet when she entered, leaving her guards stationed outside, but Dawn and Ladan were both up and eating breakfast when she walked through to the dining room. They sat close together, and some of Ladan's grim aura had softened.

"Are you just getting home?" Dawn asked with a smile.

"Yeah. The three of us had a lot of catching up to do."

"I bet. How are you doing?"

Ladan's gaze lifted to hers at Dawn's question, and Alyx sighed. "Part of me is still aching with grief and wants to burst into tears every other minute, and another part remains utterly thrown by Dashan's re-appearance. The rest of me knows Shakar is still out there to be dealt with and is both heartbroken and furious to know it was Astor all this time."

For a moment Dawn just stared at her. Then she said quietly, "I think that's the most honest you've been with me for a very long time, Alyx."

She considered that for a moment, reaching out to take a sip from Ladan's glass of juice. Her brother's green gaze lingered on her, but it was a comforting weight. "What I saw inside Shakar when he attacked me... he's so twisted up. Now I know how he ended up like that. It wasn't becoming invulnerable. It has nothing to do with being a mage of the higher order. Those things were just awful coincidence. He loved his Taliath and the council killed her. He was angry and he wanted vengeance. He bottled up his grief and anger and those emotions were so powerful they turned him." She paused. "I don't want that to happen to me."

"It won't," Ladan said quietly.

"No," she said, meeting his gaze.

"Here, eat." Dawn pushed a plate of toast at her. "Tarrick wants to meet over at the palace as soon as you're feeling up to it."

Part of her quailed at the thought. She was wrung out, empty from tears and the ache of missing her father. Her conversation with Adahn hadn't helped. But in another part of her there was a spark, a little flicker of warmth from a night spent in the comfort and safety of her two oldest and dearest friends, the only family she'd ever had before DarkSkull. So she focused on that spark, protected it so that it would grow stronger.

Then she picked up a piece of toast and stood. "Let's go."

They were all in the mage offices—Tarrick, Finn, Cario, Brynn, even Dashan and Cayr. Jenna too, hovering protectively by the door. Alyx smiled at the warm hugs of support from Tarrick and Cario. The tears in Finn's eyes as he told her how sorry he was he hadn't been there to help brought matching tears to hers. "It's okay Finn, there's nothing you could have done. Leanli was here, and he tried everything."

He said nothing for a moment, then he threw his arms around her, hugging her tightly. Closing her eyes, she hugged him back, taking the comfort he rarely offered.

Eventually he stepped back, looking a little embarrassed. "Shall we get to it?"

"Before we talk about anything, we have a serious problem," Dashan cut in before Tarrick could start. "Alyx, I'm sorry, I know this isn't a good time to—"

"There's no good time for any of this," she cut him off. "If there's a problem, we need to deal with it."

He nodded, eyes roving the room. "I think there's an informer amongst us. Someone who was reporting information to the Mage Council and maybe even Shakar—spying, essentially."

Alyx stilled. "Dashan, I—"

"No, hear me out." His jaw was set stubbornly, and she sighed. There was no getting through to him when he was like this. "You told me last night that Galien and the council came for us in Sandira, came to kill me *and* you if you'd absorbed my invulnerability."

Ladan nodded. "Right, because of their policy about Taliath."

"Exactly," Dashan said steadily "Because they knew about me and Alyx."

Alyx nodded slowly. "They knew details, specific details. Information that only a handful of people could have known or guessed."

Understanding spread over Dashan's face. "You already worked this out."

"I..." She trailed off as realisation hit her like a thunderbolt. *Now it makes sense.* Relief and joy hit her so hard she had to brace herself against the table for support.

"Alyx?" Ladan pressed.

"I figured it out three years ago," Alyx said. "The specific details Galien knew, it could only have come from one of a few people. Those in this room and my father."

A thick silence fell. Of course, it was Finn who spoke first. He sounded utterly bewildered. "You knew this and you did nothing? All that time we've been working under you, trusted with everything."

"I don't understand," Tarrick frowned.

Ladan was angry. "Something needs to be done to find out who this spy is, and if you won't do it, Aly-girl, then I will. You should have done something a long time ago."

"Being my brother doesn't give you the right to lecture me. I won't—"

"That's exactly what it does do," he cut over her. "This affects more than just you. A spy with the level of access to our planning that your closest friends have compromises our entire effort against Shakar."

"He's right," Dashan said firmly. "We need to—"

"Stop!" She lifted her hand, then glanced around the room. "Yes, I knew the council had information that could only have come from someone here. I also knew that Shakar's Hunters had been finding us too quickly and too often—it was a suspicion I held even before Sandira."

The confusion on Dawn's face matched that of everyone in the room. "Why didn't you just read our thoughts to find out who it was?"

"Because I only became certain after Sandira, when the trust between us had been completely shattered and we were trying to rebuild it." She glanced around the room, looking at each of them in turn. "I wrestled with it for days, but when it came down to it, I fundamentally could not believe that any of you was a spy. I decided to trust in that, to have faith. If I was going to build a new mage order, if I wanted you all to have faith in me, then I had to have faith in you too. So I decided that there must be another explanation. And in the end, there was."

Finn looked close to tears. "What was it?"

"Astor."

Understanding dropped over their faces with varying degrees of speed. Cayr sank into a chair, head dropping into his hands. Quicker than thought, Jenna had moved to his side, resting a hand on his shoulder.

"Astor is Shakar." Alyx's voice trembled a little as she said it out loud. "Shakar knew all about me and Dashan, and Astor knew all of our secrets.

After the attack on Sandira—*he* warned me of the spy, pointed out the specific detail the council knew. He was trying to drive us apart." Wonder filled her voice. "But he failed. I didn't let him."

The silence that followed grew so long that she began to feel uncomfortable. It was hard to read the expressions on her friends' faces. Cayr was looking at her with pride, Dashan with an amusing mix of horror and affection.

Tarrick rose slowly to his feet. There was pain in his dark eyes. "You have shown more trust in me than I ever did in you, Magor-lier."

Alyx waved him off. "Tarrick please, don't."

"He's right," Finn said. He seemed equally stricken. "I don't even know what to say."

"Fools," Dawn muttered under her breath.

Ladan gave Alyx a look that warned her this wasn't the end of him lecturing her on the topic, then cleared his throat. "There are things we need to discuss. Your Highness, it might be time to discuss your news."

"Yes." Cayr straightened in his chair and Jenna took a step back. "Amidst all the grimness of the past week or so, I have some good news to share with you."

Relieved at the attention shifting away from her, Alyx lifted an eyebrow. "What is it?"

"The Zandian emperor has sent a message offering to come to Alistriem and attend discussions with myself, Mastaran, and the leader of the Shiven rebels."

For a moment it was possible to hear a pin drop in the room as everyone swivelled to Cayr in astonishment. Alyx and her mages had been working on getting the emperor to agree to a meeting for years, and now... "He's willing to come *here*?" she asked.

A wry smile tugged at Cayr's mouth. "The emperor graciously acknowledges that given the state of the war, neither Mastaran nor myself are in a position to travel away from our homes."

She stared at him in astonishment. After the emotional hits of the past few weeks, it was difficult to accept that something good was happening. "When did this happen?"

"Sparky suspects the emperor's generals told him of the unexpected and rapid advance on Carhall by the Shiven army. It seems to have prompted him to action," Ladan said.

Alyx shot a look at Finn, he gave her a little knowing smile.

"I have already written to him to accept his offer." Cayr's voice turned firm. "The emperor has requested absolute secrecy—none bar his most senior advisors and Leopard guard are aware of his intended travel. Outside this room, only Sparky is aware. I insist that it remains that way."

"Will you invite the Shiven as the emperor suggested?" Dashan asked.

Cayr inclined his head. "I have already reached out to Tarian Astohar and King Mastaran."

"This is a good development, Your Highness," Cario said. "Even with Carhall having fallen, an alliance with Zandia could turn the war firmly back in our favour."

Cayr sighed and leaned back in his chair. "I hope so. I fear Rionn isn't going to hold much longer."

"It will hold as long as it needs to," Ladan said determinedly before rising to his feet. "We will make sure of that."

None of them spoke aloud what they must all be thinking. Alyx shivered. Shakar had been cautious and clever in his strategy so far, but how long until he decided that he could take what remained of Rionn and Tregaya by himself, especially if he got wind of a Zandian alliance?

CHAPTER 35

The ring of the doorbell was unexpected given the late hour. Not that she'd been sleeping—lingering grief and the fear of nightmares prevented that. The house seemed emptier now, even though Ladan and Dawn were living there.

As if summoned by her thoughts, Dawn came down the stairs as Alyx reached the front door, a little smile on her face. Lifting an eyebrow at her friend, Alyx opened the door to find Dashan, Tarrick, Finn, and Cario hovering, a strange kind of energy buzzing around them. All wore non-descript clothing.

"What's going on?" she asked suspiciously.

"I'm in!" Dawn answered somebody's unspoken thought and pushed past Alyx, joining the young men outside. It was only now Alyx noticed her friend had changed into a pretty sundress and light cotton wrap. *In for what?*

"We." Dashan gestured grandly to all of those behind him. "Have decided that we're in sore need of a night in the party district."

"I see." Alyx shifted to peer around him, raising her eyebrows at Tarrick. "You approve of this?"

Her astonishment deepened when he grinned. "Absolutely. Hurry and change before we leave without you."

She hesitated. This wasn't like any of them. Well, it was like Dashan. "What about my guards? And where's Brynn?"

"Brynn is resting after his recent head injury, under my strict instructions," Finn said.

You'll be safe enough with us for a couple of hours, and besides, we're going incognito." A smile tugged at Tarrick's mouth. "Just don't tell Rothai I said so."

"Will it help if I promise not to seduce any young women and start a brawl?" Dashan added, flashing her his most charming grin, and she caved, laughing.

"All right, I won't be long." She paused by Dawn. "No Ladan?"

The telepath made a face. "He muttered something about inns and drinking not being his idea of a good time, then rolled over and went back to sleep. Don't worry, we'll make plenty of noise when we come home later and insist on drunkenly telling him all about the fun he missed."

That thought had a smile spreading across Alyx's face from ear to ear as she hurried upstairs to change.

An hour later they were huddled together in a booth in the corner of a rowdy inn. All the windows and doors were open to let in the warm evening air, and the place smelled of ale, sweat and the salt of the ocean breeze.

Alyx had been tense ever since they'd arrived, waiting for the moment when Finn or Tarrick would start in on her and Dashan needing to keep their distance. But they hadn't said a word yet, neither of them even raising an eyebrow when Dashan had slid into the booth beside her.

"Interesting news about the emperor," Finn murmured, leaning in from her other side.

She grinned. The ale was beginning to soak through her, taking away her anxiety and leaving her feeling relaxed and loose. "It's what we hoped for."

"I hope it's not too late." He frowned. "And even if it isn't, this means we're now getting close to the final steps."

"Scary, isn't it?" she murmured.

"Yes, but also a relief in a way. I can't wait for all this to be over."

She nodded, meeting his gaze. "We just keep sticking with—"

"What are you two mumbling about in the corner?" Cario demanded, his face slightly flushed.

Alyx shrugged, took a swig of ale. "Finn was yammering something about the mating habits of sandbirds."

"Really?" Dawn scowled at her brother.

Finn shot Alyx an indignant look, then sniffed. "It's a fascinating subject."

Tarrick dismissed that with a wave of his hand, then started telling them a story about the time he and his brothers had gone hunting for sandbirds outside Sandira.

For a while, it was just like being back at DarkSkull Hall, when they would gather together in Weeping Stead to laugh and talk and complain about their long days. The constant tension across her shoulders and neck faded for the first time in a very long time. By Finn's flushed cheeks and Tarrick's relaxed sprawl, she gathered they were unwinding too.

A smile playing at her lips, Alyx leaned into Dashan. "Has Cayr told you yet that he wants to marry Jenna?"

Dashan choked, coughed, then spat his mouthful of ale all over the tabletop. Finn snorted, almost following suit. Dawn grabbed a napkin and threw it at Dashan, her grin only slightly wider than Tarrick's. Cario observed with his usual amused smirk.

"He's what?" Dashan demanded.

"You heard me." Her smiled widened.

"At least he'll always have a Taliath close by." Finn waggled his eyebrows. "Great protection."

"His nobles will have a fit," Cario drained his glass in one swallow, then glanced around for more. "Anyone?"

"Yes please!" they chorused at once.

Dashan shook his head in dismay. "Cayr's finally lost it."

"Unfortunately I don't think he has." Alyx sighed, sipped the remains of her ale. It was delicious, cold and frothy. She hoped Cario hurried back with more. "He says he loves her."

"I know what it is about her he loves." Dashan leered. "All that blond hair and—"

She punched him in the arm. Hard. He laughed at her.

Cario returned with a jug and refilled their glasses, receiving no end of jeers from Tarrick and Dawn about how much he spilled onto the table. Once he'd finished, they raised their glasses and cheered—rather rowdily, Alyx winced—to Third Patrol.

"I'm going to dance!" Finn said abruptly. He stood, swayed, gripped the table for support, then maneuvered his way out of the booth. "Dawn, dance with me?"

Laughing at her brother, and casting Alyx and Dashan an amused glance, she took his hand and followed him away.

"I might dance too." Cario's gaze was focused on the bar, where Casta was clustered with a few other Bluecoats. Alyx turned to Dashan, eyebrows raised. He gave her a little nod. She grinned, happy for Cario.

"Go on," she encouraged. "Say hi to Casta for us."

A few moments later Tarrick seemed to realise he was the only one at the table with Dashan and Alyx. She braced herself for the inevitable comment, but instead he muttered something about needing the privy and promptly disappeared after the others.

Dashan said nothing about the fact they'd suddenly been left alone together. He had a slight frown on his face as he considered his glass of ale. It didn't take long for her to work out what was wrong.

"You're going back to Tregaya."

He gave a sharp nod. "Rodin is capable, but I need to get back. The men will have reached their rendezvous points by now and I need to be there to start deploying them against the Shiven army before they advance further north."

She shifted to face him. "That will take pressure off our borders too."

"I'll stay in regular contact with Cayr so we can coordinate where useful." He waggled his eyebrows. "Any chance I could have those mages you promised me?"

"I'll have them come to you from our safehouse in Tregaya. I think there's at least one telepath there, and some warrior mages too."

"Thank you, your Magor-lier-ness." He sketched a mocking bow despite the cramped confines of the booth.

She scowled at him. "How soon will you be out of my hair?"

His teasing grin faded. "I hope you know that the last thing I want to do is leave you again, mage-girl." The look in his eyes made her heart do a lazy flip in her chest. And that was an easy enough truth to pull out from the tangle of emotions that had been lodged in her chest since he'd returned. No matter how much time had passed, she was never going to stop feeling this way around him—the heat in his eyes left her in no doubt it was the same for him.

"I don't want you to leave either," she whispered.

"Do you think they left us alone deliberately?" His breath was warm on her face, his leg pressed against hers.

"Tarrick should have been back from the privy by now," she murmured, and then she kissed him. Time seemed to slow and spin at the same time, the world turning to heat and overwhelming sensation. There was no hesitation as she wrapped her arms around his neck and pulled him closer, her leg sliding over his lap, his hand tangling in her hair, arms wrapping tight around her waist to press her against him. The booth was cramped, but that didn't seem to matter as they wrapped themselves together, hungry for the other's touch after so long.

She had no idea how long they were lost there, trading kisses and touches, but eventually they broke apart, breathing hard. The corner of the table was pressing painfully into her hip, and Dashan's hand was sliding dangerously high up her leg.

"We should..." He cleared his throat, but the huskiness was still there when he continued speaking. Her stomach flipped and she wanted to kiss him again. "Before they come back."

She leaned in, pressing her mouth to his one last time, a slow kiss that had her melting against him. Then, reluctantly, she broke away and began peeling herself off him, slapping his hands away with a grin when he tried to 'help'.

"What happens now?" Dashan murmured once they'd separated.

She gave a little chuckle, her emotions still too much on a high to worry yet. "No idea."

Tarrick came back not long after, his expression slightly fuzzy from the ale he'd drunk. By then Alyx and Dashan were a few inches apart and she'd managed to get her hair and clothing back into reasonable neatness. Finn and Dawn, laughing, stumbled back too.

Dawn gave Alyx a highly amused glance as she slid back into the booth, and she flushed hotly. *Damn.* Her shield had almost certainly dropped during that... intense... exchange with Dashan. Dawn didn't seem to have said anything to Finn though, and both he and Tarrick happily worked their way through the remains of the jug. Cario remained gone, and Casta had disappeared from amongst the Bluecoats at the bar.

It was well after midnight by the time they stumbled back towards Alyx's home, all either drunk or close to. Ever since the kiss, she'd been hyper aware of Dashan's presence, and as they walked through the city streets, Finn and Tarrick a little ahead, she reached out and took his hand.

It startled him, and he frowned, gesturing in the direction of the others. She shrugged—she'd promised them she wouldn't ever lie to them again about her relationship with Dashan. A wide smile—half delight, half amusement—spread across his face at that, and he tangled their fingers together before tugging her to his side.

"Finally!"

Alyx started as Dawn's voice practically shouted in her head. The telepath was smiling back at them. She summoned a mock-scowl. *"Why don't you put a lid on that amusement and start planning how you're going to manage your brother's fury over this."*

Dawn chuckled aloud, her musical laughter drawing all their attention. "Oh, Alyx, you don't have to worry about that anymore."

"Worry about what?" Tarrick turned to look back at them, his gaze on Dawn before sweeping over their joined hands. Finn turned too, eyebrows lifted in question.

She tensed, Dashan turning wary. His grip on her hand tightened.

"Nothing," Dawn said airily, throwing another smile at Alyx before continuing on. Both young men shrugged and kept walking. Alyx met Dashan's astonished look with an equally surprised one.

"Are they too drunk to notice?"

"In case you're wondering, yes we noticed," Finn called back.

"Then why aren't you furious at me right now?" she demanded, bringing them all to a halt once again. "This whole night you've been weird. What's going on with all of you?"

"We trust you," Tarrick said. "And we have faith in you. Like you had faith in us."

"It's far too late," Finn said. "But you have our trust, Alyx."

Her astonishment was so intense she literally had no words. Dashan did, remaining wary as he faced them. "What if she catches my Taliath disease?"

"Either she does or she doesn't. That's a personal choice for Alyx and you to make," Finn said. "We will follow her whether she is invulnerable or not."

"Can we keep walking please?" Dawn had begun hopping up and down. "I really need to use the privy."

The laughter that followed was, in that moment, the most glorious thing Alyx had ever heard.

Despite their boisterous spirits, they didn't make too much noise walking up the long drive to what was now Ladan's home. She wondered if he'd realised that yet. Two of her mage guards waited patiently by the front doors, Adahn and Chestin.

As they approached the house, Dashan tugged on her hand, drawing her aside onto the soft lawn under one of the trees lining the drive. Dawn was already well ahead, heading back to Ladan, while Tarrick and Finn were chatting excitedly about raiding the kitchens for cookies.

"Your guard was giving me an evil stare," Dashan said in response to her raised eyebrows. "And I wanted some privacy to say goodbye."

She hesitated only briefly before squeezing his hand. "You could come in with me."

"Not when I'm leaving you tomorrow," he whispered, drawing her into his arms. She buried her head in his shoulder, not arguing further. Besides, with or without her friends' blessing, being with Dashan had to be her choice, and she didn't want to rush into anything.

"Adahn is jealous of me," he murmured against her hair.

She nodded, pulled back a little. "You know that you have nothing to be worried about, right?"

His hand came up to frame her face. "Alyx, if I truly had died, I would hope that you would find happiness with someone else. I don't want you grieving over me forever."

She bit her lip, momentarily overwhelmed. Not by what he'd said, but what he was implying—he *wasn't* worried about Adahn. He had enough faith in her, in them, to have no need for jealousy.

"Come back soon," she whispered, then kissed him.

When Dashan had gone and Alyx turned to walk back to the house, Adahn had disappeared. Chestin remained. She gave him a friendly nod, but he merely inclined his head as she went past, gaze distant.

"Is everything all right, Chestin?"

"Yes, Magor-lier." He smiled, but it didn't quite reach his eyes.

She hesitated further, but his posture didn't invite further conversation. Trying not to be worried, she went inside and up to bed.

CHAPTER 36

The days following Dashan's departure flew by more quickly than Alyx had thought they would. On the same day he left Alistriem, Alyx reached out to the mages based in the cave network in Tregaya. It took several tries throughout the day until she found a telepath on guard duty above-ground.

Using magic over such a distance was no longer an issue for her, though the effort required usually left her with a pounding headache.

"I'm glad you reached out, Magor-lier!" the mental voice of Merial, their oldest mage and Jayn's grandmother, was filled with eagerness.

"Has something happened?"

"Nothing bad," Merial assured her quickly. *"But Master Rothai arrived two days ago. He's aware of the fall of Carhall and wants to know what your instructions are."*

Alyx thought about that for a moment, glad to hear that Rothai was well. After all these years, she still hadn't worked her way to liking him, but he remained one of the most powerful warrior mages alive and a valuable asset. Maybe it was time to bring him back to her side. *"Send him to Alistriem. There will be instructions waiting when he gets there,"* she said, but didn't explain why. She never told anyone who didn't need to know where she was.

"I will." Merial hesitated. *"Master Rothai didn't come alone. He brought several council mages with him. Parja and Dastanta amongst them."*

Alyx frowned. Mages who'd belonged to the council no longer had a master, but she hadn't expected Parja or Dastanta—both friends of Galien—to come to her. *"Are they willing to join us?"*

"I'm not sure. They seem willing to throw in with Master Rothai, so I suppose so."

The suspicion in Merial's mind was clear to Alyx, even over such a distance. Putting Parja aside a moment, she asked, *"Is Rody still there?"*

"He is, but he's driving us all to drink." Merial said in frustration of the young telepath. *"These young ones can't sit still for more than moment."*

Alyx smiled. *"Let me get him out of your hair. The militia still in the south of Tregaya are planning a series of attacks on the Shiven army as they try and push north. I want Rody to join their commander and help in any way he can. Send two warrior mages with him."* She paused. *"Actually, tell Rothai to take Parja and Dastanta with him to Alistriem. Nordan too, if you can spare him."* It might be good to integrate two potentially rogue mages with her loyal ones. Adahn would help with that too; they'd all been good friends at DarkSkull.

"Consider it done, Magor-lier. Is all well with you?"

"It is," she said, although she couldn't keep the sadness from leaking through her thoughts. Memories of her father popped up constantly. If Merial sensed it, she didn't push. She simply wished Alyx the best with a burst of cheerful thought, then let go of the connection.

Cayr received a quick response from Zandia confirming the summit, followed by a missive from Tarian Astohar promising to be there. After that, preparations began in earnest. Because of the requirement for secrecy, the entirety of the workload fell on the handful of people that knew it was happening.

Alyx was glad of it. The work gave her something to distract her from Astor's betrayal, grief over her father and missing Dashan with a constant, nagging ache. Besides, witnessing Tarrick and Finn arguing over which suite of guest rooms in the palace was most appropriate for the emperor of Zandia left her and Dawn in hysterics for hours.

Having so many leaders gathered in a single location made them dangerously vulnerable. Everyone worried about it. It proved too much for

King Mastaran's advisors—he was safely ensconced in the northern city of Ribeca, the largest city still under the control of Tregayan forces. The militia didn't want to risk his safety travelling through warring territory to come to Rionn, which was disappointing, but understandable.

"He gave us permission to act on his behalf, which is decent of him," Sparky said when he brought the news to Cayr. They were holding another late-night meeting, Cayr, Alyx, and their senior advisors clustered in his personal study. After almost five weeks of preparation, the conference loomed close—the ship carrying the Zandian contingent would dock any day. "If we agree to terms with the Zandians, Mastaran says we can agree on behalf of Tregaya also."

"Good." Cayr nodded. "Ladan, the Shiven?"

"Astohar is coming by boat via ShadowFall, that way I could make sure he has Taliath protection for the trip. They should be here any day now."

"We have to make sure the talks are completely secure." Cayr ran a worried hand through his already-tousled hair. "The level of risk these leaders are opening themselves up to by coming here..."

"We're doing everything we can, Your Highness." Since their father's death, Ladan had slowly but surely begun to step into the space Garan Egalion left at the king's side. Cayr seemed to expect it, and so far Ladan hadn't protested. "I will have six Taliath in Alistriem throughout the summit, and the Bluecoats have been drilling for weeks in preparation."

"You have warrior mages, too," Alyx promised. Rothai had arrived the previous week with Nordan, Parja, and Dastanta, and had been filled in on what was happening. Rothai had been so delighted by the Zandian developments he'd come dangerously close to cracking a smile. Parja had been polite but cool. Alyx had instructed Adahn and Tarrick to keep him and Dastanta under close watch.

"Good." Cayr sighed. "I don't mind admitting this whole thing makes me anxious."

"You concentrate on getting the emperor to agree to an alliance," Jenna spoke for the first time. "The rest of us will make sure everyone is safe."

"You should both make sure you're present at all talks," Alyx said to Jenna and her brother. "Don't forget how enamoured the emperor is of the Taliath."

Cayr yawned, breaking the silence that fell. "All right, it's getting late. Let's all get some sleep."

Cario was hovering outside waiting for Alyx as she emerged from Cayr's private quarters. "These need your signature."

She took the quill he proffered and dipped it into the small inkwell in his other hand, before signing her name to the parchment in front of her.

"I'm glad you trust me," he said in amusement. "You barely even read that. It could have been instructions to invade Tregaya for all you know."

"Well if that's the case, can we do it tomorrow? I'm exhausted."

He smiled. "Can I walk you home?"

She offered him her arm. "That sounds lovely."

Shakar chose that night to come at her with another nightmare. Panicked that he might read knowledge of the summit in her thoughts, she slammed her mental shield up and huddled underneath it.

"*Condolences on your father's death,*" he whispered. Now that he wasn't hiding from her, she heard Astor's voice in Shakar's, and it made her heart clench in pain. Her godfather was gone, just like her father.

"*Garan was a good man. I liked him.*" The hooks of his magic dug a little deeper and she whimpered, focusing everything she had on her shield. "*He spoiled my attempt on your friend Cayr, though.*"

"*How could you! You watched Cayr grow up!*" Alyx burst out, seeking to distract him from what she was hiding.

"*Just like I watched you grow up. That won't stop me from killing you if you interfere with what I'm trying to do.*"

"*You haven't killed me yet.*"

Laughter pealed through her mind and she winced—it was like razor blades across her skull. "*I told you. I don't need to. The council needed to die for what they'd done, but you—I just need to keep taking away those you rely on, those you love. Then you'll come to me. If only to make it stop.*"

Dread plunged through her, turning her chest to ice. And then he was gone.

CHAPTER 37

Alyx scanned the reception room, looking for Cario amidst the gathered guests. There were close to fifty people in the brightly lit hall, not counting the guards bristling at every conceivable entrance. The Zandian and Shiven delegations made up at least half that number, then there was Cayr and his key lords and advisors along with Alyx and her senior mages.

Chestin and Adahn stood guard on the main entrance with four Bluecoats and two Leopards. Nordan, Rothai, Parja, and Dastanta were assigned to watch the two other servants' entrances. Adahn had pointed out that keeping the council mages close was both a good use of their strong warrior skills and an even better way of keeping an eye on them.

The palace kitchens had put on a sumptuous spread, and those present gathered in small groups, talking and eating. Conversation hummed along, sounding lively and engaged.

A tall, muscular Zandian appeared gracefully at her side, his magic tinkling against her senses. "Magor-lier, it's a pleasure to meet you again."

"Hinga, I feel the same way. Tarrick is delighted you were chosen to travel with the emperor."

"Loren will forever be envious of me, I fear." A mischievous smile flashed over Hinga's fierce features. "But I am glad for the opportunity to visit your beautiful city."

"I hope the emperor is also enjoying his stay here?" She lifted an eyebrow.

"It is a shame that we cannot risk staying more than a handful of days," Hinga said. "However, I believe the emperor is pleased with the progress of our discussions so far."

"Do you think he will help us?" Alyx asked bluntly.

"That I cannot say. He does not discuss his thinking with his personal guards. If it's any consolation, Tarrick has convinced me of the need for our countries to ally against Shivasa and Shakar. Should the emperor ask for my opinion, that is what I will tell him."

"Thank you." Alyx straightened as she spotted Cario entering from the main doors. "Would you excuse me a moment?"

"Of course." He bowed and walked away.

She cut through the room, offering a smile and nod of greeting to those she passed, intercepting Cario as he headed for one of the food tables. "Everything all right?"

"Yes. I was just out making sure the Bluecoats and Leopards are getting along peaceably." Cario nodded. "How are things in here?"

"Everyone seems to be talking busily, which I suppose is a good sign."

"Cayr's done well. It was clear the emperor was dubious of his youth, but the king has ably demonstrated his strategic grasp of the war and his firm hold over his senior nobles. It helps that his most senior advisor is a Taliath," Cario noted, then frowned slightly. "What is it? You seem worried."

"Oh it's nothing." She shook her head, as if to dislodge the anxiousness that had been creeping up the back of her neck. "I had another nightmare the other night, and ever since I've been on edge. It doesn't help that the emperor leaves tomorrow and has yet to formally agree to anything."

"If it helps, I think Tarian Astohar's presentation this morning was compelling. The emperor was clearly swayed by his arguments."

Alyx's gaze moved to the tall Shiven standing with Ladan towards the centre of the room. The rebel leader towered over everyone there apart from the emperor, yet moved with characteristic Shiven grace and spoke with a quiet, penetrating voice. Both Dashan and Ladan spoke highly of him, and

Alyx had yet to see anything to cause her to disagree with them. He was clearly passionate about improving the circumstances of his people.

"His offer of a formal alliance and increased trade concessions if the Shiven government is toppled were generous," Alyx agreed.

"Generous, but necessary. If Astohar's rebels managed to topple the Shiven leader, they will have a difficult time establishing a new government while maintaining stability. They'll need all the help they can get, which is why Astohar is looking for allies now."

"Perhaps we should consider sending some mages into Shivasa to help him?"

"Let's definitely discuss it after the conference," Cario said, then glanced up. "Tarrick is waving me over. I'd better go and see what he wants."

"I'll join Cayr and the emperor. Lend the weight of the Magor-lier to their chat." Time to summon the polite charm she'd mastered in childhood.

Cario's mouth quirked in a smile. "Good idea."

"Alyx!"

She was halfway across the crowded space when Dawn's voice spoke urgently into her mind. Before she could reply the telepath moved into her line of sight, coming straight towards her.

"What is it?" Alyx asked, the words coming out louder than she'd intended. Dawn's mental voice had sounded almost panicked. A couple of Zandians nearby glanced around, and she smiled reassuringly at them. Dawn lowered her voice so that nobody but them could hear.

"I think there's a Hunter in the palace," she murmured.

A cold sliver of fear crept down her back. "Are you sure?"

"It's hard to tell, because I think there's only one of them. Can you see if I'm right?"

Alyx nodded and closed her eyes, sending her telepathic magic sweeping out through the hall and the gallery—left deliberately empty for security reasons—above. She found nothing odd on the first sweep, but trusting Dawn's instincts and ability, she did a second, more thorough search. This time her magic snagged on something.

"There's, I don't know..." Alyx murmured, shaking her head as she tried to grasp it. "A slight blankness, but you're right. There's more than one, though, maybe four, but far apart... the blankness isn't strong enough to pinpoint exactly."

"If they plan an attack, why so separated?" Dawn asked.

"I don't know." Fear uncurled slowly, and she fought to hold it down.

"Can you tell where they are?" Dawn's eyes were half closed as she used her magic too.

Alyx frowned, focused her magic as tightly as she could, but her finesse had never been good. "I'm not sure. You?"

"Inside the palace, definitely," Dawn opened her eyes and they both scanned the room. Nothing appeared out of place, and none of the alert-looking guards seemed bothered by anything.

"You two looking for someone?" Brynn's voice startled them. His teasing smile faded when he caught the looks on their faces. "What is it?"

"There are Hunters in the palace," Dawn said tersely. "Headed this way, I think."

"How did they get in?" Brynn asked in a low voice. "The place is crawling with mages, Taliath, and warriors."

"Disguised, is my bet," Alyx said. "As servants maybe. The medallions could easily be hidden under clothes. And it wouldn't be hard to do with only a few of them."

"Assassins, then. But they have no hope of getting close to anyone in here," Dawn murmured.

"I don't want to take any chances. Brynn, go and find the Bluecoat captain in charge and tell him to lock this room down." Alyx started moving for Cayr. "Dawn, tell Ladan what's going on. He can send his Taliath out to find and kill the Hunters while the leaders stay safe in here."

Dawn hesitated. "Alyx, you'll cause a panic that might put the discussions at risk. If there are only a few outside, surely we can—"

"Just do it, Dawn!" All she could think about now was her nightmare, Shakar's threat. She had to stop him. "Hurry, both of you!"

Brynn was gone without a word, pushing his way through the nobles to reach the nearest Bluecoat. Alyx looked for Cayr—he stood near the middle of the room with Sparky and the emperor, all three faces serious and focused on their conversation. Just to their left was Jenna, talking to Cario, but keeping a close eye on the king.

Anxiety pounded at her. She started moving, striding quickly towards them. He'd tried for Cayr once and failed. Shakar didn't take failure well. Still, the Hunters were outside the room—as long as they locked it down they could keep everyone inside safe.

"Finn, Tarrick, Adahn, there are Hunters in the palace," Alyx sent. "Help the Bluecoats lock down the entrances!"

At the same moment, Brynn reached the Bluecoat captain. Crisp orders echoed over the top of the hum of conversation, causing it to falter and then cease entirely. Into the silence echoed the thud of doors slamming one by one.

The servant's entrance was held open a few seconds longer for three Taliath led by Ladan to slip out, swords drawn. Swiftly and efficiently the Bluecoats lifted heavy bars and dropped them across the inside of the doors—nothing short of a battering ram would get through now. Alyx's mages hovered, staffs drawn.

Sensing something was wrong, the Leopards began moving towards their emperor. Chatter started back up, people looking around, fear beginning to fill the room. She caught sight of Tarrick, a head taller than most around him—he was shepherding Tarian Astohar towards his guards.

Silence fell over the room, each of the three leaders now encircled by guards. She told herself to calm, that Ladan and his Taliath would find and kill the Hunters. The worried bustle slowed as Tarrick and Cario moved quickly to fill everyone in on what was happening.

"You should let my Leopards out to hunt," the emperor said, his imperious voice carrying through the space.

"My Lord-Taliath and his fighters know the layout of my palace better, Your Majesty," Cayr said politely but firmly. "They will be faster in finding the Hunters."

Finn suddenly materialised at her side, white and drawn. "Alyx, this makes no sense. Why would he try for any of the leaders with only three or four Hunters?"

"Alyx there are more!" Dawn's panicked voice slid into her head.

"What?" Alyx spun on the spot, throwing her magic out in all directions. Tendrils of dread crept through her veins at what she encountered. Hunters approached from several different directions, and with a sudden instinct, she realised what was happening. What a horrible mistake she'd made.

"They're not going to try and get in!" she called into the minds of every mage nearby. "They're going to surround the room so they can cut our—"

And just like that her magic winked out of existence. Enough Hunters had come close enough to the hall for their combined number to have a blanking effect on any mage within. *There's someone already in the room.* An assassin. Someone who now couldn't be identified or stopped with mage power. With several Taliath already in the room for the reception, neither she nor Dawn would have realised the blank spots in their magic might not be one of them. A Hunter had been inside all along. And now he or she was locked inside with them.

Time seemed to slow.

Several Bluecoats closest to the doors started lifting the heavy bars at a shouted direction from Brynn, who'd caught Alyx's telepathic warning. At an order from Hinga, Leopards swarmed around the emperor, forcing him to the floor and covering him with their bodies. Cario came towards Alyx, Tarrick and Finn not far behind. Even without being able to read their thoughts she knew what they were thinking.

Protect the Magor-lier.

Jenna moved for Cayr, sliding in front of him and drawing *Huntress* in one smooth movement. Bluecoats surrounded the king on all other sides, ensuring his body was shielded.

For a single moment everything went quiet, those in the room frozen and waiting to see what would happen next. With successive crashes the bars on the main doors fell to the ground and the Bluecoats swept out, mages behind them, seeking to break through the bubble of Hunter medallions outside. The shouts and crash of steel from the fighting drifted in.

Alyx scanned the room, desperately trying to locate the Hunter that had to be inside before they could strike. They'd already tried for Cayr, she wouldn't let Shakar succeed this time either.

But Cayr wasn't the target.

She had almost reached Cayr, but the unmistakable twang of a bow had her stopping, spinning back. Cario heard it too, and he reacted instantly, fingers flicking as he tried to use his magic to send the arrow flying off course, away from its target.

Alyx.

Confusion flickered briefly over his face at the realisation his magic wasn't working. Then, before she could think, before she could *understand*, Cario leaped forward, throwing himself in front of her. The arrow ploughed into his chest, and he dropped like a rag doll, stumbling back and sending them both crashing to the marble floor.

She screamed. Time snapped back into focus, and she was scrambling, moving out from under his dead weight. Dimly, she heard more screams and shouts. Blood was pooling on Cario's chest, and his skin had turned waxen.

"Cario!" she shouted, cradling his face, trying to get him to look at her. "No, no, no. Cario!"

"Alyx! The shooter is still up there!"

Dawn's voice in her ear snapped through her daze as intended. She spun, looking in the direction the arrow had come from.

He stood on the gallery above, a man wearing a Bluecoat uniform and lifting a knocked bow. Adahn was running for the spiral steps leading up to the gallery, Chestin and Nordan close behind, but they were never going to make it in time.

As she watched, the Hunter aimed his bow at her, face taut with focus. Someone—Tarrick?—was running from her left, probably intending to throw himself in front of her too. He wasn't going to be fast enough though, and Alyx made no effort to move.

As had happened once before, on a stormy night outside a DarkSkull watchtower, utter fury consumed her. She snarled, and her anger smashed through the blankness holding back her magic like it was fragile china plate. Then she raised her bloody hand and summoned a concussion burst with every inch of power roping through her. It let loose in a burst of green light and energy, arrowing straight for the Hunter.

The bright flash of light distracted his shot, forcing him to wince and duck away even though the concussion burst dissipated harmlessly around him. He smirked then, lifting the bow, taunting her with the fact he wore a medallion. Adahn was almost at the top of the stairs but the archer was on the opposite side of the gallery.

Incandescent rage filled her, the scent of Cario's blood filling her senses, the sight of the archer's smirk unbearable. It boiled up, escaping in a scream of anger and more magic. She ripped at the columns on either side of the archer, the pure strength and power of her innate magic breaking utterly free of the medallions outside. Wind gusted, shoving Tarrick away as he tried to place himself in front of her.

The archer died with the smirk still on his face, utterly crushed as the marble columns on either side collapsed in on him. Chunks of stone and marble crashed to the floor below, taking some of the gallery with it. Guests scrambled to escape the falling masonry. Dust and debris whipped through the room.

Gasping from adrenalin, not exhaustion, she let her magic go and turned back to Cario, dropping to her knees at his side. His eyes were open and glassy, but slowly sliding closed. *No, no, no.*

"Where's Finn?" she screamed, glancing wildly around. Magic still beat at her, desperate to be let out, to do *something*. Not Cario too. She couldn't cope if he...

"I'm here, I'm already here," Finn told her. The healer mage was kneeling on the other side of Cario's body, one hand cradling the man's head, the other resting over his wound, covered in blood. His expression was as desperate as hers must have been.

"Why aren't you doing anything?" she demanded, voice thick with tears.

"The arrow pierced his heart. I can't–the Hunters are stopping my magic." Matching tears shone in Finn's eyes and his chest heaved. "There's nothing I can do."

"What if we move him?" she asked frantically, dropping to her knees.

Finn swallowed. "It nicked his heart. If we jostle him in any way he'll die more quickly."

"They're breaking through." Dawn pointed to the Bluecoats and mages fighting fiercely at the main doors. Tears streamed down her face. "Ladan has brought his Taliath back and they're cutting through to reach the servant's entrance. We'll have magic in a few moments."

Finn's stricken look told them that wasn't going to matter. Alyx's heart sank, taking all the strength of her anger with it. "Even with magic you can't save him, can you?"

His glistening eyes stood out starkly against his bone white face. He shook his head.

"Cario?" She leaned over him. "Can you hear me?"

His blue eyes flickered open, boring into hers. "M...Magor-lier."

"Stay," she whispered. "I can't lose you."

He smiled faintly. "You'll be fine... Alyx. My friend."

She bit her lip hard, drawing blood. Sobs welled in her chest, constricting her airway. Around her there was chaos, but all she could see was Cario's eyes slipping closed. She leaned down, wrapping her arms around him and hugging him as close to her as she could, uncaring of his blood smearing all over her clothes. Unbearable grief tore through her, too much to even cry.

"Alyx!"

Someone was tugging at her arm. She shoved them away, but the hand was back only seconds later.

"Aly-girl, come on. We need to leave. The Leopards and Bluecoats are clearing the corridors outside, but there could be more of them in the room."

"Then I'll kill them!" she shouted, tearing herself away from Ladan. "I'm not leaving him."

Tarrick hunkered down, his voice unexpectedly gentle in her ear, "then we'll go together." He slid his arms around Cario's body. Finn quickly followed, lifting his legs. Bluecoats and mages surrounded them as Ladan led them to the exit. She caught a quick glimpse of Adahn's face—it was as white as Finn's—and Chestin, who looked down as she passed by. Was that *fear* in his eyes?

"Alyx, here, take my hand." Dawn's face was streaked with tears, but her grip was firm. She guided them both after Tarrick and Finn, and Alyx was dimly aware of Brynn hovering protectively behind.

"Cayr?" she asked.

"Taken safely away by Jenna and the Bluecoats. The Leopards have the emperor safe as well, and Tarian Astohar is with the king," Dawn said soothingly. "Everyone else is all right. It's all right."

"It's not. It's not all right." She gasped.

He'd taken Cario from her. Just like he'd promised.

Who would be next?

CHAPTER 38

Alyx sat curled in a large armchair in the corner of the room, the cloth of her tunic stiff with Cario's drying blood. It was late, probably well past midnight. A strange kind of numbness had settled over her. Others were in the room, speaking in urgent tones ranging from angry to grieving.

Her focus didn't return until the door slammed open, cutting off conversation. Cayr stood there. His face was tight and drawn, and fury vibrated from every part of him. Jenna hovered behind.

"Why was Alyx targeted?" he demanded, and it was with a king's imperious voice that he spoke. "Why not myself or the emperor?"

"Maybe Shakar finding out Dashan is alive changed things?" Tarrick suggested. "Invulnerable, she could be a genuine threat."

"She just used magic inside a Hunter medallion bubble," Finn pointed out. "She half destroyed a room–that should be impossible. I'm not sure it's invulnerability that makes her a threat."

"Don't you dare!" Dawn rounded furiously on her brother. "Don't you dare be afraid of her."

"I'm not," he said firmly. "But I wasn't the only one that saw what happened."

"It wasn't about Dashan," Alyx said dully. "He knew one of you would jump in front of that arrow. He's trying to make me like him." And she'd made a critical mistake that led to Cario's death—if only she'd ordered them to flee instead of locking down the room... She should have seen it coming, but she hadn't and now Cario was gone. That knowledge twisted like a knife deep in her heart.

"What does that mean?" Ladan demanded.

She shook her head, unable to cope with the weight of their attention on her. It was all too much. "Nothing."

"What is the status of the emperor?" Brynn asked, neatly changing the subject. She was stupidly grateful to him.

Cayr shook his head, as if readjusting his train of thought. "He's as furious as I am, but he isn't bringing forward his departure. He'll meet with us as planned first thing in the morning."

"And Astohar?"

"The same," Ladan said. "We are fortunate."

"Excuse me if I don't see any of this as fortunate," Finn said, before walking past them all and leaving the room. The door slammed behind him.

"I meant no offence," Ladan said quietly.

"We know." Dawn took her husband's hand. "Finn is upset because he feels guilty. He's a healer, yet he had to sit there and watch as Cario died in his arms."

"Alyx, you would have died too if you hadn't killed the shooter," Tarrick said. His words trailed off, not asking the question that was in all their minds. How had she used her magic?

She shrugged. There had been no fear, only the desperate desire to destroy the person who had ended Cario's life. That anger was still there, surging like it had after Dashan's death, eating away at her like acid. It was a struggle to hold it in. Her voice was ugly and flat when she spoke. "I wanted him dead. Then it happened."

Silence fell again as they processed that. Eventually, Dawn threw her a concerned look. "You need to clean up, Alyx, and get some rest."

"We'll hold the funeral the day after tomorrow, once the Zandians and Shiven have gone," Cayr said solemnly, meeting Alyx's eyes with his kind blue gaze. "I am so very sorry for the loss all of you are suffering."

Dawn and Ladan had begged her to come home with them, but she just couldn't. She trudged down to the mage offices and stripped off her bloodied clothing, leaving it in a pile on the floor. A wash in cold water followed and she scrubbed and scrubbed until Cario's blood was gone and her skin was rubbed raw.

She paced for a while then, shivering, almost feverish as her emotions tripped from anger to fear to guilt. Grief was there too, a yawning chasm that threatened to swallow her whole. Her magic, never well controlled when she was emotional, told her Tarrick stood guard outside the door, a silent, protective presence.

By the time dawn arrived, there was only one person she wanted to see. Stepping through the door into the adjoining garden, she set off with quick strides. The golden light of morning was only just creeping across the floor as Alyx swung through the window into Cayr's bedroom.

He was waiting by the window—as if he'd known she would come to him—looking both tired and sad. She doubted he'd slept either.

"How are you?" he asked as she settled into the window seat beside him. Blue eyes regarded her with concern.

"I should ask you that." She nudged his shoulder. "You must be exhausted, and you've got your last meeting with Astohar and the Zandians soon."

"Don't do that," he said gently. "Hide how much you're hurting from me. I want you to tell me what you meant last night, when you said he's trying to turn you into him."

"Dashan's death, my father's, now Cario's." She shivered. "He tears a piece of me away each time, and he's doing it deliberately. He wants me to hurt like he did when his Taliath died. He wants the anger and need for revenge to take me over, just like it did with him."

"But it hasn't." Cayr's hand touching hers made her jump.

"I'm afraid it will," she admitted.

"It won't," he said firmly, forcing her to meet his gaze. "I know where Dashan is. I got a missive from him this morning."

She stilled. "Cayr, I—"

"I hope you've worked out for yourself by now that you could never be another Shakar," he said firmly. "There is not a single hint of doubt in my mind. Alyx, I've known you since I was six years old. You are no Shakar. You never will be. Believe it."

Something in his words broke the numbness, and she managed only a few words. "I miss Cario already. He was my friend. And I'm so afraid of losing anybody else I love." And then she broke down in his arms and cried. He wrapped his arms around her, rocking her gently.

"You're hurting, and you're exhausted and strung out." He murmured, pulling back to gently wipe the tears from her face. "We both know what you need."

"Oh, I don't know." She sniffed. "You're pretty good at making me feel better."

He smiled. "I need to get a message to Dashan quickly, it's important. Sparky's scouts think an attack is about to take place up north, close to where one of Dashan's militia units has been operating. We could use their help to push it back. Will you take the message for me?"

"I can't leave! What about the summit?"

"You can help by getting out of the city for a few days in case Shakar has a follow up attack planned—that makes us all safer," he said firmly. "Nobody but you and I will know where you are, and if you fly, no other mage or Hunter can track or intercept you."

She gave him a suspicious look. "That's a remarkably well-thought out plan."

Mischief flashed in his eyes. "I had the help of a Taliath."

"When did you have the chance to–" Her gaze flicked over to the bed, where the covers were rumpled and the pillows very clearly showed the indents of two heads. She made a face at him. "Is she hiding outside the door?"

"She's *guarding* outside the door." Cayr's sweet smile flashed at her, but it was quickly eclipsed by a frown. "It wasn't just Jenna. Finn came to me late last night—he concurred that it would be a good idea for you to leave the city for a few days."

"He's worried about a follow up attack as well?"

"I don't think that's all it is, but you know Finn, his brain is constantly working. Something was bothering him, but I don't think he was certain enough of it to tell me." Cayr rose and crossed to a table to pick up a tightly wrapped scroll. "Get this to Dash for me. He's encamped at DarkSkull. Once you're well clear I'll let Tarrick and Ladan know what's going on."

She hesitated only a single moment before taking two steps to lean up and kiss him on the cheek before taking the scroll. "Love you, Cayr."

"And you, Alyx."

She was smiling as she stepped up onto the windowsill, turning back briefly to call out, "Bye Jenna!"

Before leaving the palace, Alyx made her way to a familiar area in the residential wing of the palace. The door to Cario's room was closed, and she pushed it open slowly.

The interior was lit by the summer sun pouring through the windows, and nothing appeared to have been touched. A long maroon jacket lay neatly across the bed, and Cario's finest boots, freshly polished, sat below them. He must have been planning to wear them to this morning's session of the conference.

Grief clutched at her, and she gave it free reign as she looked over Cario's possessions, most of them familiar to her. Eventually her gaze landed on his mage staff, leaning carefully against the wall. Alyx reached out to run her fingers over its smooth surface. Tears poured unchecked down her face, blurring her vision.

Cario had made his staff from lighter-coloured wood than most mages, and when she picked it up, it felt longer and heavier than her own. It tingled with the residue of his telekinetic magic; an ability he'd wielded with such skill no other mage alive could come close to matching it. But he'd never wanted to be a warrior mage. Instead he'd been *hers*—second, friend, loyal and clever and her rock.

The air whistled as she swung the staff a few times, adjusting to its weight and feel. Eventually she hooked it to the straps down her back. It was heavier than hers had been and she shrugged her shoulders, letting it shift to a more comfortable position. After a few moments it settled, feeling utterly right.

With one final look around, Alyx made for the door. She had one more stop to make and then she could leave.

"Goodbye, Cario. I miss you."

CHAPTER 39

Apart from a little more rubble dotting the grass around the lake, DarkSkull seemed unchanged since the night they'd fled Shakar. The glow of the setting sun was at her back as she landed at the edge of the valley so as not to alarm the camp. The sentries on guard directed her to where Dashan stood in conversation with two militia soldiers by the steps of the main hall.

She paused to wait, but it only took a few seconds before he glanced over in her direction, as if sensing her presence. She sketched a wave and walked towards him. He said something to the two soldiers and they saluted before walking away.

"Alyx." Worry flashed over his face, hand instinctively falling to his sword. "Has something happened? Are you all right?"

"There was an assassination attempt at the summit," she said, voice breaking. "Cario jumped in front of an arrow meant for me. He died."

Dashan was moving before she'd finished speaking, gathering her gently into his arms and holding her close. "Is everyone else okay?" he murmured in her ear.

She nodded against his chest, allowing the tears to leak out and soak his shirtfront. "Cayr sent me with a message for you. Sparky needs one of your units to help hold back an attack in northern Rionn."

Dashan took the scroll from her and barked out an order to the nearest passing militia solider. Then he drew her back against him, holding her, giving her all the strength and support she needed. Her fingers curled in his shirt as she soaked it all in. It wasn't long before Rodin appeared, saluting sharply.

"Sir?"

Dashan kept one arm around her as he passed the scroll over. "Get this message to Captain Hoer. We've still got one of his pigeons, don't we?"

"Yes, sir."

"Tell him he's to help out in whatever way is needed. Once you've done that, ensure I'm not disturbed for the rest of the night. Someone bothers me short of a Shiven army invasion of the camp, and he'll regret it. Am I clear?"

"Yes, sir." The salute was even snappier this time, if that were possible, but Rodin didn't run off without a quick smile for Alyx.

Dashan's hand slid into hers then, and he led her past the hall and into what had once been her dormitory building. There were shadows in his eyes, his worry for her plain. Still, he didn't say anything until he'd showed her into a still-intact room. A fire crackled merrily despite the warmth of the fading day, and it cast orange shadows over the makeshift bed along one wall and a pile of Dashan's belongings in the opposite corner. Outside, the sun had finally set.

He took both her hands gently, eyes studying her. "Alyx, I know how much you must be hurting. I'll do anything to help, you know that."

She nodded, not trusting herself to speak in case she completely broke down. Dashan shifted closer. "Cario was a great man. And I know the friendship you shared was precious to you. I'm so sorry."

She swallowed. "Is it all right if I stay a day or two? Cayr and Finn both think I'll be safer out of the city in case Shakar tries again."

A smile crept over his face. "I think we can arrange a spot for you. How do you feel about your old room?"

She shook her head, trying and failing not to sway on her feet. "This one is fine."

"You look exhausted." The concern had returned to his face. "Take my bed and get some sleep. I'll keep watch."

She let him take her cloak and tug off her boots, then wrap a blanket over her as she curled up on the bed. It smelled like him and she burrowed into it, closing her eyes and using his closeness as a talisman against her grief. And then she slept.

Her eyes blinked awake. Dashan sat against the wall opposite her, dozing. The fire had burned down but it was still deep night. She'd been dreaming, for once not a nightmare but a memory from childhood. The smile was still on her face.

"Do you remember that Winter's Eve when you dragged Cayr and me out for snowball fights down in the city?" She sat up, stretching.

He blinked sleepily, roused by her voice. "Mmm. That was a good night."

"You made our childhood better than it would have been, shut up in the palace with only the other noble children for company."

"And you both gave my childhood happiness, where otherwise it would have been pain and misery." His eyes were dark.

"I'm never going to be like Shakar," she whispered. "Not even if he kills more people I love. Cario had faith in me. Papa had faith in me, and I won't *ever* let them down."

Dashan stood at her words, coming over to sit by her and wrap an arm around her shoulders. "That's not news to me, mage-girl."

She smiled, then she leaned in to kiss him.

He responded immediately, his arm pulling her more tightly against him. She tangled her hands in his hair and deepened the kiss. Every nerve ending in her body responded to his touch, and despite her aching grief, for a moment she'd never been happier.

"I'm not sure it's such a good idea for you to stay here," he mumbled, dropping kisses down her neck before returning to her mouth. For a moment she didn't respond, too caught up in the feeling of his mouth against hers.

"Dash?"

"Mmm?" He kissed her again.

She smiled into the kiss, pulling back just a fraction so she could meet his steady gaze. "If you still want me, want *us*, then I'm not afraid. I can absorb your invulnerability and I won't become a monster. I trust myself, and I love you. I never stopped loving you, not for a single moment."

"You're asking if I still want us?" He laughed softly. "Alyx, I've never wanted anyone else."

"Okay then," she murmured, then she kissed him.

As his arms came around her again, she reached between them to work on the buttons of his shirt so she could push it back off his shoulders and reach the smooth skin of his chest and stomach. Her mouth left his and began tracing kisses along his neck and jaw. His hands came up to lift her shirt over her head and then for the first time they were pressed together, skin to skin, no more barriers.

Abruptly she was overwhelmed—she'd never done this before, never felt so alive and so out of control at the same time.

"Trust me, Alyx," he murmured in her ear. "I'll take care of you."

And so she did. She gave herself up to his love and forgot about everything but the taste and touch and feel of Dashan Caverlock.

Alyx woke to sunshine warming her bare skin and shining into her eyes. She shifted slightly, trying to avoid the light, waking enough in the process to realise where she was. Dashan's large, naked body was pressed up against her back, one muscled arm tightly around her waist, his legs tangled with hers. He snored softly in her ear.

Suddenly shy, she buried her face into the blanket lying haphazardly over them, out of the sunlight. A few moments later, the hand that had been wrapped around her waist began moving over the skin of her stomach towards her breasts.

"What are you doing?" she mumbled.

Dashan chuckled and turned her around in his arms so that they were facing each other. His grin stretched from ear to ear. "What do you think I'm doing?"

She buried her face in his chest. "I don't think I can look at you."

"Why?" He sounded amused.

"You might be laughing at me, or you might be looking disappointed."

His free hand tucked itself under her chin and forced her to meet his gaze. "Why would I be doing either of those things?"

"Well, I've never—you know—and you've, quite often..."

"Alyx." He stopped her mumbling with a finger to her lips. "Do you see either of those things in my face right now?"

She allowed herself to look at him properly, seeing only warm contentment in his expressive brown eyes. Everything in her relaxed, melting into a warm puddle of goo. There was still grief and loss, and fear over what came next, but for now it was hidden behind happiness. "No."

"The more important question is how you feel?" He captured her face when she flushed and tried to look away. "You know you can be honest with me about everything."

"Well..." Alyx tried to find words for everything she was feeling, and eventually settled for, "You're really quite good."

Dashan burst into laughter at that, his chest rumbling under her hands. Seeing him laugh so freely, her shyness vanished and she grinned back at him. When he had control of himself, he flipped them over so that he was covering her with his body, and his hands began to wander again.

"You're not half bad yourself, Egalion," he murmured in her ear before kissing her. Alyx's reply was swallowed up by his mouth on hers, and very soon his touch meant that she had no room for coherent thought.

"Did you feel it?" she asked him a little while later, as they lay facing each other, hands entwined between them.

"Yeah," he said, dark eyes intense. "It was like nothing I've ever experienced."

Alyx smiled softly in agreement. She'd known the moment she'd absorbed his Taliath abilities; in coming together it had been impossible for her mind and magic to remain apart from him, and she hadn't wanted to. Their experience had been truly shared, in every way, and every part of her still rang gently with joy.

"So now I'm invulnerable."

"You're not having doubts?"

"No." She closed her eyes and curled her body around his. "It was amazing, Dash. I love you."

"Me too," he murmured, pulling her closer.

She lay there a while longer, eyes roving the room before finally falling on Cario's staff leaning against the wall near the door. Tears welled as grief ached in her chest, matched by rising anger.

"After I thought he'd killed you, I swore to hunt him down and destroy him. And then my father and Cario... I have to try harder, Dash. I want him dead. I want this over. I want a life."

His arms tightened around her, his voice soft in her ear. "I'll be standing at your side every step of the way, Alyx Egalion."

She soaked up his warmth and comfort for a moment before gently pushing him away and sitting up, the blanket falling away from her body. "We have to get back."

He eyed her. "I thought you were staying a couple of days."

"I can't," she said, her new resolve leaving her unable to sit still. Cayr had been right. Dashan was what she'd needed to calm the roiling emotions that Cario's death had caused, and now she had clarity back. She was wounded, but she could pick herself up and keep going. It was what Cario would want. "Shakar needs to die."

"Does it have to be right now?" he complained.

She glanced at the window—the sun was alarmingly high on the horizon. How long had they slept? "It's almost midday!"

He groaned and rolled away from her, rising from the bed in one smooth movement. Alyx sat there, admiring his muscular body and broad shoulders as he dressed, until he caught her looking.

"Oh no, mage-girl, both of us have to get out of bed." He leaned over and yanked off the blanket. Alyx hissed as the cool air hit her bare skin.

"No fair," she cried, scrambling for her own clothes.

"You were ogling me. I feel objectified." He winked. "Admit it, all you were after all these years was my body."

"That's easy." She stuck her tongue out at him. "And now that I find my curiosity is satisfied, I can move on."

"Satisfied?" Dashan vaulted onto the bed in one smooth movement and pinned her against the lumpy mattress. Then he leaned down and kissed her. In moments they were both breathless.

"Satisfied, huh?" He pulled back slightly, a teasing gleam in his eyes.

"Oh, shut up," she murmured, and pulled his mouth back to hers.

"What happened to *Kingsbrother*?" Finally up and dressed, they were preparing to leave. She pointed to his sword resting near the door. It looked serviceable, but nothing like the magnificent Taliath sword he'd worn before his death.

"Lost that night in Sandira," he said, shadows flickering in his eyes. "I think the council probably destroyed it in case it triggered my memories somehow."

"I thought so," she murmured, lifting her eyes to his. "I'm sorry, Dash."

"It's fine." He shrugged it off.

"No, it's not," she said pointedly, reminding him that she knew him as well as he knew her.

He huffed a breath, shot her a scowl. "Whatever. There's nothing I can do about it."

A little smile crept over her face. "I forgot to mention last night, but I brought you a present."

"You did?" His eyebrows lifted.

Alyx went to where she'd left Cario's staff and a heavy bag she'd carried on her back from Alistriem, concealed from sight under her mage cloak. Kneeling, she unbuckled the clasps on the bag and drew out a long object wrapped in velvet. He watched her curiously as she walked over to place it in his outstretched hands.

"He'd have wanted you to have it."

Slowly, reverently, Dashan unwrapped the velvet cloth, revealing Garan Egalion's Taliath sword gleaming in the sunlight through the window. *Heartfire.*

"Alyx, I couldn't." His voice caught.

"You can and you will. The sword deserves a new owner, and you're the only choice," she told him. "Ladan already has *Mageson*."

Dashan's hand slipped around *Heartfire's* hilt and he lifted it, swinging the blade deftly through the air. "I will wear it with honour."

Tears flooded her eyes. "It suits you."

CHAPTER 40

It was late afternoon when Alyx and Dashan arrived back in Alistriem. She had contacted Dawn telepathically as they approached the city so that everyone would know they were safe and not far away.

Although most of the palace staff and residents knew of Alyx and her magic, it still caused quite the stir when two people literally dropped out of the sky and into the main courtyard.

"Wait a second." Dashan caught at her arm as Alyx moved to climb the front steps. "What's our strategy here?"

"Strategy?"

"We hiding this? I mean, I know Finn and Tarrick seemed okay with it that night, but they were pretty drunk at the time."

"I'm going to be honest." She paused. "But let me do the talking."

Dashan grinned. "So we've got about an hour to live? Okay. Good. I'm prepared."

"Don't joke," Alyx said dryly. "You could be right."

"So negative," he said as they began walking up the steps. "Well, I can totally take your brother... I think. You'll just have to handle all the mages."

"You're hilarious."

"I know. That's why you agreed to marry me."

She stopped and stared at him. "I did nothing of the sort."

"But you will. Eventually." He grinned. "Speaking of which, how soon do you think it will be before we get some time alone?"

"Could be a while." Alyx sniffed. *Marry him!* "Maybe a few days."

"I hope you enjoy public displays then, because I certainly won't be able to wait that long."

"I remember you once promising to ravish me until I couldn't remember my own name," she retorted.

"All right." Dashan ran a hand through his hair. "Let's change the topic."

Alyx gave him an amused smile. "Why?"

"You know why."

She had to glance away at the look in his eyes. Any longer and there would have been a very public display which she was sure Cayr wouldn't appreciate inside his palace. She switched her thoughts to Dawn, using a touch of magic to lead them through to the lord-mage offices, where her friends were waiting.

Dawn was hovering at the door and enveloped Alyx in a hug the minute she stepped inside. "You're back faster than we thought."

"It was time." She returned the hug warmly.

"Dash!" Ladan slapped the Taliath on the back and they grinned at each other.

"Everyone is okay?" Alyx ran her eyes over the room. Tarrick, Brynn, Ladan, and Finn were all seated in the room looking tired but well. An air of sadness hung over them, though, and her heart ached. Finn had heavy shadows under his eyes. Dawn glanced frequently in her twin's direction, as if to reassure herself he was all right.

"We're fine," Ladan answered for them.

Alyx grabbed a chair and pulled it over to sit in front of Finn. "It's not your fault. Cario chose to give his life for me, Finn. There was nothing you could have done."

He stared at her for a long moment, then he gave a sharp nod. She reached out to take his hand and give it a squeeze. He squeezed back. She smiled at him—the edges of his mouth curled up. Her smile grew wider.

"What about the summit?" Dashan asked. "Good news or bad?"

Brynn made a face. "A bit of both. The emperor wouldn't agree to a full military alliance. He's worried about the Shiven push north, however, and so he offered to send his army south into Tregaya, to help Mastaran hold the northern half of the country."

Alyx sighed, rubbing at the sudden ache in her temples.

"All that's going to do is stall the invasion north an extra year or two." Dashan sounded as indignant as she felt.

"It might give us more time, though, especially if the Shiven are forced to put more of their resources into Tregaya," Ladan pointed out.

"Enough." Alyx shot to her feet. "I'm not giving Shakar another year or two. He has us right where he wants us, and we've been that way all along."

"For good reason," Dawn pointed out. "You needed to build the mage order the right way, to make it strong enough to fight him. And we had to learn more."

Finn shifted beside her. Alyx glanced at him, eyebrows raised—he gave her a little shrug. He was wearing the focused look he had when he was turning something over in his mind. She looked over at Dashan and found his gaze on her, slightly questioning. With a start, she remembered what they'd originally come here to do.

Taking a deep breath, she pushed back her chair and stood up, facing the room. "I'm invulnerable," she blurted out.

Silence fell. Dashan stepped up behind her shoulder protectively. Brynn grinned. Ladan looked horrified at the implication of his sister's sleeping arrangements being announced in front of him.

She risked a glance at Finn and Tarrick. The Zandian looked confused. "I thought you already were?"

"I..."

"Like weeks ago when Dashan was still here," Finn added.

Alyx flushed, the heat in her cheeks deepening as Dawn laughed in delight.

"I don't know why you felt the need to just announce it like that," Tarrick continued, scowling. "The topic makes me intensely uncomfortable, and I really don't need to know who you're sharing a bed with."

Alyx laughed out of sheer relief. "Oh, sorry. Are you sure you're all okay with this?"

Ladan scowled as he moved to stand in front of Dashan. "You hurt her and I kill you. Clear?"

"Perfectly," Dashan said just as soberly.

A tense moment followed before Ladan's face broke into a sudden smile, and he clapped Dashan on the back. "Good news, my friend."

"It certainly is." Dashan reached out to take Alyx's hand and tug her towards him.

Ladan glanced at their joined hands, sighed, and returned to his seat.

Brynn lifted a hand. "Is this why you're all, 'let's get Shakar now'? You think you can match him with your invulnerability."

"No. I'm not foolish enough to think invulnerability gives me anything other than the ability to last a bit longer in a direct fight with him." Alyx glanced at Finn again. He was staring at his hands where they twisted in his lap.

"I wouldn't be so sure." Tarrick was looking at her steadily, no trace of fear or doubt on his face. "After what you did to that Hunter... you could be as strong as him, Alyx. And now invulnerable too."

She shook her head. "He's been dominating my magic for years with ease. I won't underestimate that. Still, I want to end this soon, not wait for him to force us into a corner."

"Finn, will you please spit out whatever it is that's bothering you so much," Dawn said in irritation. Her gaze hadn't left her twin for several moments.

He blinked, seeming surprised to look up and see them all staring at him. Then he gave a little shake of his head. "I think we should keep news of Alyx's invulnerability secret for now."

Momentary silence filled the room, all of them taken aback. "Why?" she asked.

"We can't afford to lose mages, and some of them still hold council attitudes."

"Finn, I've been very clear about my views on the Taliath. Every mage who has joined me has known that and still agreed to be loyal. We've tested them all telepathically," she said.

"We don't do ongoing testing, and peoples' opinions change over time. Agreeing to the idea of working with Taliath is different to being faced with a Magor-lier who has become invulnerable."

"You're over-thinking this," Dawn said gently. "And we'd be just like the council if Alyx started forcing her mages to have their minds invaded on a regular basis."

"I agree with Finn," Tarrick said, and Alyx's gaze shot to him in surprise. "You don't understand mage culture like I do. The smartest thing you ever did was make Cario your second—he was pureblood mage elite, the grandson of a council member. To those who weren't entirely comfortable with you, he gave them comfort and familiarity. Now that he's gone, there's nobody to fill that void, to ease the tension. They see the twins and me as outsiders and too biased in your favour."

"What about Adahn? He's pureblood mage elite, and extremely well-liked. More than that, I trust him," Alyx said. "What if I make him my second, even though you would be my choice, Tarrick?"

"I recommend Rothai, not Adahn," Dawn disagreed. "He commands their respect, is pureblood and is the strongest mage you have."

"I won't make Rothai my second," Alyx said sharply. "Not after everything he's done. And I won't lie to my mages, either, that makes me just like the council." She sighed. "But if it makes you feel better, Finn, I won't make a huge announcement either."

"The mages have no choice apart from Alyx," Brynn pointed out. "It's not like they can leave her for another leader. She's their only hope to defeat Shakar."

Ladan rose to his feet, abruptly ending the discussion. "I think we all need some proper rest. We will resume the discussion of what comes next tomorrow."

Dawn rose to join him, lifting an eyebrow at the others. "Come and join us for dinner?"

"In!" Brynn leapt to his feet with alacrity. "I can't get enough of your wine cellar."

They crowded out together, Tarrick following, chatting happily. Alyx waved Dashan after them and lingered to pull up a chair in front of Finn.

"You had your thinking face on earlier when Brynn filled us in on the summit," she said. "Out with it."

He sat forward, the worry on his face clearing and eagerness replacing it. "What Ladan said—that Zandian help might force Shivasa to put more resources into Tregaya and give us some breathing space? It could go the opposite way, you know."

"Right." Alyx sat in the chair beside his again, thinking. "He pushed so hard into Tregaya because he wanted the council. Now, he'd be smarter to take Rionn before trying to expand further into Tregaya."

"And if he decides to do that, we have a very small window of time before the opportunity we've been waiting for is gone."

"You think it's time?"

His green eyes met hers, bright with anticipation. "You said you didn't want to wait one or two years until he has us in a corner, and you were right. And if we don't move now, we risk losing the opportunity altogether."

She rose to her feet. "Let's go and eat. First thing tomorrow I'll call a meeting and we'll see what they think."

Eagerness flashed over his face. "Finally, we might be able to end this."

"So about this marriage thing?" Dashan murmured later that night, as she lay draped over his naked body, drawing patterns on his chest with her fingers.

Alyx chuckled. "I still haven't agreed to anything of the sort, and don't for a second think I'm going to marry you without you asking properly."

He tucked a hand under her chin to bring her gaze up to meet his. "I'm not going to ask until after Shakar is dead."

"As long as you understand we might not..."

"We will," he said fiercely. "I have faith in you and me."

She smiled at him. "Suits me. Waiting longer means a bigger, more elaborate wedding. Just what I've always dreamed about."

Dashan groaned and she laughed. "What?"

"No more than ten people."

"You forget who I am, penniless Taliath. There is no way there will be only ten people at our wedding."

He gaped at her. "Penniless Taliath?"

"That's right."

Dashan moved suddenly, rolling them so that she lay under him. "I think I'd best teach you a lesson in manners, your royal ladyship."

"I love you." She leaned up and kissed him hard. "I love you so much."

CHAPTER 41

"It's time to move forward," Alyx announced. As per her promise to Finn, she'd gathered them all together in the mage offices. Cayr and Jenna sat together at the head of the table, curiosity written all over the king's face. Ladan had the seat at Cayr's other side, with Dawn beside him. Brynn, Tarrick, and Finn were there too. Dashan was at Alyx's right.

She'd looked for Adahn earlier, thinking to include him and address Finn and Tarrick's concerns about the mages, but nobody had known where he was. It didn't seem like her invulnerability was common knowledge yet, but she'd made no secret of Dashan sleeping at her home the night before. "Before I start—Dawn, we're alone here?"

The telepath's eyes slid closed momentarily. "The halls outside, plus the garden, are all empty. There's nobody within hearing distance."

"I ordered all servants to stay away, as you asked," Cayr said.

"Appropriate mysteriousness and secrecy is therefore in place," Brynn said in a dramatic whisper. "So tell us, did you dream up a perfect solution to defeat Shakar in your sleep last night?"

Alyx stifled an amused smile. "There is an idea, but it's one that Finn and I came up with, together, three years ago."

"And you didn't share your idea with the rest of us because...?" Tarrick lifted an eyebrow.

Finn scratched his head. "Because it's not so much a plan as an opportunity. An opportunity we had to wait for. If things had gone better—if the Zandians had agreed to an alliance years ago, for example—it would never have eventuated."

Also, the plan wasn't exactly foolproof. It was dangerous and risky. Alyx mentioned neither of those things aloud.

"What does that mean?" Dawn asked, an affectionate smile on her face as she looked at her twin. He gestured to Alyx, giving her the floor.

"Why did Shakar do things differently this time?" she asked the room. "Why hide his existence for decades, disguise himself amongst the mages, spend years pushing Rionnan-Shiven relations to the breaking point?"

"Because last time he was arrogant," Tarrick said impatiently. "He thought he was strong enough to go after the council on his own with only a handful of mage supporters. And he almost was."

"Right." Alyx nodded. "The council trapped him in Serrin and came very close to destroying him. So this time he hid from the council and he used his mage abilities in a far more insidious manner. He used Shivasa as a tool to weaken the council and any other opposition before moving against them. And it worked. The council is gone and within months he'll have Rionn. Tregaya won't be long after."

"That's rather a grim picture of things," Cayr said uncomfortably.

"An accurate one, though," Jenna said bluntly.

Cayr shot her a look, and Alyx had to bite down on her smile. Good—he needed someone who pushed him past his instinctive refusal to acknowledge or deal with difficult situations.

"We know this already." Ladan sounded as impatient as Tarrick. "We've known it for a long time."

"Exactly! But when Finn and I first spoke of this, I knew there was one possible chink in Shakar's armour—his hatred of the council. I didn't know then why he felt so strongly about them, but it was clear from the nightmares he kept giving me," she said. "Finn guessed that Shakar might go after the council as soon as he could, and he did. That was his first, and so far only, mistake."

"How?" Brynn looked sceptical.

"Because it placed him in the position he's in now." Finn sat forward. "A position that gives us a single, brief opportunity to bring the whole house of cards falling down around him."

Alyx pushed aside all the maps until she found the right one. Hovering over it for a moment, she found what she was looking for and placed a finger on the map. Dashan leaned over. It took him all of two seconds to catch on, a slow smile spreading over his face. "You're both geniuses."

"Excuse me?" Tarrick was frowning. "I think I preferred the bickering to the finishing of each other's sentences. What are you talking about?"

"Finn? After all, most of this was your idea."

He nodded eagerly and began talking, hands gesturing with enthusiasm as he spoke. Once he'd finished, a shocked silence settled over the room. Brynn's mouth had literally dropped open, while Dawn wore that worried look she often did when she thought Finn was being far too rational. Ladan's chair scraped over the floor as he moved to look at the map, eyebrows furrowed in a frown.

"That's your plan!" Cayr spoke, horror filling his voice. "Do you have any idea what you're suggesting? What I would have to do?"

"I'm aware," she said quietly.

Tarrick crowded in beside Ladan and Dashan to stare at the map, as if that would somehow make the plan sound better. "It would be a massive gamble."

"This is why we didn't mention it earlier," Alyx said dryly. "But Finn and I both truly believe it's worth a try."

"If Shakar does the smart thing and re-focuses his forces on taking Rionn before pushing harder into northern Tregaya, the opportunity we have will vanish within weeks," Dashan added. "And it won't come back."

Ladan appeared less certain. "If things went the wrong way, and there's a better than even chance they would, then we'd have accelerated our own demise. There are too many crucial pieces to success: your mages, Astohar's people—"

"Our demise is inevitable anyway," Finn pointed out.

"Not only inevitable, but exactly the way Shakar designed it," Alyx argued. "Yes, we're taking a dangerous risk, but if it works, we'd be on a whole new playing field. For the first time, he'd be at a disadvantage."

"I agree," Dawn said, and Brynn nodded beside her. "Anything is better than doing what Shakar expects."

"Maybe, but even if—and that's a *big* if—you succeed, there's still Shakar and we're right back at Serrin all over again," Tarrick said.

Alyx lifted her hands in the air. "He's not going to give up, Tarrick. Whether this works or not, in the end we have to face him and destroy him. I'm not going to be any more capable of that in ten years than I am today. At least this way it's only him I face, not his Shiven army as well."

Cayr shot out of his chair, unable to sit still any longer, and began pacing. "You're hardly filling me with overwhelming confidence." His blue eyes shot to Jenna. "What do you think?"

"It's a strategic gamble," she said, looking only at him. "But one that could change the landscape of the war dramatically in our favour. It could save Rionn."

Cayr turned to look at Alyx for a long moment. "But it could also destroy us sooner, couldn't it?"

"Yes," she said.

Dashan rose to place a bracing hand on his friend's shoulder. "You've always listened to my crazy ideas before. I say we do this."

A smile tugged at the corner of Cayr's mouth. "All right, Dash, Alyx. Let's end this."

CHAPTER 42

Once decided, they moved quickly. There was no telling how fast Shakar would re-distribute his Shiven forces once he learned the Zandian army was marching south to bolster Tregayan forces. Ladan left at dusk, boarding a ship for Shivasa via ShadowFall Island—Tarian Astohar's rebels would be integral to their success. At the same time, Alyx reached out to every single one of her safehouses, summoning every able-bodied warrior mage to Alistriem as quickly as they could move.

Dashan rode out too. He would use the militia to keep the Shiven army in Tregaya occupied, to harry them without respite and leave them unable to regroup with any speed. His eyes were alight with the coming challenge, everything in him vibrating with energy.

"I'm going to miss you." She wrapped her arms around his neck and kissed him.

"You take care of yourself," he told her fiercely. "I mean it."

"You promise me the same thing, and we have a deal." She spoke their now familiar promise to each other.

"Deal," he said, smiling then. "I'll see you soon, mage-girl."

He pulled her close and she buried her face in his neck, breathing in his familiar scent. When he pulled away, she felt almost physical pain.

"Love you." He gave her his familiar lop-sided smile.

She didn't stay to watch him leave.

The following morning, with ceaseless grumbling at Cayr's refusal to tell him what was going on matched with several horrified looks, Sparky dispatched orders summoning soldiers to Alistriem from every single garrison in the south and east of the country, leaving only skeleton forces behind.

"You realise if the Shiven catch on to this and attack from the southwest coast, we're done for," Sparky said to his king. "I know they don't have a navy, but they have merchant ships that can carry soldiers."

"I do realise that," Cayr said mildly. "Give the orders, Lord-General."

Tarrick, Jayn, and Finn left that morning too, riding north with a relief force of army soldiers and Bluecoats. They would take command of the mages already in the north and join the Rionnan soldiers defending against the Shiven advance—their job was to entice the Shiven into throwing more resources into their push south towards Alistriem. It would take a clever mix of fake retreat and furious rallying, and Tarrick's brown eyes glittered with the same excitement Dashan's had as he farewelled Alyx.

"We'll make them send everything they have at us," he promised fiercely.

"I'll hold you to that," she said, then glanced at Finn. "You concentrate on using your head to keep him alive."

He beamed at her. "Consider it done."

Jayn slapped Finn on the back. "Don't worry, Magor-lier, I'll keep them both in line."

Two weeks later, as her mages had begun trickling into Alistriem and taking up residence in her home, she found Brynn in the palace kitchens late at night. He was chatting with the young pastry cook assigned to keep watch on the fires overnight and wolfing down a piece of sweetbread. He smiled when he saw her, but the cook muttered an excuse and vanished into the storeroom.

"Want one?" He proffered the plate. "They're delicious."

"Sure. I haven't eaten anything since we stopped for lunch."

"It's quite the insane plan you and Finn came up with," Brynn acknowledged. "But despite the risks, I'm so glad we're finally bringing this to a resolution."

"Me too." Alyx took a seat beside him and bit into the bread. It was deliciously nutty and sweet, making her realise how hungry she was.

"Here," Brynn placed a glass of milk on the table before her. "You should look after yourself better, Magor-lier."

"Thanks." She chewed, swallowed, then looked at him. "There's another part to the plan."

He lifted his eyebrows. "You and Finn *have* been busy. This is an even more secret part, I assume?"

Alyx hesitated, pushing away her plate and glass. She wrestled with herself, whether she could do this or not. She saw the logic in it, saw clearly how it might work, but what she would be asking of one of her dearest friends—it tore at her.

"Alyx?" he prompted. He looked serious now, as if sensing what was coming.

"If this plan works, and I know that's a big if... but there will be a brief opportunity where Shakar will be at a disadvantage," she said. "We think there are two possibilities. He'll go to ground again, or he'll come for me."

"He'll come for you," Brynn said with certainty. "He knows you'll never stop hunting him if he goes to ground, and you're the only mage alive who has the abilities to do it."

"That's what Finn thinks too." She let out a breath. "And he had an idea not only about how to secure the first part of our plan, but also to engineer it so that Shakar thinks he has the advantage. A way to make sure that if we somehow succeed, he and all his supporters are dealt with for good."

"Ah." Brynn smiled grimly. "I take it this involves me, or more specifically, my mage ability?"

"Brynn, I don't..." She was horrified to find tears welling in her eyes.

His hand touched her arm, squeezing. "Tell me."

Once she'd finished explaining, he sat back, letting out a long breath. Brynn was no fool, and he understood the consequences of what she was asking him to do.

"It's your choice. I won't think less of you if you refuse." She tried a smile. "In fact, I'm kind of hoping you'll refuse."

He glanced away, his eyes distant. "I know that Shakar's army threatens the world as we know it. If he wins, none of us will like what he builds from the ruins. But for me, defeating him isn't about saving the world. I want him gone so that I can go home to Sarah and live in a little house in Fotiya and raise a bunch of kids that love each other like I love my brothers and sisters. I want to not be away from her all the time. I don't want to be a solider in a war." When Brynn looked at her, a sheen of tears made his green eyes glisten. "I think you and I have that in common."

She cleared her throat, trying to swallow around the sudden lump there, and reached out to lay her hand over his. "We always have."

"I'll do it," he said, then waved a hand as she opened her mouth. "It may not work, but I'll give it my absolute best, and if I succeed, you're the one who'll have to face down the most powerful mage of the higher order that's ever existed. I can at least do this for you."

The tears returned to her eyes. "Thank you. Brynn…"

"Nobody will see me go. Don't worry." He stood. "I'd like to write a letter for Sarah before I leave. You'll make sure she gets it, if I don't…?"

"I will." She stood up, hugged him fiercely. "Be safe."

He gave her a crooked smile. "I'll do my best."

The following morning, Alyx packed a small bag, slung Cario's staff down her back, and leapt into the skies above Alistriem, heading north. She touched down in the northern Tregayan city of Ribeca on a blustery, rainy afternoon three days later.

It took some time to locate the thoughts of a militia soldier in the city who knew where the king was being hidden, but eventually she made her way through a tangle of narrow streets and alleyways to a walled compound. Two plainly dressed men stood at the gates.

"I'm Magor-lier Alyx Egalion," she told them. "I'd like to speak with the king."

Their surprise was plain. "If you'll wait a moment, please."

One of the two went inside while the other watched Alyx carefully. She offered him a smile, careful to keep her stance loose and non-threatening. Moments later the gate swung open and Rodin appeared.

"Magor-lier, come in out of the wet!"

Rain dripped from gutters and danced over the cobblestones as he showed her through a small garden and into the house. More guards stood just inside the doorway.

"You're most welcome here," Rodin said warmly as they stepped inside. A servant came to take her dripping cloak.

"Thank you, Captain." Alyx nodded. "I'm hoping to see the king—I have urgent news to discuss, and a proposal which requires his approval."

"I'll take you straight through." Rodin began walking. "I'm currently in charge of his security. I know he'll welcome news from the south."

Mastaran, king of Tregaya, was a heavyset man in his mid-fifties. He rose from his chair as Alyx was shown through, his bulk dwarfing the handful of others in the room.

"Your Highness, Magor-lier Alyx Egalion here to see you." Rodin saluted sharply as he introduced them. "She brings an urgent matter for your attention."

"Be welcome, Magor-lier." Mastaran's voice boomed. He waved her to a chair near his before re-settling himself with the slowness of a man whose joints pained him. "You're a welcome sight, but surely you have been riding for many long days to reach us. Wouldn't you like to rest a short time before discussing what you have come here for?"

"My journey was much shorter due to my magic, Your Highness." Alyx bowed her head politely. "And my news is best discussed as quickly as possible. I need to be gone again by nightfall."

"Then sit." Mastaran waved her to a chair. "You have my undivided attention, Magor-lier."

By the time she'd finished, he was sitting back in his chair, staring at her with an interesting mix of surprise, shock, and horror. When she was done, he cleared his throat and sat forward. "You waited until all parts of this were in place before coming to talk to me."

"Yes, Your Highness. As you can imagine, it was critical that news didn't leak of what we're trying to do."

"It's more than critical," he huffed. "If even one piece of this falls over... if the Shiven army repositions before you're ready, if Tarian's rebels don't have the strength. And don't get me started on what you'd do if all this somehow works but you lost mages. It would all be for nothing."

She waited out his bluster patiently, then smiled a little. "Does that mean you're in, Your Highness?"

"Damn right it does!" he said gleefully, then fixed her with a sharp gaze. "Tell me exactly what you want me to do."

CHAPTER 43

She returned to Alistriem just over a week after leaving. The weariness of so much flying magic use tugged at her, as did a constant flicker of anxiousness. At any moment Shakar might catch on to what they were doing. All they could do was hope that he didn't until it was too late for him to do anything about it.

She landed in the palace, going straight to find Cayr. He had mostly good news. "Tarrick and Finn are doing an excellent job drawing the Shiven further and further down towards Alistriem," he said. "Scouting reports indicate Shivasa is sending fresh units across to Port Rantarin every day. Not that that is good news—it means we're past the point of no return. By Tarrick's last estimate, the army will be at our gates within two weeks."

For a moment his anxiety drew out her own. They truly were in a dangerously precarious position. Still, everything was happening exactly as they'd planned it so far. There was nothing to do now but keep going.

"I have King Mastaran's authorisation right here." She passed him the sealed parchment. "I delivered his orders as I flew back south. Units of militia from the northern garrisons are slipping south past the Shiven lines in small groups already, while the rest of the militia in the north is doing its best to keep them distracted. Dashan has the Shiven soldiers in the south so tangled up they wouldn't notice if an entire army went riding past—something we'll be testing very shortly."

Cayr sighed. "At least if things go badly here Mastaran won't be as exposed. The Zandian soldiers should reach him soon."

She hugged him in silent sympathy. He was carrying the most risk of them all, and her heart went out to him. "I'm going to catch up on some sleep. We can talk more in the morning."

"Good luck." He looked suddenly amused. "I think most of your mages have arrived. Ladan claims there's no room to move in the mansion—he and Dawn moved into the palace two days ago."

"They're both okay?"

"I think so, although Dawn hasn't done much but sit in her room using her magic—she's been invaluable ferrying messages between here and the border as well as Dashan's militia in Tregaya," he said. "Ladan worries about how tired she is, but she gets irritated when he hovers too much. And we all know how critical those messages are."

Alyx grinned. "In that case I might go and greet my mages before facing my brother."

It was dark by the time Alyx walked up the steps to her front doors, cloak swishing around her ankles. Every window in the house was ablaze with light. Although a warm bed was calling, she wanted to greet the mages first. She'd been a distant leader recently with preparations for what came next taking up all her time. A niggle of guilt wormed through her. With Cario's death and now Tarrick gone, her mages hadn't had much guidance about what was about to happen.

Surprise flickered to find the main foyer almost filled with people—surely the upper floors couldn't be so full? The hum of conversation that filled the space slowly died when they began to notice her presence. She paused just beyond the front doors, the weight of their stares making her suddenly uneasy.

Adahn appeared, pushing through the crowd to stand in front of them. "Alyx, you're back."

"What's going on?" Her voice was sharp. Something in his tone of voice, in his stiff shoulders, warned her things weren't right.

"We want to know why you've gathered us here?"

She locked gazes with him. His jaw was tight, arms crossed over his chest. There was challenge written in his eyes, and something else. Anger, perhaps.

"We have a plan to go after Shakar," she said evenly, lifting her gaze from his and sweeping over the gathered mages. "We mages are crucial to the plan. I brought you together to finally fight him."

"Are you invulnerable?" he asked flatly.

A shiver swept through the room, almost a collective intake of breath. *Adahn knew.* He knew and he'd chosen to do this deliberately. A sharp spike of panic speared through her chest. Finn and Tarrick's words of warning echoed through her memory, words she hadn't taken seriously enough. She'd been too confident in her mages' loyalty. Or maybe not. Surely she could win them to her again.

"Yes, I am," she said, facing the room without hesitation. After a long moment, as she read fear and anger, and even some horror, in the faces before her, the brief burst of hope she'd felt vanished, replaced by a creeping chill. How had this happened without her noticing?

She turned back to Adahn and lowered her voice. "I've lost you, haven't I?"

"You've lost *us*," he spat. "How could you?"

She controlled the anger that flared, using it to straighten her shoulders and infuse her voice with strength. "I have *always* been clear on where I stand with the Taliath. I never lied to any of you. And I will never be another Shakar."

"You destroyed half a room inside a Hunter bubble." Chestin stepped forward. "We saw you do it. It should have been impossible, but somehow you were powerful enough to break through. And you think we shouldn't fear another Shakar?"

"We all chose to follow you because we wanted a chance to defeat Shakar, not to watch another Shakar be formed right before our eyes," Adahn said before she could reply.

Voices murmured as someone else pushed through from the back. Rothai. He moved to stand at Adahn's side, ice-blue eyes impassive as they met her gaze. "You too," she whispered, her strength and anger vanishing as quickly as it had come. "I can't claim to be surprised, I suppose."

"The mages no longer choose to follow you, Alyx Egalion." This from Parja, the familiar sneer on his face as he stepped forward too, Dastanta at his side.

"And you're going to follow who?" She lifted an eyebrow. "Adahn?"

"He is pureblood mage and he believes in the old traditions," Chestin said.

Alyx took a deep breath, forcing back her terror and shock over what was happening. That Adahn could betray her like this, that any of them had. Without the mages they were lost. It was too late to stop the plan now. And Brynn...

"You said you joined me for a chance to destroy Shakar," she said, clinging to the little confidence she had left. "I am offering you that chance right now. Come with me and help destroy him once and for all. We can discuss the leadership of the mages after it's done."

"No." Adahn shook his head. "You are as much a threat to us as he is. I hope you destroy each other. If not, we will come for whoever survives."

"You are jealous and angry, Adahn," she said, then swung her eyes around the room, meeting as many eyes as she could. "I have built a new mage order, one that operates under principles of fairness and tolerance. One without fear. Do all of you truly want to throw that away? I am *not* Shakar, and I never will be."

Some of them were wavering, clearly doubtful of the right choice. But Parja was whispering to those around him, as was Chestin. They were too afraid. She hadn't understood the depth of that fear. And now she was paying for it.

She lifted her head, straightened her shoulders. "I *am not* another Shakar," she said. The words rang through the room, leaving a thick silence. She let it hang for a long beat, and then she stepped aside.

Parja went first, striding out the door and into the night. Mages followed him, first at a trickle, then a flood. Nordan was amongst them. Merial too. Alyx stood, stone-faced and straight backed, as every single one of her mages walked out the door. Adahn went second last, shooting her a final, angry look, followed finally by Rothai.

"Magor-lier," he murmured quietly as he passed.

And then there was silence, a cold night breeze flowing through the open doors, the house emptier than it had ever been.

White-faced with shock and lack of sleep, Alyx arrived at the palace the following morning in the midst of the hustle and bustle of the entire palace Blue Guard readying to ride out. No doubt the city barracks was equally chaotic. She squelched the surge of panic in her stomach. They'd gone too far to turn back. But now even if they succeeded, what would be the point without her mages?

Ladan shot to his feet the moment Alyx entered Cayr's private room, blanching at the look on her face. "Aly-girl, what is it?"

She dropped into a chair, voice coming out faint and disbelieving, as if it still hadn't really sunk in yet. She wasn't sure it had. "I've lost the mages."

Cayr shared a glance with her brother. "What does that mean?" he asked carefully.

The door flew open before she could answer, Dawn entering in a panic. "Alyx, the mages!"

"I know," she said miserably, meeting her friend's blue eyes. "They walked out."

"What the hell?" Ladan asked furiously.

Dawn glanced frantically between her husband and Alyx. "I was just doing a scan of the immediate surrounds of the city as I normally do. I picked them up heading northeast."

"It was Adahn," Alyx explained, raising a trembling hand to her forehead. "He was so jealous about Dashan, he turned them against me with not a little help from Parja. Rothai too."

"And we thought Finn was overreacting," Dawn breathed. "Oh Alyx, I'm so sorry. If you'd listened to him and Tarrick instead of me..."

"We can't do this without the mages!" Cayr sounded panicked.

"We don't have a choice," Ladan said grimly. "We've put all the wheels in motion. If we abandon the plan, we'll essentially be sending Astohar's people to their deaths. The militia too."

Cayr ran his hands through tousled hair. "We could get a message to them somehow, tell them to withdraw. It might reach them in time."

"No. The Shiven army is almost at our doorstep." Alyx stood up, hot anger finally breaking through the walls of her shock and despair. "The mages aren't critical for the first part of the plan. I can handle that myself. We won't get another opportunity for this."

Ladan looked at her, considering. "I agree. And if we do succeed with the first part of the plan, it puts Shakar in the most vulnerable position possible. We'll never get another chance to do that."

"But how do we face him and his mages without our own?" Dawn asked.

"I don't know," Alyx whispered.

"One step at a time." Ladan nodded firmly. "Now, to what comes next. Where's Jenna?"

Cayr jerked a thumb out the door. "You may not have noticed that it looks like the Blue Guard is fleeing the city, but my court certainly has. She's doing her best to keep a lid on their panic."

"Everyone is afraid," Dawn murmured, eyes distant. "They know the Shiven army is advancing on the city."

It was the last thing Cayr needed to hear and Alyx gave her brother a pointed look. "When did you get back to the city?"

"Yesterday." Ladan glanced at the king. "Tarian Astohar and his rebels are ready for us."

Cayr looked suddenly ill. "What am I doing?"

"We'll do our best, Cayr," Alyx said softly, voice full of sympathy. She wouldn't be in his shoes for all the gold in the kingdom.

"I'd better go and join Jenna." Cayr cast a wistful look around him, as if taking it all in in case it was the last time he saw the room. "There is much to be done before we depart tomorrow. There's no point leaving it any longer."

Alyx stared at him. "You think you're coming with us?"

"I'm the king of Rionn, Alyx. If I'm ordering a war march, I'll damn well be riding at the head of my army," Cayr said grimly, then strode for the door. "I'll talk to you later, provided there hasn't been a mutiny that has my head on a pike by the city gates."

"The soldiers are ready," Ladan told her once Cayr was gone. "Sparky told me they've been prepared for days and they're starting to eat the local garrison out of supplies. It's time he knows our full plan."

"I agree. I—"

"Magor-lier?" It was Tijer, hovering by the door. "One of the Bluecoats said they saw you come in. I heard you'll be riding with us?"

"That's right."

"Most units are already moving, only one division is left and they're about ready," he said.

"Thanks, Tijer. Tell Lord-General Caverlock we'll be riding out tomorrow morning. I'll join you on the main road outside the city."

Alyx ate with Dawn and Ladan in the pre-dawn. None of them spoke. She savoured the cook's porridge, her gaze running over the soft linen cloth over the table and paintings hanging on the wall. Her father's chair stood empty at the head of the table. Tears welled unbidden and she fought them back—after today, there was a good chance she might never see this house again.

Hearts heavy with the knowledge of what they were risking, they walked in quiet companionship through the palace gardens and down to the docks. The pink sky of dawn illuminated the ocean in the soft glow.

Despite the early hour, the docks were a hive of activity. Every single one of the long jetties was filled with neat rows of marching soldiers as division after division of Rionn's army boarded ships.

"I'll say goodbye here, Aly-girl." Ladan murmured. "I need to help Sparky ensure things are running smoothly."

She nodded, accepting his warm hug. "You take care of yourself. See you soon."

"You too."

He strode away, long strides carrying him quickly away from her. Dawn sighed. "I feel bad, not coming with you. Especially after what's happened. I can't believe they just walked out after all these years."

Alyx's jaw clenched, a horrible mix of anger and despair sinking her stomach at the reference to her mages' betrayal. "Your place is here with Ladan. And we'll see each other soon anyway."

Dawn squeezed her hand. "Bye, Alyx."

Alyx lingered on her own, half her attention on the boarding army, half on the plan she and Finn had come up with three years ago. Then, as a watery winter sun rose fully onto the horizon, the first of the ships let loose its moorings and slowly turned west.

For Shivasa.

The main road leading east out of Alistriem was filled with perfectly even columns of mounted Blue Guard. Alyx dropped out of the sky and landed where Casta stood waiting, his hand on Tingo's reins. The Bluecoat's impish spirits had been quenched since Cario's death, and her heart lurched at the faint shadows in his eyes.

"I miss him too," she said softly.

He looked down. "Yes, ma'am."

She stepped closer. She wanted to reassure him, tell him they were going to be able to avenge Cario, but the words wouldn't come out. A black despair had sunk over her—deep down she knew with terrible certainty that without the mages she couldn't defeat Shakar. She'd tried to be hopeful and positive with Cayr, but now all they could hope for was that this part of the plan worked and they would have more time to live before the inevitable destruction. It was a last-ditch effort that would never be enough. Instead, she tried for a crooked smile. "Let's go and do our best."

"Yes, Magor-lier." His shoulders straightened and his head came up. "We're ready when you are."

Alyx swung onto Tingo's back, quieting him with a touch. The waiting divisions of cavalry had seen her arrival and a wave of eagerness swept through their ranks, all gazes turning to her. She kicked Tingo forward to join Lord-General Caverlock at the head of the column.

"North through Widow Falls and into Tregaya in a week, Lord-General. It won't be easy," she told him.

She detested Caverlock, hated what he'd done to Dashan as a child. But there was no mistaking he was a veteran soldier who held overall command of the Blue Guard for a reason. "No, Magor-lier. But we're Bluecoats, and we've got the fastest and best-trained horses on the continent."

She nodded. "That's the answer I wanted. Let's go."

He fiddled with his reins, doing his best not to scowl at her, even though that's clearly what he wanted to do. "Are you planning on filling me in on where we're going, Magor-lier? And why we're taking four hundred Bluecoats and leaving Alistriem dangerously vulnerable?"

She smiled, settled herself in the saddle. "I'll explain on the ride."

And she kicked Tingo into a gallop.

CHAPTER 44

Dashan's father proved up to the task. The four hundred Bluecoats rode hard and fast, pushing their mounts to the limit each day. They passed through Widow Falls and across the narrow slice of Shivasa in a week, then angled directly west through Tregaya.

Alyx's telepathic magic was critical as they threaded the narrow gap between the Shiven troops to the north—who were fiercely battling Dashan's militia—and the army pushing south through Rionn. She ensured they avoided Shiven patrols and troop movements and allowed them to weave through the supply lines reaching into both Tregaya and Rionn.

Once Rionn was almost past them to the south, Alyx left the Bluecoats encamped and summoned her magic, leaping into the skies. The freedom of flight rushed through her, and she stayed high, well clear of any eyes below. In this fashion, she swept over the Shiven soldiers pushing south towards Rionn, though shock thudded against her ribs when she saw how close they were to Alistriem.

Reaching the Rionnan defensive lines, she slipped through camp and stopped outside one of the tents. Tarrick lay on his back, snoring, while Finn was curled up in a tangle of blankets.

With a touch of magic, she prodded both their minds with her telepathic ability, enough to wake them.

"What—" Finn came awake blinking. "Alyx!"

Tarrick scrambled up as soon as he heard her name. "Is everything okay?"

"It's all fine." She swallowed, then hesitated. "Did Dawn manage to reach you with the news?"

Tarrick's face darkened. "I will kill Adahn."

She huffed out a laugh, warmed by his protectiveness. "As much as I'd like to do the same, we're not the council. Mages are free to make their choices."

"We're not anything anymore," Finn pointed out. "Our entire fighting strength walked out on us."

"Our estimate is that Shakar has seventy or so warrior mages following him," Tarrick said softly. "We can't even get close to him without our own fighters."

"I know." Alyx hung her head.

A bleak silence hung over them, broken by a slight scratching on the fabric of the tent. Moments later Jayn stuck her head in. "I thought I heard your whispering voices. Are we plotting how to kill Adahn?"

Finn's smile flashed. "Alyx won't let us."

"Shame." Jayn sighed. "So I suppose you're discussing how doomed we all are."

The despairing silence sunk back over them, and not even Jayn's cheerfulness could stand in the face of it. Alyx cleared her throat, trying not to sound hopeless. "I just left the Bluecoats—so far we've made it without detection. The rest of the army was leaving by ship when I left Alistriem."

"So everything is going to plan." Finn joined her attempt at normalcy.

Tarrick nodded. "We'll leave in the morning."

"The Rionnan defensive lines will crumble much faster without us here," Finn warned. "We won't have a lot of time."

"We knew that when we started this." Alyx stood and moved to the tent entrance. "I'll see you all soon."

The following morning, as the Bluecoats readied themselves for the day's ride, Alyx reached out for the telepath she'd sent to Dashan months earlier. Rody was expecting her, his mind jumping with excitement as she made contact.

"Is all well?"

"Yes, Magor-lier! The Lord-Taliath has us encamped in a rugged valley well to the west of Shiven supply lines and marching routes."

"Good. I'll need you to lead me in."

It was late evening when four hundred Bluecoats wound their way down a narrow goat track and into a large valley just north of the Shiven border. Tents filled most of the open space, crowding up against a swift-flowing stream running down the centre.

Warned by Rody, the militia sentries greeted them eagerly, eyes widening at the sight of so many mounted cavalry. A tall man wearing captain's stripes came forward to greet Lord-General Caverlock and offer to show him to the space they'd set aside for the Blue Guard.

Alyx left them and rode Tingo towards the centre of the valley, flanked by her five Bluecoats, squinting against the bright orange of the setting sun. Soldiers moved around them, all flicking amazed glances at the new arrivals.

Rody must have warned Dashan too because he emerged from one of the larger tents and came striding quickly towards her. A smile spread across her face, and then she was jumping out of the saddle and running. He wore that laughing grin she loved so much, and his arms opened, lifting her off her feet and swinging her around in a wide circle.

"Alyx!" He pulled her tightly against him.

"Dash," she murmured, sinking into his embrace. Momentarily some of her despair lifted, and she clung to him tightly.

"You look beautiful." He stepped back as his hands framed her face, and then he kissed her. Alyx pulled him closer—two months was far, far too long to be apart from him.

"I love how excited you are to see me," Alyx murmured in Dashan's ear before stepping away from him. The Bluecoats were all either staring at the ground or studiously off into the distance.

"Casta, Tijer!" Dashan boomed, going over to greet them. "Roland, get that smirk off your face. And don't you dare laugh, Nario. Josha, always good to see you."

They dismounted and clustered around Dashan, old friends greeting each other excitedly.

"Your father's here," she warned once the boisterous hellos were over.

"Right, I'd best go talk to him, get the Bluecoats settled in." He frowned slightly, seeing something in her expression. "Is everything okay?"

"No," she said honestly. "But it can wait until you've spoken with your father."

His brown eyes searched hers. "All right. I'll send one of the boys over to show you to my tent."

Dashan came back not long after she'd washed and changed out of her travel-worn clothes. He came straight over, pulling her in for a long kiss.

"You seem cheerier than I expected after a conversation with your father?" she noted.

He shrugged as he sat on the rumpled covers of his sleeping pallet and began pulling off his boots. "I think he bothers you more than he does me these days."

"Really?" she asked in surprise. Even the mention of Dashan's father had always sent him into a dark mood.

"Really." He unbuckled his sword belt, resting *Heartfire* reverently on the chest by his pallet. "He's a bitter old man. I don't have to let him upset me anymore. I certainly don't need him to make me happy."

"I'm glad to hear it," she said softly.

He glanced over at her, flashing a warm smile that turned her insides to mush. She cleared her throat and looked around. "How many do you have here?"

"Only what Mastaran could spare. The large majority of the militia is engaged keeping the Shiven forces in Tregaya tied up so they can't head back home in a hurry." Dashan sighed. "Maybe two hundred in total."

"Plus four hundred Bluecoats now." She didn't like the pensive look on his face. "Hey, you've done what we needed you to."

"I have." He stood, running a hand over his face as if to dispel his worries. "Now, tell me what's wrong."

His face grew progressively stonier as she relayed what had happened, finishing with, "and don't you dare try and take the blame for this. My choices are mine, and I wouldn't have done anything differently."

"I don't blame myself," he said quietly, sadly. "I just wish we lived in a better world, where people were kinder and less intolerant."

"You and me both."

"So we're done, aren't we?" He met her eyes. "Even if we win this part, facing Shakar means death."

She nodded. "Yes."

Unbelievably, a slow smile spread over his face. "Well, at least right now, in this moment, I have you alone in my tent." He reached out to tug her closer.

She sniffed, surrendering to his warmth and love. "I see you still haven't learned to make a bed."

He shrugged. "Why would I?"

She tugged on his shirt, pulling him against her. "I missed you."

"Is that so?" he murmured, right before he kissed her.

Dashan was already moving as Alyx shot upwards in bed, waking abruptly with a gasp. He pulled her against his bare chest and wrapped his arms tightly around her.

"I'm okay." She accepted his hug for a moment before sitting back, thinking.

"You look troubled. What just happened?" His hand gently stroked her cheek.

"I felt the touch of Shakar's magic. I think he tried to give me another nightmare."

Dashan frowned. "He *tried*?"

She nodded, a weight settling heavily in her chest. "He couldn't, because I'm invulnerable. And now he knows it."

"Him knowing doesn't really change anything, though, does it?" Dashan mused. "And it meant he couldn't read the details of what we're doing inside your head."

She smiled, shifting closer so that she could drop kisses down his neck and chest. She didn't want to talk about Shakar anymore. "You know what I love most about your body?"

"No." He sounded amused.

She smiled and leaned up to murmur in his ear. "No chest hair."

Dashan stilled in her arms, and his voice was quiet when he spoke. "The thing you love most about my body is the Shiven part of me?"

"Yes." She drew back to meet his dark brown eyes. "Is that a problem?"

"No... I just." He gave her that somewhat unbelieving, but utterly happy smile she'd seen often. "It's just still hard to believe sometimes that someone loves me so much... loves all of me, even the parts that other people hate."

"Well, I intend to keep loving you like that the rest of my life, even if that's only a few more weeks. Is that all right with you?"

"I suppose I can manage," he teased.

"Good." She returned to trailing kisses down his chest.

"Shouldn't we get some sleep?" He tried unsuccessfully to slap away her wandering hands.

"Sleep is the last thing I want to do right now." She kissed him hard, then looked up at him. "Do you really want to sleep?"

He shifted, pushing them both down and pinning her to the bed, his hard body pressed against every inch of hers. "Does that feel like I want to sleep?"

Alyx laughed. "Not in the slightest!"

CHAPTER 45

Alyx glanced back as hoofbeats approached. Moments later, Finn appeared, his mare kicking up snow into a cloud.

"It's a big city," he murmured. "So much bigger than Alistriem."

"Even a little bigger than Carhall, I think," Tarrick said.

Alyx nodded and turned back to study the view that had occupied her for the past hour, despite the bitterly cold air.

Karonan sat in the centre of an enormous lake that was currently frozen over and covered in thick snowfall. It was walled, like Carhall, with four stone causeways reaching out from the north, south, east and west gates to join the city to land. Each heavy iron gate was overlooked by battlements wide enough that large numbers of archers could fire down on any attackers.

"It's hard to believe we made it here," Finn said wonderingly.

She shot him an amused smile. "It was your idea."

Finn had seen, even years earlier, how Shivasa might be momentarily vulnerable if Shakar pushed too quickly into Tregaya. Once he'd made that mistake, it had simply been a waiting game. Shivasa's army was stretched thin. Too thin. A large bulk of their soldiers were tied up in northern Rionn, pushing hard down towards Alistriem. The remaining heart of their fighting strength was in Tregaya, needed for the push to take Carhall so quickly and now caught up battling the militia as they tried to either push north or withdraw.

And ever since receiving Ladan's message, Tarian Astohar and his rebels had begun attacking garrisons in south Shivasa, not to take them, but to keep the army distracted while Alyx's Bluecoat and militia force snuck down from the north and Rionn's army marched on Karonan from the east coast.

Once in Shivasa, Alyx had ridden on ahead while Dashan led the Bluecoats and militia against the largest remaining garrison in the north on their way.

Now they surrounded Karonan.

"It was brilliant, Finn," Tarrick said quietly, his dark eyes full of respect.

Over the past day and a half, Alyx and Third Patrol had taken out every army outpost in the area. There were only a handful, and they hadn't been fully staffed. None had had time to raise the alarm. As far as Alyx or Dawn could tell, nobody in the city was aware of what was about to happen.

"Surely Shakar knows what's happening by now?" Finn spoke all their misgivings aloud. "Thousands of minds of our army out there he could have read."

"Maybe he does, and he hasn't been able to get word to Karonan? Telepath mages are rare, maybe he doesn't have one in Karonan?" Tarrick suggested. "That's why we moved so quickly, after all, to limit any warning he could give them."

"Maybe he's distracted by something else and hasn't paid regular attention to Karonan, assuming it's safe?" Alyx didn't believe it, and from the looks Finn and Tarrick shot her, neither did they. "And while it's fortunate he's not here, it makes me wonder where he is and what he's doing there." She shared a glance with Finn, and the flash of pain and worry in his eyes matched hers exactly. Maybe Brynn had succeeded, but if he had, that meant... She cleared her throat and turned her gaze away. Worry could be felt later.

The air was still and the plains around the city empty. Those few travelling along the causeways or on the roads surrounding the city appeared completely unaware of the hundreds of rebels, Taliath, and Rionnan soldiers hidden in the deep forest only a short distance away.

A touch of familiar magic brushed over her mind and she dropped her shields and summoned a touch of magic. Becoming invulnerable had made it substantially more difficult for her telepath mages to contact her—she now had to physically reach out with her telepathy to establish a connection. *If* she noticed one of them trying to reach her.

"*Magor-lier!*" Rody's excitable voice. "*We're approaching your position.*"

"*How did it go?*" she demanded. Rody had remained with Dashan's force when she rode on ahead.

"*We took the northern garrison yesterday morning. They were taken completely by surprise and our casualties were limited. Lord-Taliath Caverlock left his father behind with a skeleton force to guard the Shiven prisoners, but he's worried that word from surrounding villages could leak south quickly.*"

She worried about the same thing. They weren't equipped to stand and fight a war in Shivasa. This was a surgical strike—it needed to be done quickly.

"*Thanks, Rody.*" She sent him an image of where they were. "*We'll see you soon.*"

"Dashan's almost here. I don't think we should wait any longer. Tarrick?"

"I agree. The quicker we do this, the more chance of success. Someone could stumble across us at any moment."

She nodded. "I—" Dawn brushed over her mind and Alyx reached out again.

"Alyx, your brother is getting antsy."

Alyx huffed a laugh. "Dashan's almost here. Once he is, we're good to go."

There was a moment's silence as Dawn relayed that, and then, "He says it's time you tell us how we're going to breach those walls, because if we don't do that, Karonan can hold for months, time that we don't have." A pause. "I did tell him you were aware of that."

"Tell him not to worry. He just needs to focus on his job. Once we've—"

"I think he knows his job too, Alyx." Dawn cut over her.

"Yes, all right." Alyx sighed. "But can you also tell him to make sure our king doesn't get himself killed in the process of leading his army."

"I wouldn't worry about that." Amusement lilted Dawn's mental voice. "Jenna hasn't let him get more than half a step away from her all morning. Wait a second, I think Deskin is reaching out..."

Alyx opened her eyes, relaying her conversation to Tarrick and Finn while she waited for Dawn to talk to the telepath mage stationed with Tarian Astohar. According to Dawn, Deskin had heard of the mages walking away but had firmly declined to do the same.

"Deskin says Astohar is ready to move. He doesn't want to sit tight much longer—too much danger of discovery."

"Wait a moment, Dawn."

Alyx cut her off as hoofbeats approached. Moments later horses and riders were coming through the trees. Flashes of blue and green caught her eyes. Dashan appeared, dark Shiven eyes roaming the clearing till he spotted her with Tarrick and Finn, then he kicked his horse over.

"I don't think we can wait much longer." She recapped the situation. "Astohar and Ladan are both getting impatient. The fighters will be getting anxious too. Besides, someone is going to stumble across an army hiding in the trees sooner rather than later."

Dashan nodded. "My boys aren't too tired for a fight."

"Give the go ahead, Magor-lier." Tarrick encouraged. "Let's get this done."

Before he'd even finished speaking, Dashan was wheeling his horse, riding back to the Bluecoats, shouting orders to form up. The clearing became a chaos of noise; horses whinnying, captains calling instructions, swords ringing as soldiers checked their weapons.

Alyx looked back towards the city, reached out to Dawn. *Tell Ladan and Sparky to call for the advance.*

"It's done. Good luck."

You too. She sent a flood of warmth and affection with the thought then broke away. She needed to conserve her strength.

A horn rang out from the east, cutting over the sounds of Bluecoats forming up into neat rows in the trees around her. It rang again, louder this time. Then came a matching horn-blast from the south, where Astohar's rebels were bunkered down. Face alight with anticipation, Dashan lifted their horn to his lips and blew hard.

As the echoes of it died around them, Alyx urged Tingo forward. This first part was up to her. His hooves kicked up snow as they moved out onto the open plain, approaching the frozen lake and the entrance to the northern causeway. Movement flickered in her peripheral vision—shouts sounded in the forests surrounding the city and Shiven rebels boiled out of the trees, running gracefully for the western causeway.

Her eyes flicked to the walls ahead. Movement stirred atop them as the approach of their army was spotted. Metal screeched and the northern gate winched closed with a loud clanging sound. Running figures began to line the top of the wall.

"Alyx?" Finn raised an eyebrow. His cheeks were flushed with the cold, the breeze tousling his always too-long hair.

"You still haven't told us how you're going to bring down those walls," Tarrick added.

She glanced back. The Bluecoats were riding out of the trees in perfect formation behind her, the green-jacketed Militia arranged around them. Dashan rode at their head, and he flashed her a grin when he caught her looking at him. She grinned back.

"Well," she said. "You all know how I hate to be unoriginal... but if Shakar can do it, then I can damn well do it too."

Ignoring their queries, Alyx kicked Tingo forward a few steps, then loosened her shoulders before closing her eyes and sinking deep into her magic, gathering as much of it as she could. Then, raising her hands, palms outwards, she sent every bit of that gathered power roaring towards the northern walls of Karonan.

Two massive bursts of pure concussive energy flew towards the gates; the soldiers on the walls had a few moments to brace for impact, and then Alyx's magic hit. It ploughed into the gate and surrounding walls before exploding with a massive roar. Silver-green light flashed, temporarily blinding anyone watching, and then the concussive force expanded outwards, sweeping over all of them, before dissipating into the trees. When the light faded, the gates, along with half the northern wall, had entirely disintegrated.

"Go!" Alyx turned and shouted to Dashan.

Without waiting for him to reply, Alyx leapt up in the saddle and soared into the sky. Below her, the Bluecoats roared in unison, kicking their big cavalry horses into a flat-out gallop, streaming down the causeway towards the broken walls of the city.

High above, Alyx turned to the east. The thousands-strong Rionnan army had emerged from the trees and was marching steadily over the snowy plains towards the city. She could just make out Cayr riding at the head of his soldiers, Jenna's golden hair at his side. Sparky rode behind them, one arm raised as he bellowed orders.

In a row directly behind marched seven Taliath, swords already drawn and glinting against the snow. Alyx allowed herself a moment's fierce pride for what her brother and father had achieved.

She hovered above until Dashan and his Bluecoats hit the broken north wall and pushed through. Shiven defenders swarmed to the breach, and she sent more concussion bursts flying amongst them until they were in total disarray. Dashan dismounted, militia falling in behind him as he clambered agilely up the rubble to the top of the wall to engage the fighters there.

Alyx flew higher until she reached an apex in the sky above the centre of the city. Astohar's rebels had reached the southern and western causeways and were running unchecked towards the gates. Her staff spun again, shuddering with the force of her magic as she sent concussion blasts to blow apart the gates ahead of them, using enough force to blow them into pieces. Magic swept through her and she gasped with the rush of it.

Bright bursts of light began erupting into the sky as Shiven mages joined the defence of city. She'd wondered how many mages would be in Karonan—a focused sweep of telepathic power told her how many and where they were. There weren't many and none of them were telepaths. A bit of luck they hadn't expected. She expanded her magic outwards, sending targeted concussion balls at every single one of them.

Alyx then turned her attention to the defenders on the walls, using concussive bursts to help cover the fighters who were vulnerable as they crossed the open causeway. Once all three forces had reached the city gates and were engaged fiercely with the city's defenders, she searched for Tarrick and Finn's minds—by now they should be... and there they were.

She dropped out of the sky just ahead of where Tarrick, Finn, Dawn, and Ladan were running swiftly through one of the main streets.

"Fancy meeting you here," Finn said with a grin.

"Don't stop," Ladan barked. "We could run into Shiven at any moment."

Without another word, she fell into step as they kept running, Dawn warning them of any danger ahead. Alyx kept half an eye on her surroundings and summoned her own telepathic magic.

"Rody, tell Dashan and Deskin we're on our way to complete step two of the plan. All forces are inside and Dashan now has command of taking the city."

"Aye, Magor-lier." The telepath's voice was, for once, calm and focused.

"Dash has command of the city," Alyx said aloud.

"Good," Ladan said. "We're almost there."

Alyx's target, the one Tarian had directed them to with as much detail as he could, was walled and heavily guarded. There was only one gated entrance and it was bristling with Shiven fighters. Alyx threw her magical shield up as arrows came hissing at them.

"Dawn, find out where we need to go while I get us through," she ordered. "Ladan, Finn, watch our backs. Tarrick?"

"With you."

Alyx dropped her shield and let out a shout as she hurled a concussion ball at the gate. It exploded into the metal and sent both gates flying inwards. More echoing booms sounded as Tarrick sent his own concussion bursts into the defenders that were still alive.

"Found them!" Dawn said, triumph filling her voice.

Ladan took the lead and they ran for the now-gaping hole in the wall. He dispatched the remaining Shiven guards while Tarrick and Alyx took a moment to catch their breath. She tried not to look at all the dead, mangled bodies scattered around. More death. It made her stomach heave.

"Arrows!" Dawn shouted as they clambered over the rubble and inside the wall.

Warned, Alyx spun, settling her shield over them as more arrows hissed down around them. They shifted closer together, using the rubble and Alyx's shield to protect them.

"Dawn?" Ladan barked.

"They're in there." She pointed to the building on their left, across the open space.

"We're not going to get very far pinned down like this." Finn said.

"My reserve is too low," Tarrick said. "I can fight but not use my magic."

"Here." Finn reached out and touched his arm, and moments later Tarrick brightened considerably.

"You all run for the building, I'm going to keep the shield over you," Alyx said. "Ladan, Tarrick, you'll need to deal with the fighters guarding the front entrance to the building."

"You?" Ladan asked.

"I'm going to clear the walls of those damnable archers, and then I'll be right behind you. Ready?"

They nodded.

"Keep close to me," Ladan snapped tersely, then moved off at a run. Alyx gritted her teeth, the strain wearing on her as she struggled to keep her shield over them while they ran.

The moment they reached cover, she dropped the shield and began flinging concussive bursts. Stone gouged and chipped as her magic slammed into it, and the hail of arrows from the defenders slowed. Brute force could only do so much, though. Once the light of her blasts faded she targeted the remaining archers one by one, ripping the bows from their hands and quivers from their backs.

By the time she was done, exhaustion swamped her. She sagged, hunching over her knees to catch her breath.

"Alyx!" Ladan called across the square from the shelter of the building.

"Coming."

Forcing herself to move, Alyx ducked out from under the cover of the rubble and ran across the space to join the others inside the front entrance of the building.

"We took out the guards," Ladan said. "Dawn says there are a few more in the building, but nothing we can't handle."

"Lead the way, Dawn." Alyx hoped Dawn had the strength for it—her magic had become sluggish and slow to respond.

Dawn led them up a richly carpeted stairway to a long hall. Beautiful tapestries hung from the stone walls on either side of them, and more thick carpet covered the floor. They moved cautiously towards the double doors at the end of the hall.

"Where are the guards?" Ladan asked quietly.

"Not on this level," Dawn murmured, then closed her eyes. "They're guarding the back and side entrances. They haven't realised yet that the building has been breached, but it won't be long before they do."

"Then we'd best hurry," Ladan said. "Tarrick, Alyx?"

"I'll do it," Tarrick said with a glance in Alyx's direction. She nodded at him gratefully.

Tarrick sent the doors flying inwards with a controlled blast of his power. Ladan, sword drawn, gestured for them to wait until the dust and debris settled around the now gaping hole. Once they could see clearly, he moved forward, Alyx and Tarrick flanking him.

Alyx's fingers twitched, ready to employ her magic instantly if they were attacked. Inside, a group of Shiven men sat around an ornate table. Maps covered the surface, and several piles of parchment sat scattered over the top.

None of them moved. Their expressions ranged from terrified to angry—some wore a mixture of both. Alyx stared at them for a long moment. It was hard to believe she was standing here, right at the heart of Shiven leadership. After so long...

Ladan stepped aside so that Finn and Dawn could come in behind them, but he held his sword ready, taking up a guard position by the door.

"Which one of you is the leader of Shivasa?" Alyx asked.

"Who are you?" This from a younger man to her left. He was one of the angry ones, though his white knuckled grip on the table suggested it hid fear deep down.

"I am Alyx Egalion, Magor-lier of the mage order," she said evenly. "Now, which of you is Shivasa's leader?"

"He's not here." Another man spoke. Grey haired and composed, she guessed him to be one of their military leaders. His back was ramrod straight in his chair. "He was hidden for protection when your attack started."

"Dawn?" Alyx asked.

"He's the leader," Dawn said, pointing at a middle-aged, bearded man sitting at the head of the table. His eyes flickered at the pronouncement, but he didn't move a muscle to betray himself. The same couldn't be said of the young man to Alyx's left, however. He shifted uncomfortably, shooting a look of alarm to the others.

Alyx looked straight at the leader. "I'm sorry to inform you, but your city has been taken."

Ladan walked around the table and placed his sword at the man's throat. "On behalf of King Cayr of Rionn and King Mastaran of Tregaya, I'm giving you the chance to surrender. Accept, and you and all your military commanders will be taken prisoner and removed from power. Refuse, and I'll kill you where you sit" His face hardened, and he looked so much like their father in that moment tears shot to Alyx's eyes. "Either way, your war on Rionn and Tregaya is over."

The leader was silent for a moment, then he smiled bitterly. "I surrender."

"Get up." Ladan hauled him to his feet, while Tarrick and Finn did the same with the other men in the room.

"You might have won this battle," the leader said. "But you won't win the war. Shakar will destroy you."

She wanted to throw the words back in his face, but she couldn't. She'd lost the mages. The leader was right. The momentary surge of triumph she'd had died abruptly, turning to ashes in her mouth.

By the end of the day, Karonan was firmly under the control of Rionnan and Tregayan forces. The remnants of the Shiven army were placed under close guard at their barracks, and Sparky instituted a double guard along the city walls still standing. Rionnan soldiers patrolled the streets, ensuring none of the citizens took it into their heads to rebel, while the militia were sent out to scout the countryside for any Shiven units that might still be in the area.

Alyx found Dashan outside the Shiven barracks, speaking to the Bluecoat captain in charge of guarding the prisoners. His clothes were streaked with sweat and blood, but he looked well.

"Cayr?" he asked as soon as he saw her.

"In the old leader's rooms in the town hall. He's safe and well-protected."

"Good." Relief washed over his face. "How are you?"

"Tired, but pleased with how it all went." She caught the disquiet in his eyes and frowned. "What is it?"

"Tarian Astohar confronted the Shiven army general. He killed the man but was badly wounded in the process."

"Oh no." She sighed. "Will he make it?"

"Finn is working on him as we speak. With mage help, he might." Dashan ran a hand over his face. "I hope so. None of the other rebel leaders could easily step into his place. Respect and honour are important to the Shiven, and Tarian holds that amongst all the rebels. He's also well disposed towards Rionn."

"Do you think the Shiven will try and free their leader?"

"It's unlikely. He suffered a complete military defeat today. He's lost his standing—I don't think even the army commanders would accept him as leader any longer," Dashan said. "If we act quickly to assuage their concerns by doing what Tarian intended—holding an election for a new leader—I doubt we'll face much trouble from the army still out there."

"I hope that's true." She smiled for him. "Are there many senior commanders still alive?"

Dashan nodded. "One of them was in the room with the leader when you captured him, and a couple of others still live."

"Can you gather them and bring them to meet with Cayr and the others?" she asked. "We need to speak, all of us together, with the rebels."

Tarian had planned well for this eventuality, and his captains had already established a council amongst themselves to run things until elections could be held for a new leader. Alyx's respect for the man increased even further at how well the rebels were conducting themselves.

Dashan turned out to be right. After long hours of discussion and debate, the remaining commanders of the Shiven army agreed to accept the temporary leadership of the rebel council, on the proviso that the elections be held within six months, whether Shakar was defeated by then or not. Alyx got the distinct sense that not all of them had been comfortable with Shakar's influence and level of control over the leader—their honour had kept them loyal, but now they had strong justification to change their loyalty.

Once that was agreed, the council formally instructed them to send orders withdrawing the Shiven army from Rionn and Tregaya immediately.

It was dawn when the meetings finally ended. Alyx stepped outside and blinked at the early morning sunlight. As she stretched the stiffness from her muscles, exhaustion swamped her.

"It's hard to believe that this time yesterday we were all under attack by the Shiven," Dashan said. "And now there's peace."

"There won't be peace until Shakar is dead," she murmured, then straightened her shoulders. "I've been thinking, I should be the one to take the withdrawal orders out to the Shiven army in Rionn and Tregaya."

Dashan frowned. "Alyx, no, you're exhausted. You need to rest."

"The sooner the Shiven army retreats, the better. We both know that. Flying, I can reach them today, if not tomorrow. Written orders carried on horseback will take at least a week, longer for those in Tregaya. They're already too close to Alistriem."

He sighed, stepped forward to pull her into his arms. "I hate being parted from you."

Alyx pressed against him, closing her eyes as she rested her head on his chest. Weariness claimed her, and she wanted to stand there in his warm embrace forever.

"At least get an hour or two of sleep first," he murmured in her ear.

"All right," she mumbled. "Maybe I'll just stay here and rest."

He chuckled, then lifted her into his arms. "I don't have a problem with that, but I think you'd rest better in a bed."

CHAPTER 46

Alyx returned to Karonan late in the evening three days later, coming in slowly over the city. Everything looked quiet—rebuilding had already begun on the destroyed sections of city wall, and a mixture of green and blue-uniformed soldiers were a visible presence around the city. She breathed an inward sigh of relief.

She landed outside the stately building that had, until recently, been the home of Shivasa's leader, and traipsed wearily up the steps and inside. The Bluecoats on guard greeted her warmly. There were Shiven soldiers guarding too, big hulking warriors who were less warm but nonetheless polite.

After using a touch of power to locate Dawn, Alyx walked down the halls and opened a door leading into a plush, tastefully appointed sitting room. Tarrick and the twins were there, but her eyes went straight to Dashan, sprawled on one end of the luxurious couch.

"Alyx!" He rose instantly.

"Hi everyone," she said tiredly, walking across the room and into Dashan's arms. He hugged her tightly, then released her to peer down at her face in concern.

"You look exhausted."

"I am."

"Sit down."

He sat back down on the couch and pulled her into his side. She curled up against him, resting her head on his shoulder and slipping her hand into his.

"Have some hot tea. It might make you feel better." Dawn had risen to pull the small kettle off the fire and now she offered Alyx a steaming mug. She took it with a grateful smile, curling her hands around its warmth. It was still winter in Shivasa, and she'd been flying through bitterly cold air all day.

The door opened and Cayr walked in, Jenna at his side. His face brightened when he saw Alyx.

"Hi." She returned his smile. "I didn't expect to find you still here."

"King Mastaran is here," he explained. "Apparently he left Ribeca soon after you told him of our plan. He didn't arrive until yesterday, and is quite annoyed to have missed the battle. Both of us have remained here to formally acknowledge the rebel council as temporary administrative rulers of Shivasa and help them keep things stable."

"How did you go?" Tarrick asked, turning to Alyx as Cayr dropped into a chair opposite them. Jenna stayed by the door.

"Good." Alyx sipped at her tea and immediately felt better. "I carried the council's retreat orders to all Shiven army units I could find. As I flew back along the Rionnan border, I saw their camps being struck and a long line of soldiers marching in the direction of the Shiven border."

"Did you have any trouble?" Finn asked.

"Nothing major," she said. "Some of the commanders were not happy to be informed that the war had been lost without them even knowing about it. They recognised and obeyed the orders, though."

"I can't believe it's almost all over." Dawn shook her head. Her words echoed through the room, and she flinched once she realised what she'd said. "I'm sorry. I didn't mean to—"

Alyx waved a hand to cut her off. "It's all right."

"He doesn't have a regular army anymore," Cayr pointed out. "Which means we have time to think up a way to deal with his mages."

"Time only helps Shakar," Tarrick said wearily.

Alyx shared a miserable glance with Finn. She'd tried using telepathy to reach out to Brynn, to call him back, but had failed. She had no idea where he was, and the chances of locating him were small. She would keep trying.

"No, Cayr is right," Jenna said, surprisingly. "Shakar won't be able to build himself another army quickly. Yes, this was our best chance to take him, when he's most vulnerable, but that doesn't mean it becomes impossible."

Not wanting to spoil their optimism, Alyx shifted to look up at Dashan and Cayr. "How are things here? The Shiven guards on the entrance were almost nice to me when I came in."

"The new council is doing a good job of trying to get the city back to running as normal," Dashan said. "The causeways were re-opened this morning so that trade and travel could resume. They've sent out proclamations promising elections in six months, and the naming of candidates within a month. They want to do it right this time, make it a genuinely fair vote. I was worried that with Tarian hurt, some of his intentions might have been lost, but it seems like many of his rebel captains have a genuine desire for change in Shivasa."

"How is Tarian doing?"

"Awake and getting stronger every day." A genuine smile flooded Dashan's face. It was clear how much he liked and respected the rebel leader. "He'll be on his feet and running the council in no time."

"Mastaran and I have been giving them advice and suggestions on good governance, and they seem to be taking it eagerly," Cayr said. "There are some impressive men and women amongst the rebels."

"You'll have to go back soon, though," Jenna said pointedly. "Or you'll be facing a mutiny from your nobles."

Cayr glanced at her, affectionate irritation in his eyes. "Sparky's already taken a large part of the army back. I'll follow soon. I just want to make sure I'm leaving a stable neighbour behind."

"King Mastaran is eager to leave too—he wants to get back to Carhall and begin the process of rebuilding," Tarrick added.

"I need sleep," Alyx said lightly. She was exhausted, and simply couldn't sit there any longer pretending there was any real hope. "Tomorrow, we'll discuss Shakar."

Dashan led her upstairs to a bedroom on the top floor with a lovely view out over the frozen lake. Exhaustion tugged at every muscle in her body, and she groaned, sprawling face-first onto the bed. She didn't want to ever move again.

The bed shifted as Dashan laid out next to her, dark eyes searching hers. "Hi."

"Hi." She returned his smile.

He shifted, sitting up, and pulled off her boots before dropping them to the floor. Then he carefully undressed her before wrapping her in one of his clean shirts. Silence fell as Dashan shrugged out of his jacket.

"There's something on your mind," she said, recognising the look on his face.

He frowned and shook his head. "No there isn't."

"You have your thoughtful face on."

Dashan pulled his shirt off, tossed it over a nearby chair, and sat to begin yanking his boots off. "Alyx, it's nothing, really. There's no need for you to worry."

"Dash," she said softly. "We talk about everything. Tell me."

Dashan sighed and leaned back in the chair, one boot on, one off. "Tarian is going to win the elections. He's humble of course, keeps saying the Shiven could pick anyone. But everyone knows he'll win the vote."

"And that's worrying news?" She lifted an eyebrow.

His jaw tensed. "He's asked me to stay after the elections. He wants to appoint me as general of the Shiven army, in effect his second." He shook his head in frustration. "It doesn't matter. We both know that even though we won this battle, Shakar is still..."

He trailed off, clearly not wanting to say it aloud. Without her mages, they were lost. They might have more time now but Shakar would still win.

Alyx stared at him for a long moment, watching the orange firelight flicker over his handsome face. "I'm the Magor-lier, Dash. Even if somehow we *did* manage to defeat Shakar, I can't leave the mages to come here to Karonan."

He smiled, crossing the room to climb into bed and pull her close. She snuggled into his warmth, dropping light kisses on his chest.

"You'd be perfect for the job," she whispered.

His arms tightened. "It doesn't matter."

Alyx nodded and closed her eyes, allowing the exhaustion to claim her as she relaxed safe in his arms.

"I'm glad we had this," he murmured against her hair. "Even if only for a short time."

"Me too. Love you."

"Love you too, Alyx."

They were awoken what felt like only minutes later by a loud pounding on their door. With the reflexes of a Taliath, Dashan was rolling out of bed, sword in hand, before Alyx was even properly awake.

"What?" he bellowed as he crossed to the door.

"It's me, Ladan. Get downstairs now."

His tone brooked no argument, and still half asleep, Alyx stumbled out of bed and moved towards the door. Dashan caught her arm gently.

"Much as I love seeing you wearing nothing but one of my shirts, maybe you should put something on."

"Right." She shook her head, lucidity beginning to return. "Sorry."

Dashan looked concerned. "Why don't you stay here and go back to sleep? I can go downstairs."

"No, I'm awake now." She tugged pants on and reached for her shirt. This could be what she'd been waiting for.

The twins wore grim expressions as they congregated in the sitting room downstairs. Ladan stood next to his wife, poking at the fire in the grate, his stance rigid with tension.

"What's going on?" Dashan demanded as soon as Tarrick, the last to arrive, came in.

"Shakar has Brynn."

Dawn said the words softly. Her eyes flicked to Ladan, then Alyx. There was fear in her eyes, fear for Brynn, but also dread. Part of her knew what came next.

Alyx gasped in a breath, fear clutching at her heart. She glanced at Finn—he met her gaze miserably. She bit her lip to stop the tears wanting to spill down her cheeks. This was her fault. What she'd been afraid of ever since her mages had walked out. Her legs wobbled, and she sat abruptly in the nearest chair.

"How?" Dashan demanded.

"Shakar contacted me telepathically a short time ago." Dawn shuddered, and Alyx reached out to touch her arm in sympathy. She well knew what Shakar's touch on one's mind was like. Ladan gently pulled his wife close. "He told me he has Brynn and that he is going to kill him, slowly, unless Alyx goes to face him."

"How does he have Brynn?" Tarrick sounded calm, but his fists were clenching and unclenching at his side. "I thought he was back in Alistriem helping to run things there. Could Shakar have moved on Rionn so quickly?"

"Brynn's not in Alistriem," Alyx said quietly, raising her eyes to the room. "I sent him to find Shakar for me."

Tarrick stared at her, realisation creeping across his face. "You sent him before the mages left?"

She rubbed a trembling hand over her face. "It was the second part of the plan." She didn't bother spelling it out—it didn't matter anymore.

"We thought…" Finn choked out, then stopped, unable to continue. Dawn went straight to her twin, wrapping her arms around him. His shoulders shuddered with unshed sobs.

"It was my call, Finn," Alyx told him. "This is not your fault."

"Why didn't you tell me?" Dashan demanded.

"Because it was too dangerous for anyone to know," she almost shouted. Panic was threading through her, making it hard to think straight, to be calm. She didn't have much time. *Brynn* didn't have much time. "We have to go."

"Whoa, wait!" Dashan's grip on her arm halted her in her tracks as she spun for the door. "What does that mean?"

"If you go now, right where he wants you, he'll kill you too." Ladan's scowl matched Tarrick's and Dashan's. "He'll have his mages with him. They'll kill you before you even get close."

"I know," she whispered. "But I can't leave Brynn."

"You have to." The words seemed to tear out of Tarrick, as if causing him physical pain. A horrified hush fell over the room, but nobody disagreed with him.

Dashan shifted towards her, voice gentle. "Cayr and Jenna were right before. This was our best opportunity, but it won't be our only one. But *you* are the only one strong enough to take him one day. If you go after him now, he'll kill you. Then there is no hope for any of us."

She pulled away from him, unable to accept leaving Brynn to die. "What if we sneak in? Attack Shakar while he's alone?"

"Then the first thing he'll do is call his mages the moment he feels threatened." Ladan lifted a hand as she opened her mouth to speak. "And he's not stupid enough to be lured away from his mages either. He's just lost his army—he'll be extra cautious."

"There has to be something." Dawn looked beseechingly at Finn, who shook his head miserably, then Ladan. His grim look softened, and he reached out to draw her gently against his side. Her tears soaked into his shirt.

Alyx turned and walked out of the room.

The night air was bitterly cold, but she welcomed the way it bit into her bones and made her shiver. The physical discomfort distracted her from the pain within. There was no hope that Shakar would spare Brynn if she didn't come—her and Finn's clever plan had been turned completely on its head. The guilt was searing, and she couldn't help constantly thinking of Sarah, and Brynn's family, of the letter she would now have to deliver them.

The black despair she'd been feeling for weeks overwhelmed her. To defeat Shakar, she'd have to win the mages back, and do it before he rebuilt his strength or found another army. Her head thumped back against the icy cold stone of the low wall lining the roof as she slid to the ground.

She didn't have the strength for it—she'd thrown everything she had into building a better mage order, and she'd failed. Even worse was the thought of more years of fighting and struggle, more losses that tore away a strip of her soul each time.

Footsteps sounded on the stairs leading to the roof, and she was unsurprised to see Dashan emerge.

"I can't do it, Dash," she said. "I can't win this. I don't have any strength left for more. It had to be now."

He slid down the wall beside her, heedless of the cold, and said nothing. She didn't cry, she didn't talk, and he didn't try to push her. Even when her shivering became more pronounced, he didn't reach out. He just sat there with her.

She blinked awake into watery morning sunlight, muscles cold, aching and locked stiff. Beside her Dashan was awake, watching her carefully with his warm brown eyes.

"I don't have anything left," she whispered to him.

He smiled a little, then stood up, reaching a hand down. She took it, cursing in pain as her stiffened muscles were forced to move. "I'm not going to give you platitudes or tell you you'll feel better about all this with time," he said. "I'm just going to say that I love you, and I'm sorry you had to make the terrible choice you did last night. I'm also going to tell you it was the right one."

They were the right words to say, but even his beloved voice didn't help. She looked away. "I should wash up and change."

"You should eat something too."

"I'm not hungry." The thought of eating made her feel ill.

They'd just reached the top of the stairs when the clear ring of a horn sounded through the morning air. Dashan instantly reached for *Heartfire*.

Alyx left him to run back to the edge of the roof, slowing as she made her way down the stairs. She'd only taken two steps when an odd itching sensation scratched over her mind. Summoning magic without thought, she recognised Dawn's telepathic magic, and reached out to make the connection.

"What is it, Dawn?"

"Alyx, get to the north gate now! Finn, Tarrick, and I are on our way."

"What is it, what's wrong?"

"Just come now!"

Dawn's voice vanished from her head, and Alyx took a deep breath. Even walking up the few steps she'd come down seemed too much of an effort. Still, Dawn had been insistent. With a sigh, she traipsed back up to the roof, almost colliding with Dashan as he came sprinting back towards her.

"Riders approaching from the north!" he said tersely. "Can you get us there?"

She reached out, wrapped her arms around his shoulders, and shot them into the sky.

CHAPTER 47

S he dropped them one block from the gate to the northern causeway, just ahead of where Dawn, Tarrick, and Finn were galloping up the street.

"Is it an attack?" Alyx snapped at Dawn. She wasn't sure what she'd do if it was—she was completely and utterly drained. There was nothing left in her for another fight.

Dawn shook her head, swinging out of the saddle. Alyx almost took a step back—Dawn's eyes were aglow as she gripped Alyx by the shoulders, an odd energy vibrating from her. "Go out there, Alyx. Go now."

"We don't know that it's—"

"Dashan, enough!" Dawn firmly cut him off. "Go, Alyx. We'll be right behind you."

Frowning, Alyx turned and strode towards the front gates. At a shout from Dashan the soldiers on the walls began winching them open. A light falling snow drifted around her as she walked out onto the causeway... and came to a dead stop.

Riders filled the stone road over the frozen lake, and each and every one of them wore a royal blue cloak with the emblem of a leaping flame etched in scarlet thread over their chests. *Heartfire.*

And at their head rode Rothai.

He reined in his horse a short distance away from her and dismounted. A few others did too, but her gaze was entirely on her old sparring master.

"Have you come to kill me?" she asked, unable to hide the raw bitterness of her words.

He took three strides towards her and stopped. "On the contrary, Magor-lier. We'd hoped to arrive in time for the battle for Karonan, but despite my best efforts, it seems we failed. You have my apologies."

She stared at him. "You've got about two seconds to explain to me what is going on, or I'm going to walk away and never come back."

He gave a sharp nod. "Very well. Cario's death made you vulnerable within the mages. It didn't help that you destroyed half a room in front of those most uncertain about you, then went ahead and became invulnerable," he said tersely. "Adahn was working against you for weeks, and he used Parja's arrival to increase his efforts. If I'd spoken out directly against them, I'd have risked a permanent split of your forces."

"So you joined them instead?" she demanded.

"I made it appear so. It was hard to challenge Adahn's assertions about you directly—I had to engineer it so that I could prove without doubt to every single one of your mages that we were right to have faith in you. That you would never be another Shakar. There were those that helped me, of course." Rothai gestured behind him where Merial, Tari, and Nordan hovered. "Once we left you we immediately began to work on undermining Adahn's influence. It wasn't hard. As soon as I brought them back to your side, we came here as quickly as we could."

"It wasn't hard..." She trailed off, mouth hanging open. "You said you had to prove it to them. How?"

"*You* did, Magor-lier." Rothai's eyes blazed suddenly. "By standing there that night and letting us all walk out without retribution, you gave us our free choice. Shakar would have killed us all or found some way to bend us to his will."

Dawn's hand on her shoulder was suddenly the only thing that kept her standing. She was utterly breathtaken by what Rothai had done, the faith he had shown in her. "You planned all this, even after you knew I was invulnerable?"

"Yes. Magor-lier."

Almost as one, the mages still sitting on their horses behind him called out too, "Magor-lier!"

The sound of their joined voices echoed through the cold air, ringing with magic and certainty. She ran a hand over her face, her chest suddenly expanding, filling with bright, unbelievable hope. Spinning, she looked at Tarrick and Finn. "We can go after him. Now."

Fierce joy shined from the Zandian's face. "Aye."

Finn turned to his sister. "Dawn, did Shakar say where he was?"

She nodded, face alight. "DarkSkull Hall."

Good. "Dash, Ladan, go and tell Cayr and King Mastaran we're having a meeting right now. I'll get my mages settled and join you." Her shoulders straightened. "And then I'll tell you what we're going to do."

She turned back to Rothai as they ran off. "I kind of want to hug you a little bit, Rothai."

He fought an eye roll. "I really wish you wouldn't, Magor-lier."

She sobered. "Where is Adahn?"

"Adahn Torse is dead. As are Parja and Dastanta. I killed them in single combat, in one of the old traditions they were so fond of." There was no give in Rothai's hard voice. "You may be trying to change the old ways, but I will never stand by while my Magor-lier is threatened."

She found she didn't regret their deaths even a little bit and mourned the part of herself that had become so hard. "I won't ever forget what you've done," she said softly.

He bowed slightly, hand clenched over his heart.

The mages dismounted to bring their horses in, some with a shamefaced and genuine apology or stammering thanks for letting them back. Then there were those who beamed in delight as they passed, and those she knew were the ones who had helped Rothai.

There were many more of those than the shamefaced ones.

It took them much longer than Alyx wanted to be ready, and she chafed at the delay. She'd impressed upon them that this wouldn't just be a rescue attempt. She intended to face Shakar at last.

"There will be no better time than now," she repeated many times over the long planning session.

"If we do this now, then we're doing it right," Ladan said in a tone that brooked no argument. "I understand your fear for Brynn, but we can't allow that to push us into hasty action. That's what Shakar wants."

"I agree," Dashan said. "Ladan and I will leave within the hour. We'll ride north to DarkSkull and scout the area. We're invulnerable to Shakar's telepathic power, or that of any mages with him, so they won't know we're there. He won't be alone, Alyx. He's prepared for you, and that means he'll have mages and an army with him. We need to know what we're facing before we confront him."

Alyx heard them both out patiently, even though they were saying what she'd already been fully intending on doing. "Good. We'll follow with a combined force of mages and soldiers."

"Rothai and I will gather the warrior mages, although we'll have to leave some here to help stabilise Karonan, and I don't think we should strip the mages we left in Alistriem, either. If things go badly against Shakar, they'll be all that's left," Tarrick said.

"We'll give you some Bluecoats and soldiers as well." Cayr nodded at Sparky.

"Just Bluecoats," Alyx said. "Marching north will take too long. I'll take mounted warriors only."

"Few of my militia are mounted," Mastaran weighed in. "But those under Captain Rodin who were trained by Lord-Taliath Caverlock came with me from Ribeca. You can have them with my blessing, Magor-lier."

"Thank you, Your Highness," Alyx said. "They will be welcome."

"I will be right behind you with the rest of my soldiers," the king continued. "It is time I begin rebuilding my city and my country."

Alyx looked around at those assembled. "I want the rest of us riding out by evening tomorrow. Make it happen."

Cayr found Alyx several hours later. It was mid-afternoon and she was out on a balcony watching Tarrick and Rothai conversing below as the warrior mages milled about, preparing themselves for departure. Jayn was amongst them, along with Tari, Nordan and Chestin. She was glad to have such warriors at her back.

"What brings you out here?" she asked.

He joined her, his right hand coming to rest close to hers. "I'm coming with you."

Alyx was shaking her head before he'd even finished speaking. "No, you need to go back home and start rebuilding."

"You and Dashan are going to face Shakar. I can't just walk away from that." His voice pleaded with her. "Alyx, the both of you are my family and I'm yours. It's always been like that and it always will be."

"I know. But you are also the king of Rionn, and you are responsible for your people. You have to go back."

"Alyx, please," Cayr whispered.

Her heart tore for him, but she was resolute. "I'm sorry. You know I'm right."

He gripped her arm, blue eyes intense on hers. "Promise me you'll come back, that you'll be okay."

"I promise to do my best to come back home, Cayr, and to bring Dash back home with me."

He stepped forward to pull her into a hug. "I love you, Alyx. Always have, and always will."

"Me too." She wrapped her arms around his neck and they hugged for a long time. "There's something else I need from you, Cayr. It's big."

"Anything," he promised. "I swear it."

She took a deep breath, and told him. He flinched, the pain returning to his eyes, but his voice was strong when he spoke. "I want her to have her chance at vengeance. As much as I fear... of course my answer is yes."

"Thank you." She smiled through her tears. "Now go back to Rionn and make sure I have a home to come back to."

Dawn appeared just as Cayr was leaving. Alyx scrubbed at her face, but Dawn didn't miss the wetness on her cheeks.

"Are you all right?" she asked softly.

Alyx cleared her throat. "I hope I see him again."

"You will." Dawn linked her arm through Alyx's. "We're going to get through this. You have your mages now, heart and soul. Rothai made sure of that. You are going to beat Shakar, and everything will be all right."

"I wish I were that confident," Alyx said. "I've seen and felt his power. I don't know that I can beat that."

"It's not going to be about that, though, is it?" Dawn gave her a knowing look.

Alyx smiled sadly. "No. But even so, I'm kidding myself to think I can beat him. You haven't felt his strength, not like I have. Shakar is just a concept to you; you've heard stories that he is powerful and could not be defeated, but you've seen me, so you think I can match him. But I think we're all wrong."

Dawn frowned in concern. "Where is this coming from? You sounded so confident about facing Shakar earlier."

"Saying goodbye to Cayr... I realised I might never see him again. And I'm afraid. I'm afraid for myself, but I'm more afraid for the people I love. And when I think about it—I don't know if I can do it."

"You're not the only one. We'll all be there with you."

"Dawn..."

"Alyx, who is your most powerful telepath warrior mage?"

She managed a smile. "You are."

"I will be there, and I will help you defeat Shakar," Dawn said quietly. "One way or another, Alyx. We'll all be there."

CHAPTER 48

They left Karonan at dusk. Finally being on the move did little to calm Alyx's anxiety. It would be nearly two weeks before they could reach DarkSkull Hall and she fretted every moment that Brynn was in Shakar's hands.

Cayr had given them his entire force of Bluecoats—led by Tijer—and Taliath for the final fight, taking only his army back to Alistriem. While she appreciated his sacrifice, it only added to her worry—if she didn't manage to kill Shakar, Alistriem would be horribly vulnerable.

In addition to the Bluecoats, sixty-three warrior mages, eight Taliath and a hundred mounted militia under Captain Rodin travelled at Alyx's back. She hoped it would be enough.

After ten days of hard riding they encamped just to the west of Weeping Stead, giving horses and soldiers a rest. Dashan and Ladan found them as night fell. Alyx sat anxiously at a fire with Tarrick, Finn, and Dawn. She waved Tijer and Rothai over to join them.

"He's there all right." Dashan hunkered down beside her.

"There are at least a thousand Shiven fighters deployed throughout the valley, and I think it's safe to assume they're not listening to the new council's order to retreat," Ladan said. "It's a significant force."

"One that far outnumbers ours," Dashan added.

"With militia and Taliath help, we Bluecoats can handle it, sir," Tijer spoke confidently.

"You will have to," Tarrick said gravely. "The warrior mages will be needed to deal with Shakar's mages." He glanced at the two Taliath. "I assume he's got mages in that valley too?"

A sharp nod from Ladan. "It was hard to tell exactly because they seemed to be staying inside, but I'd guess more than seventy."

Finn sucked in a breath. "That has to be Shakar's entire mage force. He's putting everything he has into this." His eyes met hers. It was what they'd hoped for. But even then she couldn't feel satisfied, not with Brynn at Shakar's mercy.

"He's taking no chances." Tarrick nodded.

"He's making a mistake," Dashan said decisively. "If he gets beaten here, he'll have nothing left."

Exactly. She flicked another look at Finn. He couldn't smile either. Tears suddenly flooded her eyes—*Oh, Brynn, your magic may yet have won this for us.*

If I'm strong enough.

The following morning, a militia patrol scouting their back trail intercepted well over a hundred Shiven warriors in hot pursuit. They'd literally been running almost non-stop to catch up with Alyx's force.

Dashan rode out to speak with them. An hour later, she watched open-mouthed as he returned, Shiven warriors streaming behind him at a steady, loping run. When they reached the edge of the encampment, they halted and formed up in even rows. Dashan rode forward, a muscular Shiven warrior running at his stirrup.

"This is Commander Hastor. He and his boys have come to join us." Dashan told her and Tarrick with a grin.

"Really?" Tarrick was completely taken aback.

"Astohar spoke to the council for many hours after you left, Magor-lier. He argued that if we don't help you destroy Shakar, we can never be true allies," Hastor said gruffly. "The council agreed with him. Not many liked us coming, but we felt it was our duty."

She met his dark Shiven gaze. "Your countrymen are in that valley, Commander Hastor. If you join me, you'll be fighting them."

"They've disobeyed an order to retreat," he said coldly. "That makes them traitors."

Alyx offered him her hand. "In that case, you are very welcome."

He seemed momentarily surprised, but reached forward to shake. His grip was firm, as solid as he was.

"Come on, Commander. I'll help you and your men settle in," Dashan offered.

Alyx turned to see Tarrick's gaze was distant, something like pain on his face. "Hey, are you okay?"

He wouldn't look at her, jaw clenched. "My countrymen shame me. They should be here."

Her hand settled lightly on his arm. "You're here, Tarrick Tylender. And that's enough for me."

That afternoon, Dashan and Ladan led Alyx and Tarrick up the valley wall from the west, forsaking the main road. Before cresting the rise, they dismounted and left their horses before walking the remainder of the way. Then, keeping hidden within the trees, they crept up to look down at the wide, magnificent valley below.

Drifts of fallen snow lay scattered across the open space, and the lake in front of the main hall was frozen over. A bitter wind whipped up, making Alyx shiver. The presence of Shiven warriors was obvious—tents clustered at the northern end of the valley, and several hundred of them were drilling furiously by the lake, despite the cold.

"See the lookouts along the top of the valley wall." Dashan pointed.

"I can't see anything." Alyx squinted, but all she could make out was trees and snow.

"Me neither," Tarrick said. "Are you sure?"

Ladan nodded. "I'm betting he's got lookouts all through those hills to the north and south too."

"He's prepared for us," Dashan murmured. "One of the Taliath reported Shiven scouts to the east of Weeping Stead late last night. They killed two of them, but if there was one patrol, there will be others."

"Shakar has mages too, and they only need one telepath to have known the moment we rode into range," Alyx said. "He knows we're here."

"He's not moving out to engage us, though." Dashan considered.

"He has the defensible position," Ladan said, turning to give Alyx a stern look. "He wants the Magor-lier to come to him."

"As expected. Let's not keep him waiting," Tarrick said.

"Tarrick's right, there's no sense in waiting. We move tonight." Alyx nodded.

As they climbed back down to the horses, Alyx grabbed Dashan's arm, holding him back.

"Everything okay?" he asked in concern.

"We need to talk," she said steadily. "About what I need you to do tonight."

As dusk fell, they gathered together in the centre of the camp. By then, Dawn and Rody had confirmed the presence of mages in the valley. Many were shielded, but Dawn was confident there were more than fifty.

Shakar was there too. She could feel his presence like a blight on her magic.

"Let's go over it one more time," Tarrick said to the group clustered around the fire. "Dashan?"

"Under Ladan's and my command, the conventional forces launch their assault at midnight," Dashan said. "Tijer, under Ladan you'll lead the Bluecoats from the north to engage that group of Shiven. Rodin, I'll bring your boys and the Shiven from the south. Ideally, we'll force Shakar's soldiers out onto the open floor of the valley where our cavalry will have the advantage. If the battle starts going our way, it's likely Shakar will send his mages into the fight."

"That's where I come in," Dawn spoke. "I'll be positioned at the top of the valley wall, monitoring Shakar's mages. If they join the conventional fight,

I'll signal Rothai to counter-attack with our mages. If they don't, Rothai will hold the mages ready for whatever Shakar has planned."

"Your role is critical, Mage Egalion," Tijer said soberly. "Our men will be decimated if Shakar's mages attack us without the protection of yours."

"I won't let you down," Dawn said calmly.

Alyx nodded. "Once the battle starts, Tarrick, Jayn, Finn, and I will sneak in from the east, using the fighting as a distraction. We're looking to get Brynn out."

"Third Patrol, back in action." Finn smiled faintly.

"Dawn, I need you to locate Brynn and lead us to him. I could do it, but the longer I can conserve my power and energy, the better. Once we have him, Finn will get Brynn out while the rest of us go for Shakar." She glanced away, not wanting any of them to read her true intentions from her expression. Across the fire, Dashan's eyes glimmered at her. She gave him a reassuring smile. He didn't look reassured.

"Once we've defeated Shakar's conventional forces, Dashan and I will pull back from the valley floor," Ladan said.

"I believe this is when Shakar will call on his mages, not before," Rothai said. "He'll hope his Shiven army can defeat ours, but won't be overly concerned if they don't, because he'll still have his mages."

"That fight is yours, Rothai," she told him. "I won't be able to fight Shakar and his mages at the same time."

He inclined his head.

"I'd better talk to my men." Tijer stood. "If we're to attack at midnight, I want to make sure we move early enough to be in position at the right time."

A hush of silence, fraught with an intense mix of anticipation and tension, filled the camp as they waited for the appointed time to move. They all understood the magnitude of what they were about to face, and all knew the dire consequences if they failed. And in the back of their minds was the knowledge that if Alyx didn't manage to defeat Shakar, it wouldn't matter if they'd beaten the Shiven fighters and mages; they'd likely be dead by morning.

The Bluecoats grouped around their fires, quietly playing cards. The Shiven warriors carefully sharpened and polished their weapons. The militia joined the Bluecoats in their card games, and the mages talked softly, planning the best way to use and employ their various mage talents.

Alyx leaned against a log at the central fire, Dashan's arm draped around her shoulders. Dawn was curled up beside Ladan opposite them, with Tarrick and Finn between them.

"Do you remember the first time we rode through the gates of DarkSkull?" Dawn asked softly.

"I do." Half of her had been with Dashan, the warmth of his hug lingering even though he'd ridden away moments earlier. The other had been afraid of what came next. And all of her had been hungry and cold. She'd been spoiled and arrogant and utterly unprepared for DarkSkull. And now here she was, powerful mage warrior and leader of the mage order. Unbelievable.

"You were still making us call you Lady Egalion back then." Finn chuckled.

"And Ladan was scary," Jayn added, grinning wider as he scowled. "You refused to speak a word for weeks, and even though you had no magic you decimated anyone Rothai partnered you with at morning sparring."

"And I thought getting into Galien's group was the most important thing ever." Tarrick shook his head. "I had no idea."

"The moment I rode away I wanted to come back." Dashan's voice was rough. "And not just for Alyx."

She leaned into him, his arm tightening a little around her. The twins beamed at him across the fire.

"And look at us now." Dawn smiled distantly. "Mage warriors and Taliath."

There was silence for a moment as they all looked at each other.

Eventually, Ladan glanced up at the stars. "Time to go."

Alyx stood first. "We do this together."

CHAPTER 49

Almost as one, the camp moved into action when Alyx stood.

Ladan and Dashan were the first to leave, both young men giving her stern looks from the saddle.

"No stupid risks, Aly-girl."

"Promise," she said. "I will see you soon."

"You better mean that, mage-girl," Dashan muttered, leaning down to kiss her hard. She slid her hand around his neck, prolonging the kiss.

"See you soon, Dash."

Ladan barked an order and kicked his horse into a gallop. With a jaunty tip of his hat, Tijer led the Bluecoats after him at a fast trot, Casta giving Alyx a wink as he joined Tijer at the head of the column.

Tearing his eyes away from Alyx, Dashan spurred his horse over to the militia. "Let's ride!" he whooped. Affected by his enthusiasm, they cheered, urging their horses after him into the darkness. Hastor flashed a fierce smile full of teeth and he and his Shiven fell in behind the militia at an easy lope.

Once they were gone, hoofbeats vanishing into the distance, the Taliath gathered in the clearing; young men and women who had managed to escape the Mage Council's hunting and who had trained on ShadowFall Island under Alyx's father. And another. Cayr's final gift to Alyx—Jenna, *Huntress* sheathed at her waist. Around them came the mages, standing in a single, unified group.

"Mages and Taliath fight together?" Tarrick smiled at Alyx.

"As it should always have been," she murmured.

"Good luck, Magor-lier." Rothai bowed before her.

Alyx caught his gaze. "Win this fight for me, Rothai, and I'll do my best to avenge the deaths of your family."

Rothai straightened, his blue eyes flaring brightly before settling into ice-cold focus. He nodded once, then turned to call the mages and Taliath to him. Dawn joined them after a fierce hug from her twin.

"Be safe," Alyx sent to Dawn's mind.

"You too. I'll be with you, Alyx. I love you."

Then they too were gone, moving up over the ridge. They would wait at the summit with Dawn, ready to be called into the fight once Shakar's mages engaged. Only the members of Third Patrol remained now, and as Alyx looked at them all one by one, she saw only steady determination. It bolstered her.

"We'd best go," Finn said.

Alyx nodded, smiled as Jayn brought Tingo over to her. He snorted and butted her shoulder affectionately. She curled her hands in his silky mane, taking strength from an old companion.

"It will be just like old times." Finn grinned. "Tarrick and Alyx trying to see who can beat the other up the valley wall."

Jayn snorted. "I'm going to beat all of you up the wall."

They rode through darkness, carefully shielding. The echoing clash of fighting broke out as they reached the top of the valley wall. Alyx thought briefly of the soldiers fighting for them, and wished them all the best, before focusing on what was ahead of her.

"Remember last time we made this trip?" Tarrick murmured in the darkness, white teeth flashing.

"Not the best memory to recall in these circumstances." Alyx smiled. It had been the night her magic broke out for the first time—a nightmare experience of fear and pain, and yet that night cemented the friendship between her, Tarrick, and the twins. A friendship that had survived everything that had come since. Finn glanced over at her with a little smile and she hoped he was thinking the same thing.

At the edge of the forest lining the valley floor, they left the horses to move on foot. It was too dark to see much beyond the hulking shadows of DarkSkull's buildings, but the ring of steel and cries of battle from the north and south were unmistakable.

Rather than magic—detectable by any of Shakar's mages—they used their knowledge of the academy grounds to sneak from cover to cover, slowly making their way to orchards that were now overgrown and wild, despite winter having shredded the leaves. Now she had no choice but to use magic.

"*Dawn? We're hunkered down in the orchards.*"

"*I found Brynn, he's in the main hall, but upstairs. I think maybe the library but it's hard to be sure with all that thick stone. Alyx...*"

"*What?*" Her pulse picked up at the strange note in Dawn's voice.

"*I can barely sense him. I think... it's not good.*"

In the darkness, Alyx reached out to touch Tarrick's arm. He shifted closer, sensing her need for support. "*I don't suppose you can sense Shakar?*"

"*No, he's shielding. He could be with Brynn for all I know.*"

"*And the mages?*"

"*There are some in the main hall, but if you take the entrance through the kitchens and go up via the servants' stairs you'll avoid them. Most are scattered through the old dormitory buildings, but they're awake, restless. I think they're waiting for Shakar's order to move.*"

"*Thanks.*"

"*Be careful.*"

Alyx let go of the connection and turned to the others, relaying what Dawn had told her.

"I'll go first," Jayn said in a murmur. "That way if we hit unexpected trouble I can shield us."

"Check your mental shields too," Finn warned. "If you slip and there are telepaths in there, this thing will be over before it begins."

They dashed across the open space, then pressed themselves against the wall of the main hall. Jayn led the way as they crept towards the kitchen entrance and eased open the door. At the threshold, Alyx took a deep breath, gripping her staff with tense fingers. Her heart pounded. This was it.

Dawn's magic suddenly brushed over her mind, and she let the mage in. *"Dawn, what is it?"*

"It's Brynn. I can barely feel his thoughts anymore."

"I'll find him."

"Brynn's in trouble," she told the others. "We need to find him quickly."

Once inside, running as quietly as they could through darkened kitchens and then up the servants' stairs, Alyx wondered with every step whether they were about to run into Shakar. Her hands were slick with sweat, and worry for Brynn was so fierce she was barely able to keep herself calm enough to maintain her shield.

They reached the hall leading down to the library without running into Shakar or any of his mages. Light crept out of the open doors.

Tarrick groaned softly. "Could it look any more like a trap?"

"You know the plan." Alyx swallowed. "If we get caught in there, Finn takes Brynn while the rest of us fight."

Jayn led the way again, her hand raised and ready to summon a shield in an instant. They moved cautiously into the library. All Howell's beloved books were gone, burned or taken by the council after the attack. The rows and rows of empty bookshelves gave the place a mournful air. But Alyx barely noticed, her gaze going straight to the crumpled figure lying in the centre of the floor.

"Brynn!"

She sprinted across the room and dropped to her knees by his body, letting her staff fall to the ground so that she could turn him over. His head lolled in her lap, limp. Numerous cuts bled sluggishly through tears in his mage cloak, his face was badly bruised, and his arm lay at an awkward angle on the floor.

Brynn's eyes flickered open. "Alyx..." he breathed.

That effort was too much and his eyes closed again. With her limited healing power, Alyx could sense how close to dying he was; he'd lost too much blood and his skin was pale and close to translucent.

"I've got him." Finn dropped down opposite her, one hand going to Brynn's forehead, the other resting against his chest. She glanced up to see Tarrick hovering over them, staff drawn, while Jayn guarded the door.

"Oh Brynn, I'm so sorry." She took his hand, cradled it in both of hers. "I took too long, I'm sorry."

"It... okay," he whispered, then coughed. "Worked... what you wanted. Followed, captured... me... distraction from..."

"I'm here," she murmured. Finn's expression was one of deep focus and effort, and she suppressed the urge to ask him how Brynn was. Sweat beaded on the healer's forehead, and Alyx silently wished him all her strength. "Stay with us. Finn's here, he'll help. Stay with us."

A smile flickered across his face. "Did... what you needed. Tell..." He coughed again, his body convulsing as it went into shock. "Tell... Sarah..." His voice rallied. "Love her... I'm sorry."

Tears streamed down her face. "You're going to be okay. You can't die on me, Brynn."

Brynn shook his head and his eyes flickered shut again as he fought against unconsciousness. His body was trembling in hers, his breathing becoming weaker.

"Brynn, no!" Alyx shouted as he slumped against the floor, eyes closing. "Finn!"

Finn sat back on his heels, white with exhaustion. "His body has lost too much blood. I don't know if I can save him."

"You have to!" Alyx stared at him. "This is Brynn, you have to help him."

"I've done what I can for now." Finn stopped, shook his head as he fought for his own clarity. "But we need to get him out, somewhere safe, away from the fighting. If he's going to recover, he'll need more healing later and space to rest."

Alyx glanced between Finn and Tarrick, and the Zandian mage's jaw clenched. "Finn, it will have to be you," he said. "Jayn can't carry him and I need to stick with Alyx."

Finn nodded, kneeling to pick up Brynn gently in his arms. "I'll get him clear, then I'll come back to join you."

Finn turned and left, his long strides carrying him quickly out of the library. The hopeless look that he'd worn was too much. This was her fault. She'd asked Brynn to be a part of her plan and now he was probably going to die for it. She swayed on her feet and would have fallen if Tarrick hadn't been standing right beside her. The same gut-wrenching grief she'd felt on watching Cario die swept through her.

"We have to keep going." Tarrick's voice was strong. "It's what he would want. Let Finn get Brynn out while we do what we came here for."

Alyx nodded, piece by piece putting away her grief until she could stand straight-shouldered again.

"*Alyx?*" Dawn's magic brushed her shield.

"*What?*"

"*Shakar is in the main hall. He's waiting for you.*" A pause then, "*The mages are moving too. He's sending them out to engage our army. The Bluecoats have taken the northern half of the valley, and they're herding all the remaining Shiven towards the militia and Hastor's soldiers. Rothai is moving to meet them. There are so many, though.*"

"*Get the soldiers out. Tell Ladan it's about to begin,*" she said then, unable to keep the grief from her voice, "*Finn has Brynn. They're coming to you.*"

Sadness came back through their link. "*Trust Finn, Alyx, and focus on what you have to do.*"

Alyx bent down to pick up Cario's staff. "Let's go and kill Shakar."

Alyx ran back down the stairs with Tarrick and Jayn and out through the kitchens. It was well past midnight, but a full moon overhead bathed the wide valley floor in its glow. They stepped outside the kitchen door just as an explosion of fire plumed into the sky from the south, lighting up the night.

The valley floor was covered now with fighting soldiers. Voices shouted—the Bluecoats responding to the retreat order. Mage fire lit up again, followed by the bright flash of a concussion burst. Magic tingled against her senses, alive and all around her. She hoped Ladan's soldiers got clear quickly enough.

"Where's Shakar?" Tarrick asked.

She closed her eyes for a moment, took a deep breath, then turned to face them. "He's in the main hall, waiting. Tarrick, you and Jayn need to go and help Rothai."

"What are you talking about?" He frowned. "We're fighting with you."

"Tarrick, Rothai needs Third Patrol right now," Alyx told him patiently. "If Shakar's mages overwhelm us, the battle is lost. I can't fight Shakar and his mages together."

"How many times do we have to have this discussion?" Tarrick was angry. "Shakar is right there. We're your mages, Alyx, and it's our job to fight with you."

"Your magic isn't going to help!" she shouted. "He is invulnerable. If you come with me, you'll only be a liability, leverage he can use against me. He knows you're my weakness, because he knows how much I love you."

Tarrick flinched as if struck. "I'm your protector."

She stepped up to him. "And you can help me by using that powerful magic of yours to defeat Shakar's mages. We can do this together."

For a long moment he stared at her, then he stepped forward and threw his arms around her. "You're my Magor-lier and my friend. Please come back from this."

"I'll do my best," she said, utterly taken aback by his show of affection.

"I want a hug too." Jayn shouldered Tarrick aside and hugged her warmly. "You go get him, Magor-lier."

Feeling the brush on her mind, Alyx opened herself to Dawn.

"I'm with you too, Alyx."

"Finn will be back any moment. Go lead Third Patrol and win this fight for us, Tarrick," Alyx told him.

He nodded, gave her one last look, then he turned and began running towards the battle. Jayn was only a step behind. They held their mage staffs high, their profiles illuminated in the sudden flash of mage fire.

"Brynn is with us." Dawn spoke to all of them. *"So is Cario. Let's do this for them."*

CHAPTER 50

Alyx walked around to the front of the hall and up the stone steps. Her cloak was warm around her shoulders, Cario's staff glimmering in her hand. Now that he was no longer shielding himself, Shakar's presence was clear and bright. It was the presence from her nightmares. But it was also her godfather, a man she'd loved.

Unlike the last time she'd been here, the hall was lit by lanterns running along each wall. The chairs and tables that had once been used for academy assemblies were pushed to the side, cluttered together in a heap. The stone at the far end was charred from his attack all those years ago.

There was little left of the place that had once been full of mage initiates and apprentices, yet their magic lived on, in the walls, the floor, the very fabric of the place.

Shakar waited for her in the middle of the hall. He wore a flowing black mage robe, looking just like the Astor she'd known all her life, but his eyes gleamed with a power she'd never seen in her godfather, and his face was harder and far less forgiving than the man she'd loved. He said nothing when she appeared, merely watched her move inside the hall and take a few steps towards him.

"You're outdated, Astor." She pointed at his clothes. "We wear blue now."

He lifted an eyebrow. "You're going with humour?"

"I thought about threats and a promise to see you die." She shrugged. "But I don't like to brag."

"Your mother couldn't kill me. What makes you think you can?"

Alyx stilled.

"That's right," Shakar said, catching the flash of pain on Alyx's face. "She came to me, thinking she could best me, could kill me. She thought if she defeated me, the Mage Council would leave her and Garan alone."

Tears pricked at her eyes. He thought he was being clever, causing her pain, breaking her focus, but he was wrong. The knowledge of what her mother had sacrificed gave her strength.

"I won't fail where she did," Alyx told him.

"A sickeningly sweet sentiment." Shakar sounded bored. "But erroneous. Very soon, I'm going to be the head of the mage order."

Outside there was a loud explosion, followed quickly by two more. Through the windows high in the wall came bright flashes of mage power in battle. Quickly, she reached out to Dawn.

"*Rothai and Tarrick have engaged the mages. Shakar's Shiven fighters are falling back into the western foothills and our forces are attacking from behind. I think they're clear of any magical fallout.*" Dawn informed her.

"*Good. Make sure they stay back.*"

"It's not going so well for you out there," Alyx said.

He shrugged. "We both know I don't need a conventional army. Your trick in Karonan was clever, but once I defeat you here tonight, I'll use my new mage order to take it all back."

"I'm curious as to how you plan on doing that, given I'm now invulnerable." She kept her voice light, curious.

"Invulnerability only lasts as long as one's stamina. I will exhaust you, and then I will kill you." He seemed momentarily puzzled. "You were foolish to come here, to walk into my trap like this—I truly worried my ruse wouldn't work."

She chuckled then, a fierceness rising up in her. "Oh, but Astor, don't you see? The ruse was mine."

He frowned, clearly not understanding.

"I knew you would come for me once Karonan was taken. You can't afford to leave me alive anymore. I needed you to think you had the upper hand." She spoke slowly, clearly, so he would understand exactly what she was saying. "Brynn's magic is in his voice, did you know that? I'm guessing not, because to you he would just be a lesser mage. A lesser mage who gave himself up to you, who convinced you that you had the advantage, that you were trapping me. But this is exactly what I wanted."

"No." Shakar shook his head. "You expect me to believe you sacrificed one of your closest friends? For what? To walk in here thinking you can defeat me. Good try girl, but I don't buy it."

"Wrong, again," she said. "Because I didn't walk in here to defeat you."

True confusion flashed over his face and it almost made her laugh. Finn had been right, gloriously, wonderfully right.

"We're both invulnerable, Astor. I've known for years that I can't defeat you with magic." She met his gaze, forced him to look at her. "But you knew that too. And that's the real reason you suggested to the council that getting rid of the Taliath might be a good idea. You played on their fears to get what you wanted. The removal of the one thing that had the ability to defeat you."

Realisation started creeping across his face, his eyes widening almost comically.

"I'm not going to kill you," she said simply. "But they are."

Three figures moved into the light then, one from each side of Shakar and one directly behind. All moved with the sublime grace of a Taliath, and their naked swords gleamed in the firelight cast by the lanterns.

"You remember my brother, of course?" she said. "And Jenna Aridlen—you sent Casovar to kill her parents." The smile on her face widened. "Then there's the man who made me invulnerable. Dashan Caverlock. They're all invulnerable to your magic, and they're the finest warriors I've ever known."

Shakar backed up, reaching into his cloak to draw his own Taliath sword. "You can play all the tricks you like, but I wield magic with a skill you've never seen before. I can't touch them directly, but that doesn't make my magic useless."

"I know," she said, and lifted her glimmering arms into the air. "And that's where I come in."

"Too much talking," Dashan shouted, moving faster than lightning. He had *Heartfire* slashing towards Shakar's throat before Alyx even realised what was happening. Shakar's own Taliath reflexes were all that saved him, his blade meeting Dashan's with a loud ringing. For the briefest of moments they were still, two blades locked, matching snarls as they stared each other down.

And then they disengaged, and the battle began.

Ladan and Jenna wasted no time in joining the fight. Shakar danced and weaved, moving quickly enough that they couldn't close on him together. He took a few moments to test them, learning what he was up against, then he summoned his magic. When *Mageson* came swinging at him he vanished, reappearing a few steps away behind Jenna. She dodged his thrust, sent his blade flying away, then countered. When Dashan closed on him, he vanished again, getting himself out of the trap.

The three Taliath worked together, like they were all tied to the same piece of string. They stalked with the patience of a hunter seeking its prey. Alyx stood ready. Shakar couldn't keep avoiding forever—he would have to go on the attack eventually.

And then there was a loud whooshing sound as one of the chairs by the wall erupted into flame. It flew into the air, arrowing straight towards Jenna's head.

Alyx didn't think. She sank into her magic, drew on Cario's talent and used it to send the chair flying off course, crashing into the opposite wall. Jenna glanced up, cold fury shuttering her features, and then she leapt at Shakar. Frustration escaped her in a growl when he vanished again.

The Taliath blades rang and hissed as they clanged together over and over. Alyx summoned her power and lit Dashan's *Heartfire* and Ladan's *Mageson* with bright green flame and *Huntress* with bright blue. From then on, each time Dashan or Jenna got close to hitting Shakar, whenever their blades skimmed by his cloak, the bright flame would set him alight. Shakar would douse the flames instantly, but it took magic to do it.

Shakar used more magic, lifting chairs and sending them raining down over his attackers. Alyx drowned herself in her magic and fought desperately to send each flying away from its target. The temptation to strike out at Shakar directly was close to overpowering, but she fought it. It would only waste her energy.

It wasn't only his sheer power that was staggering, but the skill with which he used it. He fought three opponents and used magic at the same time as if it were as easy as putting on his shoes. He'd clearly used every one of his long years to practice and hone his craft.

And the part of her that wasn't countering everything he threw at the Taliath acknowledged what a beautiful sight was unfolding before her, four elite Taliath dancing around each other, swords blurring through the air. At one point, possibly from frustration, Shakar raised his free hand and sent a violet concussion burst erupting through the room.

Jenna, Dashan, and Ladan dropped flat to the ground, protected by their invulnerability, as the concussion wave spread out in a violet-edged circle. Alyx stood, buffeted but not touched, as the wave passed by her.

"Invulnerable, remember?" she screamed at him.

Shakar let out a cry of almost inhuman rage.

Ignoring it, Dashan leapt to his feet, closed in on Shakar's cloaked figure. His blade was a blur as he danced, ducked, weaved and slashed. Jenna's blonde hair gleamed in the light, streaming around her as she fought at Dashan's side, lunging when he pulled back, shifting when he attacked. Ladan paced, sword swinging from his hand, ready to pounce at the first opening that presented itself.

A wall of flame erupted, not unlike the one Galien had used on Alyx before she killed him. Magic couldn't touch Taliath, but fire could. The flames bore down on the fighting figures, Shakar throwing up his mage shield.

A roar of effort tore from Alyx as she ran down the steps, drawing on magic, dropping her shield down over the Taliath. Jenna grabbed Ladan's arm, dragging him to her and huddling close to Dashan, wisely giving Alyx less space to cover.

Flame licked at her shield, illuminating a frozen tableau. Alyx gritted her teeth against the drain on her magic, feet set apart, arms thrust outwards.

Shakar pushed and pushed, feeding the flames. His shield flickered. Ladan caught that, shifted as if to try and break through.

The fire vanished and Shakar with it. He reappeared a few paces away, sweating freely, chest heaving with exertion. Alyx dropped her shield, slumping. More chairs lifted into the air, Shakar summoning a wind to send them whirling through the hall. The strength of the wind forced the Taliath back, and he let go of all the chairs at the same time.

It was more than Alyx had ever had to do before, control so many flying objects at once. But she held Cario's staff in her hands, the staff of the most skilled telekinetic mage ever to attend DarkSkull. And all at once she was back in that training room, Howell watching with a small smile as she and Cario used yellow and green balls to chase each other around the room, delighting in each other and the competition. She'd wished then for his exquisite skill and now it flooded her.

Cario, my friend. Thank you.

Her eyes closed and her magic reached out, not as a sweeping force, but as tendrils of power. Each one wrapped around a chair, pulling it from its orbit. But Shakar countered her, his power wrapping the chairs too. He hopped around the hall, flashing in and out of existence, avoiding the Taliath that came after him in an unending wave.

Sweat poured down her back, legs trembling. Everything she had was tied up in countering Shakar's magic.

"Alyx has him almost fully engaged!" Dashan realised it first, his voice rippling through the wind and sounds of battle outside. "Go at him!"

Shakar had to let go to defend himself. Chairs crashed to the ground all around, one barely missing her. Ladan stepped forward, *Mageson* licking out quicksilver fast. And Shakar stumbled, blood pouring from a long gash down his arm. Ladan's triumphant roar rang through the hall.

"Alyx!" Jenna's cool voice, tinged with weariness. "You can do what he can do, remember!"

I can!

She let out a shout of effort as she dragged up every inch of mage power she had and used it to send chair after chair at Shakar in one continuous stream. The Taliath worked with her, weaving with unbelievable agility around the flying chairs, attacking each time Shakar had to move to avoid one.

Magic roped through her. She felt herself *become* her magic. Her mind floated, almost separating from her body, as the true strength and power of what was inside her came sweeping out and around, clashing with a roar into the incredible power that was inside Shakar.

Her awareness expanded outwards, her mind let loose on the searing tide of her telepathic magic. There was Tarrick; he stood, legs planted firmly apart, face set deep in concentration as he sent concussion burst after concussion burst at three opponents at once. She heard the great roar he gave as he broke through the shielding of the first and then the second, killing them both. Bright red flame lit up the sky near him, and he ducked, rolled, and came up shouting orders.

She saw Nordan then, the ice mage back to back with Finn as they fought fiercely against more mages; sensed as Finn sent a steady flow of strength into Nordan while he flung spears of ice at anyone who came near, his face a mask of weariness and fierce determination.

Then there was Rothai, his form almost a blur as he fought with the sublime power of a pure warrior mage, his staff spinning and dealing death as his power exploded around him, killing anything in his path. He broke through a knot of Shiven mages, and called back to those behind him, running forward to widen the breach.

Jayn hunkered down beside the fallen bodies of two injured mages, concentrating with a steely focus as she held her shield steady over them. Fire and concussive energy slammed repeatedly into the shield, but she held it, despite the exhaustion lining her face and the trembling of her hands.

And Dawn, drained of energy now but there in Alyx's mind, sending her nothing but pure confidence that Alyx could win this, that she *would* win this.

"YOU CANNOT DEFEAT ME!" The shout seemed torn from Shakar's very soul.

The ground began shuddering under their feet. Gasping for air, Alyx temporarily let go of her magic, glancing around. Shakar stood in the centre of the room, surrounded by a wall of flame the Taliath couldn't penetrate. His hands were lifted towards the sky and he was summoning magic, so much magic.

The ground rocked again, and then there was an almighty crack in the roof above.

He was bringing the roof down on them.

For a moment Alyx quailed—she couldn't combat this depth of power. He was going to win and they were going to die.

"Alyx."

Dashan's voice. His gaze was on her, steady and reassuring. "What can't we do, together?"

She nodded, licked her dry lips. Above them the roof cracked open, stone and debris already beginning to fall. Ladan and Jenna prowled the fire circle, glances shifting from the roof, frustration evident in every move. Dashan stood still, watching Alyx. The idiot was smiling.

She closed her eyes and drew up everything she could, every bit of power her mother had given her, every bit of love and support her father and brother had given her, the faith Dawn had in her, everything Dashan meant to her and the love she felt for her friends. Once it was gathered, she focused it with Jayn's sheer grit and determination, refined it with Finn's intelligence and cool logic, bolstered it with Tarrick's heart and Brynn's warmth then let loose with Dashan's reckless courage.

"This is for my mother," Alyx whispered as she threw it all at him.

The roof stopped caving in, the stones halting mid-flight as her magic caught them. Shakar bellowed, pouring more of his strength into ripping at the roof. They strained against each other for what seemed like an age, neither giving in.

Alyx hung on, eyes closed, everything in her refusing to let go, to back down.

Then Shakar staggered backwards half a step. The flames around him flickered as he drew energy from the flame wall to fight Alyx.

Dashan didn't hesitate.

He leaped straight through the flames with a roar of anger. Shakar was exhausted, drained of magic and weakened from his duel with Alyx. Dashan disarmed him in a single move. Shakar's sword clattered to the ground and Dashan didn't hesitate in stepping forward and running *Heartfire* through Shakar's chest.

The darkmage staggered, coughed.

The flames disappeared. The pull on her magic disappeared. Dashan yanked his sword out and kicked the mage contemptuously, forcing him to fall hard to the ground, grievously wounded. Then, with one graceful move, Dashan stepped forward and drove Garan Egalion's sword down through Shakar's heart.

"Alyx!" Ladan shouted, running for her.

"I can't move," she said through gritted teeth. Shakar's incredible magic had done too much damage before dying. The whole structure above her was fatally cracked through, thick stone ready to collapse into rubble.

And her magic was the only thing holding it back.

"You have to go," she said. "I can't hold this much longer."

"What about you?" Jenna's beautiful features were dusted with soot and dust, but Alyx thought she'd never looked more magnificent.

"If I let go we all die here. Please!" she gave a shout of effort as her magic began to waver. "Go."

"I'm not leaving you, Aly-girl." Ladan's face was set. "There's nothing you can say to change my mind. We'll think of something."

"There's no time." Her breath sobbed out of her. Magic was beginning to burn through her muscle and bone. There was a groan above and a single boulder crashed to the floor. Jenna hovered, clearly torn. "This whole structure is coming down. Please, go."

"Alyx." Dashan was there, dark eyes steady on hers.

"Dash, please," she whispered. "He's my brother."

He gave her a single nod, and then he turned. *Heartfire* was still drawn and he lifted it, bringing the hilt down hard on the back of Ladan's head. Shock and fury flashed through her brother's green eyes in the moment before he crumpled to the ground, unconscious.

"Jenna, help!" Dashan bent to lift Ladan's shoulders.

She took his legs and they lifted him, but then she hesitated. "Alyx..."

"Go!" she said, "Tell Cayr I love him, that I'm sorry."

"I will," Jenna promised.

Alyx hung on, sucking in breaths, shoulders sagging under the weight of what she was holding up. Her magic was draining quickly. Another piece of stone slammed into the floor, hard. Dust flew, showering Dashan and Jenna as they got Ladan to the door.

She watched, waiting for the moment when they were clear. They disappeared, and she began counting. A count of twenty should give them time to get far enough away before the whole building came down. Everything hurt, her breath panting in and out too fast, a scream of effort building up inside her. She just had to hold a few more seconds...

She'd reached ten when a tall figure came running back through the door, light and graceful on his feet as he dodged chairs and boulders to come and stand before her. His eyes were warm as he regarded her.

"You didn't seriously think I was leaving you to die, mage-girl?"

"I can't—" Tears flooded her cheeks.

He stepped forward, wrapping his arms around her, his voice soft in her ear. "I've got you. Focus everything you have on the magic holding this building together. Focus on my voice. I'll hold you up."

She did as he asked, letting the strength go out of her legs, allowing him to keep her standing. But even then it was too much. "Too hard," she mumbled.

"Just a little bit longer," he soothed. "Dawn's outside. I need you to let her in, sweetheart. She needs to talk to you."

There was no strength for shielding anymore, and once Dashan made her aware of Dawn, it was easy to let her mind in.

"*Alyx, I've got you.*" Dawn filled her mind, wrapping it in strength and determination. "*Can you hold on a little longer? I'll help.*"

Everything in her was burning, muscles trembling, her magic beginning to flicker and die. Thousands of tons of stone were bearing down on her. Another stone smashed to the floor, terrifyingly close. She didn't even have the strength to respond to Dawn. Dimly she heard running feet.

"Can you do it?" Dashan's voice.

"I'll give it a damn good try." Jayn's voice, as cheerful as always.

Alyx whimpered and Dashan's arms tightened around her. Dawn soothed her distress, sending her constant encouragement. A hand rested on her shoulder and a trickle of strength supplemented her draining power. Finn.

Then Dashan's voice at her ear. "You can let go now, Alyx. I'm right here."

And she did.

CHAPTER 51

S he woke to darkness and a mouth full of dust. Everything in her body hurt and her magic was gone. Not even a spark lived inside her.

"How are we doing?" Incredibly, Dashan's voice.

"A little cramped," Jayn rasped.

Alyx tried to stretch, but found herself hemmed in by rough stone. Panicked, she struggled to move, and was stopped by a warm hand grabbing hers.

"You doing okay, mage-girl?"

She swallowed. "What...?"

"Try not to think about the fact we're currently buried under the remains of DarkSkull Hall," Finn said. His voice was ragged with exhaustion.

What!

"Well, it's not like we had time to come up with a more detailed plan," Dashan said, pebbles tumbling around them as he shifted.

"*He's hilarious, your future husband,*" Dawn's voice slid into Alyx's mind. "*Just be patient. We've nearly got you.*"

Alyx became aware of a distant thudding sound. Another followed it, and another, the sounds growing closer and closer. Then a blast went off so close it sent dust and shards of rock raining down on them. The breath left Alyx in a rush as Dashan scrambled on top of her. Once it stopped, a bright shaft of light shone down on them.

Above them stood Tarrick, haggard, trembling, Dawn's hand on his shoulder as he sent concussion blasts into the stone around them. Jenna hovered, sharp gaze watching Tarrick's progress. She was the first to see he'd broken through and stopped him with a shout.

"Aly-girl!" Ladan scrambled down.

Dashan let out a whoop so loud she almost winced. "It worked!"

She pushed him aside and dragged herself over to where Finn was sitting, a dangerously pale Jayn tucked in his arms. His green eyes glittered against the heavy shadows under them.

"Third patrol wins again," he said tiredly, head slumping back against the rock.

"Thank you," she told them both, meaning it with everything she had.

Ladan landed with a thud, Tarrick barely a step behind. She found herself being caught up in her brother's arms and carried to the surface. Dashan came right after her, then Tarrick carrying Jayn, and lastly Finn. Dawn flew at her twin and the two of them wrapped each other in a fierce embrace.

"I'm all right." With Ladan's arm helping she managed to stay standing, but it was an effort to catch her breath. "I just used too much magic. I'm okay. I'll be fine."

He pulled her hard against his chest. "Really, you're okay?"

"I'm okay." She pulled back to smile at him. "You?"

"I'm good," he said, and then an expression of awe came over his face "We did it."

"Yeah, we did it." Excitement and joy bubbled up in her chest.

Ladan's face softened and for the first time ever she saw tears in her brother's green eyes. "We avenged her, Aly-girl. You and me. For Mama."

She was too choked up to reply and simply nodded, clutching her brother's arm so tightly he would likely have bruises later.

"Look," Dawn said with a gasp, pointing at the sky.

Alyx looked where she was pointing and a slow smile crossed her face at the sight of a bright orange dawn lighting up the horizon.

"What's the status?" Dashan asked, looking at Tarrick.

"Shakar's Shiven warriors are dead or captured." Tarrick's skin was barely visible under the layer of blood and grime that covered his face. "We defeated their mages too. Some are captured but most are dead."

"So it's over?" Jenna asked wonderingly.

"Yeah, I think it might be," Finn said, turning practical as always. "And now Alyx and Jayn need to see a mage healer. I've got nothing left, and they've both overused their magic horribly."

It didn't take long for those gathered nearby to see Alyx and the others emerge from the rubble. Like a stream charting a new course, they all began moving towards her—Bluecoats, mages, Shiven, militia, an eager mass of tired, wounded fighters. Grinning, Dashan leapt up on the nearest piece of fallen stone.

"He's dead!" he told them in a loud, gleeful shout. "Shakar is dead."

There was a moment of silence as the news sank in, then a shout of triumph went up that quickly echoed across the valley. Cheers and claps and whistles reverberated around and through them, and Alyx felt giddy from a combination of exhaustion and joy.

Rothai was the first to reach Alyx. Blood trickled down his cheek from a nasty-looking gash, and he was limping, but his face was alight with triumph, and he couldn't stop smiling as he stared down at Alyx. "Thank you, Magor-lier. Thank you from the bottom of my heart."

"You held up your end, Rothai," she told him with a smile. "I saw you fighting with everything you had. You all did."

"Together, right? Wasn't that always the plan?" Dawn said, tears in her eyes.

"From that very first day at DarkSkull." Finn wrapped an arm around his sister, looking close to tears himself.

Alyx squeezed Dashan's hand in hers, again unable to speak. He squeezed back, similarly struck.

Hoofbeats sounded then, five showy cavalry horses galloping across the open ground towards them. Casta was off his horse first, but Tijer was only a step behind. Both saluted sharply.

"Allow us the honour of escorting you to the healer, Magor-lier?"

"Granted." She nodded, smiling helplessly, and the five Bluecoats formed up around Alyx and her friends, Rothai and Jenna falling away gracefully.

She was beyond weary—her thoughts weren't entirely clear and she suspected her overuse of magic was going to have consequences. Already she felt a touch feverish, and her muscles trembled uncontrollably. But there were things she had to do before she could rest... she tried to think... Brynn!

She spun to look at Finn. "Brynn?"

"Still alive," Finn told her, his voice tinged with exhaustion. "Leanli has been working on him since the fighting out here ended. I'll show you to where he is. You should let Leanli look at you too."

Ladan left them to go and begin rounding up the Bluecoats and militia, Dashan reluctantly joining him on Alyx's insistence. Finn led her, Tarrick, and Dawn to a large, hastily-erected tent which was being used to treat the injured.

Brynn lay on a pallet alongside the other injured mages and soldiers. His skin was deathly pale, and he looked thin and fragile. Leanli came straight over at Finn's call.

"Will he be all right?" Dawn asked.

"It's hard to say," the healer murmured. "He's deeply unconscious, and he lost a lot of blood. Even if he survives the night, it's unclear if he'll ever wake up."

Alyx sat down beside the pallet, taking Brynn's cold hand in hers. "You did it," she whispered. "He's gone, Brynn. I'm so sorry for what I asked you to do."

"He did it willingly." Tarrick's hand landed on her shoulder. "As you would have done for him. That's what our friendship means. It's what Shakar could never understand."

"It's why we beat him," Dawn added.

"And now you must let me look at you, Magor-lier," Leanli said in a tone that brooked no argument.

"Jayn first," Alyx said, pointing to where Finn was already helping her onto a spare pallet. "I wouldn't be alive if it wasn't for her."

She sat as her legs went suddenly weak under her. The moments of Shakar's death replayed through her mind unbidden as she leaned forward to rest her face in her hands. His prone body was clear as day, in death his face losing all its bitterness and hate and becoming that of her beloved godfather.

Astor was dead.

Her shoulders shuddered and she fought back a sob. Shakar had deserved to die. But Astor had loved her. He'd been the man Shakar would have been, if only he'd made different choices. And he'd died too.

CHAPTER 52

Despite their wounded and exhausted force, Alyx didn't want to linger at DarkSkull any longer than necessary. She wanted to get home, as did her brother and the twins. Brynn was alive but still in a deep coma. She, Tarrick, and the twins rode out to Fotiya on the morning after the battle. Telling Sarah and Brynn's family what had happened was one of the hardest things she'd ever had to do.

"We'd like you to come with us," Tarrick said to them. "Brynn will recover much more quickly with his family around him."

"We will leave him here with you if that's what you want, but there are more healer mages in Alistriem," Alyx added.

"And I am his friend and a healer. I promise to do everything I can for him," Finn said.

"We will come," Sarah said firmly. "Of course we will."

Astonishingly, as they were preparing to depart on the third day after their victory, their scouts alerted them to a large force of militia marching up from the south. It was King Mastaran, on his way back to Carhall from Karonan.

"We thought to come via DarkSkull in case you could use extra men," Mastaran boomed when he was escorted through their camp to see Alyx and her brother. "I see that wasn't necessary. Congratulations, Magor-lier, Lord-Taliath. I very much look forward to hearing your account of the battle."

"It was good of you to come," she said, meaning it. "Had we not won, you would have placed yourself at serious risk."

"You were fighting for my country. I could do no less," he said soberly, then cleared his throat. "You will come to Carhall soon, I hope? We four countries, along with the mages and Taliath, need to hold talks. I want to ensure this never happens again, and it is best to do it while the horror is still fresh in our minds."

"I agree, Your Highness, and I'm sure King Cayr will, also." Ladan inclined his head.

"Good, and if the Zandian emperor doesn't agree to come, I'll ride there and drag him back to Carhall myself."

She laughed, and even Ladan's mouth twitched. "I don't think that will be necessary, Your Highness."

Two weeks after the battle, they rode into Alistriem. Alyx and her mages led the way, with a weary force of Bluecoats in neat rows behind them.

It was a bright, sunny day, the air warm and vibrant and heralding the onset of spring in Rionn. Alyx, riding beside Dashan, reached out to take his hand. Riding Tingo, with Dashan's hand in hers, it finally began to sink in that Shakar was gone and her future was free. Tears welled in her eyes, and she let them fall.

Word quickly spread through the city as their force rode in through the gates, and people came out of their homes and businesses to find out what had happened. The Bluecoats were all too eager to shout out the news to anyone that asked.

Cayr was coming out of the palace at a run as Alyx rode in, warned by her telepathic contact with the mages at the palace. His gaze went straight to Alyx, and then Dashan, and his shoulders slumped in relief. Alyx dismounted and ran to him.

"We won, Cayr. We did it. He's dead."

An unbelieving smile broke out across his face. He held her gaze for one, joyous moment, then he lifted his eyes, searching behind. "Jenna!"

Hearing him shout her name, she slid down from the saddle and broke into an undignified run towards him. Cayr swung her into his arms with a relieved laugh. For the first time Alyx saw Jenna's cool exterior snap, vanishing as she buried herself in Cayr's embrace, clinging fiercely to his shoulders.

"It feels more real now, doesn't it?" Dashan murmured to Alyx. "Now we're home."

"Yes. For the first time, it's real." She squeezed his hand. "We're free."

Alyx lay on a cushioned lounge on the sand, Dawn stretched out comfortably beside her. Finn, Cayr, and Dashan were messing around in the water. Tijer and Casta were there too, supposedly on protection detail, but far more involved in the water fight. While an unusually bright winter sun shone above, it was still far too cool for swimming as far as Alyx was concerned.

"This is nice." Dawn sighed. "I don't remember the last time I felt this relaxed."

"It was probably the day before we were told we were being sent to DarkSkull Hall," Alyx said dryly.

Dawn's musical laughter rang out. "True. Why isn't Tarrick here?"

"He's still at the palace, organising the mages that have been arriving in the city," Alyx said. "You know how he is. Finn says yesterday he was talking about starting a new academy; he said mages need to be trained, the sooner the better."

"I suppose he's right. He could at least take a day or two off to relax first."

Alyx smiled. "Will you and Ladan stay here in Alistriem?"

"Yes. This is our home. Besides, he's not just responsible for Widow Falls anymore, he also has the Egalion lands now."

"I'm glad to hear it. Cayr will need a Lord-Taliath and senior advisor, and Ladan is pretty much already filling that role. I can't think of a better team to lead Rionn, particularly when you add them together with our new warrior queen."

Dawn looked at her. "We just assumed that Dashan would fill your father's old role now that the war is over. He and Cayr have been best friends since children."

Alyx shook her head. "Once I manage to talk him into it, Dash is going to be the commander of the Shiven army and senior advisor to the new leader."

Dawn stared at her in shock. "You're serious?"

"Yes. Tarian Astohar has asked him to do it. I think he'd be perfect." Alyx gave her a pointed look. "Cayr is going to need a new lord-mage too, you know? I've already told him he should choose you."

Dawn froze, astonishment filling her face. "Alyx that's—"

"Absolutely perfect, and there is nobody who could do a better job."

Dawn frowned. "What about you?"

"Me being Magor-lier shouldn't hold Dash back. We'll be apart for a while, but we'll sort something out."

"So that's what you want to do now?"

Alyx laughed. "What do you mean? I'm the Magor-lier."

"Yes, but Shakar's dead now. You can do what you want," Dawn said. "No more expectations."

Alyx looked at her friend, wondering at her words. She hadn't really considered that. Ever since that first moment she'd entered DarkSkull, her life had been overtaken by the fact she was a mage of the higher order, then Magor-lier, the only one who could defeat Shakar.

Dawn took her hand. "Alyx, you've done what everyone asked of you. You get to have the life *you* want now. If that's leading the new mage order, I'm sure they'll welcome you with open arms. But if not…"

Alyx turned and looked back towards the ocean, where Dashan was chasing Finn through the shallows, splashing water everywhere. As if sensing her attention on him, he looked up, giving her a warm smile and a wave. She returned both the smile and the wave, luxuriating in the warmth she always felt at his regard.

"Maybe you're right." She stood suddenly, and Dawn looked up in surprise. "I'm going to go and have a chat with Tarrick."

They ate together that night in Cayr's private quarters with Jenna and Sparky. As had been the case since their return to Alistriem, the atmosphere was light and convivial, although this evening Tarrick was quiet and had a dazed expression on his face.

Things broke up late, and she asked Dashan to walk her down to his boat. "I want to spend the night with you out there," she told him. "It holds so many good memories."

They walked in companionable silence, hand in hand, down through the city and out to the docks. Dashan's boat bobbed gently against its moorings, and Alyx smiled as he helped her aboard. He ducked inside the wheelhouse and came back out carrying blankets and pillows.

"A bit dusty, but perfectly good." He told her as he laid them out on the deck, then came to join her at the prow.

"Remember that night in Carhall when you told me about the stars?" she asked him, leaning into his body.

"I wanted to kiss you that night," he admitted.

She smiled up at him. "Why didn't you?"

"You would have freaked out, which is what you did do when I eventually kissed you a few weeks later."

"I'm glad you did," she told him. "I'm glad you didn't give up on me."

"I'd never give up on you."

"By then, I wanted to kiss you too," she admitted softly. "I was just refusing to admit it to myself."

He smiled and kissed her, a slow, deep kiss that told her how much he loved her.

"You'll have to leave for Karonan soon," she told him.

"Alyx, I—"

"Dash, you have to do this." She laid a hand on his chest. "You *want* to do this, and Tarian needs you. More than anything, stability in Shivasa is key to building a strong alliance between all four countries and recovering from what Shakar did."

"I don't want to be apart from you." His eyes were dark.

"You don't have to be," she told him. "I'm going to be away, the next couple of months. Tarrick needs help with the mages, and they need me too. We need to re-establish some sort of order for them."

"I understand that. But you're talking about more than a few months," he said. "I want to be with you, there's nothing I want more than that. If you need to be Magor-lier, then I'll be living with you wherever you are."

"No, Dash," she said softly. "I'm going to come and live with you in Karonan."

"What?" he asked, confused.

"Our whole lives you have sacrificed everything for me. You've done what I needed, no matter what." She smiled. "My turn. You're going to be right hand man to the leader of Shivasa."

He stared down at her for a few moments. "What about the mages?"

"I've spoken to Tarrick. From this afternoon, he's the new Magor-lier. I'm not their leader anymore."

"Alyx," Dashan breathed, his hand coming up to touch her cheek. "What are you going to do? You can't just be my wife, I know that's not enough."

"DarkSkull was destroyed and the mages need a new academy, one that's brighter and better than before. I'm going to build a new one, in Karonan." She smiled. "Tarrick wants to form a new Mage Council, where everyone has an equal vote and the Magor-lier can be overruled by a majority of the council. I'll sit on the council, and I'll be head of the new mage academy. I'm pretty confident I can do a better job than Romas did."

"Really? You mean this?" he asked.

"I mean it." She laughed and leaned up to kiss him. "Your turn to shine. I can't wait."

Dashan laughed aloud and pulled her into his arms. "I love you, Alyx Egalion."

EPILOGUE

Alyx rode a tired, dusty Tingo back into Alistriem with Nordan, Finn, and Tarrick beside her. The steady ice mage had effectively replaced Adahn's role as her personal protector, and she had quickly come to rely on his experience and steady nature. And of course her five Bluecoats trailed behind, Nario, Tijer, and Josha in hysterics over some joke Roland had just told. Even Casta was smiling, and she was glad at the signs he was beginning to heal from Cario's loss.

As they made their way through the city, it was clear things in Alistriem were much livelier than when they'd left—trade was slowly starting to come back to life, and the city squares were busy with traders and their stalls.

Alyx knew from Dawn's letters that Cayr and Jenna were working hard at managing the rebuilding of Rionn at the same time as negotiating new trade agreements with Tregaya, Shivasa, and Zandia that were advantageous for the much smaller Rionn. Tarian Astohar had won the elections in Shivasa in a landslide victory and had been officially sworn in as their leader a month and a half earlier, Dashan at his side.

She'd wanted to be there with him, but the mages had needed her, and she'd been working non-stop with Tarrick and Finn in the months since they'd beaten Shakar.

They clattered into the palace yard and grooms came running to take their horses. Alyx dismounted, releasing the Bluecoats to a night at the

Party District. Tarrick and Finn followed her inside, but all three came to a halt at the sight of Jayn running madly down the hall towards them.

"I can't believe your timing," she said excitedly. "Quick, come with me!"

"What is it?" Alyx demanded.

She was smiling from ear to ear. "Brynn just woke up!"

Alyx sprinted down the hall, flying past Jayn and down to the palace room where Brynn had been lying in a coma since coming to Alistriem. Heart pounding in her chest, she opened the door with trembling hands and went inside.

Her eyes welled with tears at the sight of Sarah, on the bed, her arms wrapped around Brynn as she sobbed into his shoulder. He was pale, with deep hollows under his blue eyes, but he was awake and alert and clearly knew who he was.

Alyx couldn't move as she stared across the room at him. Tarrick, Finn, and Jayn burst into the room behind her and stopped still, just as she had.

"Hey, guys!" Brynn smiled. "Can someone please tell me if we beat Shakar or not? Sarah hasn't managed a coherent word since I woke up."

Alyx laughed, then sobbed, then flew across the room to clamber onto the opposite side of the bed from Sarah and hug him too.

"Dash killed him," Finn filled in when Alyx couldn't speak. "You really okay, mate?"

"I feel tired, and like I've been really sick, but good," Brynn replied. "So Shakar's gone? Really?"

"He's gone." Alyx sat back, still grinning and wiping tears from her face.

"Did they tell you that I was the one who killed him?"

Alyx looked up, unbelieving, as Dashan appeared in the doorway, cocky grin firmly in place, eyes alight as he looked at her. She gave a shriek of delight and flew across the room into his arms.

When they managed to untangle from each other, Dashan went straight to the bed to slap Brynn on the back. "Good to see you up and about."

"Thanks, Dash." Brynn winced at the force of the slap. "How are you?"

"I'm good."

"He commands the Shiven army," Tarrick said with a grin.

"He *what?*" Brynn gaped.

Dashan groaned. "I'd like to quit already. Nothing but paperwork and policy advice and bureaucracy. Give me a good fight any day."

"Don't listen to him, he loves it," Alyx said.

"And, from what I hear, is very good at it," Tarrick said.

"Also, Tarrick is the new Magor-lier!" Finn announced with glee.

Brynn's eyes rounded further. "You fired Alyx?"

She laughed. "I quit. I think we all know I never wanted to be Magor-lier."

"How is the mage stuff going?" Dashan asked.

"Good," Tarrick said. "I think everything is settled. I'll be operating out of Carhall with most of the Mage Council. All the mages still alive have been tracked down and invited to join the new order. Most have signed up and have received their assignments. Others preferred to retire."

"So you're done?" Dashan looked hopefully at Alyx.

She smiled. "Yes, I'm all done. I'll have to travel to Carhall for Mage Council meetings once a year, but I'm ready to start building the new academy in Karonan. Jayn is going to come with me."

"Do you need a master?" Finn asked diffidently, though his eyes flickered to Jayn. She beamed at him.

Alyx lifted her eyebrows in delight. "Seriously?"

He nodded. "There's nothing I'd love more than to teach and rebuild Howell's library."

"I'd love to have you with me. Yes, absolutely!"

He shrugged, eyes again straying to Jayn. "Plus, it means I'll be close to Alistriem, where Dawn is, which is important too."

"Speaking of, where is my brother?" Alyx asked Jayn.

"They'll be here in a moment, I'm sure. I sent a message over to the Egalion mansion before coming out to meet you."

Sure enough, Dawn appeared shortly after, hesitating at the door and clearly unsure as to who to hug first. Eventually, she decided on Brynn, who beamed at all the attention. Alyx was grinning stupidly at the sight when her brother's gruff voice sounded and she found herself hauled into his arms.

"Aly-girl."

"Big brother." She hugged him fiercely. "It's good to see you."

"And you."

Tarrick clapped his hands and went for the door. "Such a reunion needs ale!"

"Get some snacks too," Finn called after him.

An hour later, Alyx wandered through the palace gardens, a small smile on her face. She was lost in thought, and so it took her a few moments before she recognised the familiar figure seated on a bench seat by a tinkling fountain.

Curious, she went to join him. "Is this seat taken?"

Rothai turned to her, then shrugged slightly. "Not at all."

She sat down, quiet for a moment as she enjoyed the peace of the garden and the sweet scent of flowers. The sun was warm on her back, and a slight breeze toyed with the tendrils of hair that had escaped her braid.

"I was wondering where you'd gotten to," she said at last.

"I heard Brynn was awake. I didn't want to intrude," he replied. "I figured you wouldn't be leaving for a couple of days at least."

Alyx smiled. "I'll be leaving for Karonan with Dash soon."

"So this is it? You're no longer the Magor-lier?"

"That's right. I'm now the new head of Temari Hall."

"A fitting name," he said quietly.

Alyx's mouth quirked in a smile. "I thought it was appropriate. What will you do now, Rothai? I remember you promising to keep an eye on me to make sure I don't turn into another Shakar."

"Actually, I thought I might try farming."

Alyx stared at him in astonishment. "You're serious?"

Rothai shrugged. "Ever since we met, Alyx Egalion, you've been a means to an end, the only way to destroy the monster that killed my family. I did whatever it took to make sure you were able to defeat Shakar, and I tried desperately to keep you from becoming him."

"I know, I was there," she said dryly.

He glanced down at his hands. "Somewhere along the way I finally learned to trust you. You will do good things for the mage order. And I think, after everything I've done, the best thing I can do is to go and leave you to live your life."

"You could contribute to the new mage order too. You're one of my strongest warrior mages."

"No. I'm done with the mage life. I want some peace. My sister still lives in Serrin, and I'm going to go home and help her family run our farm."

"That's good." Alyx smiled again. "Because there's no way I was going to let you teach at my new school."

He looked up at her, startled, then burst into laughter, astonishing her.

"I've never seen you laugh before."

"I think it's about time I learned." Rothai stood. "Allow me to properly apologise to you, Alyx."

"Apology accepted, Rothai. Go and be happy."

He nodded, smiled slightly, and walked away.

Alyx watched him go until the arrival of Dashan caught her attention. Smiling, she rose from the bench seat and walked down the hill to meet him.

"Alyx." He pulled her close before swinging her high into the air. "I missed you."

"Me too." She laughed as he put her back down. "No more. I'm with you to stay now."

"I very much like the sound of that," he said, leaning down to kiss her softly.

"I love you," she murmured into his chest.

He released her eventually, stepping back a little and taking both her hands in his. His dark Shiven eyes were serious on hers. "I promised I would ask properly, so here goes. Lady Alyx Egalion. How do you feel about marrying a penniless Taliath?"

She bit her lip, tears welling unexpectedly in her eyes. After so long, after all the pain and heartache and lingering grief, Dashan Caverlock was standing in front of her and asking her to marry him. "Yes," she whispered.

"Good," he murmured, voice hoarse. "That's very good."

He kissed her, pulling her close while she wrapped her arms tightly around his neck. *I'm betrothed to Dashan Caverlock.* Her heart sang.

"Now." He cleared his throat, pulling back a little, eyes dancing. "How about we get married, now, before we go to Karonan?"

"Now?"

"Well, maybe tomorrow. While all our friends are here together."

She arched an eyebrow. "You think we can get a state wedding organised by tomorrow?"

"Oh no," he murmured, kissing her. "We discussed this. Ten guests maximum."

"Ten people?" She kissed him back, tracing her fingers over his shirt.

"It's a perfect number." He dropped kisses down her neck. "Brynn, Sarah, Cayr, Jenna, Ladan, Dawn..."

She laughed and pulled away from him. "Jayn, Finn, and Tarrick? You're one short, Dash. And what about Casta and Tijer and the others?"

"I've never been good at math." He waggled his eyebrows at her. "But what do you say?"

She grinned at him. "I say yes."

"What are you two grinning about?" Alyx looked up as Cayr came walking down one of the paths towards them. He had one hand in his pocket, his blonde hair tousled and a touch too long as always.

"Cayr!" Dashan said in delight, reaching out to clap him soundly on the back.

"I've missed you." Alyx hugged him.

"Me too," Cayr said. "I love my life; since Shakar was defeated, I can barely believe sometimes how happy and content I am, but I miss the three of us together."

"I don't think we could ever have imagined, growing up together as children, how our lives would turn out," Dashan murmured.

"I think we'll be connected always," Alyx said. "So the two of you need to make sure you have plenty of state visits."

"Well, I don't know about that." Cayr smiled as he slung one arm around Dashan and the other around Alyx, and the three of them began strolling down the path. "I'm slightly afraid that I'll run out of the royal store of ale if I invite Dashan and his Shiven here."

"I'm taking offence to that." Dashan sniffed. "Besides, if you bring your fancy royal court to Karonan, we're likely to run out of the velvet carpet you and your nobles like so much."

Cayr laughed, then stopped. "Isn't that the tree you challenged Alyx to climb when we were kids?"

"The one I fell out of?" Alyx said dryly. "Yes, I think it is."

"Bet I could beat you up it," Dashan said to Cayr slyly.

Cayr raised his eyebrows. "Is that so? I remember winning most of our races up that tree, my friend."

"Right, that's a challenge." Dashan began rolling up his sleeves.

Alyx laughed as Cayr determinedly began rolling up his own sleeves, then watched in amusement, as—keeping up a steady stream of good-natured bickering—Dashan and Cayr ran for the tree and began climbing up it.

Her mind flashed back to a bright sunny day just like this when they were children. She saw Dashan's young face, his Shiven eyes dark and sparkling as he laughed and followed a tousle-headed Cayr up the tree. She saw herself too, seven years old, green eyes and a serious face, breaking out into delighted clapping as Cayr beat Dashan to the top.

The memory faded, and Alyx began clapping in echo of that perfect day as a fully grown Cayr beat Dashan to the top by a mere fingertip.

HERE ENDS *THE MAGE CHRONICLES*

Return to the world of *The Mage Chronicles* in Lisa's latest series, *Heir to the Darkmage* - available now

THE DOCK CITY CHRONICLE

Want to delve further into the world of *The Mage Chronicles*?

By signing up to Lisa's monthly newsletter, *The Dock City Chronicle,* you'll get a FREE novella – **A World at War**: a collection of short stories from the world of *The Mage Chronicles*. Each story is set before the beginning of *DarkSkull Hall.* You'll also get exclusive access to lots of subscriber-only special content, updates on Lisa's books, her writing process, the books she's reading, and more!

You can sign up for the *Chronicle* at Lisa's website: lisacassidyauthor.com

ALSO BY LISA CASSIDY

The Mage Chronicles
DarkSkull Hall
Taliath
Darkmage
Heartfire

Heir to the Darkmage
Heir to the Darkmage
Mark of the Huntress
Whisper of the Darksong
Rise of the Shadowcouncil

A Tale of Stars and Shadow
A Tale of Stars and Shadow
A Prince of Song and Shade
A King of Masks and Magic
A Duet of Sword and Song

CONSIDER A REVIEW?

'Your words are as important to an author as an author's words are to you'

Hello,

I really hope you enjoyed this story. If you did, I would be genuinely thrilled if you would take the time to leave an **honest** review on GoodReads or Amazon, or both (it doesn't have to be long - a few words or a single sentence is absolutely fine!).

Reviews can be absolute game changers for the success and visibility of a book, and by leaving a review you'll help this story reach others. Not to mention you'll also be helping me write more stories.

Thank you so much for reading this book,

Lisa

MORE ABOUT LISA...

Lisa is a self-published fantasy author by day and book nerd in every other spare moment she has. She's a self-confessed coffee snob (don't try coming near her with any of that instant coffee rubbish) but is willing to accept all other hot drink aficionados, even tea drinkers. She lives in Australia's capital city, Canberra, and like all Australians, is pretty much in constant danger from highly poisonous spiders, crocodiles, sharks, and drop bears, to name a few. As you can see, she is also pro-Oxford comma.

A 2019 SPFBO finalist, and finalist for the 2020 ACT Writers Fiction award, Lisa is the author of the young adult fantasy series *The Mage Chronicles* and *Heir to the Darkmage*, and epic fantasy series *A Tale of Stars and Shadow*. She is currently diving into a brand new series.

As part of her writing journey, Lisa has partnered up with One Girl, a charity working to build a world where all girls have access to quality education. A world where all girls — no matter where they are born or how much money they have — enjoy the same rights and opportunities as boys. A percentage of all Lisa's royalties go to One Girl.

You can follow Lisa on Facebook and Instagram, where she loves to interact with her fans. Lisa also has a Facebook group - Lisa's Writing Cave - where you can jump in and talk about anything and everything relating to books and reading.

If you want to learn more about Lisa and her books, head on over to Lisa's Website - lisacassidyauthor.com

www.ingramcontent.com/pod-product-compliance
Lightning Source LLC
Chambersburg PA
CBHW030646120726
47905CB00001B/79